Wolf Pelt

Cold War in Greece, Love, and Trust Revealed

Wolf Pelt

Cold War in Greece, Love, and Trust Revealed

by

Steven James Hantzis

Alinet, LLC

Alexandria, Virginia USA

2026

Alinet, LLC
P.O. Box 7353
Alexandria, VA 22307

ISBN: 979-8-9986067-6-2

Lécythe vessel from Athens circa 460 BCE from Musée du Louvre, Département des Antiquités grecques, étrusques etromaines.

Contents

Marauding Through the Night

from The Iliad by Homer

But no sleep for the headstrong Trojans either. Hector would not permit it. He summoned all his chiefs to a council of war, all Trojan lords and captains. Mustering them he launched his own crafty plan: "Who will undertake a mission and bring it off for a princely gift? A prize to match the exploit! I'll give him a chariot, two horses with strong necks, the best of the breeds beside Achaea's fast ships. Whoever will dare—what glory he can win—a night patrol by the ships to learn at once if the fleet's still guarded as before or now, battered down at our hands, huddling together, they plan a quick escape, their morale too low to mount the watch tonight—bone-weary from battle."

So Hector proposed. All ranks held their peace. But there was a man among the troops, one Dolon, a son of the sacred Trojan herald Eumedes. He was rich in bronze, rich in bars of gold, no feast for the eyes but lightning on his feet and an only son in the midst of five sisters. This one volunteered among the Trojans: "Hector, the mission stirs my fighting blood—I'll reconnoiter the ships and gather all I can. Come, raise that scepter and swear you'll give me the battle-team and the burnished brazen car that carry great Achilles—I will be your spy. And no mean scout, I'll never let you down. I'll infiltrate their entire army, I will, all the way till I reach the ship of Agamemnon! That's where the captains must be mapping tactics now, whether they'll break and run or stand and fight."

How he bragged and Hector, grasping his scepter, swore a binding oath: "Now Zeus my witness, thundering lord of Hera—no other Trojan fighter will ride behind that team, none but you, I swear—they will be your glory all your life to come!"

So Hector vowed—with an oath he swore in vain but it spurred the man to action. Dolon leapt to it, he quickly slung a reflex bow on his back, over it threw the pelt of a gray wolf and set on his head a cap of weasel skin and taking a sharp spear, moved out from camp, heading toward the fleet—but he was never to come back from the enemy's beaked ships, bringing Hector news. Putting the mass of horse and men behind him Dolon picked up speed, hot for action now, but keen as a god Odysseus saw him coming and alerted Diomedes: "Who is this? A man heading out of the Trojan camp! Why? I can't be sure— to spy on our ships or loot the fallen, one of the fighters' corpses? Let him get past us first, into the clear a bit, then rush him and overtake him double-quick! If he outruns us, crowd him against the ships, cut him off from his lines, harry him with your spear and never stop—so he can't bolt back to Troy."

No more words. Swerving off the trail they both lay facedown with the corpses now as Dolon sped by at a dead run, the fool. Soon as he got a furlong's lead ahead, the plowing- range of a good team of mules—faster than draft oxen dragging a bolted plow through deep fallow ground—the two raced after and Dolon, hearing their tread, froze stock-still, his heart leaping—here were friends, yes, fellow Trojans coming to turn him back, yes, Hector had just called off the mission! But soon as they were a spear-cast off or less he saw them—enemies— quick as a flash he sprang, fleeing for dear life—they sprang in pursuit as a pair of rip-tooth hounds bred for the hunt and flushing fawn or hare through a woody glen keep closing for the kill, nonstop and the prey goes screaming on ahead—so Odysseus raider of cities and Diomedes cut him off from his own lines, coursing him, closing nonstop with the Trojan about to break in on the line of sentries, racing fast for the ships—when Athena poured fresh strength in Tydeus' son so no Achaean could beat him out for the glory of hitting Dolon first, Diomedes come in second. Rushing him with his spear in a sudden surge Tydides shouted, "Stop or I'll run you through! You'll never escape my spear—headlong death—I swear I'll send it hurling from my fist!"

He flung his shaft, missing the man on purpose—over his right shoulder the sharp spearpoint winged and stabbed the earth. Dead in his tracks he stopped, terrified, stammering, teeth chattering in his mouth, bled white with fear as the two men overtook him and panting hard, yanked and pinned his arms. He burst into tears, pleading, "Take me alive! I'll ransom myself! Treasures cram our house, bronze and gold and plenty of well-wrought iron—father would give you anything, gladly, priceless ransom—if only he learns I'm still alive in Argive ships!"

Odysseus quick with tactics answered, "Courage. Death is your last worry. Put your mind at rest. Come, tell me the truth now, point by point. Why prowling among the ships, cut off from camp, alone in the dead of night when other men are sleeping? To loot the fallen, one of the fighters' corpses? Or did Hector send you out to spy on our ships, reconnoiter them stem to stem? Or did your own itch for glory spur you on?"

Dolon answered, his legs shaking under him, "Hector—he duped me so—so many mad, blind hopes! He swore he'd give me the great Achilles' stallions, purebred racers, his burnished bronze chariot too! He told me to go through the rushing dark night, to patrol the enemy lines and learn at once if the fleet's still guarded as before or now, battered down at our hands, huddling together, you plan a quick escape, your morale too low to mount the watch tonight—bone-weary from battle."

Breaking into a smile the cool tactician laughed, "By god, what heroic gifts you set your heart on—the great Achilles' team! They're hard for mortal men to curb or drive, for all but Achilles—his mother is immortal. Now out with it, point by point. Hector—where did you leave the captain when you came? Where's his war-gear lying? Where's his chariot? How are the other Trojans posted—guards, sleepers? What plans are they mapping, what maneuvers next? Are they bent on holding tight by the ships, exposed?—or heading home to Troy, now they've trounced our armies?"

And Dolon son of the herald blurted out, "Yes, yes, I'll tell you everything, down to the last detail! Hector's holding council with all his chiefs, mapping plans on old King Ilus' barrow, clear of the crowds at camp. Guards, my lord? Nothing. No one's picked to defend the army. Only our native Trojans hold their posts—many as those with hearth fires back in Troy—our men have no choice, shouting out to each other, 'Stay awake! keep watch!' But our far-flung friends, they're fast asleep, they leave the watch to us—their wives and children are hardly camped nearby."

But the shrewd tactician kept on pressing: "Be precise. Where are they sleeping? Mixed in with the Trojans? Separate quarters? Tell me. I must know it all."

And Dolon son of the herald kept on blurting, "Everything—anything—whatever will satisfy you! To seaward, Carians, Paeonian men with bent bows, Leleges and Cauconians, crack Pelasgians—inland, toward Thymbra, camp the Lycians, swaggering Mysians, fighting Phrygian horsemen, Maeonian chariot-drivers—but why interrogate me down to the last platoon? You really want to raid some enemy units? There are the Thracians, look, just arrived, exposed on the flank, apart from all the rest and right in their midst Eioneus' son, King Rhesus. His are the best horses I ever saw, the biggest, whiter than snow, and speed to match the wind! His chariot's finished off with gold and silver, the armor he's brought in with him, gold too, tremendous equipment—what a marvelous sight. No gear for a mortal man to wear, I'd say, it's fit for the deathless gods! There. Now will you take me to your ships or leave me here— bound and gagged right here?—till you can make your raid and test my story, see if I've told the truth or I've been lying."

But rugged Diomedes gave him a grim look: "Escape? Take my advice and wipe it from your mind, good as your message is—you're in my hands now. What if we set you free or *you should slip away? Back you'll slink to our fast ships tomorrow, playing the spy again or fighting face-to-face. But if I snuff your life out in my hands, you'll never annoy our Argive lines again."*

With that, just as Dolon reached up for his chin to cling with a frantic hand and beg for life, Diomedes struck him square across the neck—a flashing hack of the sword—both tendons snapped and the shrieking head went tumbling in the dust. They tore the weasel-cap from the head, stripped the wolf pelt, the reflex bow and long tough spear and swinging the trophies high to Pallas queen of plunder, exultant royal Odysseus shouted out this prayer: "Here, Goddess, rejoice in these, they're yours! You are the first of all the gods we'll call! Now guide us again, Athena, guide us against that Thracian camp and horses!"

So Odysseus prayed and hoisting the spoils over his head, heaved them onto a tamarisk bush nearby and against it heaped a good clear landmark, clumping together reeds and fresh tamarisk boughs they'd never miss as they ran back through the rushing dark night. On they stalked through armor and black pools of blood and suddenly reached their goal, the Thracian outpost. The troops were sleeping, weary from pitching camp, their weapons piled beside them on the ground, three neat rows of the burnished well-kept arms and beside each man his pair of battle-horses. Right in the midst lay Rhesus dead asleep, his white racers beside him, strapped by thongs to his chariot's outer rail. Spotting him first Odysseus quickly pointed him out to Diomedes: "Look, here's our man, here are his horses. The ones marked out by the rascal we just killed. On with it now—show us your strength, full force. Don't just stand there, useless with your weapons. Loose those horses—or you go kill the men and leave the team to me!"

Translation by Robert Fagles, 1990

Wolf Pelt is the story of an American spy in Athens. The story unfolds in the fall of 1951, a formative time in the Cold War. Greece and Turkey are on the cusp of NATO accession. The Marshall Plan is winding down its shower of money on Europe. And the disparate functions, departments, and personalities of the adolescent CIA are jostling for bureaucratic equilibrium.

My protagonist, Stavros Theofanis, has a history. For a full background, I invite you to read *The Greek Boxer* and *American Andarte*. Stavros is fictional. But other primary characters are historic. Here's a brief biography of each reduced to one paragraph but deserving of volumes.

Frank Wisner was the father of the CIA's covert action arm. He influenced America's Cold War undercover work more than any other person.

Hod Fuller worked with Frank Wisner and ran Operation FIEND, the covert war in Albania. He was a World War II OSS veteran, as is Stavros Theofanis.

Thomas Hercules Karamessines was CIA station chief in Athens. He reformed the Greek intelligence service into a look-alike CIA. He too was OSS, though office bound. Much later in his career, he played important roles in the Chilean elections of 1970 and Watergate.

Of these three historic figures, only Wisner and Fuller come into play throughout *Wolf Pelt*. I didn't know these men and only know their character from books. I have used the ages-old ploy of authorial license to create their dialogue and strive to fit it into reported personalities and historical context. There was an Operation FIEND, fighting between CIA's OSO and OPC, Stay Behind Armies, Holy Bond, NATO subversion, Cultural Influence Campaigns, and . . . .You'll get the drift. I've provided a bibliography if you want to flesh out any of these fascinating themes.

There are plot points I lifted from CIA annals. Igor Gouzenko's defection to Canada following World War II is one. And Nesti Josifi Kopali's defection to the Italians from Albania in 1949 is another. I've kept these accounts as close to fact as I could. If a turn of plot is factual, it is likely noted.

And, speaking of notes, *Wolf Pelt* is less notated than *The Greek Boxer* or *American Andarte*. This is because the plot is fictional. I don't know whether the CIA tried to recruit the Soviet GRU rezidentura in Athens and run him as a mole or, in the lexicon of spy craft, a double. But they could have. The CIA Reading Room verifies enough irons in the fire that this fictional operation might have risen in some smoldering corner.

I like Greece. I have a loving family there and have visited many times. The devastation wrought on this small country by fascist occupation during World War II and the stalking Civil War that followed sets the stage for *Wolf Pelt*. In 1951, Greece began stepping away from the worst years of torture, fratricide, and deprivation thanks to the funding and political guidance of the United States. Its strategic sea lanes and proximity to the Soviet Block gave it two personalities. On the surface, things were getting better in 1951, and peace prevailed. But not far beneath that placid patina, a domain of spies, espionage, and anything-goes noesis percolated. The Cold War was just that, a war by other means. But not that different from traditional war. Operation FIEND, the CIA and British effort to undermine the communist government of Albania by infiltrating armed cells, was Frank Wisner's first effort to field a surrogate Cold War army. He did it from Greece. You could call FIEND a Greek tragedy with Albanian actors.

It is trite to say that geography is destiny. Perhaps not when Napoleon uttered it before invading Russia, but trite today. Where Greece falls on the globe has presented Greeks opportunities and perils like few other countries. The dichotomy played out in 1951 as the world's superpowers sought to arrange geography to their advantage. I offer in *Wolf Pelt* a pawn's advance on the chessboard of the Great Game for your enlightenment and entertainment.

Chapter 1

Rain came early in October and washed away the dust of an Athens summer. The city shone anew under the season's soft sun. The drive from Tripoli had taken three hours, an interval of anticipation and speculation. It had been a trip of necessity, not choice.

He was a day late. The downpour in the Peloponnese had waylaid him in Tripoli for the night. The Galaxy Hotel was serviceable, but the thunder and pouring rain made sleep impossible. When the storm passed in the early hours, he too passed into the silence. Come morning, he awoke abridged and muzzy. Consulting the dressing mirror, he took stock of a thirty-eight-year-old man, six foot tall and athletic. He buttoned a pressed white shirt from his grip and put on his charcoal-gray suit. The tie would come later.

He ordered coffee and a grilled ham and cheese in the hotel's taverna. He was stirring sugar into his coffee when a liquid baritone called from his left, "*Ypolochagós.*" Then in English, "Lieutenant."

Greece is a small country where news travels fast. It is easy to believe that every Greek talks to every other Greek every day. Greece, with all the modern impersonal conveyances— telephones, telegraphs, and radios—somehow maintained intimacy in all communication. Man-to-man, woman-to-man, no matter how transmitted, messages landed leavened with urgency and merit. It was The Greek Way.

Stavros set his spoon on the coffee's saucer and turned in his chair to a tall, clean-shaven man in a scuffed and faded MQ-1 field jacket and khaki pants. He wore the boots of a worker. Even without his guerrilla growth, Stavros recognized Nikolas at once. Nikolas had been second in command of the Chómori andartes that Stavros and his OSS Operational Group had coordinated and collocated with during the German occupation. He was a brave fighter, a seasoned tactician, and an educated man. His family ran a small olive oil plant near Missolonghi, and the last Stavros knew, from six years earlier, Nikolas had been in the Nafpaktian Mountains harassing retreating Germans.

Stavros had left Greece in September 1944 when the OSS recalled his commando group to Italy. From there, he volunteered to go to China. In the desolate mountains north of Xi'an, he'd teamed with Loyal Patriotic Army guerrillas. They had radioed weather reports, harassed the Japanese, and rescued downed American airmen until the end of the war.

The Germans left Greece in October 1944. The swastika fluttered its last in Athens and retreated from the heights of the Acropolis. The jubilant hoisting of the "blue and white" returned Greece to the Greeks and unleashed a bloody battle for political ascendence. The contested soul of Greece had yet healed.

Nikolas had been a partisan in the Greek National Liberation Front, EAM, a political coalition with the Greek Communist Party at its core. He'd fought as second in command of Chómori ELAS, the Greek People's Liberation Army. From high in the Nafpaktian Mountains, his ELAS fighters had ranged the breadth of Greece. They had battled in the Plains of Thessaly to the east, the peaks of Roumeli between, and Epirus on the western border with Albania. Most ELAS andartes had fought against the fascists, against the return of the king, against British imperialism, and for Greece. But a core, a motivated minority, had fought for communism and initiatory socialism. They were internationalists. Nikolas had fought for Greece. EAM-ELAS had welcomed the OSS commandos, schooled the Americans in The Greek Way, and provided impenetrable operational security. Not once were Stavros or his commandos betrayed or abandoned in Greece.

Stavros remained in touch with only one of the Chómori andartes, the captivating, elusive Dimitra, former kapetánios of the andarte band. It was a connection more personal than professional. They were in love, distant and circumstantial, but love. She was why he looked forward to Athens.

"Nikolas, what a surprise. *Ti kanis*, you look well. What are you doing in the Peloponnese? I thought you might be in Missolonghi."

"It surprises me, Lieutenant. I thought that was you, but your suit and smooth face gave me pause. Are you not *kataskopeía*? What is it called today, Central Agency?"

Nikolas loved American slang and idioms. Stavros corrected, "You mean CIA, Central Intelligence Agency. And no. I'm not. I left the OSS and kataskopeía after the war. Now I teach, and I'm in Greece doing research. The suit . . . I have a meeting in Athens that requires it. I must drive there after breakfast."

Stavros hated lying to Nikolas, but his mission demanded it. Nikolas was a potential source of information and a trusted acquaintance, a point of contact and a known quantity. Nikolas and Stavros had fought shoulder to shoulder in close combat, each man protecting the other. But his *need to know* about Stavros's employment did not rise to providence. Besides, it was complicated.

Nikolas probed, "They say that a man so initiated never leaves kataskopeía. Espionage is an old and binding fraternity, no?"

"I have heard the same, my friend. But in the OSS, we were soldiers. In the beginning we were United States Army. In Greece, did we not wear the American uniforms? Spies would never wear uniforms, no?

"Yes, you speak true, but Greece is full, its kataskopeía decanter spills over with spies. They come from Albania and Russia and Britain and Bulgaria and Turkey, even Yugoslavia. And, of course, America, no? Very shady people, Is that right? Would Americans say shady?" asked Nikolas.

"Yes, that is proper usage, and I believe you are right. But I steer a path far from the shadows. My roads all lead to well-lighted universities and libraries. There, I have met no spies, only librarians and curators, boring people who stick their noses in books and dusty artifacts. The excitement of kataskopeía would humble their existence. And you, do you still sling your Beretta and fashion ambushes?" chided Stavros.

"No, no. I ambush only my wife on nights when this is allowed. I ambush my son for play."

"A wife and a son! Congratulations, my friend. When did all this take place?"

"Four years ago. We married in Missolonghi, and my son arrived a year later."

"What are their names?"

"My wife is Diana and my son, I named him Yiorgos. Yiorgos Nikolas."

"Yiorgos for Chómori Yiorgos?" asked Stavros.

"Yes, he is my child's godfather. Kapetánios Yiorgos saved my life after you left Greece. We marched to Patras to escort the British Second Airborne Brigade, paratroopers landing by boat. What do I know? Along the way, just before Antirrio, swine of the Security Battalion took up a sniper's position in the hills. I was leading the main column and would have received a bullet. But Yiorgos was in the hills with a detachment, moving silently and watching for just such danger. He saw the glint from their binoculars. He circled their hide, found there were two swine, and killed them both. You know the area. It was near the Church of Saint George, north of Molykreio. Where you escaped the Messerschmitts, no?"

Stavros nodded, and with remembrance, a charged tingle rose in his spine.

"Yiorgos is a good man. Where is he?"

"He tends his bees in Kato Dafne. Golden, smooth, good honey. He says the best. He has many customers; some even travel from Athens. He has a following that believes his product improves their breathing. Some suffer from the asthma; others smoke too many Papastratos. They take the honey for a cure."

Chómori Yiorgos had been fierce, grizzled, and as hard as the granite in the mountains. Stavros smiled. His reaction raced from fanciful to absurd to risible picturing Yiorgos a docile apiculturist in blanched canvas and veil.

"Yes. I see you smile. It is funny to picture Yiorgos so tame, but he is a cultured man. He attends the opera at Odeon of Herodes. He has heard Maria Callas every time she has performed. The war, the Italians, and the Germans made him a wolf, but now he has regressed to a puppy. He is a dear friend," said Nikolas.

"What of you, Nikolas? What is your work these days?"

"My wife, she is from this town. Her family owns a machine shop north of here. It is not so big, but we have twenty employees. We do fine work, shipbuilding components. I spend the week here at the fabricating plant and travel to Missolonghi Saturday and Sunday. Thus, begins my ambush, no?"

"Are you a machinist?" asked Stavros.

"No. Not a true journeyman. The journeymen let me play with their machines, but no. I am not a machinist. I oversee the business.

"My wife's family has no son to hand the business to. The Germans killed her brother when the British retreated to Crete in 1941. He was fighting in the hills with a band of local men. It was a time before EAM-ELAS. Her father is a man who worked every day to build the business and he, he is a true machinist. But he is old and cannot manage as he has. Now it falls to me. It is good work, I am fortunate."

"Do you still process the olives in Missolonghi?" asked Stavros.

"Indeed. This my wife looks after. My mother and father rebuilt our factory after the Germans left. The Italians set fire to it after they killed my brother in forty-two. But they are Italians, so they only did half the job. Most of the machines were still working. The building they burned, but the machines we salvaged. It is a good business, but not all the year. Only at harvest is it busy."

The news of the machine shop stirred Stavros. But he maintained his composure, smiled, nodded, and revealed nothing to his old friend.

Stavros and Nikolas talked, drank coffee, and reminisced for two hours in the taverna. They caught up on old comrades and relived blood and thunder. When the bells of Saint Basile tolled noon, Nikolas said he was going to the machine shop to meet a shipyard representative.

Nikolas said, "I must go now to the business. You should follow along. It is on your way to Athens, no? I will show you the shop."

"It would be my privilege," replied Stavros.

Stavros checked out, paid his bill, and met Nikolas in front of the hotel. Nikolas drove a well-worn, white-over-green Bedford OY with a canvas-covered bed. Stavros assumed it was 1930s vintage that had survived the British retreat, the Italians, the Germans, and landed in the hands of a loving Greek. In his mind, Stavros compared the old lorry to a laden village donkey or the stout mules they had packed for OSS actions. Stavros was driving a gray 1950 Morris Oxford MO saloon, a tepid excuse for an automobile. Stavros preferred his Ford flathead V-8 convertible in Missouri. The Morris forty horsepower four-cylinder engine propelled the car to seventy miles per hour. Stavros had to admit, that was plenty fast for most Greek roads. The Morris was his issue by economy and circumstance. The United States Embassy in Athens had inherited a fleet of these diplomatic cars from the downscaling British, who had fought as hard as they could against the Greek communist insurgents after the Germans fled. When the British ran out of money, they handed the cars and the insurrection to their American cousins. The CIA station chief in Athens appropriated part of the fleet and refitted the cars with standard issue plates and civilian registrations. The Morris was, as Stavros strove to be, unremarkable on Greek streets and roads.

The friends drove in tandem three kilometers north to a corrugated building set in a field off the road to Kalavrita. The Bedford chugged at a steady speed and only issued a rare puff of blue smoke. There was a tidy painted sign at the entrance to the property that read TRIPOLI METAL FABRICATION. They walked through the front office and past Nikolas's secretary, a pretty, shy young Greek woman. Inside the machine shop, Nikolas introduced Stavros to the workers, men in their forties and fifties with a few younger and only one much older. He said Stavros was an old friend and an American Greek who fought with the andartes. The workers nodded their appreciation. Nikolas called him Professor Stavros. This took Stavros by surprise, and Nikolas saw his expression. Nikolas said, "Come now, Lieutenant, did you not know that your men and some of our fighters called you professor? Was that a secret? I may have offended some pledge by telling you, no? I believe Kapetánios Dimitra was the first to call you such." Then he laughed at Stavros's embarrassment.

Nikolas went on, "What are you researching in Greece, my friend? We never discussed this at the taverna. Something ancient?"

Stavros faced the group. He said, "I am studying the Athenian Navy from the time of Themistokles, the fifth and fourth centuries BC. I hope to author my PhD dissertation from the research. I might like to interview some of you. Your ancestors built the triremes, no?"

The assembled workers met his chide with puzzled looks. Greeks have a robust sense of humor, but not all American comedy translates well.

He spent the next half hour touring the plant. Nikolas needed to attend his meeting and handed off Stavros to the old man, Epaminondas. It was an ancient name shared with a Theban general. Stavros tried to converse and said, "I have come across your name in Xenophon's *Hellenica*. Epaminondas was a prominent leader, a great man."

His taciturn guide nodded and smiled, revealing a litany of missing teeth.

But when the pair arrived at their first machine station, Epaminondas was a fount of narration and wisdom. He explained in detail and duration the equipment and the processes. The plant was tooling and balancing propeller shafts for reworked liberty ships. Greek shipping magnates, most of whom weathered the war in London and New York, had purchased these mass-produced American workhorse vessels following the war. Those in New York got a jump on the investment, while their countrymen in London waited on the cash-strapped British government and banks to release insurance payouts.[1] The liberty ships were sturdy boats for their day, but now needed retrofitting and rebuilding. With the outbreak of the Korean War in June 1950, only a year before, Greek shipping flourished, and owners scrambled for seaworthy vessels to meet demand. Nikolas was in a sound position and negotiated a healthy contract, certain to keep Tripoli Metal Fabrication busy for months.

Epaminondas lectured Stavros on acceptable bearing misalignment limits, uniform load distribution across bearings, shaft strength limits, crankshaft deflections, and coupling bolt strength.[2] Then he spent five minutes talking about misalignment tolerances for clutches and flexible couplings and concluded, "But, for this work we have not to worry about such things."

When the old man started a monologue on hull deflection and thermal deviations, Stavros interrupted his host. He said, "Sir, Epaminondas, your knowledge is vast. You are a walking encyclopedia. I wish for more time to absorb your expertise. However, I have an important meeting in Athens, and I must leave now for the drive. Thank you for your patience and valuable time. I hope someday to visit with you again and we can continue my education." Little did Stavros know of his need for education.

Nikolas walked up behind Stavros as he tried to uncouple from Epaminondas and asked, "Has our foreman made of you an apprentice?"

Stavros smiled and nodded. He said, "Epaminondas is a stream that overflows with knowledge. I am too shallow to contain it."

Nikolas smiled. Then he told Epaminondas, "You better check on the others. We may work this weekend. The shipyard wants to speed up our delivery schedule."

Epaminondas nodded, bowed, then set off to supervise the work.

Stavros said, "Thanks for showing me around. This is an impressive operation. You have good men at work here and plenty of work to do, no?"

Nikolas said, "We will be busy for months. The shipyard agreed to pay the overtime and a premium for the quick delivery. Still, there will be no ambush in Missolonghi this weekend.

"Here, this is my address and telephone at the shop. In Missolonghi, you can ask anyone, and they will know of the olive plant."

Stavros took the paper and said, "You can reach me through the American Embassy. I've been staying at the Grande Bretagne in Athens. There you can leave a message."

"The Grande Bretagne, eh? College professors are well cared for, no?" chimed Nikolas.

"I am fortunate to be working on a special grant from my Uncle Sam," revealed Stavros.

Nikolas smiled. He knew well the reference to Stavros's benefactor.

The old friends shook hands and hugged. They promised to stay in touch and not let another six years pass before talking once again. Nikolas walked Stavros to the parking area. Stavros fired the Morris, turned right on the road to Kalavrita, and began three hours of dread and anticipation.

Ten kilometers north, Stavros left the road to Kalavrita and joined the road to Corinth. As the road straightened, he reached for the radio and turned the power knob. A crackly noise escaped from the dashboard speaker, and Stavros finessed the tuner until he found the band for Ethniko Idryma Radiofonias, EIR, the Greek National Radio Federation. From the two o'clock news update, he learned the EIR had joined with twenty-two other stations to form the European Broadcasting Union. This registered as a positive development to Stavros, who believed that Greece and Europe needed all the unity they could muster. Unity, on the side of America, was his reason for being in Greece. After the news, EIR began broadcasting a series of recorded concerts from young composers of the Athens Conservatory. The first selection was from 1949 entitled *Study for Two Violins and Cello* by a promising composer, Mikis Theodorakis.

The lilting chorus lifted his spirits. He slid his hand under the center of the dashboard and found an unremarkable bolthead, part of the dashboard frame. With a quarter twist, a padded compartment dropped. Stavros removed a .45 Colt M1911 pistol. He steadied the oversized steering wheel with his knees, held the gun in his right hand and press-checked the slide just far enough to be reassured by the brass in the firing chamber. He slid the weapon back into the compartment and secured the secret panel. A profound cello registry accompanied his thoughts, and the asphalt's hum conveyed the Morris.

Chapter 2

"I thought I'd never find this place. Sorry I'm late. I've spent more time in Istanbul than Athens and even less in the Plaka. Besides any symbolism attached to meeting here, do they have decent food?" he asked in a soft southern drawl.

Frank G. Wisner wore a tan, conservative summer-weight suit. He was stocky and well traveled. Stavros rose at his chair to shake his hand. When Wisner pulled his chair back from the two-top table under the leaning lemon tree, the wooden legs grated against the rough cobble. The commotion scared away the black-and-white cat begging at Stavros's feet.

Stavros said, "Sir, good to see you. Yes, the food is fantastic. Great salads and grilled octopus. I wasn't thinking about symbolism when I picked the place. But a restaurant named for the world's first actor might qualify. Everything in this corner of the Plaka relates to the theater." Stavros looked over his shoulder toward the Theater of Dionysus, only yards away on the eastern slope of the Acropolis.

"What was his full name? My classical history fails me," asked Wisner.

"Aristotle called him Thespis of Icaria. He developed tragedy as an artistic style," said Stavros.

"Actor and tragedian. We might use that as a position description, right? Only sad actors need apply? I'll send a note to Personnel and Administration and see what they say. They'll send back a ream of rules and regulations it would trample."

Stavros nodded at his boss's levity, relieved at his good mood. Frank Wisner was fair, educated, practiced, and driven. But the driven could overshadow the practiced. He was a man who ran warm and cool, high and low. The world was on his shoulders with a war to win, cold though it might be. Stavros respected Wisner without reservation and felt honored to have one-on-one time with the CIA Deputy Director of Plans. Wisner's title diminished his all-knowing role as chief of covert operations and intelligence. His promotion was the latest snapshot of the fast-forward bureaucratic whirlwind that was America's intelligence services following abolishment of the OSS.

Stavros first met Wisner in Cairo in early 1944. Wisner had entered Egypt just before Christmas 1943 on a following wave of *beautiful people,* Americans working for the Red Cross, the OSS, and the Office of War Information. He was part of the ballooning American Mission.[3] He was a reports officer, an analyst. He worked with paper and sorted half-truths and lies from usable intelligence. His work at OSS HQ consumed him, but it would never be mistaken for exciting. He sought the company of Secret Intelligence Branch spies and Special Operations Branch commandos, people like Stavros, people with stories he wanted to hear.

Even before Cairo, Wisner had been a devotee of cultural immersion. From a wealthy and cultivated Mississippi family, he had been treated to a grand tour of Europe before entering college. Cairo only reinforced his notion that analysts couldn't understand a country and assess intelligence without knowing the people and their ways. The British Special Operations Executive officers he worked with only confirmed this. In understated caution, they warned the energetic greenhorn that it was important to study foreign cultures but to guard against *going native.* Thus, it was in the spirit of cultural expansion that Wisner met Stavros.

On a day trip to Camp Huckstep, the sprawling Allied supply base near Cairo where the OSS Greek Operational Groups were awaiting deployment pretending to be truck drivers, Wisner overheard a conversation. Stavros and his commandos were bantering about a Greek dance on the sidelines of a basketball game. Interrupting a vivid projection of how the local girls would find them irresistible, Wisner asked if he could tag along. He said official Cairo bored him.

Stavros liked the man and saw no harm in him coming. Having someone from the American Mission and the OSS head shed might help if any of his cocksure comrades found their way into the clutch of local police.

They hit it off that night, but the dance was a bust. The commandos, in their British paratroop boots and new Eisenhower jackets, cut a dashing cast in the ballroom of the Grand Hotel. But the Greek girls kept a haughty distance, stuck on themselves. It disappointed the Americans that there were no line dances, no Kalamatianos. The Greeks in Egypt only danced American style. Stavros and Wisner met at Huckstep two more times. Over coffee in the mess, they discussed everything from women to world views. Then Stavros's Operational Group shipped out to Italy in February.

Stavros held a master's degree in world history. He taught at Park College in Kansas City and lectured at the Army Command and General Staff College at Fort Leavenworth. In April 1943, he relinquished his draft exemption and volunteered for the Army's 122nd Greek Battalion. When that unit disbanded in September, the OSS recruited Stavros and 186 other Greeks for commando service in the Old Country. OSS commissioned Stavros a first lieutenant and gave him command of an operational group.

Wisner was two years older than Stavros, with a wife and two children. He had earned his bachelor's and law degrees from the University of Virginia. He practiced law on Wall Street but never fit in. He joined the US Naval Reserve six months before Pearl Harbor and earned the rank of commander. But reviewing legal briefs and managing the censorship branch offered little challenge. He transferred to OSS just prior to meeting Stavros in Cairo. He was engaging, motivated, and full of ideas. Stavros liked him.

So did Wild Bill Donavan, the head of OSS. In June 1944, while Stavros and his commandos were learning The Greek Way by ambushing Germans in the Nafpaktian

Mountains, Donavan appointed Wisner chief of OSS Secret Intelligence Branch Istanbul. In neutral Turkey he made fast work cleaning up Operation Dogwood, an OSS chain gone to seed that the Nazis were using to sow disinformation. In August he transferred to Romania in charge of OSS SI operations in all southeast Europe. In Bucharest, he evacuated 1,350 British and American airmen scattered throughout the country and held prisoner by the quisling government. With a successful coup d'état by King Michael, Romania moved into the Allied Camp. In the chaotic shuffle, Wisner evacuated the POWs just hours ahead of the Soviet Army's advance and under the noses of the retreating Wehrmacht and Luftwaffe. The Germans left in such haste that Wisner came to possess a trove of sensitive oil production data and shipping records. Romania was the largest supplier of Axis oil during the war, and most of the Allied airmen were downed trying to bomb it to rubble. The industry data allowed analysts to infer much about Nazi war capabilities. It was an intelligence coup alongside King Michael's, and Wisner's reputation grew, as did his promotional appeal.

With evacuation of the airmen in Romania, Stavros and Wisner's OSS careers overlapped once more. Stavros infiltrated China in the fall of 1944 and led guerrillas rescuing downed American flight crews. When President Truman abolished the OSS in October 1945, Wisner first went back to his legal practice, then to the Department of State. In September 1947, President Truman signed the National Security Act creating the Central Intelligence Agency. Wisner left State and reentered the world of mirrors in 1948 as CIA assistant director of policy coordination. He developed expertise in downed airmen and tactics of evacuation, escape, and evasion. He wrote Stavros, a subject expert in downed airman, who after the war returned to teach at Park College and work on his doctorate.

Late in 1948, Wisner took over the misleadingly named Office of Policy Coordination. The OPC's charter was as robust as its name was innocuous. A National Security Council directive put OPC in charge of "propaganda, economic warfare, preventive direct action, including sabotage, anti-sabotage, demolition and evacuation procedures; subversion against hostile states, including assistance to underground resistance groups, guerrillas and refugee liberation groups, and support of indigenous anti-communist elements in threatened countries of the free world."[4]

Wisner set out to recruit Stavros and others like him. He targeted former OSS operators and spies, men who lived clandestine lives and knew survival. The pitch was simple. The world is divided into good and evil, light and darkness, freedom and slavery. America stands for dignity and progress and the USSR for enslavement. In this epic struggle for the soul of civilization, the Soviets would leave no avenue uncontested.

He recited the 1948 bombshell that *Time* magazine editor, Whittaker Chambers, had confessed to spying for the Soviets. Chambers then implicated Alger Hiss at Department of State, unveiling a shadow war. Communists had breached America at the highest levels of government, and Uncle Sam was playing catch-up.

Nuance abounded, Wisner admitted, but the big picture was clear. The initiation of the Cominform, the Communist Information Bureau, in 1947 had been a springboard for international revolution and a reincarnation of the Communist International disbanded in 1943. Wisner pointed to the February 1948 Soviet-backed coup d'état in Czechoslovakia, then the Blockade of Berlin in June. That same year, France and Italy tottered under communist-led strikes, and the Partito Comunista Italiano appeared poised to win Italy's general election. Greece was still fighting communist guerrillas in the country's north.

In 1949 the Soviets detonated an atomic weapon, and the Chinese Communists came to power. In the jungles of Central Luzon just north of Manila, communist and Huk rebels advanced with little resistance. In June 1950, the Soviets and Chinese supported the invasion of South Korea. Wisner saw communism threatening, not only because of its military might, but for its insidious ideological appeal.

Wisner foresaw a strategic battle for cultural and ideological supremacy amid a concurrent counterinsurgency and political war. That was his world. He commanded a bottomless budget with minor oversight. He would oppose Soviet influence in political and cultural circles anywhere and everywhere, in Europe and America. His Operation Mockingbird planted CIA-sourced stories throughout American newspapers, television, wire services, and radio. His network touched leading outlets from CBS, *The Washington Post, Newsweek, The New York Times*, and *The Christian Science Monitor*.[5] Similar cultural tendrils he seeded across the globe.

His offshore clandestine work, active measures, direct-action projects, were impersonal, targeted, and unrestricted. Thus, the need for hardened operators, people who would do what needed done.

On the world stage, the US offered economic support to the ravaged, war-torn European economies through the Marshall Plan. Military support radiated through a new alliance called NATO, the North Atlantic Treaty Organization.

Stavros bought the appeal in early 1949 and entered his own world of mirrors. His cover was as natural as the feral feline weaving between his legs. He was a professor. He stayed at Park College, teaching, and researching. In late 1949, the President of Park College received two well-dressed visitors from "a government agency." They suggested a healthy educational grant could be forthcoming if the college arranged for the "loan" of Stavros. The president allowed an indeterminate sabbatical, and Stavros began orientation and training in Washington.

Downed airmen were important, but Wisner saw Stavros in another role. Those plans and modifications thereto were the tedious predicate for their meeting. At Thespis in the Plaka on a warm October night under an ageless full moon, conversation veered from friendly to business.

"We've got a lot to talk over. Do you have the time?" asked Stavros.

"You are the last thing on my list for today unless either of the two men around the corner comes by and whisks me away for something urgent," answered Wisner.

Just then, a server in his fifties brought a tray to their table and placed in front of Stavros a beer and a basket of small fried fish. Both men were silent as the waiter set the table. Then the waiter asked Wisner if he'd like to order. Wisner told him a beer would do for now, and they could order dinner in a few minutes. The waiter left, and the conversation resumed.

"First, how did your trip to Crete go?" asked Wisner.

"Interesting," offered Stavros. "Souda is a near-perfect location for naval staging. The Greeks have been using it since before time. The Venetians used it, the Ottomans, the Germans. It's deep water and defensible.

"The wind can be tricky when it blows due west. There's a funnel effect over Chania between the Akrotiri Peninsula and Cape Drapano. But this is rare, and at twenty-five knots, it's not prohibitive for larger vessels. Otherwise, it's fifteen kilometers east to west and two to four kilometers north to south and protected. I'll file the report tomorrow.

"The Soviets have an anchorage south of Crete, about seventy kilometers. It's their Black Sea picket. It's under command of their Operational Formation Mediterranean Sea. They have supply vessels and maintenance units there, and only eight warships, Komar class. Wooden hulled fast boats with the Termit missiles.[6] That's what the photos looked like to me. I've sent the film per channels. My contact reported no sub conning towers. The rest were all supply ships, two dozen in all.

"The rain waylaid me in the Peloponnese. I spent the night in Tripoli and ran into an old andarte friend. I'm ninety-nine percent sure it was happenstance. His name is Nikolas. He runs a machine shop doing marine contracting. He showed me around the plant, and it's impressive.

"Nikolas is a good man. The Italians killed his brother, a monk, and burned his family's business. He joined EAM-ELAS and rose to stratiotikós in the Chómori unit. He was never KKE, so I doubt he's palling around with them now. He could not have known I would stay in Tripoli. Hell, *I* didn't know. His business, Tripoli Metal Fabrication, is as legitimate as they come, so I think he's clean, no attachments.

"I'll write up a contact report."

"What about your NATO contacts in the Circle? It looks like the Greeks are onboard and we'll formalize their ascension early next year. They'll come in along with Turkey. Their entry will anchor a three-thousand-mile defensive line from Gibraltar right up to the Soviet border," stated Wisner.

"Our Athens Group is supportive. They like our aid and they like Americans. They are not always comfortable with our military approach to the communists, but they like that the communists have lost and that the British have left. The population, at least in Athens, is hungry for peace and economic recovery. They've been at war for over a decade," answered Stavros.

"Who came up with the name?" asked Wisner.

"*O kýklos érevnas kai proódou*? The Research and Progress Circle?" asked Stavros.

"Right," said Wisner.

"A friend of mine suggested it. She knows how Greeks think," answered Stavros.

"That would be Dimitra?" asked Wisner.

"Right," answered Stavros.

"You know we've got concerns about her and your, um . . . connection?" prodded Wisner.

"I've been up front, sir. We met in Chómori, fell in something approaching love, and separated in 1944. Now she lives her life, and I live mine. She earned her PhD and digs artifacts for a living, and I, as far as she knows, research ancient navies. We see each other when it's convenient."

"It's her past, Stavros. Her membership in KKE that sends up red flags, no pun intended."

"I understand. But I was with her when she renounced party discipline. I know the danger she was in. She worked her magic with social democratic friends and VIPs. They cut a deal with the KKE to get her out without a trial or inquiry. I was there.

"She has great insight and contributes a pro-American voice to the group. Plus, her contacts are invaluable. The Circle has movers and shakers from political organizations, publishing, academia, and cultural groups. They hold sway. Just what we want, right? Influence among those who create culture, thoughts, policy, and ideas."

Wisner nodded, then said, "You understand why we're cautious."

Stavros nodded.

Wisner kept his thoughts to himself. He knew Dimitra from photos and appreciated Stavros's attraction. Dimitra gave suitable cover for his detached, love-sick professor circulating in Greece to research shipbuilding and ancient nautical prowess.

Wisner went on, "Just keep up the contact reports. You don't have to pen anything salacious, just who, what, where, when, and why. Okay?"

Stavros nodded.

"Back to NATO," offered Wisner before launching into a recitation of postwar events.

"The Brits told Truman in February 1947 that they were finito. They couldn't afford another war in Greece. The KKE had reorganized and rearmed, and the Brits didn't want the fight. Truman told the world in March that the US would stop communist expansion, and his first order of business was Greece. In July, Griswold came to Athens, set up the American Mission, and began weeding out rightists. He got rid of Zervas and installed Sophoulis, reined in the torture and atrocities, and set them on a political and military strategy. The Greeks liked American money, which I believe came to four hundred million above the board.[7] He controlled the money, so he controlled the Greeks.

"General Van Fleet took over in February 1948. He spent two hundred million and organized a hundred local militia battalions. He freed the Greek Army from positional defense and used them to pursue the KKE.[8] He pounded the guerrillas wherever they popped up and pushed the communists out of Central Greece in a month. They retreated north, and he crushed them in late 1949. That's when NATO came to the front burner."

Stavros thought about the communists he'd fought alongside against the Germans, members of the KKE. They were good men and women. Not once had his American commandos been betrayed, exposed, or abandoned. But things change. Now, the KKE was a puppet of the Soviets and Yugoslavs. And when the Yugoslavian support withdrew in 1949, they had fallen. Stalin and the Soviets had abandoned them even earlier. He felt sorry for them, at least for the individuals he knew to be Greeks first and communists second. The thought of their last stand on Mount Grammos under the hell of napalm B sobered him.[9]

Wisner went on, "The Greeks have never been the problem for NATO. The problem was that the Brits didn't want them included. They wanted a separate Middle East defense pact. The Scandinavian and Benelux countries feared Greece would drag them into an unwanted Mediterranean war.

"Then, enter the Soviets and Chinese communists. The Soviet bomb and the Korean invasion changed the calculation. When the Greek government sent troops to Korea, it was the cherry on the cake. The Brits relinquished their objection and both Greece and Turkey will ascend early next year. I understand General Bradley is standing by for the initial integration planning.

"We expect the Greeks will allow military installations. That's our interest in Souda, among other places. We'll set up airfields and support bases, some monitoring stations, and other infrastructure.

"So, I'm here to say excellent work. Your Circle and their influence has helped with the friendly acceptance of NATO. And NATO is the linchpin to containing the Soviets.

"Now, we should talk about something delicate. First some good news. I want you in Washington with me. I want somebody who knows Greece right next to me. I plan to work you out of this assignment over the next year and put you behind a desk at HQ. It's a promotion and a raise.

"What are your thoughts?"

Stavros was dumbfounded. He had never saw himself behind a desk at CIA HQ with the bluebloods and ivy leaguers. He'd never pictured himself living in Washington. What would he do about his dissertation and his PhD?

This was dread, but it wasn't the dread that Stavros had expected. Since being summoned to this meeting, he'd worried Wisner would give him something off the books. A face-to-face with the deputy director of plans on your home turf meant . . . trouble. A promotion to CIA HQ was gift-wrapped trouble of another sort, but trouble, nevertheless.

Stavros picked a small fish from the basket, dropped it for the cat, and tried to maintain his outward composure. The cat worried not at all about composure and attacked the plunder like a ravenous beast.

Wisner said, "Okay. I can see you need time. You have a day. Here's how I see things."

Just then the waiter reappeared with Wisner's beer, and his customers went silent. He asked if they would like to order.

Wisner said, "Go ahead. I ate a late lunch, and I need to work when I get back. I'll just snack on these fish and drink this beer."

Stavros asked the waiter to bring an appetizer of grilled octopus, a Greek summer salad, and a bowl of avgolemono soup with the salad served last. The waiter nodded and walked back to the kitchen.

"You'll stay in Greece for a few months. A year might be too long, but we'll see what happens. Wind down your work in Athens Morale Group and keep reporting through FB-1. The merger of OSO and OPC into the Directorate of Plans is a work in progress. Nothing official yet. Keep reporting status quo. OPC structure will stay the same at the field level, for now.

"Our friends in OSO were supposed to be intel only, but they've crept into operations. They think their title entitles them. Guess again. I'm just getting a handle on what they've been up to. Keep your eyes open and your ears to the ground. Let me know if you ferret any Office of Special Operations *operations*."

This was the injunction that made Stavros's head spin, the headquarters merry-go-round. Wisner was asking, ordering him to spy on the CIA's own spies. His was justified dread.

"You will need to help with Project FIEND. I don't like where that is going. The Albanians are on to us. Or onto the Brits, definitely on to somebody. The Pixies write more letters than a New York publishing house. They tell Aunt Besjana everything—where, when, how many. The Sigurimi reads all Albanian inbound mail. The operation leaks like a colander. Now that the Greeks have KKE under control, and Albania is not running resupply, I'm not sure why we're there. Albania is cut off. Tito's stiff-arming Stalin, so Yugoslavia is no help. They're cut off and not much of a threat.

"Hoxha has a sixty-five-thousand-man army and a fifteen-thousand-man security force. The Soviets field over five thousand advisers and technicians. It's a police state. We keep losing recruits, and the Brits aren't doing any better. God help us if we've got a mole. The minute our recruits land, and I don't approve of the Brits calling them Pixies, they're snatched up. The Brits are haughty, but any time we need an island to stage an operation, they seem to have one right at hand.

"Albania is a beautiful country, but they live in the Dark Ages. The people care more about their clan than their government. They're still fighting blood feuds that go back centuries. And by dark, I mean no electricity. They turn it on for two hours in the evening in the parts of the country that are wired.

"Still, we may need another airlift, maybe two. You might have to pull some strings, move some people from Kifissia to Corfu. The Polish aircrews are already onboard at Elefsina. Work with Hod Fuller, he's running logistics. I'm rotating new training staff to Manetta, but they'll come in through the embassy. They shouldn't be a problem.[10]

"This will give you time to finish your research, right? You should have plenty for a dissertation by now?"

Stavros nodded. Then he realized Wisner had asked a question.

"Right. Lots of material, less dissertation," he answered.

"Midnight oil, my friend. Just like your undergrad days," chided Wisner.

Stavros didn't mention that he had burned his undergrad midnight oil in Kansas City's West Bottoms Stockyards, prodding manure-crusted cattle from pens into railcars.

"So that was the good news," said Wisner.

To Stavros, the good news had landed as something less.

"Now for the bad," confided Wisner. "We've got a problem in your Circle. Lochagos Christakis is GRU. We have him on film meeting with the rezidentura. His trail goes all the way back to Gouzenko."

Stavros remained silent and again kept his thoughts to himself. Captain Christakis was a staff officer in the Greek Army assigned to the Ministry for Public Security. In Circle discussions and signed publications, he was a supporter of all things American. He was younger than Stavros, reserved and stiff if not formal. If Wisner said there was film of him meeting with the Soviet's chief spy in Athens, then he was a problem.

"When Gouzenko defected right after the war, the Canadians didn't believe him. He walked into an Ottawa Mountie post with a codebook and a story. They told him to get lost. He went to *The Ottawa Journal,* and the editor told him to try his luck at the Canadian Department of Justice. He went there, codebooks and cipher in hand, but they were closed. It was months before the government figured him authentic. The Canadians called in the Brits and, sometime later, they briefed the FBI. We played hell getting the material from Hoover.[11] He hates us. Anyway, Gouzenko's archive and debrief confirm that Christakis died in the battle for Crete, and a KKE impostor assumed his identity. We're still working on the agent's actual name. The impostor Christakis fled to Turkey and then to Egypt and into the exile Hellenic Army.

"He was in Palestine in April 1944 when the Greeks expanded their Sacred Band unit to a full regiment. He passed muster, and that's the legend he's been living since. His story is that his entire family was murdered by the Germans and their village burned. Hence, no family in Greece. It's plausible enough—God knows the Germans killed their share of innocent Greeks. I'm sure you know all too well.

"Anyway, he's a problem. What do you want to do?" asked Wisner.

Stavros thought in silence and sipped his beer. If the GRU had penetrated the Circle, it was bad for the mission, bad for him, and worse, it could be bad for other members. Including Dimitra. He knew now why Wisner had called this unwelcome news.

"Sir, we have options. We can leave him be and watch him. We can try to turn him. We can feed him misinformation and see where it goes. Or we can neutralize him. Those are the obvious choices," answered Stavros.

"The GRU is a tough nut. Soviet Army intelligence trusts no one. Hell, they frisk politburo members and the general secretary before letting them in their Moscow headquarters. Our odds at turning him are long. We'd have a better shot if he were MGB," offered Wisner.

"If we roll him up, take him off the chessboard, we stop the leak. Then we could interrogate him and see what he gives up. But to be honest, the problem is bigger than the Circle. We don't deal with elevated secrets and strategy in the Circle. It's public consumption product, journal articles, newspaper editorials, position papers. Pretty harmless stuff. He must have another source he's working, something with more meat on the bones, at the Ministry," said Stavros.

"Right, that's a bigger problem. We need to know how far his chain extends. Can you pal up to him and find an angle, see what he's made of?" asked Wisner.

"It's possible, sure. I'm friendly with him in the Circle, but I've never socialized with him. He's remote and guarded. I've never seen him with anyone else," answered Stavros. After a moment of silence, he cautioned, "If he's GRU, he'll know the pitch. I'll be on their list pretty quick if I'm not already."

Wisner nodded agreement.

"What would you think of bringing Tommy in on this?" asked Wisner.

Tommy was Thomas Hercules Karamessines, a Greek American and former analyst on the OSS Greek Desk working counterintelligence. He was CIA station chief in Athens, and it bothered Stavros that Wisner had suggested that Tommy not be read in. This was the off-the-books dread that haunted his anticipation of this meeting.

Stavros had no issues with Tommy. They weren't friendly, but there were no grudges. Stavros thought Tommy might be envious of his commando experience. Desk jocks could be that way.

"That's your call, sir. You outrank us all," said Stavros.

"Tommy's got his hands full reorganizing the KYPE. He's got the Greeks focused on a CIA model and they are buying in, lots of politics. Plus, the CIA model is a moving target, right?" chided Wisner.

"Yes sir," answered Stavros.

"Let me think about it. The fewer who know, the less likely a leak," said Wisner.

Stavros thought, *The fewer who know, the more I'm on my own.*

Wisner said, "Come by the embassy tomorrow, and I'll leave the Christakis file with the duty officer in the reading room. I'm off to Rome early. Have the station send a crypt about your DC decision.

"I want you with me, Stavros. You're savvy about this country, and that's scarce. HQ is full of smart people, but they can overthink a problem. I need someone who sees a problem and produces a plan. Speaking of plans, we plan to teach your ferry operation at Camp Peary."

Stavros smiled. "You mean ''Devil's Cauldron.' That was our code for it."

The cryptonym had emerged from a dressing down Kapetánios Dimitra had given Stavros for infecting her andartes with *big American ideas.* His smile broadened remembering her words, "Ferries, water, tides, storms, Germans, these all stir the cauldron and make a tempest of your devils' brew, no?"

The improbable operation had been a success but at the cost of the lives of two brave andartes. A calculation of war that sent a ferry full of Germans and their vehicles to the bottom of the Gulf of Corinth. Stavros thought of the sinking as his late contribution to the 1571 Battle of Lepanto.

Wisner said, "That makes you happy? Then you must station in DC so you can drive to Peary and teach the class, eh? You'll want to get it right, right?

"Anyway, let me know by tomorrow evening, and don't overthink it."

The decision had already been made. Stavros was sorting the details. He thought of his life in Missouri. Alex and Marta, his father and stepmother, lived in St. Louis, an easy drive from Kansas City. He would give up his teaching positions at Park and the War College. He could submit his dissertation from anywhere. He'd have to go back to defend it. Where would he live in Washington? How would this change things with Dimitra?

Dimitra. She had been a never-ending enigma and unfinished chapter even before Wisner's latest provocation. His fascination with the raven-haired beauty went far beyond skin-deep. They had fought side by side. He'd watched her command andartes and master political maneuvers that would have destroyed lesser players. They were intimate. When she perplexed him, he thought his compulsion . . . what? Pathological? When they connected, which was most of the time, he registered his feelings manageable, bordering on distracting. He would not sort the Dimitra puzzle tonight. He just nodded to Wisner and accepted the deadline.

He reached into the woven basket, withdrew a fried scimitar, and dropped the morsel, much to the delight of his fugacious friend.

Chapter 3

Rock shrapnel exploded from eager tires. Punished Pirellis spun and clawed into loose gravel and packed dirt, seeking purchase for the engine's torque. Stavros doffed his fedora, turned his head, and covered his face with the Stetson. The rally-fitted Fiat drifted into the apex of the curve. As the rear of the car pivoted toward the spectators, the fevered engine blasted an overwrought signature from the glowing throat of the exhaust. Stavros smelled gasoline and melting rubber. Then the gray Fiat vanished, invisible in a retreating cloud of dust to further its conquest of Agios Elias.

At 1,900 meters, the mountain was one of the highest in the race, and the highest on this stage, the fifth of twelve. Stavros watched with a small group of locals and rally enthusiasts at the sharpest turn on the course. Where he stood, the road veered three hundred and sixty degrees before continuing its precarious climb. Here drivers negotiated a gritty about-face, the trickiest turn on the stage. Picket pines kept cars from launching into the abyss, but peril and mechanical failure loomed in every moment and movement.

Stavros turned to his companion and said, "That is amazing driving. He handled that hairpin like he was on rails."

Lochagos Alexis Christakis nodded, then offered, "That was Petros Peratikos. He is among the best. Many think he will win, if his Fiat holds up. This is the first time Fiat is racing its fourteen hundred with its self-supporting body. Its first race on dirt. It's a modern design. Many think it will not hold up. But the design makes the car lighter, eliminating much of the heavy iron frame."

Stavros had followed Wisner's suggestion that he pal up to Christakis and take his measure. As a result, Stavros now knew that Christakis was a knowledgeable rally enthusiast. After that week's meeting of the Circle, Stavros asked the suspected GRU operator what he was doing over the weekend. It pleased him that

Christakis mentioned the rally and suggested Stavros tag along. Christakis said the first ever sanctioned Greek road rally excited him. The race had no official name in 1951. But in two years it would organize as the Acropolis Rally, draw top European competitors, and forge a legend for its demands on drivers and cars.

As the Fiat climbed out of sight, Stavros thought, *these crappy Greek roads have found some value.*

Other cars followed, racy J2X Allards, stylish Jaguar XK 120s, ponderous Mercedes salons, and cars Stavros couldn't name. One hundred and twenty in all. Most entrants featured bulging, add-on headlights fitted with screens. It was quite a parade, and Stavros, an American interested in cars with a passing knowledge of Indianapolis-style racing, relished the spectacle. It was a lovely day and, other than being pelted with road shrapnel, an enjoyable one.

The two men scrutinized the action and made small talk for the rest of the afternoon. With the cars still arriving, Stavros told Christakis he was getting hungry and asked if he would like to join him in Amfissa for dinner. The men were halfway between Karoutes and Amfissa, with Amfissa to the east on the road back to Athens. Stavros could tell that Christakis was not quite ready to leave but after a thoughtful moment, he nodded his head in agreement. Stavros asked, "Do you know a good place in Amfissa?"

Christakis registered the question and answered without hesitation, "Yes. Kaísaras Psitopoleío. One block south of the plateia in front of the church, the Mitropoli Church. Here they roast a fresh lamb every day on weekends. Very good. But they have poultry. If that is your preference."

"Caesar Grill?" asked Stavros.

"Yes, yes. Years ago, the owner was an Italian who came to the Greek ways. My family would eat there on holidays. It is a small place, not special. But the food is exceptional," Christakis assured.

"Then Caesar it is," said Stavros.

Both men had driven to the rally via a road that was even less of a road than the racecourse. When they retrieved their cars from the parking area, Stavros told Christakis to go first and he would follow. Although Stavros feigned ignorance of the locale and Amfissa, he knew it. He had visited before with Dimitra when she was working a dig near Delphi, twenty kilometers southeast. She was the dig boss at a settlement believed to predate the Pythia, the oracle established in the eighth century BCE. They had spent an exuberant and lustful night at the Hotel Amfissaeum but hadn't bothered with dinner, so his ignorance of where to eat was real.

One thing kept coming to Stavros's mind on the eight-kilometer drive to Amfissa. Why would Christakis mention his family if they were part of his GRU legend? It was an opening for discussion that no cagy agent would ever offer. Unless he was good and wanted to throw Stavros off the track or learn how eager Stavros was to explore his background. To follow up or not, that was the question.

Caesar Grill was much as Stavros expected. It was a small, tidy business with indoor and curbside seating for maybe fifty people. A husband, wife, and daughter attended. There was a smattering of locals and a table of tourists who appeared continental, but Stavros couldn't tell their nationality.

A big man in a kitchen-soiled apron walked from behind the service window and entwined Christakis in a bear hug. He lifted the soldier off his feet, all the while chiding him for not visiting more often. "I never see you, my friend. Where do you go? Why not visit more? Are you too good for us peasants now that you live in Athens? And why the uniform? Are we to be invaded again?"

Christakis flinched and pulled his head away, an involuntary reaction to the big man's unshaven stubble and the smell of a day's sweat earned in the kitchen. He grimaced at kisses on both cheeks. Chagrined, Christakis deftly disentangled from the hug. He regained his distance from the owner, then reached for the big man's substantial hand with both of his, shaking it with reserve and warmth.

"Elias, I want you to meet a friend of mine. He too is staying in Athens, but he is a professor from America. Stavros Theofanis, meet Elias Stergiopolous. Elias is a dear friend of the family. This is his wife, Fofo, and his daughter, Angelica," offered Christakis, nodding toward the women near the kitchen pass-through.

Stavros removed his hat and shook hands with the owner, nodded and smiled at the matronly Fofo and her pretty, bright-eyed daughter. Both women smiled in return.

"Come, come, sit here, unless you want to sit outside? Sit here, this is better, this way I can work and talk with you at the same time. Our business is not so good tonight, but it is early. We'll get busy later," Elias confided.

The owner showed the men to a table to the right of the kitchen doorway. As they took their chairs, Angelica brought table service wrapped in cloth napkins and smiled again at Stavros. She set the service to the left, then returned with a pitcher of water and glasses which she poured three-quarters full and set to the right of the placemat. Then, looking at Stavros, she asked in a cheery tone, "Can I get you something to drink? Alexis, I know what he wants."

Stavros looked across the table at Christakis and asked, "What are you having?"

Christakis said, "Cellar red."

Stavros looked puzzled, and Angelica interpreted, "Cellar red is the wine my father makes. He keeps it in the cellar. He thinks it is special. Me, not so much. He makes it with a white grape that has grown at our house since he was a boy. Maybe longer. He ages it in an ancient oak cask, more a barrel than a cask, so it turns red. He adds sugar and a little something else. It's more a tradition than a fine dining experience."

Stavros liked this young woman. She was confident and charming. He said, "Then, make it two. I like tradition."

The little something else was tsipouro and anise, but not too much.

When Angelica left to retrieve the order, Stavros smiled across the table at Christakis and then let his eyes take in his surroundings. On the rear wall hung family photographs and religious iconography. There was a Greek flag on the wall to the right. To their left hung an oversized map of classical Greece, a map that stretched from Sicily to India. It was not academic quality but conveyed the lore and pride of times long ago. Just inside the grill's entranceway was a plaster bust on a pedestal of Alexander the Great.

Angelica returned with two fruit glasses filled with dark, syrupy liquid. She set them before her customers and said, "I'll give you a couple of minutes to look over the menu." She pointed to a blackboard to the right of the kitchen pass-through. Again, she looked at Stavros and said, "If you have never tried Fofo's skordalia, you should. It is the best. People come from miles for it."

Christakis nodded at Stavros.

"Fine, sounds great. Maybe a double order?" he asked, looking at Christakis.

Christakis nodded, then suggested, "Better one skordalia and one fava."

"*Kala*! I'll be right back," assured Angelica. And she was off to the kitchen like a force of nature. *She moved like Terpsichore in a glen*, thought Stavros.

Christakis saw his admiration. He said, "She is a delight, no?"

Stavros nodded.

Christakis raised his fruit glass and Stavros followed. The young soldier said, "*Ya mas!*"

Stavros answered, "*Yassou!*"

They sipped from their glasses, and the first taste on Stavros's tongue was sweetness, then a hint of anise and pepper. The drink was not distasteful, but one glass would be plenty. It reminded him of the more conventional dessert wine, Mavrodaphne, or the wine used in communion.

Christakis sipped his drink without reaction, then took a second, more substantial swallow.

Stavros said, "Thank you for inviting me to the rally. It was exciting. Have you been a fan of racing for long?"

"Yes. Since I was a boy. My father worked on cars and trucks and owned a garage, though he was a farmer. I do not know where he learned mechanics, but he was good. He even owned a welder's set. He dug out a pit in our garage so he could work underneath vehicles. I would hide there when we played, my brother and me. My clothes would get so oily that my mother withheld my dinner.

"One day, a friend brought my father a Mercedes roadster, a 1936 model, I believe. It didn't belong to my father's friend; no one in our village had such money. The driver flagged my father's friend and asked where he could have a wheel straightened.

"It was sleek and black with a red leather interior. Never had I seen such fine coachwork and upholstery. It was to me like a dream. The car was something beyond my imagination. The speedometer registered two hundred kilometers per hour.

"My father trued the wire wheel and the owner, I believe a German, thanked him, and paid. Then he started the engine, a supercharged, straight-eight with dual outboard exhausts. The power and the presence. I remember the respect born at that moment. I was eleven years old. Cars have fascinated me since."

The next conversational leap would be for Stavros to ask where Christakis grew up, what village. But he hesitated. He didn't sense a trap or an agenda. Just the opposite. Words between the men had flowed with a natural rhythm all day. Christakis seemed reserved but never standoffish. Never guarded to the point where Stavros felt he was hiding something or dodging the truth. But the best at this game were better than anyone. The GRU and all Soviet spy agencies were world-class deceivers.

It was the spontaneous familiarity at the grill, the unrehearsed fondness of the owner and this family. Stavros knew the GRU capable of this level of legend, this level of reinforcement. He had read the files and after-action reports. The Soviets went to unfathomable lengths to snare targets. They crafted lifelong legends and vivid vignettes. They wove fantasies to make Hollywood green with envy. But there, sitting at Caesar Grill with Angelica flirting, her inviting dark eyes beaming across the dining room, the moment seemed very Greek, very real. *And it would*, thought Stavros, *if that's the way the GRU wanted it.*

He took another sip of the sweet red wine.

Angelica returned with the appetizers and set the skordalia before Stavros and the fava in front of Christakis. Then she placed a basket in the middle of the table and uncovered the red checkered cloth, keeping the fresh bread warm. The smell wafted to Stavros, and his hunger turned urgent. She nodded to Stavros, smiled, and said, "*Apolamváno!*"

Stavros smiled back, and Angelica whisked away to return her server's tray to the ready station.

Still smiling and reaching for a piece of bread, Stavros asked, "How did you come to enlist in the Army?"

"It is not surprising. I joined the call-up after the Italians attacked in 1940. I left my family in November, and that was the last I saw of them. I was sixteen years old.

"I fought as an enlisted man in a rifle battalion in Epirus. A most lowly rank and difficult fighting. We drove the Italians back into Albania, but it was hard. It was a freezing winter, and the Hellenic Army lacked provisions. But the Italians lacked the heart for the fight. They fielded better arms and equipment and more men, but their leaders told them Greece would be easy.

They said we would fold like a paper army. When we fought them with determination, they lost heart. What do I know? Then came Hitler in the spring.

"In the winter they promoted me to *lochías*. I was seventeen and a sergeant of men who were twice my age. Our unit joined the defense of Athens, then the Peloponnese, then Crete. When the Germans overran us in Crete, I fled in a caïque to Turkey, then to Egypt, then to the Middle East. That is where I joined the Sacred Band. By then I was Ypolochagós Christakis. I came to understand that surviving was the best guarantee of promotion.

"In October 1944, when the Germans left Athens, we transported there and fought the KKE. Then they sent us back to the Dodecanese to rout the remaining Germans from the islands. We were under British command. The British had been in charge since Egypt, though some Greek commanders thought otherwise.

"The Germans surrendered in May 1945, and they recalled the Sacred Band to Athens. They disbanded the regiment in August. I was Lochagos Christakis and assigned to the Ministry, or the remnant department that became the Ministry after Papandreou reorganized the government."

Scripted and well-rehearsed, or succinct and well-lived? Stavros couldn't tell. Christakis recited the tale in his military briefer's persona. Stavros knew the countenance well. Every military of every country groomed this type of hierarchical communication. Keep it short, to the point, and accurate. No more, no less.

Then the tables turned.

Christakis asked, "What is it like in Kansas City?"

He impressed Stavros with his correct if over articulated pronunciation.

Christakis continued, "I know little of American geography, but I know that Kansas City is not in the state of Kansas? I believe it is in the state of Missouri, no?"

Stavros smiled, "You are knowledgeable. More so than many Americans. Yes, Kansas City, the big city, the city where I live, is in the state of Missouri. Just across the junction of the Kaw River and the Missouri River, there is another city named Kansas City in the state of Kansas. It's easy to confuse. Park College, where I teach, is north of the city on the Missouri River."

"Then the United States Army base at Fort Leavenworth is in Kansas, no?" asked Christakis.

"Yes," answered Stavros, unsure if Christakis knew about his lecturer's position at the Command and General Staff College or if he was curious about the military installation. Stavros couldn't remember if it were public information that he lectured there. Dimitra may have mentioned it at an early meeting of the Circle. His CIA legend didn't avoid this detail, but he never brought it up. His standard story was that he was a Park College professor working on his PhD, researching ancient Greek navies and shipbuilding.

Stavros picked up on his life in Kansas City, avoiding talk of Leavenworth. "Kansas City is a great town. I love it there. Plenty of culture, jazz, sports—you name it, it's got it. The people are friendly, they're ambitious but not rude, and it's easy to get around, not congested. The saying goes, Kansas City was settled by people going west to the land of milk and honey. But when they got to Kansas City, they said, Oh well, this is good enough."

Stavros saw in Christakis that this attempt at humor again landed in a Greek no-man's-land.

"Are their many Greeks in the city?" asked Christakis.

"A few. We have a church, Annunciation, and an active AHEPA chapter. Most Greeks work in industry, the railroads, or stockyards. Ford opened an auto assembly plant this year. A few own businesses—there's a candy company, grocers, a few restaurants, a florist, a shoeshine parlor, a photography studio, that sort of thing."

Christakis seemed to register the list Stavros offered. He was so thoughtful that Stavros wondered if he were committing the list to memory. Was Christakis trained in memory retention techniques? Stavros was.

Stavros knew that friendly interrogation was a delicate and nuanced engagement, not to be overdone. The goal was to get the target to talk about themselves and offer useful information without ever asking the question. It was the Socratic method level one. Never reveal your intention by prodding for a specific response, but lead the target toward the general discussion and hope they take the bait. It was interrogation masked as conversation. A friendly encounter, nothing more. The technique played on a basic human failing, love of talking about oneself.

"I asked about Leavenworth Army base because I would like to be assigned there as an international student. General Van Fleet told me of the program, and I found it most appealing. The United States Army is the best in the world. We Greeks, we fight like tigers, but too often, we think like mice. It would honor me to attend," stated Christakis.

There it was, thought Stavros. Christakis sought entrée to Leavenworth. But why? Personal desire, legitimate career advancement, or GRU mission-driven determination? An American tour of duty was not an uncommon request of Greek military officers. They considered time in America a vacation in the promise land. Stavros thought the resort that was Leavenworth might disappoint.

Stavros was uncertain about how much Christakis knew of his involvement at Leavenworth. This was an opportunity for Stavros to mention it, make it public knowledge, or stay quiet and, if Christakis knew, signal Stavros's less-than-forthrightness. Christakis would know he was covering and likely an agent. Stavros took a middle path.

"I've visited Fort Leavenworth and lectured there. It is a high-quality program, and you would find it most appealing and informative. Have you applied?" asked Stavros.

"Yes. This I have done. I have written my commander and received information from the United States Army. It is a delicate matter now, that I must ask you about. Can I depend on your discretion?" confided Christakis.

Stavros felt himself being sucked into dangerous water, a perilous riptide of overcommitment.

"Of course. So long as it's nothing illegal or unethical," offered Stavros, hearing his sanctimony.

"This matter in Greece is neither. But in America. . . ." Christakis said, rolling his shoulders.

Stavros nodded.

Christakis continued, "Who should I present with a *fakelaki* to further my application to Leavenworth?"

Stavros chuckled. This puzzled Christakis, who had just asked whom he should bribe to get the assignment. Fakelaki was Greek slang for a small envelope of money. Greeks thought of it as a tip. Christakis was right, this offering was customary in Greece, and Stavros could draft a dissertation on its ageless cultural origins.

"No one, not in America. No reason to.. . . ." Stavros struggled to find the less offensive word. "No reason to *encourage* a decision in America. They might look down on a fakelaki."

Christakis nodded. He said, "Yes. I know this is different in America."

Stavros nodded and thought, *in America, it is not what you know but who you know.* No small envelopes, just small favors. A step above menial bribery with the comfort of civility.

Their discussion concluded when Angelica returned with a pad. Pushing her gentle curls behind her ear, she smiled at Stavros and asked, "Are we ready?"

Both men ordered spitted lamb.

The men talked and enjoyed their main course. The lamb was tender and fell from the bone. They dipped hacked chunks of the succulent meat into tzatziki and savored the lemony roasted potatoes with garlic. They talked of motor racing, and Stavros told Christakis he had visited Indianapolis but not the race. He didn't mention that he'd stopped in the city on the heels of his World War II OSS deployments. There he had met Harry Hantzis, the man who, along with his father, Alex, and their friend Dimitri, had hunted the murderers of his birth mother, Eléni. His time in the OSS was not a part of his CIA legend. Christakis said he dreamed of going to the Indianapolis 500 Race. He said he also hoped to attend Le Mans and the Mille Miglia.

Elias came from the kitchen to ask about the lamb. His following questions and conversation shed light on Christakis, or his legend. It could have been rehearsed. Stavros remained wary. But it felt genuine. It felt like these two men went back years and shared the conviction of lives lived in proximity.

The conversation livened when the subject turned to a rascal named Piero. "How is Piero these days?" asked Christakis.

At the inquiry, both men lapsed into flawless Neapolitan. Their exchange lasted only a few seconds, ending in belly laughs. Stavros, fluent in the Italian Lombard dialect learned from his stepmother, picked up on the switch but didn't let on that he spoke the language.

It was nine o'clock when they finished the main course. Ceasar Grill was buzzing with new arrivals and a waiting line at the door. Angelica's inviting eyes now hardened and scanned the room, darting from table to table. When she asked Stavros and Christakis about dessert, she managed only a perfunctory smile. Both men declined. Then Mama Fofo arrived beside her daughter with two plates of baklava and set them on the table. She said to her daughter, "Bring the gentlemen some coffee." Then, looking at the men, she said, "Compliments of Elias."

Both men looked up at Elias in the pass-through window and waved their appreciation. The big man smiled. It all seemed authentically Greek. Stavros replayed the evening frame by frame on his drive back to Athens. He replayed Angelica's flirting as he drifted to sleep in his fresh bed at the Grande Bretagne.

Chapter 4

"She was swimming, there," he said, pointing to the placid Ionian just below the Strait of Corfu. "She was two hundred meters from shore, from the beach. The monster took her. The boy she was swimming with, her fiancé, escaped. Fishermen rescued him. People on shore saw it all, but they could do nothing. The monster came from below and pulled her under, and the sea boiled red. Her name was Vanda Perri. She was the daughter of the director of the National Bank of Kerkyra. That was two months ago, in August."

The report chilled Stavros to the bone. It was sad news for the young woman and her family and sadder news for wayward Pixies.

The gory narration supplemented Stavros's interview of the elderly Kosta, a knowledgeable if interminable historian whose field of study was Kerkyra, the Greek name for Corfu. Stavros and Kosta stood before arched stone ruins, the remains of a Venetian arsenal in the town of Gouvia, only meters from the sea. The site was thirty meters wide and forty meters long, framed by fifteen conjoined arches creating three berths for Venetian galleys and traders. The shipyard, or what the Venetians called an arsenal, dated from 1716. It was one of many built in Venetokratia Greece. Corfu fell under the rule of Genoa, Sicily, and Greeks from Epirus following the Byzantine Empire. In 1386, the Venetians imposed control that lasted through the Middle Ages until 1797.

Kosta's stooped frame made him look half the height of Stavros. With his long silvery hair, he looked like a hoary hermit. But he was a well-informed man, a published author. Stavros listened with one ear for the facts and one ear for the lore.

"Are sharks common?" asked Stavros.

"Yes. Three or four a month, maybe more. Mostly in summer. Now, not so many. Maybe one or two. They are called white sharks, but colored gray. They can weigh five hundred kilos and be four meters long. The Greek patrol boats shoot them. Only last year, they dragged one to shore that measured four meters," declaimed Kosta.

"Are they drawn to the Strait?" asked Stavros, referring to the channel between Greece and Albania, where the countries are separated by only two kilometers.

"This is not known. Some say yes, since the narrowing of the waterway forces prey into easy reach. Others. . . ?" Kosta shrugged. "They are soulless monsters, the devil knows how they think, no?"

Stavros did a silent calculation of the greater danger. The soulless Sigurimi on the far shore, or the soulless denizen between. Surviving the first would earn the Pixies the chance to survive the second.

Stavros asked, "Do the sharks feed at night?"

"Indeed. At night they attack monk seals. The seals feed on the tide, day or night. Their prey, the Cephalopoda and small fish, move with the cycle of tides. Then the sharks go after the seals. On a calm night you may hear an eruption, then a splash like the gods dropping a boulder into the sea. Then, nothing more. The sharks attack from below and deliver the seals to Poseidon. Some seals weigh two hundred kilos, and they fight, but it is useless. The sharks drown them, then feast," offered Kosta.

"My cousin fishes for octopus. This he does at night. He has seen a shark attack a seal, and he swears its jaws were larger than the mammal, and its teeth glistened like pearls in the moon's light," confided Kosta.

Stavros shook his head. Kosta thought he was registering the horror of the natural world. But the natural world and the man-made both host horrors. Stavros was considering the latter.

Stavros motioned to a stone bench north of the ruins and asked, "Should we sit? I'd like to make some notes on the arsenal. Your account of marine history is extensive. I want to make sure I get it right."

Kosta nodded, and the two men walked to the bench. Stavros flipped to an empty page in his notepad and pulled a pen from his coat pocket. He asked, "Did the Greeks build ships on Kerkyra before the Venetians?"

"It is certain they did, but confirmed locations are elusive. In 709 BCE, perhaps the earliest Greek naval battle ever recorded, the Corinthians sailed here to put down a rebellion. Kerkyra was then a colony of Corinth.

"Thucydides notes that Ameinocles of Corinth built four triremes for the Samians around 700 BCE. Ah, but then he adds that triremes were built earlier on Sicily and Kerkyra!"[12] At this inflection, Kosta pointed his index finger to the sky and beamed a smile of satisfaction.

Stavros nodded his appreciation, then asked, "How many Venetian arsenals were built in Greece?"

Kosta answered, "Of the known sites, Methoni and Koroni in the Peloponnese. Chalkis on the island of Euboea, northeast of Athens. Preveza in Epirus. And Chania and Heraklion on Crete. And, of course, Gouvia on Kerkyra. Gouvia came near the end of the Venetian era. They built others much earlier.[13]

"The Venetians began building arsenals in 1104 CE. They started, of course, in Venice. In 1320, they built a new arsenal in Venice and began using modern production practices, practices that would not appear again until the Industrial Revolution. Here they used interchangeable parts and components. They advanced from the old Roman hull-first technique to a frame-first building order. Their arsenals were factories, organized as assembly lines. They could build one new galley every day.

"The minds of the Venetians were their strength. Galileo advised their engineers. So legendary were the arsenals that Dante writes of them in the *Inferno,* Cantos Twenty-One."

Kosta began a dramatic rendition, his gray and milky eyes far in the distance:

"As in the Arsenal of the Venetians
Boils in winter the tenacious pitch
To smear their unsound vessels over again
For sail they cannot; and instead thereof
One makes his vessel new, and one recaulk.. . . . "

Stavros interrupted, uncertain of the intended length of Kosta's recital. He said, "Sir, I must return to the hotel for a telephone exchange, and time is running short. If you don't mind, could you tell me about the galleasses? Were they built on Kerkyra? The ships were important in the Battle of Lepanto; they may have been decisive, no?"

"We do not think they built the ships on Kerkyra. This arsenal is not so old. Galleasses were used to profound effect in the sixteenth century. You mention Lepanto. That battle was 1571. They also accompanied the Spanish Armada in 1588. So no, they were not built on Kerkyra. Some later hulls were maintained here, cleaned, and caulked. It is likely they served as merchant ships by then.

"These were massive vessels for their time. They employed five men per oar with thirty-two oars. With their three main sails, they were fast with the wind and deadly, with more guns and bigger bore. But alas, they were ponderous, so they were difficult to maneuver. It was hard to plan an attack with precision. A commander could not be certain that when the time came, they would take their position as a ship of the line."[14]

Stavros wrote and thought, but not about galleasses.

The two men talked another twenty minutes before Stavros excused himself, thanked Kosta, and drove north along the coast. He had lied to Kosta. He was not staying at a hotel but at a CIA secure location, a safe house. One of a handful on Kerkyra.

The narrow road along the coast wove through thickets of scrub and elegant Cyprus trees known to the Greeks as fingers of God. Through flighty gaps in the foliage, Stavros looked down on the sea, blue and bottomless. Just beyond a humble stone shrine to Saint Arsenius, Stavros turned left onto an unmarked dirt road. In two hundred meters, out of sight of curious travelers, the road became steep and paved. He drove on and came to an electrically operated iron gate. Stavros waved to the sentry carrying a scoped rifle and standing watch on the terrace of Villa Agni Stefania. The gate slid open, and Stavros drove his Morris to a parking area aside the circle driveway.

The villa was modern and well-appointed. The architecture was typical for Corfu, simple coral stucco construction with a terracotta tile roof. Italianate iron railings proscribed both porticos. The lower-level railing extended around an eight-by-five-meter swimming pool. Both porticos gave unobstructed views to the Strait of Corfu. The CIA had fenced the entire property in high decorative ironwork outfitted with Doppler ultrasonic motion detectors. Two muscular and attentive German shepherds patrolled, their civilian-attired handlers restraining bred-in vigilance.

Stavros entered the villa to a pleasant, open, two-story sitting room with white marble flooring. A limestone fireplace rose from floor to ceiling in a far corner, and an open-design, three-level staircase climbed to the top floor. From the kitchen hallway, a tall, trim, and fit man in his thirties dressed in khaki pants and a white T-shirt walked toward Stavros. Wiping his hands on a dishtowel, he asked, "How'd your interview go?"

Horace Williams Fuller, better known as Hod, was the CIA officer in charge of logistics for Operation FIEND, the infiltration of Albanian agents. He was a senior officer to Stavros, having earned his OSS stripes in France and China. He held the rank of brigadier general in the Marine Corps Reserves but was not in Stavros's chain of command. Stavros was on Corfu to move exfiltrating Albanian Pixies on the run dodging Communist secret police, the Sigurimi.

Hod said, "I love this country. I feel alive here. Everything is new and exciting; every day is a storybook. How are you doing, Professor?"

Stavros wondered how far his nickname had traveled since Nikolas first called him that in Tripoli.

Stavros said, "The interview went fine. He is a fount of knowledge. He raised a problem I'm not sure we have considered."

"Oh, what's that?" asked Fuller.

"Sharks," said Stavros. "They populate the Strait and attack people and seals, day or night."

"Yes, I heard about the girl. That was a couple months ago, right?" asked Fuller.

"Right. In August," answered Stavros. "The historian said that there are not so many now but still a threat."

"Well, let's hope our boys steal a boat and don't have to swim. The Brits buried a Goatley over there. If the Pixies can find it and figure out how to put it together, they'll be home free. What could go wrong in a canvas boat in a sea full of sharks, eh?"

Stavros nodded, then asked, "Have they made contact today?"

"Nope, not yet. They're on the run, so who knows when they'll be able to set up and transmit. At least they have the new radio, the RS-One. Those old sets were worthless in the mountains. Heavy, clumsy, only operate in the clear. These new units are much better. Much better," repeated Fuller.

Stavros nodded again.

Fuller went on, "These poor devils have been in Albania for five months. They dropped eleven of them into Mirdita on May Day, the theory being that the commies would all be drunk and celebrating. They're down to three: Airtight, the leader; Domino, the wireless telegraphy operator; and, Airmail, the guide. They're banged up. Airtight has dysentery, Airmail was injured in the drop and has hobbled since May. And Domino broke his sending hand somewhere along the way. The W/T codes we've been receiving are suspicious. They don't fit Domino's sending profile. His timing is off, his delays atypical, his error pattern incongruous. So far, they've sent the correct responses to our challenges, signaling they are not under control. No duress. So far."

Stavros sized up the odds of the Pixies' safe return as slim to none. He knew they would not be the first Albanian team to vanish, victims of treachery and fate.

A young man, the station radio operator, called down from the second-floor landing. "Sir, Airtight just called. They're in Ksamil, Vlorë County. They're on the Cape."

"The Albanian Riviera. Good for them," replied Fuller.

Stavros knew the Cape meant the spit of Albanian land across from Corfu.

"Airtight said they would wait for dark, then search for a means of transport and transmit when they start across," said the operator.

"Did you tell them about the Goatley? The Brits left a location. If they're close, they might want to look around," said Fuller.

"Yes, sir. I sent the coordinates, but Airtight seemed confused. I'm not sure he can read a map. He said they'd be in touch when they found a way across," answered the young man.

"Did they confirm pickup at Kassopei?" asked Fuller.

"Yes, sir. I gave them a bearing of two-ninety degrees, west-northwest."

"Okay. I'll start a team up there. It's almost dark," said Fuller.

"Sir, there's one other thing," interjected the operator.

"What is it?"

"They did not confirm that they were not under control. They didn't respond to my challenge. It may have been hard for them to transmit. I couldn't tell. I sent the challenge, and they didn't respond. It was the last part of my transmission. They might have turned their set off. It wouldn't be the first time they've broken protocol," said the operator.

"Right. Let's get the team moving and we'll deal with whatever comes our way," said Fuller.

"Yes, sir," responded the operator.

Fuller looked at Stavros and asked, "You want in on the fun? It's not in your assignment but, for old times' sake?"

Stavros smiled.

Fuller said, "Outstanding! Get out of those street clothes and into some fatigues. I'm coming, too. Just for grins."

Operation FIEND was America's first clandestine challenge to Soviet Cold War ambitions. Albania was a ripe target. Cut off from the USSR and bordering only anti-Stalinist Yugoslavia and western-friendly Greece, the poor country of one million people was an outlier. By infiltrating teams of anti-communist, native Albanians, the theory went, Americans would gain intelligence and activate an armed resistance to the Enver Hoxha regime. FIEND would restore Albania to the western fold and serve as a model for defeating Soviet domination.

The British began infiltrating agents into Albania in 1947 in a project they called VALUABLE. Their results were scant, and their agents fell into the many traps set by the regime. In 1949, the British approached the Americans about funding VALUABLE. Frank Wisner and his budding Office of Policy Coordination jumped aboard with both feet. The OPC needed a pilot project to exercise its newly granted, broad, clandestine authority and tap its bottomless, unregulated budget. Wisner designated the effort Operation BGFIEND, shorthand FIEND. The project fit Wisner's mantra, "We are people of action; we do what needs done." But in the new CIA, nothing was simple.

Prior to initiation of Wisner's OPC, the CIA Office of Special Operations (OSO) had come to an arrangement with Italian Naval Intelligence. The partnership went by Operation CHARITY. The OSO fielded spies and tasked them with gathering and analyzing intelligence. Covert action was not their ambit. Covert action was OPC's purview. OSO photographed bridges but left them standing. OPC blew them up. Or so CIA organizational charts professed.

Operation CHARITY began in 1947. In 1949, agents began infiltrating to report on political trends, military installations, transportation facilities, and leading personalities. The Italians recruited CHARITY spies from displaced persons' camps in Italy and Greece and didn't shy away from former Albanian fascists and collaborationists.

Stonewalls, confusion, leaks, and canards hounded Albanian operations. While both OSO and OPC were a part of CIA, they might have operated on different planets. Communications and coordination were neither organization's forte. And for good measure or bad, the British didn't want to share information with Greece and Italy, snootily citing security concerns. That was rich.

In 1963, with the defection of Kim Philby to the Soviet Union, Britain won the deserved but unwanted title of the biggest leaker. Philby, recruited by the Soviets in 1934, had risen through the ranks of the British Secret Intelligence Service (MI6). He arrived in Washington, DC, in 1949 and as first secretary to the British Embassy, he was the top British spy in America. At his office in the Pentagon next to the Joint Chiefs of Staff, he learned precise coordinates and drop details for all Albanian operations. He was in on all FIEND and VALUABLE planning. His primary source and drinking buddy had been James Angleton, himself a rising star and well on his way to CIA chief of counterintelligence.[15]

In July 1949, British MI6 instructors and American CIA OPC advisers began training a "better class of commandos" at a base on Malta. Soon after, a well-funded political front group, Free Albania National Committee, launched in Paris.

Italy and Greece came onboard through diplomacy and promises of aid. The Americans enticed the two countries, threatened, cajoled, and bribed them into the swirling orbit of American and NATO commitments.

Both countries asserted long-standing interests in Albania. Italy maintained a network of collaborationist agents, holdovers from Italian occupation in World War II. The Strait of Otranto, the narrowing of the Adriatic where it meets the Ionian Sea, separated the two countries by only forty-five miles.

Greece nursed historic territorial claims to the southern fifth of Albania, what Greece called Northern Epirus. Greece was poised to invade the ethnically friendly territory for no other reason than Albania had given haven and arms to KKE guerrillas. Greece and Albania never signed an armistice after World War II, so they were still at war.

FIEND Pixie teams began infiltrating late in 1949 by parachute, overland from Greece, and by boat. New teams went in every few months, and the results were not promising. Albania was more a prison than a country. The survivors of one such team, Orange Team, brought Stavros to Corfu. Their deliverance was his.

To construct a Goatley after finding one under the camouflage and debris of an expert burial requires only two men. A Goatley is simple genius. The two men raise its sideboards and insert vertical spars. The plywood floor is one piece, and the canvas becomes taunt with the spars inserted, giving the sides the appearance of an accordion at full bellows. Paddles, rations, flotation vests, and lines are part of the kit. The craft weighs three hundred pounds and will transport ten. Two healthy men can move it, or three banged up Albanians. Luckily, they didn't have to go far.

The Cape, the land closest to Greece, saw constant patrols. The Sigurimi directed local communist militia, shore patrol units, units of the Albanian Army, and spotter aircraft. They weren't only after western agents but noncombatant Albanians trying to escape the land of their birth. Dense brush and squat trees blanketed the coast, and the vegetation grew right to the shoreline. Concealment, once inside the forest cover, was good. Movement was possible, but best when traveling light. Movement in the dark with a three-hundred-pound Goatley, the three components of the RC-1 radio, arms, and ammunition was not ideal.

The Pixies discussed commandeering a boat but decided that all such craft would be under guard. Thus, the Goatley became their transference of choice. When they reached the rocky shoreline, they assembled their RC-1 and signaled Corfu. Corfu again confirmed pickup at Kassopei Beach, northwest of their position on the Cape and two

and a half kilometers away. Corfu sent a challenge code and again received no response. The radio operator confirmed the transmission to Hod Fuller. He and Stavros belted on M1911 Colts and grabbed M1 carbines from the arms closet, then climbed into a Jeep for the short drive to Kassopei. There they joined the CIA team already in position waiting to retrieve the Albanian agents. It was 0345 hours on a clear but moonless night.

International conventions divide the water between Greek Corfu and Albania down the middle with a slight offset to the east in favor of Greece. Thus, if everyone played by the rules, the escaping Albanians would be in Greek waters a little more than a kilometer from the Albanian shore. Their expected rate of paddle was three kilometers an hour, putting them out of Albanian water, beyond the iron grip of the Sigurimi, about twenty minutes after launch. The full trip to Kassopei could take an hour, maybe more, depending on wind, current, and tide. The CIA tethered a motorized, twenty-one-foot runabout on the beach. They planned to meet the Pixies upon sighting them, throw them a line, and tow them to freedom. That was the plan. Once in Greece, they would return to Villa Agni Stefania, receive medical attention, and get a cursory debrief. When they were healthy, Stavros would see them to Italy for further debriefing. Only he knew the exact conveyance.

Fuller and Stavros stood on the sandy beach and peered into the darkness with powerful binoculars. The ambient light of the stars and a faint phosphorescence from the sea revealed nothing. It was a sound that first alerted them, the sound of a high-pitched outboard engine approaching at full throttle, maybe a kilometer away. It couldn't be the Pixies.

The CIA boat crew heard the same and started their engine. Fuller waved them off. He needed to hear what was going on. At the first sound of gunfire, the unmistakable metallic burst of a Soviet RPD machinegun, Fuller ordered his boat crew into action. The engine fired, the helmsman shoved the throttle to full open, and the boat came up on plane in seconds. Armed with two Thompson machineguns and a BAR automatic rifle, the two crew and helmsman tore over the chop toward the sound of firing and distant muzzle flashes. Over the sound of the muffled Mercury inboard, Fuller and Stavros made out return fire from the less potent Sten guns of the Pixies. It sounded like two Stens firing, not three.

The encounter took place in Greek waters. The more powerful and better-armed CIA boat disabled the Albanian craft with a burst from the BAR that riddled the outboard engine and set a fuel line afire. With their targets illuminated, the CIA operators neutralized all four Sigurimi. They boarded the eighteen-foot metal boat, searched the bodies, photographed the carnage, then sunk the craft, consigning the Sigurimi to shark bounty.

The CIA boat crew secured a line to the shredded Goatley and towed it the half kilometer to Kassopei Beach. They couldn't board the canvas craft because it was barely afloat. The Pixies' bodies rode in the Goatley, sloshing in a bloody blend the final few meters to freedom. On the beach, a medic pronounced the men dead and assigned them to body bags.

Fuller oversaw the retrieval and muttered to Stavros, "Damn! I should have gone with the boat crew. They had all the fun."

As the first hint of rose blushed the eastern horizon, a solitary figure watched the solemn retrieval. Hidden behind a divine cypress rising on a less consecrated knoll, the figure peered through field glasses and adjusted the Moschetto Automatico on their shoulder.

Chapter 5

Elegance surrounded him, overwhelming but never overstated. He contrasted the opulence and serenity with the art before him. A rare eighteenth-century tapestry of Alexander the Great entering Gavgamila hung behind the densely stocked marble bar. Three Doric columns rose on either side of the forty-foot-long textile depicting Alexander at the reins of a gilded chariot harnessed to Bucephalus, the greatest horse ever sired in Thessaly. He arrives as the victor, clean and composed. Supplicating figures offer loyalty and riches. Stavros thought about the battle that delivered Alexander to Gavgamila and to the greatness won from Darius and his army.

The 331 BCE engagement had been anything but clean and composed. Bloody, nightmarish, and chaotic, he knew to be better descriptors. But it was elegant, as battles go. The clash of 100,000 Persians, mercenaries, and subjugated conscripts against 47,000 Greeks on a battlefield of Darius's choosing should have ended differently. The fight began with Alexander ordering a phalanx against the Persian center. Then Alexander led an inspired flanking charge on Bucephalus, outpacing his own cavalry. The maneuver mystified Darius, who overreacted and exposed his flank. Thus Alexander sowed the kernel of confusion that led to the Persian rout and the erasure of his biggest obstacle to world domination.

His deep leather chair was comfortable. The fine wood paneling and warm, rich marble, the high ceiling, the ornate mirrors and flawless crystal were never garish. No need. Their essence infused the atmosphere with quality and taste. Alexander's Bar in the Grande Bretagne was the nicest place Stavros ever visited.

He lifted his Mandarine Napoleon Select and sipped. Then, just as carefully, returned it to his table. The blend of Dubonnet Rouge, Grand Marnier, gin, and fragrant essential oil of Sicilian tangerines took residence on his palate and lingered with no relinquishment. He didn't deserve this refinement. He was not of this world, a world of privilege and fortune. He was the son of a Greek coal miner turned railroader turned businessman. His fortune was his circumstance. Unaccountably, Stavros found himself in a fine hotel, shouldering unpardonable responsibility, and at that moment, in the gaze of the most beautiful woman in Greece.

Dimitra was striking, whether dressed in shapeless, unflattering EAM-ELAS fatigues or the simple black sheath and heels she wore now. It wasn't her form that drew you in. It was her eyes, her soul, dark pools offering reflection and mystery but no promises. After processing her countenance, only then could you take in her presence, her form. This was a pleasure, not a task. As a freshly minted OSS first lieutenant in the mountains of Greece, Stavros had stumbled and stuttered in her presence. For all the years and knowledge of this woman, he still felt . . . what? Insecure? Undeserving? Enraptured? Excited? That was it. Simple excitement, physical and emotional. Adrenal secretion, nothing more. He cautioned himself to get a grip and smiled like a hyena.

She crossed the marble floor in the soft light of late afternoon. Her heels made a persistent dull click, each step planted with purpose and aim. Her raven hair was longer now than when they met in Chómori. When she had been kapetánios, leader of andartes, she had worn it short, and most of the time it was under her ELAS campaign cap. Now her soft curls flowed to her shoulders and moved with the rhythm of her stride. She would never be mistaken for a runway model. She was direct, poised, and purposeful. No middle-distance stare. No sway and sash but a posture of unmitigated steel. Stavros thought he was on a movie set filming its star.

He rose from his chair, and the couple exchange cheek kisses, first to the right, then to the left. Dimitra said, "I need to go back to Chómori and dig up my pistol. The one I buried before moving to Thessaloniki."

Stavros knew she was referring to her Beretta M1934, her kapetánios sidearm.

"I take it the meeting didn't go your way?" he asked.

"Yes, yes. I will get the dig, but we wasted five hours talking about everything under the moon. Wasted time. Had I my pistol, I could have gained their attention and saved hours of tedium."

"Well, it's good to see you. You look—"

Dimitra cut him off. "I look preposterous. These heels are antiquated implements of torture. But this is Athens, no? We expect this in such a civilized environment, no? This dress and shoes are a costume, nothing more. A uniform for the occasion, like my dungarees on a dig or my ELAS fatigues. These clothes are to further a mission. My mission was to get old codgers who haven't soiled their fingernails in years on the Ephorate of the Archaeological Society of Athens to support my dig at Aphaia. And it worked! It worked too well! They want me on the Ephorate! The price we pay."

"Well, congratulations. We should drink to your . . . what?" Stavros stumbled for the word. "Here's to your success?"

"Yes, yes. I will drink, but success is not an exact science. It has consequences not always intended. A position of the Ephorate means I must travel to Athens every month. And they meet for two days, sometimes three. What a waste," replied Dimitra.

Stavros smiled. This was the direct, ambitious, self-confident woman he had fallen for in 1944. No longer did she plot and plan to ambush fascists, but her drive and intolerance of delay lived on. Now her ambush of the Archaeological Society of Athens had rendered a victory plus an obligation. It pleased Stavros that she would be in Athens on a monthly schedule. This should make their time together more manageable, if there was anything about Dimitra that was manageable.

"White?" asked Stavros.

"Yes, yes. Gavalas Katsano, if they have it," offered Dimitra.

Stavros motioned to the waiter and ordered the drink. Then he returned his lost puppy gaze to Dimitra and asked, "So, will you be the first woman on the Ephorate?"

"This I do not know. I doubt it. They organized in 1837, so they must have included a woman before now. Harriet Boyd Hawes, perhaps. She was American, that might have disqualified her. I do not know. But now, now I will be the only woman. The only woman in a room of Papastratos and pipe-smoking university pensioners who have forgotten how to sharpen their trowels."

Stavros chuckled. Then the waiter returned with Dimitra's wine.

"So, tell me about the dig at Aphaia."

"What is there to tell? I will recruit a team, sail to Aegina, and begin sifting."

Stavros shook his head. He said, "I know there's more to your plan than that. You have sought this assignment for years. What is your mission? I'm sworn to secrecy." And he pursed his lips.

Dimitra took her second sip of wine, and she too shook her head. She asked, "Do you know of the Epic Cycle and the *Cypria*?"

Stavros recognized the tone. He had received Dimitra's instruction many times, and he foresaw the lecture. He said, "No. Please fill me in."

Dimitra shook her head and rolled her large Cimmerian eyes. He knew that to be shorthand for her ongoing disdain for the shallowness of American higher education.

She again sipped her wine, then stared at Stavros. She asked in mocking curiosity, "You have, of course, heard of and perhaps read *The Iliad* and *The Odyssey*? These were great poems attributed to a Greek called Homer, no?"

Stavros sighed and nodded.

"Then this is good. This is where I will begin your instruction. Pay attention, please. Do not make me retrieve my sidearm."

Stavros chuckled. Dimitra continued, "The Epic Cycle is a collection of eleven such poems, a chronology of the origins and struggles of Greece ending with the famous works of Homer. *The Cypria* is the poem leading to *The Iliad*, an account of Greece from the apple of discord to the Trojan War.

"The apple of discord was, of course, the contest between Hera, Athena, and Aphrodite caused by Eris's offer of a golden apple to the most beautiful woman. Perhaps they wore high heels then. No one knows this.

"The three goddesses fell prey to their divine vanity and, voilà, the Trojan War. The details of how this came about you must read on your own. This is your homework assignment."

Stavros nodded.

"We believe that the poems of the Epic Cycle do not appear in chronological order. *The Iliad* and *The Odyssey* appeared first. Then, the other nine poems authored to predate the works of Homer. *The Cypria*, authored by Stasinus of Cyprus, is dated from 700 BCE. Of this there is little controversy. Scholars accept his authorship.

"What is, however, controversial is where this happened. Most say Cyprus. That was his home. But, he may have written it on Aegina, near Aphaia, though the temple dates from two hundred years later. I have my reasons, but they are far too technical for your wayward American mind.

"There. These are my reasons for digging at Aphaia. Only time will tell if I am correct. If I am, my reward will be a glossy photograph in a scholastic journal of undetermined weight and merit.

"Oh, and the next time you report to Mr. George C. Marshall in Washington, DC, thank him for me. It is his money that the Greeks will spend on my deserving dig."

"Funny you should mention DC. I may move there in a few months," Stavros offered as a maladroit segue.

Dimitra caught the waiter's eye and nodded to her empty glass. Then her gaze of puzzlement and irritation fell on Stavros.

"They have offered me a job in the government, but I have to move to Washington. I'll still be traveling to Greece, but I can't say how often."

Dimitra and Stavros never discussed Stavros's CIA employment. Dimitra was savvy. She knew Stavros was doing more than preparing research for his dissertation. His grant, his travel, his extended sabbatical, and his OSS background all added up to more than an itinerant college professor on an academic glide-path.

Dimitra knew discipline. The KKE and she had survived on it. Metaxas banned the party in the 1930s, killing, jailing, and torturing its members. Secrecy became their way of life. The intervening years of clandestine organizing prepared the party for their fight with fascist occupiers, first the Italians, then the Germans. The KKE brought to the Greek resistance a forged and proven discipline like no other guerrilla force. Their resolve and leadership, faced with Nazi barbarity and brutality, had drawn fighters of varied political persuasions, including Dimitra. The communists had made a play for Greece and had failed, twice. She knew the secrets of the party, and only through political skill and cunning did she leave KKE discipline with her life.

Dimitra knew combat, close and personal. She fought beside comrades whose blood splattered her face. Discipline defined war. Those with it won, those without fell. Now came a new war shrouded by the facade of peace. Turmoil beneath the calm. They fought the new war with spies, not soldiers, and they came from everywhere. They walked the halls of her university, Aristotle of Thessaloniki. They joined in the Circle where she and Stavros shaped the thoughts of opinion leaders and policymakers. She knew this. Stavros was a spy; only the details were unknown to her. She was happy to leave things that way.

"Then we are both victorious and our unintended fortunes complicating, no? How soon do you plan to begin your new job with *the government*?" she asked with a conspiratorial lilt.

"A few months, maybe a year. It's about funding and that sort of thing. It's the government, you know?" answered Stavros.

"Of course. *The government.*"

The waiter returned with her second glass of wine. She said, "A toast," and held the glass high.

"To our victories and accidental fortunes."

The clink of their crystal rang in the air like a starting bell. The beginning of a new chapter, the interrogation of Stavros.

"How was your trip to Corfu?" she asked.

"Productive, but not a complete success. I interviewed the historian I mentioned, Kosta. He has a wealth of knowledge about Kerkyra and the Venetians and sharks."

At the mention of sharks, Dimitra raised an eyebrow.

"Yes. Sharks feed on the seals and sometime swimmers. They killed a young woman in August, and he filled me in. Very sad and a horrible way to go.

"Kosta gave me details on the arsenal for my draft. I may visit a few of the other sites he mentioned. There are two big ones on Crete. I'm most curious to find out if the Venetians built arsenals on sites that had been Greek shipbuilding locations? Do you have any insight?" Stavros asked.

"The Greeks have built ships for so long, it would be hard to find a location where they did not build," chided Dimitra.

Stavros chuckled.

Dimitra asked, "By what route did you arrive at Corfu?"

"I drove and took the ferry at Rio and again at Igoumenitsa. The drive brought back memories."

"Oh, I have no doubt," agreed Dimitra.

"Right. It wasn't just the Rio ferry. I thought about Devil's Cauldron, sure. But the road to Igoumenitsa passes Angelokastro, and I remembered blowing up the Papastratos railroad and Johnny breaking his leg. Then Amfilochia, where we first dodged the Messerschmitts. Then Ioannina, our first action. And Parga where we came ashore, and I met Yiorgos and they warned me about you," said Stavros.

"Who? Who *warned* you? Why have I never heard this before now! I know you keep secrets, but this you should have shared," Dimitra reprimanded.

Stavros made the universal gesture of surrender. He said, "No. No. It was a good warning. Colonel Barnes, the New Zealander with the British Military Mission. He met me when we came ashore. He said you were smart, brave, a rising star, and pleasing to look at. He said the Greeks used women like mules but that you were not of that breed. And he said you were KKE."

"Not of that breed? Do they breed women in New Zealand? Preposterous!" she fired back.

Stavros rebutted, "Oh, come on. Other than the breed comment, everything he said was true and complimentary, no?"

Dimitra stiffened, and her voice hardened. She said, "The British and their colonial serfs are not of my concern. They were eating mud while we built the Parthenon. Please continue with your travelogue."

"Not much to add. Took the ferry at Igoumenitsa. Corfu is lovely but very Italian in its architecture and food."

"Where did you stay?" asked Dimitra.

"A place north of the armory, near the Strait."

"Near Albania, no?"

"Right across the channel," answered Stavros with hesitation.

Dimitra sensed he would reveal no more. She reached the wall of their confidence. She didn't want to know. She was a curious woman, but smart. She knew there are things that people should not know.

Stavros said, "Oh, did I tell you I ran into Nikolas on my drive back from Crete? He's running a metal fabrication shop in Tripoli. He's married with a son."

"Nikolas? From Chómori?"

"Yes, yes. He told me Yiorgos was tending bees in Kato Daphne."

"This I know. Yiorgos writes twice a year. He is doing well, and he always thanks me for breaking him out of the jail in Nafpaktos. He said I have earned free honey for life!"

"Nikolas is managing a machine shop, and his wife tends the olive presses in Missolonghi. I thought about stopping there on my way to Corfu, but I didn't want to miss the ferry and my appointment. Another time, I suppose," said Stavros.

"And now Nikolas knows you are in Greece. And he knows you were OSS. Will this be a problem? You have forbidden me to tell anyone in the Circle about your commendable if brief tour, no?" asked Dimitra.

Stavros didn't think five months was brief. But Dimitra had organized and led combat units since the Italian invasion in October 1940. She had been in the line of fire for four years when she left to finish her doctorate.

"I don't know. It may be a problem, it may not. The OSS ordered that we keep all our assignments secret. I swore to that," Stavros said, his secrecy now more about his CIA cover than honoring his OSS pledge.

"Indeed. A secret it will remain. Until Nikolas tells Yiorgos, who tells the honey seller from Athens, who tells. . . . This is Greece. The only secret in Greece is why Greeks can't keep a secret," said Dimitra.

Stavros nodded. Dimitra was right.

"Well, it was good to see Nikolas. He looked healthy and happy. Married life suits him."

Dimitra only nodded.

They had talked about marriage.

Both were in their late thirties, and time was not on their side. Especially if they considered having children. But things never went further than talking. Now, with Stavros set to move to

Washington, he worried that his time in Greece might come to an unwanted end. The problem was that neither Stavros nor Dimitra would put their fondness, love, attraction, or whatever it was, above and ahead of their work. Dimitra was passionate about Stavros, and he was whatever the next state above passion is about her. But she was more passionate about her work and about staying in Greece. She, unlike so many Greeks, did not want to go to America for a new life. Her life in Greece was rewarding. She was where she wanted to be. Her mother, Eva, was with her in Thessaloniki. They owned a pleasant house with a well-tended garden where Dimitra joined her when she was not on a dig. Stavros did not want to give up his life in America. His biological parents were Greek, but he was as American as any red-blooded Midwesterner. It was complicated.

Dimitra had set Stavros straight before his OSS unit left Greece. On the bank of a mountain stream, he had pleaded his case for them to fashion a life together. Her words remained true all these years. "We are what we make of ourselves. Nothing changes. Today you make of yourself an OSS lieutenant. I a kapetánios. Tomorrow will be different.

"This is the thing. We will separate. We will miss each other. We will write. You will take another lover in America or wherever the OSS sends you. I will study in Salonika. That is all. My nails will grow dirty searching for relics of an ancient past, clues to my country's greatness and misfortune.

"Why is *this* not enough?"

This was still the impasse and philosophical gulf that found Dimitra reposed on her shore and Stavros left to the Sisyphean task of rowing her way. They made of their love what they could. He didn't push, and she didn't give. They enjoyed each other's company as they did in Alexander's Bar and in Stavros's suite all the night to follow.

Chapter 6

A three-masted sloop sailed out of the gloom into the light, her port bow slashing a contentious sea. Leading the way, a golden spread-wing eagle figurehead at the base of her bowsprit stared into the future. She was rigged with fifteen sails drawn from the cloth of each country's flag. Her hull implied by the stylized word EUROPE. The text below the art implored, ALL COLORS TO THE MAST. Stavros wondered why the artist, Reyn Dirksen, treated the Greek "blue and white" to prominence atop the mainmast, the uppermost flag in the art. The poster was aspirational, visually moving, with a succinct message. It was well-done propaganda. Stavros wondered not at all why Yiorgos had chosen to hang it in his otherwise tidy but unadorned waiting room.

Yiorgos Vedros was a friend of the family, but much more than that. He was now the director of sociology curriculum at the Hellenic Ministry of Education, Research, and Religious Affairs. His had been a winding road to this post, an epic escapade, variants of which many a Greek might tell.

Yiorgos was a spy but cut from a different cloth. Educated at the University of Athens, he had traveled to America and found work as a railroader. He had been cleaning locomotive pits in a roundhouse when he took a job with the Colorado Fuel and Iron Company. They needed an educated Greek.

Colorado Fuel and Iron, CF&I, was owned by the Rockefeller family. Its headquarters and steelworks in Pueblo stood at the pinnacle of their vertically integrated conglomerate. The company employed thousands of coal miners, coke smelters, and steelworkers, many of them Greek immigrants. CF&I created a corporate Sociology Department to control the Greeks and dozens of other toiling nationalities. They hired Yiorgos as their Greek representative, a company man, someone to report on his rabble countrymen. They instructed him to develop programs and literature to keep workers sober, hygienic, and away from the union. This he accomplished, except for the union.

In 1913 and 1914, the coal mines of Colorado had reverberated with gunfire, death, and cruelty in the service of destroying the United Mine Workers of America. Yiorgos was a double. While posing as a loyal company man and an enlightened Greek, he fed information to the strike leaders. He attended university with the leading Greek unionist, Louis Tikas.

Tikas suggested Yiorgos befriend Stavros's father, Alex. His insight and information gave critical clues in the hunt for the murderers of Stavros's birth mother, Eléni.

Stavros had met Yiorgos only once before his CIA assignment to Greece. During the Assumption Day furlough in 1943, Stavros had taken the train from Camp Carson in Colorado Springs to Pueblo. There he'd met the people who helped raise him after his mother's murder thirty years before, the Georgallas family, and Yiorgos Vedros.

Yiorgos was a little older than Alex. As World War II ended, and Greece struggled to recover, Yiorgos had taken his pension from CF&I and in 1950 returned to the Old Country. Yiorgos applied himself without reserve to the country's reconstruction. He worked longer hours in Greece than in Colorado. From his post in the Greek Ministry of Education, Research, and Religious Affairs, he authored a modernized national sociology curriculum.

Yiorgos appeared in the doorway to his office, shaking hands with another gentleman. The man left and Yiorgos opened his arms to greet Stavros with a hug. He was a head shorter than Stavros, stocky with dark features and a trimmed mustache. Yiorgos seemed shorter to Stavros than when Stavros had seen him in August. But as always, Yiorgos was well-dressed.

If Yiorgos had shed an inch, he had lost none of his insight and cunning. These served him in Colorado as he navigated the pitfalls of the strike and CF&I politics and bureaucracy. He was smart and devoted to the Socratic method;

it informed every conversation and defined Yiorgos's character: classically educated and curious. Stavros promised Alex that he would look up Yiorgos in Athens, and he did. It was excellent advice.

"How is the son of Alex?" asked Yiorgos.

Stavros nodded.

"You look well and fit. Greece suits you, no?"

Stavros said, "Greece is a good fit. Great food and people, and this weather has been outstanding."

"Yes, yes. In autumn, when we finish with the rain, it is always beautiful. Come in, sit. We can talk in here," he said, motioning Stavros into his office.

Stavros knew Yiorgos's role in Colorado, and he knew Yiorgos was a spy but of a different stripe than himself. As Nikolas opined, "They say that a man so initiated never leaves kataskopeía. Espionage is an old and binding fraternity, no?"

Stavros maintained his CIA cover with Yiorgos. There was no talk of OSS days and no talk of current missions. Only discussion of dissertation, weather, women, politics, food, and whatever topic the Circle found of interest. All the same, Yiorgos was smart and practiced at deduction.

Soon after arriving in Greece, Stavros had invited Yiorgos to join the Circle and host a few meetings. After consideration and weighing conflicts with his government position, he agreed. So long as the Circle was not supporting a political party, he would join its deliberations and perhaps endorse position papers, essays, and editorials he supported. Yiorgos was to host the coming meeting of the Circle at the Ministry, and Stavros was there to discuss topics.

Yiorgos asked, "How goes your dissertation research? You are fortunate that your university allows long sabbaticals for its preparation."

"I have volumes of research. Some I have cataloged. A draft outline is to follow, and the dissertation and defense still to come. Greece is replete with shipbuilding history. Mine is a burden of riches," answered Stavros.

"Without ships and their brave sailors, there would be no Greece, only scattered islands and mountains speaking Farsi. Ships and sailors birthed Greece," reflected Yiorgos.

Stavros nodded agreement. Then asked, "I came to talk about this week's meeting of the Circle. Do you have a topic for discussion?"

"I have thought about this. There are many current political matters that might spark interest. For example, the ambitions of Field Marshal Alexander Papagos, and his Greek Rally party. Will his attempt to model Greece on De Gaulle's du Peuple Français take root? He received thirty-six percent of the vote in September but failed to form a government. Nonetheless, he and his party are a rising power.

"Papagos is fascinating talk for a kafeneion, but I believe a greater concern is the inescapable rise of anti-American sentiment. Or what some have called *neutralism*. America has been generous to Greece. This is well-established and appreciated. But you extended generosity for an outcome, no? America wants a friendly Greece, and soon in the coming year, a Greece in NATO.

"With a cut in aid from $182 million this year to $81 million in 1952, friendship is taxed, no? And with another cut to $22 million in fiscal year 1953, we might expect the balloon you have blown full, to deflate and fall back to earth, no?[16]

"What will be the political ramifications? What of the military expenditures? Is Greece prepared for self-governance? Self-reliance? Have we reformed not only the government but the minds of Greeks? Self-reliance and neutralism are strong rhetorical levers, but Greece is Greece. Change does not come because a government snaps its fingers and promulgates a new law.

"So, I would suggest we offer the topic as *Greece and America, Beyond Dollar-Patronage*."

Stavros nodded, engaged by the forward slant of the topic.

"Then all is set. This should be a good discussion. We can expect maybe a dozen people. Dimitra and I will be there. I believe Alexis Christakis is coming. You will be there, so a dozen? Any other thoughts?" asked Stavros.

"No, no. It should be worth an editorial and perhaps a position paper on the size of Greek armed forces. I've heard the Ministry of Defense is suggesting a cut from 140,000 to 120,000 because of the decreased funding. I suspect bureaucratic blackmail, an attempt to manipulate America," answered Yiorgos. Then he added with a smile, "Now for the big question of the day. Where do you want to eat lunch?"

Chapter 7

"I don't believe her. I believe she is a weak attempt to fool us. Maybe a honey trap that took a wrong turn. She looks the part. But an embassy staffer? Why would they target an attaché who really was an attaché? She'd qualify for a bigger target than that.

"The communists want us to inform the Athens police of the plot. The police will overreact. They will round up a dozen low-level cadre, torture them, and the KKE will have its propaganda.[17]

"First, Alepoú knows nothing about the Central Committee; she can't name their current members. She is low-level. Too low to be in on planning such an assassination. Second, why would the KKE target the Deputy Chief of the Economic Cooperation Administration Mission, Paul Jenkins? He is important, true, but he's no symbol. He has no psychological value. Why not target the ECA Chief, Nuveen? He is much better known and a prominent symbol. Third, her identification and recruitment were dubious. A pleasing young woman presents herself to embassy staff in a bar and professes disenchantment with the KKE within fifteen minutes of meeting?

"We cannot confirm her legend. She is a student in Athens, but we could not confirm that she joined the party after Grammos. She's old enough, barely. She could have joined during the Civil War.

"She and her reports are a weak attempt at provocation, run by the local KKE without MGB or GRU oversight.

"Either that, or she's after money.

"Alepoú says they plan the attack to coincide with VIP communists arriving from abroad, date unknown. Chief OSO Athens has informed the ambassador. The ECA and Jenkins are increasing security and taking precautions.

"I suggest we run her status quo, allow her to report that she is fooling us, and put her in the bag when her story crosses up. Then we can decide if she has any further utility. That could be soon if their operation is as slipshod as it looks.

"Have we paid her more than the standard inducement?" asked the OSO man.

"No. She received two hundred dollars; we called it an advance. We got her signature and fingerprints, so she's in the system, but nothing came up," answered Alepoú's handler.

"Let her sit for a few minutes; then tell her to carry on. Pat her on the back for her bravery and send her on her way. If she asks for more money, tell her we'll talk at her next meet. Got it?" ordered the OSO man.

Alepoú's handler nodded.

"Keep it snappy. I know you've got to get across town to the Ministry for the Circle meeting," reminded the OSO man.

Alepoú's handler nodded again.

Alepoú was nervous. She fidgeted. She sat at a wooden table on a wooden chair in a room devoid of hangings, art, pottery, or anything that might serve as a weapon. Two large, meshed windows lit the space but revealed only a high garden wall covered with ivy and wisteria beyond. A camera mounted in a ceiling corner above and to her right transmitted closed-circuit television to a control room on the third floor. The CIA OSO safe house in the Kolonaki neighborhood of northeast Athens was unremarkable. The quiet community was well-off, and well-tended, and large gated homes were common.

She was twenty years old, shapely, and well-favored in the way of a northern Greek. Her medium-length, honey-blond hair was natural. She wore a leather motorcycle jacket and blue jeans, with no harsh or garish jewelry. She was bohemian without the badging. She stood five foot seven inches in her heeled boots. It would be hard to ignore her in a crowd, as it was at Taverna Elia where she had presented herself to a young Italian Embassy cultural attaché. Her name was Calista. The OSO had coded her Alepoú, Greek for fox or vixen.

Her handler waited fifteen minutes, then entered the room with a smile. They spoke in Greek, the handler with a formal, academic countenance. Alepoú thought, "Faculty?"

"Sorry for the wait. We talked over your report."

Alepoú nodded but remained silent.

"You are doing fine work. We will forward your report to the Greek authorities. But we need more details. We need names of the assassin team and date of the planned attack and information about the method. These are most important. We will contact you for a meet in two days. You will know the messenger by the phrase, 'The sky is beautiful at sunset.' You will respond with, 'Beauty is in the beholder's eye.' Do you have that?" asked the handler.

Alepoú nodded.

"Questions?"

"I need more money to pay my party dues and my rent," Alepoú urged.

"We'll discuss that at the next meeting. For now, do as you are told and get the information. We will reward any other party documents you gather, too. Do you understand?" asked the handler.

Alepoú nodded. Then she asked, "Do you have to blindfold me when I leave here? That is humiliating."

"Yes. That is standard procedure. No one will see you. The car's windows are darkened," answered the handler.

Alepoú's handler rose and said, "We'll talk again soon."

Alepoú flashed a flirtatious smile and batted her big green eyes. This registered with the handler who noted Alepoú's raw talent, then thought, "She'll need training to bring her to full potential."

The handler left the room, and two strapping men in dark suits and large aviator-style sunglasses entered. The man to the right dangled a black blindfold.

Chapter 8

"We need to talk after we finish," Dimitra stated cooly.

Stavros knew something was wrong.

The Circle drew eleven people and lasted an hour. The dialogue remained direct and personal, with only intermittent descents into speech-making. The publisher of the *Athens Journal of Social Sciences* agreed to draft the consensus. He was a friend of Yiorgos. The consensus was that America might see a decline in popularity over the coming five years. But the organic relationship between Greece and America was strong. Only the political class, often under the influence of hostile nations or motivated by corruption, sought to leverage American aid and manipulate Greek foreign relations. The Circle resolved America should continue promoting economic reforms and political liberalization, and provide aid for critical infrastructure projects and the military. This America might do with less public fanfare.

Stavros spoke sparingly. Dimitra insisted Greece was far from ready for self-governance. She said, "Greece is bound by the lingering barbarity of Ottoman autocracy. In 1453, the Turks gifted us primitive habits that we have yet to shed. Then, for four hundred years, these habits baked in our souls. Until we purge these, Greece will never be free. Look no further than our treatment of women. In the mountains, women are treated as mules. How can such a country be free if it enslaves half of its population? America is not perfect, but it is a towering beacon alongside our cave of darkness."

Two other women attended the meeting. One, a young professor from the Athens University School of Economics and Business, nodded her assent. The other, older and matronly, was a lawyer with a prominent Athens firm. She said, "Efharis Petridou was the first woman admitted to Athens Bar in 1925. Only twenty-six years ago.[18] Still, to this day, women cannot be judges in Greece. So, not only are the women in the villages abused and relegated to inferior lives, so does it happen in Athens. Here we are burdened not with bundles of wood or dirty laundry, but a burden is present all the same. Women have been lawyers in America since 1869. In 1925, when Athens admitted Petridou to the bar, American women were arguing before the United States Supreme Court. America is our friend, if for no other reason than the modern example she sets."

Yiorgos, Socratic to the end, asked thoughtful and probing questions, like "Why does Greece pretend we are independent when we cannot feed ourselves?" And "If a country seeks aid from a friend, is it not proper for the friend to seek a favor? Is not freedom the recognition of necessity?"

Christakis was circumspect, as usual. He spoke only once. He warned, "America is our only hope for the future. Our pride and national hubris is worth less than the material support and security we receive for being their junior partner. Are we to demand our *independence* only to become again occupied vassals?

"Our geography defines us. As always throughout our history, the sea is our bounty and because of its value, prized by our enemies. Given the opportunity, the Soviets, in search of a mighty navy and bases to stage it, will swallow us for dinner at the first bell. And if not them, the Turks. And if not them, the Yugoslavs. We will fight, as we did against the fascists, then perish before their tanks and aircraft. We are ten million and they are ten times that. Independence is an illusion, a clarion for opportunistic politicians."

Stavros agreed.

A young man, A Greek of Slavic extraction, began speaking. Stavros knew him to be a marine engineer. He echoed Christakis's argument but added, "While America is in charge, we will be at peace, not only with the communists, but within our borders. The Americans will not allow adventures into Macedonia or Albania. They will prevent Greeks from being our own worst enemies."

The draft consensus would circulate for comments, and then its rewrite would circulate once more. The Circle would vote up or down on the rewrite. If a majority voted to endorse the draft, the Circle steering committee would decide if a public product was viable. That product might be an editorial, a public statement, a policy position paper, or a submission to a magazine or journal. If the Circle's publication produced enough interest, they might assign a point of contact for radio or print interviews.

The Circle worked well. Over the past year it turned out a dozen well-informed and reasoned pro-American, pro-NATO products. In the early days, Stavros had exerted a leading personality, but now, the Circle had a life of its own. Participants believed that publishing costs, the cost of meeting rooms, and the cost of drinks and food were paid from a generous grant from Marshall funds. They weren't. The money came from Frank Wisner's OPC's slackly audited, bottomless budget.

After the meeting, the group enjoyed a round of wine and appetizers. Stavros suspected some came for only this reason. He circulated and talked with everyone. He said to Christakis, "I trust the wine is up to the lofty standards set by Cellar Red?"

Christakis smiled.

Stavros said, "Thanks again for inviting me to the rally. That was fun. Maybe we can do it again?"

Christakis said, "Do you hunt?"

Stavros noted the abrupt change of subject. Then he said, "Sure, but I don't have any guns in Greece."

Christakis went on, "We will hunt the boar this coming weekend. The guns are not a problem. I can provide them. Would you like to come?"

Stavros did a quick calculation. Guns, a suspected GRU agent, remote hills, dangerous cliff faces, and dense woods . . . He said, "Sure. It sounds like fun."

Christakis, a literalist, replied, "Fun, not so much. The terrain is rough, and it will be cold in the mountains. But the reward is worth it. Do you have rough boots and outdoor clothing?"

Stavros said, "I'm sure I can borrow some from the Embassy staff and the Marines stationed there."

Christakis said, "Good. We will leave early Saturday morning. I will pick you up at the hotel. We will meet the others in the team by noon. We will drive to an area west of where we watched the rally."

Team? Thought Stavros. Now this is getting interesting. He said, "Right." Then he thanked Christakis for his contribution to the dialogue.

Stavros circulated to Yiorgos, whom he thanked for arranging the meeting and suggesting the topic. He said, "Your questions, as always, were provocative and stirred the dialogue. Well done."

Yiorgos smiled and said, "Good." Then with mocking flourish added, "I have added to the tree of knowledge, may it bloom forever."

Stavros approached Dimitra and the female lawyer engaged in a passionate conversation. The passion came from Dimitra, but the logical and dispassionate words of the lawyer landed with equal weight. Dimitra held the glass of wine in her right hand and gestured with her left.

Stavros decided not to interrupt and moved on to the younger woman from Athens University. She stood alone at the edge of the group and seemed lost for social skills. She was new. Stavros had seen her at the Circle only one time, and other than nodding agreement with Dimitra, she didn't speak during the dialogue.

"Do you approve of tonight's wine selection?" he asked.

The young woman was pretty but unadorned. She was trim, but every feature—her clothes, her jewelry, her shoes, her hair—was mousy. She wore tortoise-shell cat eyeglasses that framed her lustrous but diffident hazel eyes. She was young but refined. Stavros pegged her in her late twenties. Her name was Penelope, and she wasn't wearing a wedding ring.

Penelope said, "Oh. The wine is superb. I should thank you for providing it."

"No need to thank me. You can thank Uncle Sam," smiled Stavros.

Penelope looked puzzled.

Stavros said, "Uncle Sam is American slang for the United States."

"Oh. I see," she said.

Stavros concluded she was not a conversationalist.

After a pause, he asked, "What field of economics do you teach?"

"I lecture in economic development and labor economics," she said, again letting the conversation drop.

Stavros waited then asked, "Do you have your PhD? I teach world history in America, and I'm here to research my dissertation."

"No. We are the same. I am working on my dissertation. This I hope to have by autumn of this coming year," she shared.

Now Stavros felt like he was pulling teeth. He asked, "Do you have a title or a topic?"

She smiled just a bit, and Stavros thought that perhaps the wine was loosening her. She said, "My advisers and I agreed on *The Development of Greek Labor Relations in the Twentieth Century and The Impact on Wage Rates*."

Stavros nodded. Then Penelope surprised him with, "If that title doesn't put you to sleep, you suffer from clinical insomnia."

This made Stavros smile. Penelope warmed and offered her first encouraging eye contact.

Just then, Dimitra arrived at his elbow. Stavros looked to her, and she was stern but managed a smile to the young woman.

Dimitra said, "Professor, may I speak to you before I leave?"

Stavros said, "Excuse me, Penelope. I look forward to talking further about your dissertation."

He nodded to Penelope and he and Dimitra made for a quiet corner in the room away from the others.

Dimitra turned her back to the others and started the conversation, "If you control your American spies, call them off."

"What are you talking about?" asked a disbelieving Stavros.

"Do you know Dr. Charles H. Morgan?" asked Dimitra.

"No. Never heard of him," answered Stavros.

"He is a prominent, though I believe overrated, American archeologist. He lectures at the American School of Classical Studies in Athens. He has published works on Byzantine pottery and other uninteresting drivel. He was an American air intelligence officer in Europe during the war.[19] Don't ask me how I know. I know people who know these things.

"He sought me out last week. While he pretended interest in my plans for the dig in Aphaia, he hinted I might still be in touch with the KKE! He is not good at hinting. Americans are as short on guile as they are on history.

"Tell him to stop the interrogation and mind his own business!"

Stavros was shell-shocked. He knew nothing of Morgan and nothing of ongoing efforts to vet Dimitra. He said, "I . . . I don't move in those circles. I don't know the man, and I don't control any spies. I can ask around the embassy and see what's up."

"Do not bother. Embassies are for politicians. Tell your fellow spies to leave me alone. That is all."

With that last command, Dimitra turned to Penelope standing alone ten feet away, smiled a pleasant smile, and strode from the room, leaving Stavros slack-jawed.

Chapter 9

Frank Wisner, CIA Deputy Director of Plans, replied to Stavros's inquiry the following day.

> ***Top Secret—From Director's Log 8:30 AM, 12 Oct.–8:30 AM 13 Oct.***
> *On debriefing by the OSO case officer, Dr. Charles H. Morgan, prominent classical archaeologist who was briefed prior to a three-week visit to Greece in September–October, reported that his stay had been too short to permit the broad contacts he had hoped to make among Greek officials or to allow him to collect significant intelligence information.*

The reply revealed only that Dimitra was on an OSO list of targets to monitor. Stavros didn't expect more information until he could meet with Wisner in person. If Stavros learned more—who ordered the contact, what prompted the interest—there was still little he could do. If he defended Dimitra to OSO brass, his flashing cape would only madden the bull. She was on a watch list. An order from above, from Wisner, was the way to free Dimitra of OSO surveillance. He wondered how far OSO would take their scrutiny. It worried him all night in bouts of shallow, anxious dreaming.

He woke at 4:30 a.m. and put on the rough clothes on loan from US Embassy staff and the Marine Security Guard. He waited in the tasteful lobby of the Grande Bretagne as Bulgarian maids in crisp black-and-white uniforms polished and dusted around him. Had the concierge, security, and desk staff not known him; they would have asked him to leave. He didn't look like he belonged.

A little before 5:00 a.m., Christakis rolled into the reception parking area ahead of two waiting taxis in his Simca 8 Sport Coupé, a car befitting a rally enthusiast. The two-door was stylish, rounded and set on wire wheels. It was glossy black with a red leather interior. It sported a civilian license registration and, Stavros thought, so does my Morris.

Stavros opened his door, placed his hunting jacket in the rear and sat in the sporty bucket seat. He said, "Good morning."

Christakis nodded.

"This is a fine car. How long have you owned it?"

"For one year. This is a 1950 model," answered Christakis.

"At the rally, you drove an old Morris like mine. Why didn't you drive this?" asked Stavros.

"The road from Amfissa was rutted. The road to our vantage too rough. This car cannot travel such roads. It is too low to the ground. No clearance. We will not drive this car into the mountains. We will meet our team in Lidoriki and from there go by truck into the hills," answered Christakis.

Stavros knew of Lidoriki, although he never visited. The village was on the Mornos River. He was familiar with the river from his OSS operations near Nafpaktos. To the east of Nafpaktos, the Mornos emptied into the Gulf of Corinth. And Lidoriki was on the southwestern slope of Mount Giona. He knew that name from stories of the British Special Operations Executive commandos who landed ahead of the Americans. Colonel Eddie Myers and his team had parachuted onto the mountain to begin their campaign in Greece on a moonless night in September 1942. Stavros knew the mountain rose to over two thousand meters and wondered how far up they would climb. He asked, "So we are hunting near Mount Giona?"

Christakis nodded.

"Will we climb the mountain?"

"No. Not to the top. But we will climb so your legs know the challenge. The boars stay in the wooded areas and these only rise to fifteen hundred meters."

"Just so you know, I've only hunted rabbits and deer and a few ducks, never boar," confessed Stavros.

"Yes. But you know how to handle a gun. The OSS taught you that, no?" answered Christakis. Then he went on, "Hunting boar is much like hunting Nazis. We will start the animal on a path not of their choosing, then ambush them at a location we select. The only difference is that we will use dogs to make them run."

Stavros wished for his Colt. Christakis knew he was OSS.

Christakis went on, "We will use twelve-gauge slug ammunition. I brought for you a pump-style weapon. Does that suit you?"

Stavros nodded, now realizing that his silence acknowledged his OSS connection. Then he thought about his gun and ammunition. The combination was deadly at short range. The kinetic energy of the twelve-gauge slug round at thirty meters was enough to knock down a charging boar, no doubt. But hitting a raging animal in thick brush, that was the trick. Then he thought about the dogs. Greeks loved their dogs. He envisioned a pack of snarling hounds chasing the boar, gnashing at its heels, and hoped like hell he could hit the boar and, God forbid, not a dog. He remembered when Gus, his friend and a sergeant in his OSS Operational Group, shot a mother boar north of Thermos with his sidearm. Her demise had led to the recitation of the Caledonian Boar myth over glowing wood embers and a welcome roasted dinner. The episode gained Gus the nickname Meleager. The hint of a smile formed on his lips.

Christakis saw his smile. He asked, "Good memories?"

Stavros said, "Some, yes. Tell me more about the hunt. I don't want to be a hinderance."

"Yes. We have the time. Our drive will take four hours, maybe more," assured Christakis. "But first, would you like to tell me more about your OSS service?"

Stavros played it straight. What else could he do? He asked, "How did you come to believe I was in the OSS?"

Christakis said, "Stavros, we are friends, no? We work together in the Circle, no? The product of the Circle is political manipulation, no? Perhaps you call it influence or public relations, this I do not know. I work for Greek Public Security; do you believe we do not have the means to investigate? Of course, you don't. Americans play this game well, but you have one weakness. You underestimate the ability of other services. Greece is a small nation recovering from terrible times, but some skills endure, some arts are never forgotten."

Stavros nodded. Then he said, "So, I'm sure you understand that if I were in the OSS and spent time in Greece, I would be duty-bound not to speak of it."

Christakis nodded, and they drove on for a few kilometers. Then Christakis said, "Here is what we know. You arrived in Greece in April 1944 with a unit called Operational Group II. You led the group. You departed Greece in September, and during your stay you encamped at the village of Chómori and this is where you met your friend, Dimitra. Also, during your time in Greece, you completed a handful of successful antifascist operations notably sinking a ferry on the Gulf of Corinth. The Greek resistance fighters you collocated with and fought alongside were EAM-ELAS partisans. Dimitra, at the time KKE, was their kapetánios.

"Stavros first let me say, bravo. Well done. I was marching to nowhere and drilling in the sands of the Middle East while you were killing Germans in Greece. My hat is off to you. I bring up your OSS service to clear the air between us and allow us to further our cooperation. Cooperation in the Circle is easy, but not all operations are so . . . civil, no?"

Stavros admired his information. But from where had it come? The Greek Ministry of Public Security or the Soviet GRU? Stavros stayed as calm as he could. He said, "I'm sorry I cannot confirm or deny your information. As far as further cooperation, you must be more specific about what you have in mind. And, again, I can only offer my support as a friend, not as a representative of my government. I'm a simple professor working on my dissertation in a country I love, a country I will help in any way I can."

"That is good," said Christakis. "We can talk further but for now, allow me to explain the hunt."

As they drove farther from Athens, the roads became rougher and reduced to a double lane. Christakis drove in the Greek fashion, envisioning a notional third lane down the crown of the road. When he wanted to overtake a slower vehicle, he moved to the invisible center lane regardless of oncoming traffic and gunned the engine to pass. Other cars then moved to their notional outside lanes using the road's narrow shoulders, allowing Christakis to speed on. This was nerve-racking to the uninitiated, but Stavros had witnessed this technique driving through the country and was mostly immune.

Christakis began his description of the hunt. He told Stavros that they would meet two men in Lidoriki, men that he knew from his days in the Sacred Band. They were local men, one a farmer of olives and tobacco and the other the owner of a small grocery store in the town. He said his friends would travel with at least three dogs, two bay hounds and one catch dog, maybe two. The bays were Schwyz hounds, a Swiss breed in its pure form but, in Greece, mixed with cur, mongrel dogs known for their bravery and fearlessness. He told Stavros the bay dogs would be friendly and harmless. But he warned him about the catch dog, a Cane Corso. This animal, he said, was a well-bred Italian dog, never neutered and fifty kilograms. This dog stayed with the ambushers to be unleashed only when the bay dogs drove the boar close enough for him to attack. Then, the catch dog would rush the boar, latch on to its ear or neck, and stop it long enough for the ambushers to finish it with slug rounds.

His friends knew the boar runs. They would drop Christakis, the catch dog named Dante, and Stavros at the bottom of a run. There the two men would fashion a hide and wait for the action. The other two men would drive farther up the mountain to the top of the boar run, perhaps a kilometer away, then fire their guns to roust a boar. The bay dogs would take after the boar and chase it down the run. They would signal with howling all the way to the ambush.

Christakis finished his description with, "That is all. We shoot the boar, give the dogs their rewards—an ear, a tail, the entrails—and when we have gutted the animal, we carry it to the truck. We drive back to Lidoriki, have a celebratory dinner with my friends, then drive back to Athens with stories to tell."

Stavros asked, "Should not your friends be the ambushers? They are bringing their dogs, providing the truck, scouting the run. It seems like they should have the honor of killing the boar."

Christakis smiled, "You think like an American. You must learn to think like a Greek. Who will carry the boar to the truck? This could be half a kilometer and not good footing. Some boars, the big ones, can weight two hundred kilos. And even after gutting, perhaps one hundred and fifty kilos. We will do most of the work. Greeks will trade work for honor any day of the week!" Then he laughed out loud.

Stavros laughed as well.

They arrived at Lidoriki a little after nine in the morning. The town was just stirring with shopkeepers opening stores and a few women in black village dresses and shopping bags walking about. North of the town, Christakis turned into the parking area of a building supply business. At the far end of the lot, two men leaned against the front fender of a truck smoking cigarettes as three dogs frolicked around them. Stavros recognized the vehicle as a Beep, a half-ton four-wheel-drive Dodge. These were the World War II trucks GIs had used when Jeeps weren't enough to get the job done. The vehicle was topless, doorless, and the windscreen lowered to the hood. A power winch rode atop the front bumper, and a steel grill protected the radiator and headlights. Painted in its war colors, its faded olive drab made it indistinguishable from the background of woods and rock.

Christakis said, "Good. They are here. We don't have to wait." He pulled the Simca next to the Dodge and he and Stavros got out. Christakis walked to the two men, who smiled and shook hands. The bigger man slapped Christakis on the shoulder and said something familiar that Stavros couldn't make out. Christakis turned to Stavros and said, "This is my friend Stavros Theofanis; he is from America, but he knows Greece. He was here during the war. But do not ask him about his adventures, he is a sealed envelope. A monk pledged to silence.

"Stavros, this is Atticus," he said, nodding to the man on the left, "and Basil."

Stavros shook their hands and smiles remained all around. Basil, the larger man, taller than Stavros, said, "These worthless pests are Sigma," and he snapped his finger at the name. The first bay hound came to heel alongside his left leg. Then he snapped, "Daphne," and the other bay hound lined up alongside her partner. Then he spoke in a rougher tone, "Dante," and the large dog quit romping like a puppy and lined up with the others.

Dante was massive. His breed, Cane Corso, derived from Molossus dogs, a Greek breed that originated in Epirus. In Dante's veins flowed much of the breed. Greeks bred Molossus as war dogs and guardians of livestock, protecting flocks from wolves, jackals, and brown bears. The Romans imported the animals and bred them to modern standards. The Greek Molossians were ancestors of the mastiff breed, and Dante's one hundred pounds cast an aurora of contained aggression.

Basil pulled three chicken feet from his hunting vest and fed each dog, praising them and patting their heads while jaws crunched gristle and bone.

Stavros said, "Your dogs are impressive, especially Dante."

Basil replied, "Aristotle wrote of them in his *History of Animals*. He said the bigger dogs, like Dante, were used to tend flocks because they fought off wild beasts.[20] Today he will get to show his breeding."

"How old is Dante?" asked Stavros.

"Seven years. He is in his prime. He is a star athlete and, like some, a little stubborn," answered Basil.

Dante looked up at Stavros when he heard his name slobbering while he chewed.

Christakis called sharply, "Dan-te."

The dog first looked up at Basil, who nodded, then ran to Christakis and came to heel. He looked up at him like he deserved another chicken foot. Christakis padded his head. Dante's ruddy brown fur was short and well groomed. His muzzle was black running back to his browed eyes where it turned grayish then black again on his stubby ears. His muzzle, head, eyes, and ears evolved as weapons and any beauty in Dante rested in this purpose. He looked to Stavros like a masterpiece of death.

Christakis asked Basil, "You have been working on his commands, I can tell. He is alert this morning."

Basil said, "He is excited. He has not hunted for three weeks. His only excitement comes from chasing squirrels and rabbits. He knows that a trip in the truck means boar. When you want him to catch the boar, use the command, the same as we used our last time on the mountain. Until then, keep him leashed. Release the leash, shout the command, and be ready to shoot the boar when he brings it down. Whistle him to make him release. If today we get a boar, it will be his tenth kill. This is what he lives for."

Christakis nodded, still padding the dog's head.

Basil looked at Stavros and said, "Dante is an obedient dog. He will see you are a friend. Let him smell the back of your hand. He knows Alexis, and he respects his commands. But do not stare Dante in the eyes. To him, that is a challenge to his dominance and a threat to his pack. If you see his upper lip roll away from his left incisor, back away and do not look him in the eyes. That is the only warning he will give."

Stavros forced a smile and said, "Right. Thanks for the warning."

Then Basil said to no one, "Let's mount up and bring home a boar!"

The two hounds at his feet began circling in anticipation.

Basil called Dante and walked to the truck's tailgate.

Christakis went to the boot of the Simca and retrieved two worn leather gun carriers and a hatchet he hung from his belt. He handed one gun to Stavros and said, "Let's carry them for now and we'll ready them when we park."

Then he and Stavros climbed into the bed of the truck with the animals.

They drove north on the road to Kastriotissa with the Mornos River to their west. After five kilometers, they turned right onto a dirt trail. Just off the main road, Basil stopped the Dodge and got out of the vehicle to lock the four-wheel-drive hubs on the front axle. He climbed back into the driver's seat, shifted into low range, and set off up the steep, furrowed packed earth. Cedars and firs rose to forty feet on either side of the vehicle. Uncountable needles filtered the morning sun, casting a green glow. Stavros looked at the terrain and saw little undergrowth, only a dense forest of trunks and rocks with most of the branches starting above a man's head. He braced himself to mitigate the jarring in the steel bed and saw Christakis do the same. The dogs wanted to stand, to scent the air in anticipation of an adventure, but they gave up and lay down.

Two kilometers up the path, Basil stopped the Dodge and turned in his seat. He said, "This is a new hide, Alexis. We scouted this run less than a week ago, and it looks fresh. Walk in about three hundred meters bearing due east. You will see the run. Set your hide and when you hear Sigma and Daphne get ready. Here's Dante's leash," and he handed over a well-worn leather tether with a quick-release hook that Christakis attached to Dante's collar. Dante stood in the truck bed ready for action but stayed at heel.

Christakis said, "Let's assemble our guns and leave the carries in the truck."

Stavros nodded.

Still sitting on the fender well, Stavros unzipped the carrier and found inside a Remington 870. He recognized the gun. This model was not fancy but one of the most reliable shotguns ever made. He worked the pump slide before assembling the barrel and felt it move smoothly along its guide.

Christakis said, "I oiled it, it should work well."

Stavros removed a twenty-inch barrel from the carrier and fitted it to the receiver; then he screwed the stay-bolt into the mount. The barrel, designed for slug use, featured sights both front and rear.

Basil handed back a carton of twelve-gauge ammunition, and Stavros put five rounds in the weapon and took another handful for his pocket.

Christakis pulled from his carrier a double barrel Stavros thought he recognized. Stavros asked, "Is that a Smith?"

Christakis answered, "Yes. This is field grade, nothing fancy. I've cut the barrels down for quicker presentation in brush."

Stavros knew this gun. L.C. Smith was a legendary American manufacturer, their guns coveted since the late 1800s. Not only did they make reliable weapons, but their high-end models offered some of the finest engraving in the world. Field grade was the least adorned, but still remarkably reliable. Stavros noted the side-by-side barrel's single front sight. He asked, "Any problems   sighting?"

Christakis, inserting two shells into the Smith, answered without looking up. He said, "No. I'm practiced, and I shoot the British style."

He looked up to see Stavros's questioning expression. He continued, "Just as Fairbairn, Sykes, and Applegate instruct, no?"

Christakis's mentioned British SOE and American OSS commando training to elicit a reaction. Stavros, instead, let the provocation slide without comment.

Christakis took a handful of shells from the carton and put them in his hunting vest. He mated the receiver with a muted clink that reminded Stavros of a safe closing. Christakis thumbed the safety atop the grip to "*S*" and looked again at Stavros. He said, "Shall we find our hide?"

The two men climbed out of the truck bed with Dante, and the two chase hounds followed. Dante tugged at his leash and Christakis jerked back. The dog came to heel. It looked to Stavros like a spiteful and vehement command, but Dante received it as a slight rebuke.

Basil called Sigma and Daphne to the truck and they climbed aboard over Atticus into the bed. Basil said, "Good hunting. About two hundred meters due east. This road runs north and south. We will drive up the mountain another kilometer and flush the boar. When you hear Daphne—she's always the first—you will know something is moving. Sigma will join in, and they will sound all the way to your hide if they have the scent or the boar in sight. If their calls become distant, the boar has outsmarted us."

Atticus spoke, "We saw deep tracks when we scouted. Two hundred kilos, perhaps. A big target, no?" Then he smiled.

He's big because he's outsmarted many Greeks, thought Stavros.

The Dodge pulled away, and the two dogs in the bed swayed with the ruts, then lay down for the ride.

Christakis said, "You should rack a shell, have one ready in the chamber. There is boar here, also bear. One time I came between a mother and her two cubs, and she charged. Better to be ready, no?"

Stavros nodded, then worked the pump to charge a round.

With Dante straining at the leash, Christakis set into the tall firs at a right angle to the road. Stavros followed. Although he had sized up Christakis as something other than a GRU agent, he was glad to have him in his sights and not the other way around.

The two men and dog walked deeper into the firs and came onto a track through the fallen needles. The run was worn enough to leave a rut, and on closer inspection, Christakis found scat. The hardened, squeezed pellets first caught Christakis's eye. Their black gnarled clumps stood out against the brown, gray, and green of the forest floor. Then Christakis saw the splotches of lighter gray colored droppings and said, "Fresh. The boar was here only a day ago."

Christakis stood up, looking around in a circle. To their right he pointed to a fir with the bark rubbed off to a meter high. He said, "There. That is his rub. He is tall."

Dante rose from scenting the scat, and his stubby ears perked and swiveled like radar.

Christakis said, "He's on alert. We should hide."

The two men looked around and Christakis said, "Over here. This will do. You take the hill, and I'll stay on this side of the run behind this boulder with Dante. Stay behind the tree trunk and don't let the boar see you until I've released Dante. You should have a clear shot from the rise. Twenty meters, maybe thirty. I'll release Dante and fire from here, but you may have a better shot while the boar is broadside. Aim for just behind the shoulder and low. If you hit the shoulder blade, the round will deflect."

Stavros asked, "Should I fire before Dante grabs him if I have a shot?"

"Of course. If you have a clear shot, kill him. But it is likely he will run and dodge and not be an easy target. Dante will slow him and bring him to a stop, although if it's a big boar, even

Dante will find that difficult. But Dante will slow him and make for us a better target."

Stavros nodded.

As Stavros and Christakis separated to take their hides, they heard shots up the mountain. Stavros looked back at Christakis. He said, "They are rousting the boar. They shoot to make him move. When he moves, the bay hounds will sense him, and the chase is on."

Stavros nodded.

Then Christakis added, "Stavros, when we approach for the kill, remember that the boar is much faster than he looks. Stay at least three meters from him, always. We will know when he is dead and only then will we approach him. Understood?"

Stavros said, "Right." Then wondered what he had signed up for.

Christakis took one step, turned back to Stavros, and said, "This will happen fast."

Stavros turned and nodded.

Stavros knelt on a rise behind a large fir tree. He took a knee and heard the first bay coming from, he presumed, Daphne. Then the second. He estimated the dogs and whatever they were chasing to be five hundred meters away. The muffled sound was of indistinct direction because of the heavy woods. All he could tell for certain was that the baying grew louder. They were getting closer.

Christakis and Dante waited behind a boulder twenty meters on the other side of the run. Stavros saw Christakis unleash the dog and grab him by his collar. Every muscle in Dante's body tensed and tightened, and the dog looked like a coiled spring.

It was a blur, but even in that instant, Stavros registered the bristle on the boar's back and the saliva flying from beneath the animal's razor tusks. He materialized from the trunks like a phantom. He was a splotchy brown that melded with the forest floor and moving fast for his awkward stature.

The bays, whom Stavros envisioned nipping at the beast's ankles, were nowhere to be seen. He heard their yelps, but the boar was fifty meters ahead of the dogs and thirty meters from Stavros. The animal dodged on the path, making him an impossible target.

Christakis released Dante and yelled, "Fermo!" at the top of his lungs.

Dante needed no command. This was his blood. The dog raced from the boulder and matched every weave and dodge the boar made. Dante dove full speed into the left side of the boar, lips pulled from his gums and his teeth gnashing. Stavros heard a yelp as the boar's tusk entered Dante's right hip. In the snapping and tugging, Dante locked onto the boar's right ear. The animal halted, moving only to drag Dante with him in a blur of blood, dust, and fir needles.

Christakis stood from behind the boulder and moved to its side for a clear shot. Stavros rose and took a firing position alongside the tree where he took cover. Christakis fired first, but the boar was head on and not at a good angle. He missed.

Stavros's target was better, but he was farther away. He took aim and knew that his shot would be as much intuition as marksmanship. Everything was in motion, Dante, the boar, dust, a cloud of fir needles. He fired one round that went wide. He pumped the Remington, and his second round found the boar's hind quarter, high on its hip. He heard the beast gasp and squeal. Stavros knew the shot was not fatal. But it hobbled the boar, and Dante, his muscular legs searching for traction, brought it to a stop.

Christakis advanced, and when only five meters away, he fired the second barrel. His shot grazed the boar's hind quarters. This seemed to enrage the crazed beast and with an impossible jerk of its head; Dante flew to the forest floor with most of its ear in his bloody jaws. Then it sighted Christakis and pawed the earth with its right hoof.

Christakis opened the breach of the Smith and brought two shells from his vest. Before he could reload and lock the breach, the boar was on him. The strike knocked him off balance and as he fell, he brought the Smith across his chest for protection. He landed hard on his back. He smelled coppery blood and foul breath and felt saliva on his cheek. He was defenseless. The heft of its body was insufferable. It gasped into his face through its deadly tusks. A moment passed before Christakis realized the monster had landed as dead weight.

Stavros placed his shot perfectly. The round entered behind the shoulder blade low and passed through the brute's lungs and heart.

Dante was having nothing of it and reengaged on the left ear. Christakis squirmed from beneath the bleeding carcass and yelled in a strained voice, "Whistle! Whistle so Dante will release!"

Stavros put two fingers to his lips and hailed the dog.

Dante looked around at Stavros, still locked onto the boar's ear. It surprised the dog that the command came from Stavros. He knew Stavros to be a friend and a member of the pack, but of undetermined status. Just then the two bays arrived and stood off barking at the kill. Dante released the lifeless appendage. Stavros called, "Good, Dante."

Christakis squirmed under the boar. Stavros tried to push the carcass off but found the lifeless creature to be not only heavy, but impossible to grip. With great effort and strain, Christakis worked his way free. Stavros asked, "Are you okay?"

"Embarrassed but unharmed," he answered. "I should have reloaded before I approached. Thank you for killing this monster. I am certain he weighs at least two hundred kilos. He would have killed me; of this I am certain. I am in your debt."

Christakis stood and favored his left leg.

Stavros asked, "How's the leg?"

"The beast landed on my knee. It may be bruised. I can walk," answered Christakis.

Stavros looked him over for cuts and only saw blood from the boar. Then he looked at Dante. The dog was gashed the length of a tusk in his right hip. He asked Christakis, "Should we tend to Dante's wound?"

"We'll let Basil handle him. Dante's moving well, no limp. The wound is congealing, perhaps not too deep. Basil will know what to do," said Christakis.

Dante circled to the side of the boar, lay on a patch of fir needles, and licked the wound.

Christakis moved better now. He pulled a folding knife from his pocket, extended its five-inch blade, and cut the remaining ear from the boar. He gave the ear to Dante, who relished the treat. He cut away the stub of the left ear and gave it to Daphne, then severed the boar's tail for Sigma. He said, "That will hold them while I gut him."

Gutting the animal was as unpleasant as it sounded, but it lightened the carcass by at least fifty kilos. Stavros helped roll the boar onto its side. Christakis began by stroking the blade at the base of the animal's scrotum, cutting away skin and fat but careful not to puncture the intestines. After he cut the skin away from the entrails, he turned the knife over and inserted it under the skin and fat, cutting edge up. He ripped the tissue all the way to the diaphragm and ribcage, again making certain not to puncture the stomach or gut. He cut away the diaphragm and severed the carotid artery and esophagus in the base of the boar's head. He reached into the cavity and pulled out the intestines and organs, cutting away connecting tissues. He cut away the heart and liver and put them in a canvas sack he pulled from the back pouch of his vest. Then he replaced the sack in his vest. He said, "He is at least two hundred kilos, now maybe one hundred and fifty. We will leave his head here and lose another twenty. I will cut that off. You take the hatchet and find a carry pole. We'll strap him to the pole to get him out of the woods."

Stavros found a straight cedar and began hacking at its trunk. Christakis looked up from cutting and called to Stavros, "Better that you strip away the limbs first, then cut the tree."

Stavros said, "Right. That makes sense." And he did as Christakis suggested.

Stavros returned with a sturdy limb cleared of its branches about three meters long. Christakis said, "I need the hatchet."

Stavros handed it to Christakis who chopped into the base of the boar's skull and after three swings, severed its backbone. He finished cutting the head from the body, and it rolled away from the carcass to the delight of the three dogs.

The two men were tying the boar's legs over the carry pole when Basil and Atticus called from the run. Neither Stavros nor Christakis heard them coming. The dogs heard but made no fuss since the two flushers were of no concern.

Basil called, "Good for you! He is big, no?"

Christakis called back, "He is big, and we are lucky to be carrying *him* away and not me."

Christakis told the tale as Basil looked at Dante's wound. Basil pulled a flask from his hip pocket and splashed a good portion of tsipouro over a handkerchief. He held Dante by the collar and dabbed the wound. Dante whimpered at the sting, his ears laid back, and he fought being held to the ground. But Basil was Alpha. Soon the sting subsided. Dante stopped licking the wound and his ears perked. Then he stood tall at Basil's side, wagging his stubby tail, pleased with his day.

Chapter 10

"Do you know the name Nesti Josifi Kopali?" asked Christakis.

Stavros, downshifting into third gear as he entered a tight left turn, shook his head. "Never heard of him."

"He is an Albanian defector. He came across late in 1949, in Rome. He was posing as a press officer in their legation but serving as chief of the Albanian Sigurimi in Italy. They recalled him to Tirana. He feared torture and execution for his failure to kill off the Albanian resistance movement in Italy. He turned himself over to the Americans. You rejected him.[21]

"Italian Naval Intelligence interrogated Kopali for two months. Then the CIA flew him to Washington, DC, listened to his story, and decided he was a fish too small for their net. He provided some information in Washington about Albanian security and military operations. But not enough for the US Government to offer him political asylum. It disappointed him; he wanted to resettle in America. He had visited Boston in 1947 to establish liaison with an Albanian weekly newspaper, *Dielli*. At this he failed, but he liked America. The CIA sent him back to Rome.

"He became erratic. He fashioned himself a great asset could bring down communism. He drank and whored. He couldn't be left alone; he knew too much. He claimed to know a great deal about the GRU in Athens and said he knew the rezidentura, Colonel Dmitriy Chernov. He said Chernov was playable. But by then, neither the Italian nor the American service took him seriously.

"The CIA moved him to a detention camp in Germany. There he bedeviled your US Army Counterintelligence Corps. Kopali schemed and drank and hounded his captors with plans to resettle in America and even return to Albania. No one has ever confirmed it, but I understand they moved him to a mental hospital in Athens."

Stavros listened. Christakis was full of details. But it was true, Stavros had never heard of Kopali. Christakis took Stavros into his confidence, yet Stavros never confirmed that he was OSS, let alone CIA. The approach bemused Stavros.

The Simca hummed along on a stretch of straight road with Stavros at the wheel. The men had enjoyed a celebratory meal with Basil and Atticus after bringing the boar down from Mount Giona. While Christakis sat motionless at the table, his wound stiffened. When the meal finished, Christakis tried to drive, but the road was twisty with many hills. Depressing the clutch with his bad leg was painful, and the knee was swelling. He asked Stavros if he wanted to drive. Stavros was sorry for Christakis, but happy to oblige. The Simca was fun.

"It is a fascinating story. Why tell me?" asked Stavros.

"Stavros, I tell you because I believe we should work together for a grand prize. Something that both our services will value," answered Christakis.

"And what would that prize be," probed Stavros.

Christakis answered, "I believe we can play back the rezidentura against the GRU. That is the correct terminology per your service, no? I believe we can provide false information to the enemy while gaining accurate information from the rezidentura."

Stavros remained unmoved, but his thoughts raced. Playing back the head of Greek GRU was big-time, high-risk. He wanted to hear more but not blow his cover, although Christakis knew a great deal already. Stavros felt childish pretending otherwise.

"So, how can I, as a private citizen unattached to any United States Government agency, help in this project?" Stavros asked.

"The whereabouts of Kopali and permission to talk to him must come from, um . . . a friend of yours," answered Christakis.

"Who might that be?"

"Mr. Frank Wisner, the CIA Deputy Director of Plans. I believe you are acquainted, no?"

Chapter 11

"Frank, it's hard to know what to make of him. Christakis is the most buttoned-up legend I've run across, or he is what he seems. His story about Kopali holds up. Right?" asked Stavros.

Frank Wisner nodded.

"Then his request for a face-to-face seems logical. If Kopali has a hook for the GRU rezidentura, and we can confirm it, it could be a strong play.

"Do you know where he is?"

Frank Wisner nodded.

"A hospital in Athens?"

Wisner did not respond.

"So, Frank, here are three things you might help with. First, double-check Christakis. There might be a mistake in the file. Maybe he was misidentified. He seems bona fide to me. Second, think about letting us interview Kopali. A move on the GRU would be big league. And third, can you tell me why OSO has Dimitra on a watch list? What's going on there?"

In a secure room in the basement of the US Embassy, Wisner spoke for the first time, "Let's talk Dimitra first. She is on a list, but it's not top priority, not active. Morgan, the professor, is an asset. He was in Greece for an archaeology conference. He's a fellow or faculty at the American School of Classical Studies. Dimitra's name came up as former KKE. Now she's on the board of the Archaeological Society, right? They get American funds, right? My understanding is that he sought her out less for her intelligence value and more for . . . well, let's say her aesthetic value."

"Wait! So, he tried to pick her up?" asked an incredulous Stavros.

Wisner shrugged. He went on, "Dimitra's always going to be on somebody's list. God knows there's a million lists. I'm the DDP, all knowing and omniscient over all things OSO and OPC, and I can't tell you all the lists. I'll talk to Morgan's chain and tell them to clear her. But if she shows up somewhere she shouldn't, she'll be fair game. Understand?"

Stavros nodded.

"Kopali. What I can do there is review his status. I haven't thought about him since we sent him to Germany. Let me investigate."

Stavros nodded.

"Now, about Christakis, or whatever his name might be. I'll order a review of his file. Let's check him out. I trust your instincts but . . . the GRU is good at fiction. You stay close to him. If he adds up, and Kopali is not a basket case, we'll talk about a face-to-face. If Kopali can give a hook on the GRU, we'll talk then.

"Meanwhile, you stay plugged into FIEND, monitor Christakis, keep the Circle going, and humor Tommy. If we decide to move on the GRU, I'll run that from HQ. Got it?"

Stavros nodded.

Chapter 12

The noise hammered. Stavros cringed. He reached for his ears and put his fingers over them. Dimitra handed him a small yellow box with red lettering that he recognized from OSS training. It read "Ear Warden Medium V-51R, Mine Safety Appliances Company, Made in USA. " He opened the end flap, removed two plugs, and put them in his ears. Still, the concussion of the compressor powering the sandblaster, pelting the steel hull of the trawler on the hard behind Dimitra's slip, jarred his senses. Dimitra motioned to the companionway of the boat. She pointed down, then led the way into the Atlantic 70's cabin. Stavros followed, turned on the steps, lifted the companionway board into its runners, then closed the hatch above. The cabin wasn't soundproof, but it was better than going deaf in the cockpit.

A chill was on Piraeus, and the moist air from the Saronic Gulf clung. Dimitra, dressed in her dig dungarees and a bulky gray deckhand's turtleneck, removed her earplugs. Stavros did the same. He said, "How do you stand the noise?"

"It does not last. The compressor will malfunction soon, and peace will return," she said.

Then, as if on cue, the compressor chugged its last, and the Greek boatyard worker cursed.

"There, it will take him twenty minutes to sort the problem," she said with assurance. "Tell me what you have to say while I finish this letter to our geologist. He is a specialist on the Pleistocene. I must tell him it is unlikely we will need his service on this dig. More likely Holocene, wouldn't you say?" toyed Dimitra.

Stavros nodded, not that he could date either of the epochs.

He said, "I came down here to tell you I talked to someone at the embassy. You were right. Your colleague, Dr. Morgan, was on a fishing expedition, clumsy though it might have been."

"Fishing? I don't understand."

"He was looking for information, he was fishing. You are a new member of the Ephorate, the Archaeological Society gets US dollars, and Uncle Sam wanted to make sure you aren't KKE. That's reasonable, right?" asked Stavros.

"What is reasonable is that *Uncle Sam* should mind his own business. And should *Uncle Sam* need to know something, he can send someone who speaks directly, does not stammer, and looks me in the eye, not the breasts."

Stavros chuckled, then caught himself. Dimitra remained unamused.

He said, "I'll let them know."

"Good. Then we must finish because soon the yardmaster will fix his compressor, and we will be unable to hear ourselves think. This boat is almost ready. I need to replace some lines and repair the davit and bring stores aboard. I need two more days to finish her preparation before we sail to Aphaia." Then she looked up from the chart table and asked, "Will you be at the hotel this evening?"

"I should be, yes. If I'm not there, you have a key," answered Stavros. "Let yourself in."

"I will not be late; perhaps we can have dinner, no?" Dimitra smiled.

"I will look forward to it," answered Stavros.

He reached for the companionway hatch and Dimitra said, "Thank you for looking into this unpleasantness. Please tell your friends at the *Embassy* that I am not a threat."

Stavros nodded, "Right."

He started sliding the companionway hatch forward when the compressor chugged back to life.

Dimitra yelled over the noise, "I have to finish letters to our paleontologist and Bourne Brook Educational Films. I will be along. I will go deaf if I stay here much longer."

Stavros nodded, climbed up the companionway, then replaced the board and secured the hatch. He stepped ashore on the gangway, pleased that he would see Dimitra later. From the parking area, he looked back at the stern of the sixty-foot sailboat tugging at its lines and rolling in its slip. It was a sturdy vessel, broad of beam, built for durable service, not for racing. In his mind, he translated her hail, *Chorís Anchos*, to *No Stress*.

On the drive back to Athens and the Grande Bretagne, Stavros thought about Christakis and his legend. He wanted to believe that Christakis was who he said he was. He fought against it. If Christakis was GRU, then there was nothing Stavros knew about him that could not have been staged.

And what of Kopali? Why would Christakis profess an interest in the Albanian to find a hook for the GRU? Was the GRU a ruse? A way to get Stavros to put Christakis in touch with Kopali? Did Christakis intend to kill the Albanian, to silence him and tie off a loose end? If the Albanian knew too much, it would solve a problem. The Americans had made this mistake before and failed to believe a source because the information didn't fit their preconceived notions. And they always paid a price.

Stavros handed the valet the keys to the Morris at the hotel reception. He was walking to the elevator as a group of well-dressed businesspeople descended the stairs from the mezzanine. He noticed one. He recognized her but couldn't place her. She was graceful, willowy, and fashionable in a tailored business suit and heels. And . . . those cat eye glasses. It was Penelope, and she was no longer mousy.

The group passed him in the lobby when he caught Penelope's eye. She startled for an instant. Then she broke off her conversation, motioned the group on, and walked to Stavros.

She said, "Professor, are you meeting here, too?"

Stavros smiled and said, "No. I live here. For now, anyway. Did you have a meeting?"

Penelope nodded, then said, "A subcommittee for the Ministry of Labor and Social Affairs. I'm here to consult."

"Any big news?" asked Stavros.

"Oh, no. We don't make news, we issue recommendations. The full committee and the minister make the news." She smiled and adjusted a strand of her chestnut hair that had fallen out of place.

Her conservative, tailored, dark-blue suit revealed her form. Stavros pegged her as a dancer or a swimmer. Perhaps too tall for a dancer.

"Do you have time for a drink? Alexander's is right here. It's the best in Athens. Would you join me?" he asked.

Then Stavros thought to himself, "Okay playboy. This is business, dial back the charm."

Penelope said, "How kind. Thank you, yes."

They found a table against the far wall with a partial view of the lobby. Stavros sat with his back to the lustrous paneling. Penelope ordered a champagne cocktail and Stavros a Napoleon.

Conversation seemed to flow much more smoothly than in the Circle. Penelope said, "I believe I bored you with the title of my dissertation. Now you have the same opportunity."

Stavros smiled and recited, "*The Athenian Navy from the Time of Themistokles.* And if that doesn't grab you, I plan to add an appendix on *Greek Influence on Venetian Shipbuilding.*"

Penelope said, "Your title is more dramatic than mine, but perhaps of less clinical value to remedy insomnia."

Then she offered her drink for a toast, and Stavros followed.

Stavros asked, "Where are you from?"

"Greece, of course," answered a now playful Penelope.

Stavros thought the cocktail had kicked in.

"Right. But, where in Greece? If you don't mind my prying."

"No, you can pry all you wish. My family lives in Athens, but we are from a small village in the Peloponnesus. We have a house there where we go back on holidays and August to mix with our ancestors and descendants. My father says that when he retires, he will live there in the summers. He says Athens is too hot, and the air polluted. And you?" asked Penelope.

"I was born in Colorado. My parents are from Crete. They left for America early in the century. Now my family lives in Saint Louis, and I live in Kansas City, Missouri. Park College, where I teach, is just north of the city on the Missouri River," answered Stavros.

"Do you like America?" asked Penelope.

"Sure. I mean, it's the only place I know, other than Greece."

Stavros didn't mention his time in Egypt or Italy or China or a half dozen other countries he'd visited making the rounds for OSS and later the CIA.

"What's your father do?" asked Stavros.

"He, too, is an economist. He retired from the university, and now he works for the American Mission, the Economic Cooperation Administration Mission. Do you know it?" she asked.

"Yes, of course. I spend a fair amount of time at the embassy," answered Stavros.

Penelope cocked her head and said, "Oh? And what is your business there?"

Stavros realized his slip. Perhaps the Napoleon had snuck up on him.

"I'm here on a grant, a study grant. They administer the grant at the embassy. I have to check in every so often."

Penelope nodded, removed her eyeglasses, and for an instant, recognition beamed in her perceptive hazel eyes. Stavros noted the expert eyeliner and brow makeup for the first time. The mouse had vanished.

Penelope again fingered her loose curl of hair and tucked it behind her ear.

"And this hotel? Is it part of the grant?" asked Penelope.

"Yes. American dollars go a long way in Greece. And I believe the embassy gets a reduced rate," said Stavros.

"You are fortunate," said Penelope.

"Yes. Very," answered Stavros.

Stavros had launched into a series of questions about Penelope's likes and dislikes to move the conversation off the embassy when he saw Dimitra only steps from their table. Somehow, she had snuck up on him, just like the Napoleon. Still dressed in her dig-boatyard outfit, she strode with confidence and poise.

Stavros stood. He did not show affection because he and Dimitra were keeping their relationship secret from the Circle.

He said, "Ah, Dimitra. Would you like to join us?"

He sounded impersonal and rehearsed. Stavros saw Dimitra roll her dark eyes.

Dimitra smiled at Penelope. She said, "I came to leave you papers for the Circle. They are at the front desk. I saw you on my way out.

"I cannot join you; I have a previous engagement. Please enjoy yourselves and let me know your thoughts on the draft. Another time, perhaps?"

Then she smiled, turned, and walked away unperturbed.

Stavros took another drink of his Napoleon, and Penelope sipped her champagne.

After a moment, they spoke at the same time. Stavros to ask about Penelope's likes and Penelope to comment on Dimitra. Stavros looked at Penelope and said, "You first."

"I was going to say that your friend Dimitra is a forceful personality. How did you meet?"

Stavros nodded and thought, *If you only knew.*

Chapter 13

Dimitra did not join Stavros for dinner. And she did not stay with him that night.

Stavros did, however, part company with Penelope after a second round of drinks. At the coat check, she gave Stavros her university number. Penelope presented every sign that she would have stayed for dinner, but Stavros thought he was engaged. He was, but that changed.

Just before nine that evening, Stavros received a visitor. A bellman came to his room with an accordion file folder, the kind with a ribbon closure that secures a flap over the contents. There was no writing on the outside. The bellman said, "The bartender at Alexander's said that you may know the young lady who left this behind. It was on the seat at your table. Should I leave it with you, Mr. Theofanis?"

Stavros said thank you, handed the young man a tip, and returned to his room service dinner. He remembered Penelope clutching the folder as she came down the stairs. After that, she must have set it on the seat of the chair next to hers in the bar. Two champagne cocktails might have made her forgetful.

He considered opening the file. He was a spy, after all. He looked at it and entwined in the center of the ribbon's bow was one chestnut-colored, human hair. The bow was brown, and the hair was brown; it was an inconspicuous security tell. Someone less practiced might have tugged the ribbon, released the hair, and signaled the owner of their meddling. Now Stavros was curious.

The setup might have been happenstance. Women do shed hair like everyone. And one strand might have fallen into the middle of the knot. But Stavros believed it was intentional.

He untied the bow and placed the hair on a white napkin. Only a few papers inhabited the file. None looked to him important. There was a packet of charts and data for wage rates in the shipbuilding sector and a meeting agenda sheet. The only other document was a one-pager entitled *Schedule ECA Chief, 05-Nov-51—18-Nov-51.*

The next morning, he dressed and went to the embassy. There was a crypt from Wisner, and the news was mixed.

Wisner said that Kopali was institutionalized at the Dromokaition Psychiatric Hospital of Athens. Access to him would be through American security at the facility. They would challenge with *Who's the best minor league team on the East Coast?* He was to respond with *the Portland Seadogs.* Wisner said he would message the security unit and let them know to expect Stavros and, perhaps, Christakis.

The news on Christakis was inconclusive. Wisner left it to Stavros to decide whether to include him in the contact.

Wisner ordered a review of Christakis's file. The review said that Christakis was an assumed name based on transcripts of the MGB defector Igor Gouzenko. But there was a problem. The transcript was secondhand, maybe even thirdhand. The Canadians had interrogated Gouzenko, then informed the FBI. That was in 1946. Then, Hoover and the FBI turned over some of their information to the CIA in 1948. Wisner's file was three levels from pristine with no confirming sources.

Transliteration of Greek names is difficult. No international standards exist for substituting Greek letters and their phonetics into English. Thus, a Greek name that starts with the letter Chi, *X,* could in English start with an *H* or a *CH* or something else. Stavros had observed this problem many times in the OSS as his unit reported actions or enemy movements, and spelling Greek roads or villages caused confusion.

But Wisner sent something that was helpful, a photograph of Christakis meeting with the GRU rezidentura, Colonel Dmitriy Chernov. The date was July 3, 1951. The photo showed two men standing in a stone archway, talking and pointing. The man in Greek military uniform looked like Christakis. But to be honest, Stavros was only 80 percent sure. Chernov, with his signature oversized eyebrows, dressed in a baggy civilian suit hanging untailored on his bulky frame, was unmistakable. All CIA and embassy staff in Athens knew this man.

Stavros needed to feel out Christakis further before deciding what to do about Kopali. He called the Ministry for Public Security and left a message when he was told that Christakis was unavailable. The secretary said she was not sure when Christakis would return.

Wisner asked Stavros to get in touch with Hod Fuller. That meant Operation FIEND needed him. He asked the embassy to send a crypt to Fuller and request a meeting per Wisner.

Then he called the Penelope's number at the university. The secretary said she was in class, but she could take a message. Stavros declined and said he would call later.

With all his duties on hold, Stavros drove to Piraeus to mend things with Dimitra. She would leave for Aphaia in a few days, and he didn't want to part in anger.

Dimitra was not the jealous type. Quite the opposite. She told Stavros that she did not own his body, and he did not own hers. Still, they were involved. They were in love.

If Stavros told himself the truth, he was flirting with Penelope; it wasn't just business. She was an attractive young woman, and he was eligible, sort of. He rationalized his behavior as cultivating a potential recruit, bonding with an asset. That was bunk. He was taken by her, intrigued. A polite way of saying he wanted to sleep with her. He capped his introspective interrogation with, *I can't help being a healthy male. Get it together, Stavros, and get back to business.*

Chapter 14

The trawler was gone, and so was the compressor. And so was *Chorís Anchos.* Stavros looked around the boatyard and the marina and did not see the Atlantic 70. It was mid-morning. He looked up at the sock on the flagpole next to the office and judged the wind to be fifteen knots out of the southwest. An ideal day for sailing. Still, Dimitra would not take the boat out by herself. The Atlantic 70 required a crew of at least two experienced sailors.

He turned and walked back to his Morris. He put the key into the ignition, then looked up and spotted the arch over the cockpit that was the visual giveaway of the Atlantic 70. The boat was rounding the seawall, entering the calm waters of the marina basin. She was under diesel power with her sails furled. From a stern halyard flew the Greek flag and under it a white banner with a red encircled bust of a figure Stavros knew to be Aristotle. Embossed below the bust in Greek was SACRIFICE TO THE MUSES AND CHARITES. This was the logo and motto of Aristotle University of Thessaloniki. Dimitra was forward on the bowsprit, tying off a line and setting fenders.

In the cockpit, a young man expertly helmed the boat. When they arrived at the slip, twenty meters away, he lowered the anchor, and Stavros heard the chain passing through the bow roller. Then he reversed against the rode, and docked in the European manner, stern in. Stavros went to the float to help with the lines. He crossed the stern lines and secured them to the cleats. The spring lines the same. The young man positioned the gangway and stepped ashore to shake Stavros's hand. His smile beamed as he introduced himself as Kosta. He was lean and handsome, clean-shaven, and in his mid-twenties. His skin was brown from time at sea and his hand calloused.

Dimitra walked around the cabin on the narrow deck, using the boat's cable guard to ensure her footing. Then she used the dodger frame to steady her long step down into the cockpit.

She came ashore on the gangway and greeted Stavros without a smile. She said, "Hello. I see you have met Kosta. This young man is a worthy captain, and someday I hope to make of him a worthy archaeologist. He is one of my graduate students."

Kosta smiled.

Dimitra was in the same clothes she had worn the day before, and her hair was in a ponytail. She wore no makeup, and her eyes were not attentive.

Stavros sensed he had interrupted something.

Kosta looked at Dimitra and said, "The davit should work well now. It should be good to bring aboard stores and the dinghy, no problem. Do you have anything more I can help with this morning?"

Dimitra shook her head. She said, "Thank you for coming. We should be ready to leave the day after next. You are bringing someone to help with the sailing, no?"

"Yes. I will bring Linda. She is a skilled mate. We have been out many times together. She knows the ropes." Kosta smiled.

"Good. Thank you again, Kosta," Dimitra said, nodding.

Kosta pulled a red baseball cap from the rear pocket of his blue jeans. He put it on at a jaunty angle and smiled again at Stavros and Dimitra. He walked to the far side of the parking area then into the Pikrodaphnē train station.

Stavros and Dimitra stood together on the dock and watched him leave in an uneasy silence.

Stavros spoke first, "I'm sorry we missed our connection last night. I was looking forward to dinner and your company. I won't see much of you when you leave for Aphaia."

"Yes," was all she said.

Stavros's eyes played around the marina, waiting for . . . waiting for his punishment to stop.

She outlasted him, again. He asked, "Would you like to try for dinner tonight?"

"Are you certain you will be free?" she asked without emotional engagement.

"Yes, of course. I was free last night," he answered.

"I see. Perhaps I mistook your freedom at the hotel. It seemed you were occupied and might remain so well into the night, no?" she asked in a question that was more of a statement.

"I'm sorry you thought that. I saw Penelope. She was leaving a meeting at the hotel, and we shared a drink. It was all very proper and social, nothing more," he lied. He knew it had been more.

He went on, "Look, Dimitra. I want to be with you. I love being with you. I wish there were a way we could be together more, a lot more. But until that day. . . ." he shrugged.

She drilled a gaze as cold as ice into his soul. She said, "You are free to be with whoever you want, as am I. But you can't betray me with someone else. This is humiliation and I will never stand for it."

"I . . . I didn't betray you. I would never humiliate you. You are . . . jealous. . . ."

Before he could finish, she lit into him. "Jealous! You have the nerve. I am the least possessive woman you will ever meet. And jealous? Jealous of that mouse? Please. You insult me."

Stavros was losing this round. His only salvation was utter, unabridged surrender. He pleaded, "Of course, you are not jealous of Penelope, and I would never compare the two of you. You and I have been through times that are incomparable. She could never understand what we've been through. Please, let's let our blood cool. You do what you need to do here, and we can meet back at the hotel. Or, if you'd rather, we can meet here at the boat. Whatever you want to do. It's up to you."

Dimitra seemed to consider his offer. It was a good sign. He pushed on, "Look, we don't want to part company in a bad way. I love you, and in your own, detached, stoical way, you love me. Let's cool down and get together for dinner. You can tell me about the sail to Aphaia and how you plan to organize the dig. I'll be your sounding board. Free. Okay?"

"Do not speak to me of Stoicism. We have confirmed long ago that you know nothing of classical philosophies," Dimitra said.

She was berating him, which was a good sign. Progress. She discharged a bit with the mouse comment.

She said, "I have much to do here. The boat is ready, but I have a great deal of paperwork for your generous Uncle Sam. I will call the hotel this afternoon and leave a message if you are not there. We will see how the day goes."

There it was. Stavros was on probation. She was yet deciding his sentence. Unresolved, unnerving, but he'd take it.

"Good. I need to make some calls and start drafting my appendix on Greek Influence on Venetian Shipbuilding. Please call and we can talk further, or not, this evening. Okay?"

He heard his own words. They weren't quite a beg, but more than a plea. He knew a parting kiss was a bridge too far. He turned toward the Morris and started walking. With his back to Dimitra her parting words drifted to his ears, "A treacherous mouse."

Chapter 16

The king bed was luxurious. Fresh sheets smelling of the hotel laundry mixed with the seductive scent bathing her warm body and perfect, moist skin. The glow of finishing was upon him. He hadn't died and gone to heaven, but he was visiting. Dimitra was sound asleep, depleted by her stimulation and a restless night before in Chorís Anchos' rolling berth. His mind was drifting back to earth when the phone rang.

"Hello?"

"Professor, you left something for me that is not mine. I'm here in the lobby. Can I bring it to your room?" asked Penelope.

The request confused him; he was off guard. He said, "Um . . . can you leave it with the desk? I'm working on something . . . um?"

He looked at the clock. It was only nine.

"It is best that I hand it to you. It might be something important, no?" said Penelope.

"I guess. I'll be down in a minute."

He swung his legs out of bed, his descent from heaven. He put on his jeans and a crumpled white shirt he wore that day. Dimitra rolled and asked, "Where are you going?"

"I have to get something from the lobby. I'll be right back." Then he walked to her side of the bed and kissed her on the forehead. "Why don't you order room service if you're awake. I'll be right back."

Stavros took the elevator to the lobby. Penelope waited on a sofa near the entrance. She looked mousier than her last appearance. Stavros wondered if the university saw one Penelope and the Grande Bretagne, another.

He said, "So that's not yours? The bartender thought he saw you leave it. They brought it to me to return it to you."

"I am sorry, it is not mine. I thought it might be something that you were working on, and you delivered it by mistake. So, I thought I should return it in person. I have not looked inside." She handed over the folder and beamed.

Stavros smiled back, then caught himself. He was certain, somehow, that Penelope knew he just had sex.

"Thanks . . . um." He looked over his shoulder back to the elevators and went on, "I was just working on something that I need to stay focused on. . . ."

"That's okay. We can, perhaps, catch up another time. Maybe next week?" she asked.

"Right," he nodded.

"Good. I'll call and we can plan from there." She smiled again, and this time her eyes drifted toward his abdomen.

He was embarrassed and flushed. He held the folder over his crotch and said, "That'll work. I might be out of town for a couple of days, so just leave a message with the desk. I'll leave this with the concierge. The hotel has a lost and found."

She smiled again, then rose from the sofa. She buttoned her beige trench coat, tied the belt, smiled again, and walked out the entrance. Stavros noted tonight was mouse plus heels.

Stavros shook his head.

Back in his suite, Dimitra sat up in bed against the headboard, bare breasted, talking on the phone. Her raven hair flowed over her left shoulder to just below her collarbone. She was magnificent. Stavros put the folder on a table and lay down on the bed next to her. She hung up the phone, and he asked, "What are we having tonight?"

"I am having the branzino and you are having pork. American-style chops," she said.

"Did you order more champagne?" asked Stavros.

"No. This is not allowed. My head must be clear tomorrow. I am accepting equipment for the dig and the stores we've ordered. I must be at the boat by eight in the morning, not that the delivery will be on time, God forbid. What did you bring back from the lobby?" she asked.

"Just a file folder," he said.

Dimitra looked across the room at the table where the folder lay. She said, "That is the mouse folder."

Stavros felt goodwill leaching from the moment.

He asked, "How do you know that?"

She said, "I saw it on the chair between you and the mouse the other night. It is the same folder, no?"

"Right. I mean, I think it is. The bartender thought she forgot it, but she said it's not hers."

"So, you have talked to her?"

"Well, just briefly. She brought it by and. . . ."

"And you got out of our bed together to go fetch it?"

Stavros felt the temperature rising.

"Right. She called from the lobby and. . . ."

"And you came running," said Dimitra. A look rose in her eyes that foretold the brewing storm.

There was only one way out. He said, "I need to look into it. I need to see what's inside of it, or I would have told her to leave it with the concierge."

"Why do you need to see what is inside?"

"It's part of the job," he said.

"Oh, you mean the spy job," she said.

"Come on, you know I can't. . . ."

"Well, let us see what the mouse brings, shall we?"

She got out of bed, pulling the plush hotel robe over her toned body.

Stavros said, "Wait."

Then he got out of bed too.

He said, "There's a certain way to open this."

He turned the table light on and held the folder by the edges, looking at the bow.

It was still in place. The chestnut hair was still entwined with the bow, but he could not be certain it was the same as before. The bow was smashed and moved around in the normal course of transmission and carriage.

Dimitra watched him, puzzled.

He sat the folder on the table, untied the bow. Then he went to the bathroom and returned with a white hand towel. He picked up the hair and placed it on the towel, and Dimitra squinted as she watched.

He opened the folder and inside were the same documents as before, a packet of data and graphs and a schedule. But this time, it read *Schedule ECA Deputy Chief, 05-Nov-51— 18-Nov-51.*

She asked, "What is wrong?"

He said, "This is different. When I opened it before, the schedule was for the Economic Cooperation Administration Mission chief. This one is for the deputy."

"What does that mean?" she asked.

"Good question," was his preoccupied reply.

He put the papers back into the folder and retied the bow with the hair intact. He said, "I'll be right back."

She watched him leave the room.

He left the file folder with the concierge and said, "Someone may claim this. I don't know who it belongs to. But will you please pay close attention and describe the person to me? It's a business matter."

Stavros handed him a folded ten-dollar bill. The concierge knew Stavros well and would have done him a favor for free. But Stavros knew the Greek mind well enough to know that business was business.

Stavros returned to his suite to await room service and perhaps another heavenly visit.

Chapter 17

They were up early. They showered together, dressed, then climbed the ornate spiral staircase one story to the eighth-floor roof garden for breakfast. As they waited for the caffeine to enter their systems, the panoramic view of the ageless Acropoli mesmerized. The Parthenon seemed close enough to touch. Stavros ordered coffee and Dimitra tea. Their meals finished, they walked onto the patio facing Syntagma Square. To their left they looked beyond Leoforos Vasilisis Amalias to Parliament and the Monument of the Unknown Soldier, guarded by two proud, stock-still Evzones. Dimitra felt pride, Stavros admiration. They could have watched much longer; Athens was waking up, but it was time to go.

Stavros drove, and they arrived at the marina a few minutes before eight. He walked Dimitra to the gangway and asked if he should stay and help. She told him no. They kissed, he wished her luck, and they promised to see each other in two weeks when Dimitra planned to return by commercial ferry to meet the Ephorate.

Stavros drove to the safe house in Kifissia. The duty officer told him that Hod Fuller had left for Corfu earlier that morning and that he needed to talk to Peter. Peter was in the vault.

The vault was a room that served the estate as a kitchen pantry. The CIA had fitted a heavy door and heavy locks. It wasn't a large room, but it didn't have to be. Its shelves circled the space lined with stacks of banded currencies from many countries and bags of gold coins. The door was open. Peter stood at an island table banding bills and looked up at Stavros. He said, "Are you ready to move some funds?"

Stavros said, "At your disposal. Am I too early?"

"No. No. We have what you need," and he nodded to three unadorned, used shoeboxes on a low shelf in front of him.

"That should keep them for a while. Two contain currency and one gold sovereigns. That one is heavy."

Stavros asked, "So, I deliver these to the duty officer at Elefsina, right?"

"Yes. He will secure them until the order to launch. Oh, and take this envelope. This is zloty for the flight crew. They want sovereigns, but Hod says to pay them in Polish currency. They would be suspicious spending the gold. You can leave this, too, with the duty officer."

Stavros asked, "Are you read in on this component?"

"No, not really. Just what I've picked up from Hod hanging around here for the past week. I leave tomorrow," said Peter.

"Right. Okay, just wondering," said Stavros.

"The scuttlebutt is that Hod doesn't like the feel. He's got a sixth sense, you know? And he's usually right," confided Peter. "He's a unique fellow, Hod. A longtime friend. He's superb at this game. Did he tell you how we met?"

"No, he never mentioned it," said Stavros.

"I'm not telling tales out of school. It's almost a legend; some think it's myth. I'm surprised you haven't heard.

"The OSS dropped Hod into the South of France in 1944, and he went missing. They sent me in to find him, or his remains, because everyone assumed he was dead. I drove around in a beautiful Cord 812 and never found him. I enjoyed a grand tour of the region, though. Lovely countryside.

"The reason I didn't find him was that he didn't want to be found. He had bought a small farm with the gold sovereigns he dropped into France with. Michael Burke was the one who found him. Hod was pissed. He was in the middle of harvest, and he'd just started restoring an old boat. He planned to sail the Mediterranean, living as a vagabond. A grand life, but Frank wanted him in Greece for FIEND. He reactivated. He was sore for months. Now, he professes to love Greece and says it was the best thing that ever happened to him."[22]

Stavros smiled and shook his head. He said, "Everybody's got a story."

"Some larger than most," answered Peter.

"Should I just walk out of here with these boxes?" asked Stavros.

"You need to count the money and sign for it. Then it's all yours to Elefsina. Don't buy a farm. The leks are worthless outside of Albania."

Stavros nodded, opened the first box, and began counting. He asked Peter, "Will the CIA ever run out of money?"

Peter shook his head. He said, "That is not at all likely. Do you know of the codicil?"

Stavros shook his head and searched his vocabulary for the little-used word.

"Along with our congressional budget, we receive five percent of matching local currencies set aside for Marshall funding."[23]

Stavros shrugged.

Peter went on, "It's money laundering, but sanctioned. Every country receiving Marshall funds must set aside an equal amount of local currency. If Uncle Sam puts up a billion dollars, you put up a billion pounds, or deutschemark, or drachmas, or whatever. Of this, we take five percent. Better than a bookie, no? All very secret."[24] Then he put his finger to his lips and shushed.

Before he left Kifissia, Stavros called Christakis at the Ministry. He got the same message from the secretary. Christakis was away, and she did not know when he would return.

The drive to Elefsina was twenty-five kilometers across the northern suburbs of Athens. Elefsina was a military airfield under heavy guard and controlled by the CIA. A Greek security unit patrolled the perimeter, and staffed the gate, but all command and traffic decisions fell to the CIA. Elefsina was the last stop for Pixie teams parachuting into Albania.

Stavros produced a pass at the gate and issued a challenge response. He drove to a building near the control tower and parked the Morris. He left the three shoeboxes in the trunk and walked into the entrance, where he asked the guard to see the duty officer. Two minutes later, a plainclothes man arrived looking like a bristle-hair Marine drill-sergeant and introduced himself as Captain Smith. The two men exchanged challenges, and the phrases synced. They stepped into Smith's office. Stavros asked, "What should I do with the funds?"

"Wait here. Give me the keys and I'll have someone get them," said Smith.

Stavros handed over the keys and Smith picked up his telephone. A minute later a young man arrived, took the keys, and returned with the three shoeboxes. He gave the keys to the Morris back to Stavros. Stavros said, "Oh," and he reached into his jacket pocket for the envelope. "This is for the aircrew."

"Great, let's count it and get you signed out," smiled Smith.

Stavros and Smith both signed a receipt and Smith said, "I understand that you'll be staying with us for a day or two."

"Right. Fuller asked me to brief the outbound Pixies. It shouldn't take more than a day," said Stavros.

"Good luck with that," said Smith with a tinge of irony.

Stavros let it go. He asked, "When can I talk to them?"

"Any time. They're not training or in class. They seem to spend most of their time playing cards, smoking, and kicking a soccer ball. You can bunk in the officers' quarters. The Pixies are in a Quonset near the flight line. I'll go over there with you."

"Great. Can I leave my car here?" asked Stavros.

"No problem. It's fine where it is," said Smith. "Let's go in my Jeep."

The two men climbed into the Jeep and headed south, paralleling the flight line. Stavros noted a row of eight Douglas C-47 Dakotas, a couple of old Hawker Hurricanes that Stavros assumed were there for restoration and display, and two

Canadian-badged Curtiss Helldivers. The rest of the wing, he assumed, was away from prying eyes in the low-slung hangers to the west. He was right. Two of the hangers hosted the new Boeing B-47 Stratojets equipped for reconnaissance. They could also carry atomic bombs.

They stopped at a thirty-meter-long Quonset building at the end of the flight line. A dozen men sat on picnic tables and folding chairs, watching a handful of their comrades kick a soccer ball on the tarmac. They were not in uniforms, but their shirts and trousers looked military surplus, tan, and olive drab. Heads turned toward the approaching Americans.

Smith walked up to the nearest man sitting on the picnic table and said, "Ringchief, this is Colonel Madison. He's here to brief you. I'll leave you to it. Madison, I'll see you back at base later."

Stavros detected no warmth in the exchange, and the chill between the men seemed mutual.

Stavros offered his hand and said, "Ringchief, I'm pleased to meet you."

Ringchief was short and stocky. He looked to Stavros to be in his forties. His bushy mustache, long hair, and crumpled features conveyed neither wisdom nor wile. It was sleepless worry hidden in the furrows of his forehead and the bags under his eyes. He looked bloated. His eyes were a cloudy blue and sunk into their sockets, obscured. He said, "My name is Agon. You can call me Ringchief, but I will only answer to Agon. On the radio, I will be Ringchief."

Stavros thought better to humor him than to pick a fight.

"Right. You can call me Madison and skip the Colonel," he replied.

"So, Madison, what are you here to teach me about my country? Should we speak in English, Albanian, or Greek? It is your choice," offered Agon.

"Greek, if you don't mind," said Stavros.

Agon signaled surprise by pushing his lower lip away from his chin. He said, "All right, Greek it is."

Stavros said, "I understand you have some maps of Epirus. I would like to go over some exit plans we might use when it's time for you to leave Albania."

"We are going to Albania to start a revolution, to overthrow the communists. We will not leave until we are victorious, no?" asked Agon.

Stavros noted the Greek manner of turning a statement into a question. He said, "It is always best to prepare for all possibilities, no?"

Agon asked, "Your Greek? You are American, no?"

Stavros nodded.

"How is it you speak with the inflection of a westerner? Say for me the name of the port city on the west coast of the Peloponnesus," instructed Agon.

Stavros said, "Patras," dropping the last letter, sigma.

"See. Ah-ha. You speak the name as would a western Greek. How did you come by such inflection?" asked Agon.

"A good tutor," answered Stavros.

Stavros turned the tables. He asked, "And you? Where did you learn Greek?"

"My mother, she is Greek. She *was* Greek," he corrected.

You spoke Greek in Albania?" asked Stavros.

"No. Never. I grew up in Chameria. I am a Cham," stated Agon.

Stavros knew of the Chams. An early OSS action near Ioannina in Greek Epirus saw Operational Group II retreat through Cham territory. It was not friendly ground. The Chams whipsawed through alliances and betrayals for the duration of the Italian and German occupation. They fought against and sided with both EDES, the right-wing resistance, and EAM-ELAS, the left-led partisans. The Greeks had no love for Chams and wanted them gone. They were Muslims who had sided with the Turks as far back as the thirteenth century.

In Albania, where thousands were forcefully moved after the war, the communists gave them citizenship but treated them as lesser Albanians because of their Greek origins. It was more complex than that. Chams were a mix of Greek, Albanian, and Turk. Enver Hoxha and his communist police state mistrusted them, seeing them as infested with Greek agents.

To be honest, Stavros could draw no straight lines with the Chams. Their loyalties were murky and viscous, ever changing and flexible. The Greeks were Christians and fighters, and Greeks above all. Stavros knew these immutable characteristics. The Chams were binders. They attached to whoever was strongest in their presence. Their sense of nationhood was nominal, not the burning identity of Greeks. The Chams were an orphaned and misplaced people floating on the turbulence of history, century after century, in a land where roots would never grow.[25]

Stavros asked, "Where are you from?"

"Filiates," said Agon. "Do you know it?"

"I know the area. It is mountainous and beautiful. I have visited the Kalama Gorge, but I have not visited Filiates," said Stavros.

"The beauty of the earth remains, but the beauty of the town is gone, burned to the ground in 1941 by Cham fascists. Këshilla, do you know the name? The Dino clan?" Agon asked.

"I've heard of Këshilla. The Dino clan, no," answered Stavros.

"Këshilla were fools. They believed the Italians and then the Germans would gift to them Chameria, a nation of their own. So, these fools sided with the invaders against the Greeks. They killed their own people, Chams, and burned our towns. The Greeks never liked us. The Chams have no friends.

"My family fled to Albania when Këshilla burned. My mother, who was Greek, died running from her home. She was not well, but she made it over Sarakina. She climbed the mountain. Then she drowned crossing the Bistricë River. My father and sister went on to relatives in Vlorë. Two letters I received, that is all. I have not seen them since 1941," Agon recited the tale in a tone of detachment.

"What did you do after the Italians invaded and Filiates burned," asked Stavros.

"I hid. For months, I hid with other men of our clan. We stole food and livestock and lived as bandits, klephts. Everyone hunted us; everyone wanted us dead. Our group numbered twenty, that was all.

"One day, three men from Balli Kombëtar came to us under a white flag. They said they would provision us if we fought the invaders. Later, Balli Kombëtar signed an accord with LANÇ, the Albanian communists. We were allies, they said. Together we would free Albania. Then, in 1943, Balli Kombëtar ordered us to fight the communists and the British who were supplying them.

"All the while, we were in a truce with EDES and Zervas. These are names you know, I am certain. EDES told us to kill Germans and Greek communists. Then, as soon as the Germans left, EDES killed us. They burned our villages and drove Chams into Albania. EDES received weapons and supplies from Great Britain, and again we were fired upon all sides.

"I fled to Albania and tried to find my family. They had moved north with many other Chams. After that, I went to Italy and Rome. It is there the Italian Naval Intelligence found me in a camp. Now, I am here, awaiting my return to Albania. Perhaps reunion with my family," Agon offered flatly. Then he added, "Your CIA has heard this story many times; why do you ask it again?"

"I have never heard it, and I want to know your background. As you said, it is your country, and I do not wish to tell you what you may already know. That is a waste of your time and mine, no?" said Stavros.

"Hmph. . . ." grunted Agon.

Stavros gained an impression, and it wasn't good. He didn't believe the story because he didn't believe Agon. Everything Agon said *could* have happened, just as he said. But even if Agon were telling the truth, his story was of bending loyalties and unclear motives. Agon conveyed emotional connection only when he talked about his family. Stavros sensed that reuniting with them was his true motivation. This could be detrimental. He knew Hoxha manipulated expatriates by holding family members hostage. The Sigurimi could have approached Agon in Rome with an ultimatum. The Albanian community was close-knit and easy to track.

Stavros pried, "What do you know of your family?"

"As I have said, I know nothing. I received two letters in the days following their escape to Vlorë. The first told of my mother's death, and the second said they had moved north, away from the Dino clan. My father said he would write when they settled, but that letter never came. But I was difficult to find. The first two letters I received in Filiate, at the mosque they left standing when they burned the village. Good Muslims, eh? After that, I was hiding, and I never went back." Agon's voice softened and he saddened, beyond the tormented melancholy of displaced people.

Stavros pushed further, "How will you go about finding them once you are in Albania?"

"This is not important. This is personal and not a part of the mission," said Agon, returning to his flat tone.

Stavros had heard enough to make him cautious. Agon commanded fifteen men. If the Sigurimi controlled him, they would parachute into a trap. They would all die horrible, torturous deaths, and so would their families.

He told Agon, "I will spend the night, and tomorrow morning we can go over your maps, if that is all right with you."

Agon nodded and looked away into the distance of the flight line as an Italian-badged Douglas took to the air and banked to the west. Christakis watched the group of men outside the Quonset from his seat on the port side of the aircraft.

Chapter 18

Stavros called from a secure line before he left Elefsina the next day. Hod Fuller listened at the Corfu safe house. When Stavros finished his report, Fuller uttered a long, drawn-out, "Yeah . . . I'm getting the same take from another source. Untrustworthy, under discipline, no clear allegiance. I'll put them on hold. That's the safe thing. Hell, we've lost so many Pixies, it's like sending them into a meat grinder. The commies know way too much about our operations.

"I'll tell them the hold is weather, then get face-to-face with Ringchief. I'm not sure he's been fluttered. Like I said, he was an Italian and OSO candidate. I'll get a technician and a machine and wire him. That should get him sweating.

"Thanks, Stavros. I knew I could count on you. Greatly appreciated."

Stavros drove back to the hotel and waited until all guests were out of earshot to approach the concierge. The impeccably dressed, polite young man told him that a woman, blond hair, early twenties, and medium height had claimed the folder the morning after Stavros left it. He said she was attractive, but he could not see the color of her eyes because she wore smoky green sunglasses. She wore jeans and a black motorcycle jacket. He said she was Greek; he believed from the north. He'd asked her to sign for the folder and leave an address, and this she did.

He folded the information and handed it to Stavros as Stavros handed him his tip. Stavros thanked him, started to the elevators, then turned around. He came back to the concierge and asked, "Did you see how she arrived?"

The young man answered, "No, sir, Mr. Theofanis. But I will discuss it with the doorman. He may have information."

"Thank you. You have been most helpful," said Stavros.

Stavros returned to his suite and perused the room service menu when there was a knock at the door. He answered, and the concierge told him the doorman had seen her leave in a cab. The doorman recognized the driver, an old friend. The doorman said he would know more after he talked to his friend. Stavros said, "Excellent!" and presented the young man with a five-dollar bill.

He ordered the braised leg of lamb, poured a short glass of fiery ouzo, added water, then a squeeze of lemon. He sat at the desk, sipped his drink, and opened the folded paper. It read "Calista Fox, University of Athens."

Chapter 19

"I care not about tobacco acreage or estimated exports of unmanufactured crop! Greece produced fifty thousand metric tons in 1950 and sixty-two thousand this year.[26] Why am I hearing this? Greece has tobacco. We have timber, fertilizer, and sewing machines. Our soldiers need cigarettes. We barter like merchants in a bazaar. That is all.

"Comrade, from this day forward when you brief me, I need only essential information. Information vital to the well-being of the homeland and Soviet advancement. Do I make myself clear?" It was not a question but a command from GRU Rezidentura, Colonel Dmitriy Chernov.

In the bowels of the Soviet Embassy in Athens, the flabby Chernov was growing agitated with his new aide. The young man was a princeling, the nephew of Matvei Vasilevich Zakharov, the head of GRU. Chernov reminded himself that the aide was not to be fatally offended, only bruised. Still, Chernov was waging war, not buying tobacco.

"Comrade, you will come to understand that we are under attack in Greece, every minute of every day. The capitalists and their lackeys are everywhere. They are invasive, and, like boring beetles, they seek to eat away at our house.

"This is your first posting outside of Moscow, so your education will continue. This is typical. But remember, GRU is here to subvert the subverters. We are here to know what they know. Complicated, but simple. No?"

"Yes, comrade Colonel. I only mentioned the trade negotiations because we have an additional source on the Greek side. An economist." The aide beamed.

"Another economist," Chernov flatly acknowledged. Then, with a flip of his backhand, dismissed the aide.

Chapter 20

The Douglas touched down at Pratica di Mare Air Base on the Tyrrhenian Sea southeast of Rome. Christakis, the only passenger, wore a tailored navy-blue, double-breasted uniform. Three bands of blue on a field of gold circled his cap, ranking him as a capitano di corvetta, or lieutenant commander. A young Italian tenente di vascello met him on the airstrip tarmac in a virgin, olive-drab Fiat Campagnola Jeep. As Christakis approached the vehicle, still walking with a limp, he asked the lieutenant, "How do you like your new transport?"

The young naval officer took Christakis's duffle and replied, "It is like the American Jeep, sir. Maybe not so much power, but better looking, no? A smoother ride, too."

Christakis, ever the motoring enthusiast, nodded his approval and said, "Fitting for an Italian vehicle."

The ride to the Ministry of Defense and SIFAR HQ took thirty minutes. Along the way, Christakis was silent, and his driver did not impose. Christakis gathered his thoughts.

In 1949, the Armed Forces Information Service, SIFAR, had formed with American blessing and funding. SIFAR conglomerated all Italian military intelligence services. Christakis worked for Naval Intelligence. His service competed with the former Ministries of War and the Air Force.[27] The merger was still fresh, as was the new SIFAR director. Intra-agency competition simmered, and enmity roiled the roost in Rome, buffeted by a stream of demands from Washington.

It was midday, and the evening traffic in Rome was yet to build. They drove past the Basilica Papale di Santa Maria Maggiore. Then a few blocks later, Christakis saw the Fontana delle Naiadi in the center of the busy traffic circle that controlled the flow to the train station. A few blocks farther and they turned into the guarded entrance of the Ministry of Defense off Via Firenze. The lieutenant dropped Christakis at an entrance where Christakis stated his business and asked for an aide to the SIFAR director. He carried no paper pass or SIFAR identification. The aide came a few minutes later. They exchanged challenges, and the aide escorted Christakis to an opulent office on the fifth floor with a view to the Palazzo Barberini and the National Gallery of Ancient Art.

General Umberto Broccoli was Director of SIFAR. Christakis saw him as an ophthalmologist or somebody in a medical specialty. His dark, thick-framed glasses magnified his eyes. He was not a gruff man, but Christakis, or anyone else in his presence, conceded his authority. His silver hair was quaffed and tight, and his suit and tie looked coordinated but not fastidious. His calm belied the hot seat on which he sat.

"Capitano, I called you to Rome for a status report and to share some information with you that is most delicate. First, I see you are limping; are you injured?" asked Broccoli.

"No, Director. It is minor, a minor inconvenience," answered Christakis.

"Good. Please tell me about Kopali," instructed Broccoli.

"I expect to hear something soon from our CIA contact, Theofanis. Director Wisner and he have been in touch, Wisner is the key to accessing Kopali. My office reports that Theofanis called but did not leave a message. I will talk to him when I'm back in Athens," reported Christakis.

"Good. It is best that Wisner does not know that SIFAR and Naval Intelligence is interested. Otherwise, I would inquire about interrogating Kopali."

"Yes, sir," answered Christakis.

"Now, this I must ask that you keep in the strictest confidence."

Christakis nodded.

"Have you heard of Sheepskin?"

Christakis shook his head. He said, "No, sir."

"Do you know the term Stay Behind?"

"This I have heard, but only in the rumor mill. Once in the halls of the Ministry, and it was hush-hush, minister-level only," said Christakis.

"Stay Behind is the brainchild of the British, but now an adopted offspring of the Americans. Mr. Wisner envisions a network of secret armies in each NATO country. These armies will activate, arm themselves, and resist any Soviet invasion and occupation. Sheepskin is the Greek force and Gladio is the Italian.

"The Stay-Behinds will hide cashes of arms and explosives throughout the countryside and in the cities. They will predesignate sites for muster. They will conceal radios and supplies, have prearranged codes, and thus be ready to act as coordinated paramilitaries and partisans when the Soviets arrive.

"Either the British or Americans will train these clandestine armies. The British are the better trainers, more experienced, but the Americans will give us free arms if we allow them to train. The British want us to pay for the training and buy arms from them.

"Regardless, I tell you because we need to know more about the Greek force. We need to know who the Greeks are recruiting. We need to know if they include the Greek Holy Bond or if Holy Bond has infiltrated Sheepskin. And we need to know if the Americans support this recruitment.

"We have a problem in Italy, and the Greeks may have the same. Some of our Gladio force is to come from undesirable elements; I speak of former fascists and mafioso. The Americans have been in league with the Mafia since they came ashore in Sicily. These undesirable elements are a minority but dangerous, no matter how small their number. Do you agree?" asked Broccoli.

"Sir, I agree," said Christakis.

"We can control our force, or I wouldn't support Gladio. But I need to know more about the Greek force. Report to me and bypass regular channels. Do you understand?" asked Broccoli.

"Yes, sir," answered Christakis.

"Transmit from our naval liaison office at Salamis. Use the code as always. But do not transmit from the Embassy and avoid going near it. Understood?" asked Broccoli.

"Yes, sir," answered Christakis.

"Now, tell me more about your plans to deal with Kopali," instructed Broccoli.

"Sir, if I can talk to him, and if he is coherent, I will see what he knows of Chernov. That was the carrot that I offered Theofanis. If he confirms our understanding of Chernov's predilections and offers an approach, all the better. The GRU is always a worthy target.

"The other matter, the logistical matter, I will have to investigate. I presume Theofanis will be present during our interrogation. If Kopali is cooperative, I will take no further action. If he is incoherent and still dangerous to the service, I will take other measures," answered Christakis.

"Good. He is too knowledgeable of our methods to allow him to blather and spout. Someday, someone will believe him, or worse, they will set him free. We are lucky that the Americans think he is psychotic and of no consequence.

"Make it clear to him he will live so long as he is quiet. If he is defective and he cannot understand his circumstance, silence him," ordered Broccoli.

"Yes, sir," answered Christakis.

On October 8, 1951, Broccoli wrote Efisio Marras, the Italian Minister of Defense, with a plan for the best of both worlds. He maneuvered to have the British train Gladio and the Americans provide free arms.[28] He was playing a devious game on the CIA's home pitch. The British, as they say, were not amused.

Launching the consolidated Italian intelligence service, SIFAR, was concurrent with Italy's ascension to NATO. For funding SIFAR, America demanded and received a top-secret protocol. Through NATO planning and coordination, SIFAR would make available to the CIA all intelligence collected, and Washington demanded approval of all SIFAR personnel.[29] A branch of SIFAR called Office R ran Gladio. This secret network of armed anti-communists failed to dent Soviet military ambition. But in the years to come, their impact on Italian politics proved pivotal just as its counterpart network in Greece.

Chapter 21

"Let's drive there tomorrow. How's your knee?" asked Stavros.

At his office in the Ministry, Christakis cringed a bit as he pulled his leg closer and flexed the joint. He said, "It's getting better, thank you."

"Put some ice on it. Ice it, then eat some garlic. Then drink some mountain tsái. That'll bring down the swelling. Greek field medicine one-o-one, eh?" said Stavros.

"I will eat the garlic, drink the tea, and, maybe later, the ice. Thank you again for your concern. What time should we leave?" asked Christakis.

"I'll pick you up at ten. At the Ministry?" asked Stavros.

"Excellent. We can discuss our approach on the drive. It is not wise to talk over the phone. Our trip will take thirty or forty minutes," said Christakis.

"Oh, wear civilian clothes. Your uniform might provoke," suggested Stavros.

"Certainly," answered Christakis. Then he wondered if Stavros was worried about agitating Kopali or other patients at the hospital. If Stavros had said nothing, Christakis would have worn his uniform, a visible symbol of his authority and a reminder to Kopali of his power over him. But this was Stavros's meeting, and Christakis would be there at Stavros's invitation.

"Have you ever been there?" asked Stavros.

"No. I have not. I've only heard stories, none of them pleasurable," answered Christakis.

"Right. The Dromokaition Psychiatric Hospital is well known, both admired and dreaded. Respected for its clinical practice, yet no one wants to be a patient," said Stavros.

"A prison by another name," said Christakis.

Stavros hung up the phone and returned to a table stacked with notes and loose papers. He began sorting the tangible record of his dissertation research in Greece. The phone rang five minutes later.

The hotel switchboard operator said, "Mr. Theofanis, I have a Penelope on your line. Will you accept the call?"

He hesitated, but only for a moment, before saying, "Thank you. Put her through, please."

He heard the operator say, "Thank you for holding, I'm connecting you with Mr. Theofanis."

"Hello, Stavros?"

"Yes, Penelope. How are you?"

"I am fine. And you? Did your travels go well?"

"Yes. Very productive. I was just sorting some of my research." That was a lie. There was something about Penelope that made lying easy.

"Are you busy this evening? Perhaps we can have dinner? You can fill me in on your progress?"

"Um . . . I supposed that would work. I still have a lot of sorting and filing. Do you have a place in mind? Should I meet you at your office?"

"Do you mind coming to the university, instead? Here we have many good places, none so fancy as the Grande Bretagne, but excellent food priced for the likes of poor students and underpaid faculty."

"No, I don't mind. That should work."

"Meet me at the Museum of Mineralogy and Petrology at eight o'clock. I'll be at the entrance. Use the Geōlogia bus stop or take a taxi. Parking there will be not so good."

"All right. I'll see you then."

"Oh, Stavros. Whatever became of the folder?"

He lied, "I don't know. I'll ask the concierge before I leave."

"I'm curious. See you at eight."

Stavros was more than curious. Wittingly or not, Penelope had facilitated a transfer of intelligence with the folder swap. Dimitra voiced reservations about her, too. And Dimitra's instincts for whom to trust and whom to avoid were unassailable. But Dimitra was jealous, if only slightly, her impression perhaps clouded. Was Penelope playing Stavros? If she was, for whom? And to what end? She was alluring in a refined, innocent way, but not the bait for a typical honey trap. The women in that game were sultry with irresistible seduction techniques. The Soviets were unparalleled. They used knockout beauties, highly trained, with flawless legends. These temptresses were elite recruits with the rank of MGB or GRU colonels. No, Penelope wasn't under discipline. To Stavros she was a puzzle, one to solve for sake of a bigger picture. It was his job, right?

On his way through the lobby, Stavros saw his friend the concierge. The young man gave a look of recognition and held up a single finger to the tourist couple he was talking to. He walked to Stavros and said, "My friend, the cab driver, remembered the young woman and said she rode to an apartment building near the university. He watched her go into the building, but he couldn't tell which apartment she entered. This is the address." He handed Stavros a folded sheet from a Grande Bretagne notepad.

Stavros put the note into his jacket pocket unopened. When he reached for his wallet, the young man ever so slightly shook his head. Stavros nodded, shook his hand, and thanked him. He'd make it up to the concierge later.

Penelope was waiting at the entrance to the museum. She wore the same beige trench coat with a blue scarf and stylish black heels. This wasn't mousy Penelope. She said, "Do you mind a walk?"

Stavros said, "It's a beautiful night, I'd love a walk."

She smiled broadly, and as they stepped onto the sidewalk, she put her arm through his.

This didn't surprise Stavros, Greeks often walked arm in arm. But Penelope's contact felt more intimate than friendly. She seemed happy to be with him. He relaxed.

They walked west past the School of Modern Greek Language and the Department of Theology. The university sat amid wooded acreage and public parks. To their left, the

Aesthetic Forest of Kaisariani stretched for nearly a kilometer. They walked in silence until Penelope nodded to an unmarked gate and a dirt road into the park. She said, "That is the path to the Kaisariani Monastery of Saint John. Do you know the place?"

Stavros shook his head.

She went on, "This mountain, Trellóvouno, Crazy Mountain; do you know the name?"

Again, he shook his head.

"The French named it during Ottoman occupation. The Greek name is Hymettos. At the summit, there was a sanctuary to Zeus, or some say Aphrodite. Who knows? They built it well before Pericles. Then came the Byzantines. Around 1100 current era, they decided Christianity needed an outpost. Today's buildings date from the sixteenth century. The monks maintain magnificent frescoes. My favorite is the Virgin Platytera arms orans on a throne. She's usually pictured standing, so this is rare.

"The monks enjoyed earthly rewards, as well. Among their buildings is a bathhouse. The monks relished bathing, together. One wonders what the clean and holy talk about in a bath, no?" Then she winked at Stavros.

She went on, "You can tour the monastery, but only with permission. Our School of Theology coordinates with the order, so if you'd like to see it, this I can arrange."

Stavros said, "Thank you, that's nice of you. I'll put it on my list of things Greece can teach me." He returned her smile, and she beamed.

They came to a traffic circle and followed the road to the left. This road separated the Aesthetic Forest from the Walking Park to the west. They turned right on Nasou into a commercial area with the Walking Park to their right. They passed car parks, apartment buildings, motorcycle repair shops, and restaurants. Traffic was steady with the occasional bleating of horns.

Penelope pointed to a restaurant across the street, Akri. They watched for traffic and crossed, still arm in arm. Akri was a small, unassuming establishment with a few tables set on the patio at the entrance. Only one person, a young man in a heavy coat, like that of a sailor, sat outside. His hands were not rough, and his face not weathered, so he wasn't a deckhand. A book sat on the table with the title obscured. He was writing in a journal, drinking coffee, and smoking a cigarette. He looked up at Stavros and stared intently from behind round wire spectacles as the couple entered.

Akri was small, only twelve tables. A man in his fifties whom Stavros assumed to be the owner greeted them at the door. The man bowed politely to Penelope and said, "Welcome. Two tonight?"

Penelope said, "Yes. Andreas. This is my friend Stavros. He is also a professor, in America."

"A pleasure to meet you, sir. I hope Athens is to your liking?"

"Indeed, it is. I like Athens very much," answered Stavros.

"Come, this table at the window is the best I can offer."

They took off their coats and handed them to Andreas. He said, "I'll hang these and be back with menus. Can I get you anything to drink?"

"Gavalas white, if you have it," said Penelope.

This registered with Stavros, Gavalas was Dimitra's white wine of choice.

Stavros said, "The same for me, please."

Andreas nodded and headed away for the cloakroom.

They sat at the two-top only a couple meters from the studious young man on the other side of the glass. Andreas returned promptly with two glasses and menus. He said, "Take your time. No rush tonight. Roasted lemon chicken is our special."

Both diners nodded.

When Andreas left, Penelope lifted her wineglass for a toast. Stavros followed suit and asked, "To what do we toast?"

Penelope was giddy. She said, "Let us toast to the mysteries of bathing monks."

Stavros thought that was clever and said, "To the monks."

They touched glasses, and Stavros caught the young man watching from the corner of his eye. His head was toward the street, but Stavros knew his quick, sideways glance. Peripheral vision, if practiced and honed, could be remarkably effective. Stavros took note.

But instantly his attention sprang back to Penelope. She was captivating. She dialed her allure up and down, much as a cook might adjust the heat on a stovetop. Yet she seemed unaware. She seemed coy but not manipulative, flirtatious but not teasing. Stavros thought perhaps she was what she seemed, a young woman with a crush on him. That's what it felt like.

She said, "Have you spent time at the university, for your research?"

"Not yet. I need to contact a curator or someone in the Ancient Studies Department."

"That would probably be the Faculty of History and Archaeology," Penelope suggested. "I can help. It would be my pleasure to make introductions."

"Great. Thanks. That would be helpful. I would have the embassy recommend a contact but if you know someone, all the better."

"How soon would you like to meet?" she asked.

Was Penelope pushing? She alternated between disinterest and gung-ho resolve. Stavros was off balance.

"Um . . . whenever you can arrange it. I've got some travel coming up over the next few days, so . . . maybe next week?"

She said, "Good. I will ask around."

"May I ask a question? About your university."

"Sure. What would you like to know?" said Stavros.

"In Greece, we offer full professors sabbaticals. Sometimes a semester, but seldom beyond that. You have been away from your school for more than a semester, no? Are American universities so lenient?"

"Um . . . no, not really. I'm on a leave of absence, not a sabbatical. I qualified for a government program, and my university allowed me the absence; and for that, the university receives a grant."

"When is your grant up?" she asked.

"Probably in the coming year. It's flexible. I'm a *fortunate fellow* if you will."

Stavros's pun about being a university fellow landed flat like most of his attempts to translate American humor.

"I see," she said, not really seeing at all.

He asked, "How is your dissertation coming?"

"Slowly. I have numbers and notes and statistics piled to the ceiling. Wage rates for sailors, wage rates for shipbuilders, wages for restaurant workers, teacher salaries, and taxi drivers. Much correlation and much tedium. I want to explode. I want to free myself of the smallness and closeness of concentration. My mind demands freedom, yet I am trapped in a cell of ambition. Do you know the feeling?"

Stavros didn't know the feeling, but he knew her description. His PhD was part of his cover, but also a personal goal. But it always came second to his work. He said, "You need a hobby."

Penelope didn't understand. Greeks didn't have hobbies; they just lived their lives. Greeks may love birdwatching, hunting, or car racing, but these were integral, not hobbies. They were part of someone's life. *Hobby* was an American construct.

Stavros saw the confusion on her face. He said, "Do you have anything that takes your mind off your studies?"

"Sometimes, I walk in the woods. And I take along my camera. I like photography. Would you care to see some of my pictures?"

"Sure. Do you have them with you?"

"No, silly. These I frame and hang. My apartment is near, we will go there after dinner, okay?"

Stavros was only 50 percent certain this was a good idea when he said, "Sure."

The chicken was succulent and splendidly spiced, and the many glasses of Gavalas light and liberating. Somewhere between the last morsel of roasted potatoes and the galaktoboureko, a dessert they split, the sailor impostor left. Stavros didn't notice in which direction. The Gvalas, Penelope's more and more animated expressions, and the enticing conversation stole his attention.

He was helping her with her trench coat when she asked, "Did you ask about the folder?"

"Yes. I saw the concierge, but he knew nothing. Do you think it was something important?"

Penelope pursed her lips and shrugged her shoulders.

The feel of her shoulders through her coat, her perfume, the scent from her chestnut curls as she cleared them from under her collar, deflected his thoughts. Stavros the spy was slipping. She was harmless. She was a smart young woman with a crush. Dimitra was the most important person in his life. Penelope was no threat. His pact with Dimitra was simple: neither owned the other's body. They were agents of thought and reason. No jealousy, no possessiveness. Together when they were, and free when they weren't. That's the way Dimitra wanted it.

"Are you up for another walk? It is not far." Penelope asked as she tossed the scarf around her neck.

"Sure," answered Stavros, forgoing any depth in his decision-making.

They walked arm in arm up Antistaseos for a block, then crossed the street to Tantalidou. They entered a pleasant neighborhood with the border of the Walking Park on the right with a playground and a tended memorial. Penelope's apartment entrance was at the street's end just around the corner.

Penelope's apartment was on the top floor, the fourth. As she pushed open her door, she said, "Please excuse the mess, I was not expecting a visitor."

The apartment featured an awning-covered patio overlooking the park. Her furniture was modern and matching, and despite her protestations, it was tidy. It was a delightful place. She turned on the light, and on a wall to the left, hung six black-and-white photographs, all matching and framed in forest green. They were nature scenes and well done. The lighting and focal points were expert, allowing the viewer's eye to center on the subject: a grotto here, an ancient, gnarled olive tree, a startled miniature goat. Penelope explained the goat. "I took the photo in the Samariá Gorge on Crete. They call the small goats with their oversized horns kri-kri. They are rare because, during the war, the resistance fighters hunted them almost to extinction."

He said, "Penelope, you have a trained eye, you are talented. How did you come to know photography?"

"It is something that grew from my love of the outdoors, my love of nature. When I was a young girl, I would hike and find things I thought were magical. The way animals behaved, a school of fish swimming as one, the leaves of trees warning of a storm. As I grew older, I understood these to be spiritual signs, signs of something more than what we expect on the surface. I sensed truth behind the objects, the earth, the plants, the animals. Even the insects. An invisible universe connecting everything. I hope I don't sound mystical?"

"No. You sound . . . you sound lovely, very evolved," said Stavros.

"My photography grew from that. I do not know where my father found it, but he gave me a thirty-five-millimeter camera when I turned sixteen. That was the first I ever used a camera. I spent a few years toying with it and then, a few years ago, when I started university, I began studying photographic technique.

"I prefer shooting out of doors in natural light, but . . . come here, these I took indoors with lighting equipment. I'd like your impression."

She put her hand on Stavros's elbow and led him into her bedroom. On the wall opposite her tidy bed hung six more photographs. These were different. Framed in natural wood, three were in color. But it was the subject that surprised Stavros. All six photographs were of a young woman, Stavros guessed, eighteen years old. She was blond with green eyes. Green eyes and the look of someone hiding a smile, but only partly succeeding. She was beautiful, her toned body flawlessly proportioned, suggesting to Stavros an athlete.

She wore clothes that complemented and highlighted her sexuality. The dresses and blouses evoked curiosity of hidden glory. Every pose was seductive with artful emphasis, suggestive but not slutty. Slutty was easy. No, these images were studied and nuanced, both by the artist and the model. One featured her legs, one her breasts. In one she leaned against a wicker chair, her tight skirt slit far up her sculpted leg. She looked back into the camera. Her blond hair hung over her far shoulder with only a hint of backlighting framing her wary indifference in a balmy phosphorescence. Again, from the perspective of technique, the work was flawless. From the perspective of a man, it was provocative.

Penelope smiled and asked, "What do you think?"

"I think your subject is remarkable and your technique outstanding. You are talented, Penelope. Are you certain you want to be an economist; photography might be your calling?"

Penelope shook her head, "Photography will never pay the bills, sad to say."

"Your subject, is she a friend?"

"A model from the School of Fine Arts. She is beautiful, no? I wish I looked like her. She is so vital."

"Why would you say that?" asked Stavros. "You are lovely and lively. Don't compare yourself to a model. You are an accomplished, fascinating, and appealing woman."

Penelope's eyes widened with the compliment. She blushed. Then she stepped close to Stavros, kicked off her high heels, stood on her toes, and kissed him full and deep.

Chapter 22

"Telephone for a taxi. This time of the morning, they will all have fares. You will not hail one on the street," Penelope advised from under the covers as Stavros pulled on his pants.

"But first, I will make you some coffee. I have some bread and cheese, but no pastry. Would you like eggs?"

She rolled onto her back and pulled the covers just above her breasts. She was winsome in the light of morning. Rumpled but not disappointing, a fascinating young woman.

Stavros said, "You don't have to do that; I'll get something at the hotel."

"Do you think I should just send you into the streets of Athens, undernourished and hungry? You insult my manners." She tossed the covers, and she rose from the bed. She wore her nakedness without embarrassment, and Stavros felt a physical response rising. She was young, trim as a gymnast, and vivacious. There was no mouse in her this morning.

She walked to a closet and lifted a robe from a hanger. It was flimsy and revealing. She went barefoot into the kitchenette and began boiling water. She said, "I trust you can drink Greek coffee? You have attained that level of refinement, no?"

Now Stavros was lusting. He struggled for control. He said, "Yes, I like Greek coffee."

Penelope called, "*Sketos, metrios* or *glykos*?"

"Metrios, please."

"For your next visit, I will have pastry and ham. I promise to be a better hostess."

Stavros thought, *My welcome has been near perfection, ham, or no.*

He looked at his watch. It was nine. There was just enough time to return to the Grande Bretagne, change clothes, retrieve the Morris, and meet Christakis.

She said, "You should call the taxi company. It will take them fifteen minutes to get here. The number is on the pad near the phone, on the desk."

Stavros sat at the tidy, wooden writing desk with a view to the park. He found the number and dialed the cab company. The dispatcher answered and asked Stavros for an address. He held his hand over the mouthpiece and asked Penelope. She called back, still stirring the *briki* and said, "Anatolikis Thrakis, Eastern Thrace, number 38."

The taxi arrived and tapped his horn. Stavros kissed Penelope at the door and walked to the cab. As he rode, he thought about the evening and Penelope's innocence. Nothing in their night together made him believe she was other than a young woman, sometimes overstrung, ambitious, with a crush on him.

At the Grande Bretagne, he reached into his jacket pocket for cash, and along with the money he pulled the concierge's note. He handed the money to the driver, then unfolded the note. It read, *Anatolikis Thrakis # 38.*

Chapter 23

"His English is not so good. He prefers Albanian, of course, and he speaks understandable Italian," noted Christakis.

Stavros did not want to reveal his fluency in Italian. He said, "How's your Albanian?"

"I know enough Tosk for an approximation. Gheg, not so much. Kopali is from Tirana, so he should converse in Tosk."

"So, I'll let you lead the interrogation. Does he speak Greek?"

"This I do not know. It would be unusual for him to not understand some Greek. But his fluency, I do not know."

"So maybe we should switch between English and Greek when we talk among ourselves. Okay?"

"Certainly. I will question him in Albanian and Italian."

Christakis went on, "Our primary goal is to learn the vulnerability of the rezidentura, agreed? We need a hook, I believe that is the American term, no? Is that your priority?"

Stavros nodded, then downshifted the Morris into second gear as he descended a hill near the National Archaeological Museum on the road to Dromokaition.

"Do you have any orders from CIA?" asked Christakis.

Preoccupied, Stavros was still swooning over Penelope. He savored their night together and speculated about the matching addresses. He answered, "Not really." Then he caught himself and added, "Of course, I have no connection to any United States Government agency or department. I am facilitating this meeting as a private citizen hoping to build a constructive relationship with our host country."

Christakis smiled.

The hospital compound was walled, fenced, and gated. Enclosed in its thirty-five acres were a dozen clinical buildings made of stucco, some with barred windows. A church sat in the middle of the layout, its dome and cross rising above all. An olive grove, outside the fenced perimeter, spread at the far corner. Figures in white and gray busied about the trees.

Dromokaition occupied the eastern edge of Mount Aigaleo Park. The park contained the Diomidous Botanical Garden, the Daphne Monastery, areas for children to play, and tended walking trails. Its sparsely wooded expanse and barren peak reached for five kilometers all the way to Skaramagas. At the center, Mount Aigaleo rose to 450 meters above the placid Gulf of Elefsina.

Uniformed guards, local police, met them at the gate. Christakis showed his Ministry identification, and the guards directed them to the administration building. Inside the building, Stavros asked to see the American security chief, and the receptionist behind a partial glass window told them to have a seat. Five minutes later, a burly man in his forties arrived and introduced himself as Mr. Smith. That was fine with Stavros.

Stavros said, "We're here to talk to Kopali. And who is the best minor league team in America?"

Smith answered, "The Portland Seadogs."

And with that confirmation, Smith led them out of the administration building and across the campus to a nondescript, three-story stucco building with barred windows. Inside, they entered an open room of gray-and-green walls with pockmarked plaster. A few chairs and tables were arranged in exaggerated spacing. Board games and checker boards scattered around gave the room its only personality. It was empty. Smith said, "Wait here. I'll bring him down. How long do you need with him?"

Stavros shrugged, "An hour, maybe. It depends on how cooperative he is."

"Cooperation won't be your problem with Kopali. Not now. He got the procedure," said Smith.

Stavros looked at Christakis, both shrugged. Stavros asked, "What procedure is that?"

"About a week ago, I thought you knew. He had a lobotomy; you know, scrambled eggs in the head," replied Smith.

Neither Christakis nor Stavros knew the term.

They had practiced lobotomies or leucotomies at Dromokaition since 1948.[30] The procedure severed nerve tissue in the brain's prefrontal lobe and rendered the patient, docile or, sometimes, vegetative. The procedure did not enhance mental acuity.

Stavros asked, "Who ordered that?"

Smith said, "Above my pay grade, sir. You can talk to his doctor if you like. I don't think it will do much good. He's following orders. I'll bring him down."

Christakis and Stavros waited in the recreation room for an apprehensive ten minutes. Neither felt at ease in his surroundings. Smith arrived with a short, stocky, bearded man whose age was hard to call. His gray eyes, dark and sunken, were vacant and, if not lifeless, soulless. He wore a wrinkled gray smock and khaki pants. His slippers were in tatters. He walked with a stoop and shuffled his feet like he was in chains, although he was unrestrained.

Stavros looked at Christakis and saw reflected puzzlement.

Smith said, "Mr. Kopali, these gentlemen are with a United States Government agency, and they are here to talk with you. Do you wish to speak to them?"

Kopali lifted his head, stared into Smith's eyes for an uncomfortable spell, then nodded his head.

"Fine. I will leave you together, and I will be outside the doorway to make certain you are undisturbed." With that, Smith left the room and Stavros and Christakis wondered how to proceed. After an uneasy pause, Christakis said in Tosk, "Sir, would you like to sit, perhaps at this table. We can be more comfortable, I think."

Kopali perked up at the strain of Albanian, as if it freed his mind of the burden of translation.

Christakis put his hand on Kopali's elbow and led him to the nearest set of table and chairs. He helped Kopali into his chair, then he and Stavros sat.

Christakis began, "Sir, Mr. Kopali, we are here to talk to you about your time with the Sigurimi and Albania. Do you understand?"

Kopali nodded and remained silent.

Christakis asked, "When you worked with the Sigurimi, do you remember speaking to a Russian colonel, Dmitriy Chernov?"

For the first time, Kopali spoke. His tone was hushed, as if to avoid anyone else hearing. His voice was firm. This surprised Christakis, given his frail appearance. He said, "Yes. I remember Chernov. He was liaison with the Sigurimi. He liked women and booze, vodka. He is smart, difficult to fool."

Kopali's response set Stavros back in his chair. He couldn't understand Tosk, but Kopali's unexpected lucidity registered.

Christakis raised his eyebrow in a quick glance at Stavros. He looked back at Kopali and asked, "Sir, we are here to help you, if you can help us. Do you understand?"

Kopali nodded, then said, "Yes, I understand. You are here to free me if I tell you what you wish to know."

Christakis spoke to Stavros in Greek, "He wants to know if we can free him for his cooperation."

"Tell him only if his information is accurate and helpful," said Stavros.

Stavros couldn't free Kopali. But dishonesty in the conduct of CIA business was not a moral failing. On the contrary. Kopali was of mixed allegiance. He would work whatever side of the street was most likely to get him what he wanted. That was the reason for his institutionalization. He was not trustworthy, not a sympathetic figure. If he had not killed them, he had ordered the death of anti-communist countrymen exiled in Italy. At this he was subpar. That was the reason he had come over, the reason he'd defected. The Sigurimi believed he soft-pedaled these assassinations and failed for reasons of ineptitude or treason. It was his death warrant.

The United States had turned him down for asylum and relocation. Americans from the CIA and Department of State had grilled him then and determined he was not important enough to bother with. The Italians used him for what they could, extracting secrets of Sigurimi tradecraft and operations. They learned about Albanian defenses and secret bases. But in their care, Kopali became incorrigible. He spoke of returning to Albania. He cursed the Americans and demanded relocation there in the same stroke. His behavior became so destructive with drinking, whoring, and interrupting meetings, that the Italians gave him over to the Americans. They sent him to a camp in Germany where the US Army would have none of him and asked the CIA to take charge. He was their project, after all. The CIA sent him to Dromokaition a year earlier. There were others like him here, but Stavros did not know how many. Now someone at CIA had ordered a surgery to render him incapable of threatening their methods and sources.

Christakis continued, "We can free you if your information is good, something we can work with, something we can use to turn Chernov."

Without hesitation, Kopali asked, "Where would I live?"

"Where is it you want to live?" asked Christakis.

"I want to go to America; this is the only country where I will be safe. Otherwise, I should return to Albania. There I will take my chances and meet my fate. The life in his hospital is unacceptable. I am a prisoner except for the few hours we work on the trees."

Christakis was certain that the man speaking to him was not of diminished mental ability. Kopali was controlled and metered. He spoke without error or hesitation. In rapid Greek, he said to Stavros, "He wants to go to America. And there's something else. He is speaking without confusion. This is unexpected, no?"

Stavros replied, "Tell him it is possible, but only if he gives valuable information. And it will take time."

Christakis nodded, then turned to Kopali. He said, "America will have you in time, but only if we get the information to turn GRU Rezidentura, Colonel Dmitriy Chernov. Is this understood?"

Kopali nodded. Then he said, "I can give you a profile of Chernov. We worked together for a year before he went to Greece. But there are other matters, as well. Bigger fish to fry, as the American might say." Then Kopali tilted his head toward Stavros, keeping his eye contact with Christakis.

"He likes young women, young blond women. Fair skin and fair hair. Virgins. These cannot be too young or too blond. He is married to a babushka back in Russia. He has three sons, two in the GRU, the third I know not. I don't know their stations.

"He has an apartment near the Soviet Embassy, I have an address. This is where he takes his women. Remember, I have not seen him in over a year, closer to two years. Things can change. And remember, the Russians are expert at using women. They are better than any other service. He will spot a trap like a wise old wolf. Unless . . . unless it is someone he thinks is clear, someone in his orbit of control.

"But the rezidentura is himself a small fish. This I have tried to tell the Americans and the Italians. The big fish are submarines. Soviet submarines. These they plan to base in Albania, and I know where. Perhaps when you have confirmed my profile of Chernov, you will want to know more of the submarines?"

They talked for an hour, with Christakis digging into details about Chernov and reporting Kopali's responses to Stavros. As their time lagged and Kopali's responses became repetitive, Christakis switched subjects and language. In Italian, he asked, "When you were in Italy, do you recall your interrogators?"

This puzzled Kopali. He looked over to Stavros for a clue. The question was not about turning Chernov. For the first time, Kopali switched to Italian and said to Christakis, "My interrogators wore masks. But one man I recall, although I'm certain he used a false name. He used the name Dominic and said he was with Italian Naval Intelligence. He did not wear a mask. It was unusual. This meeting was at a naval base, somewhere near Rome, an hour away, perhaps. They blindfolded me for the trip."

"What do you remember about the meeting?" asked Christakis.

When they spoke Italian, Stavros understood, but he didn't let on.

Kopali switched back to Tosk. "Dominic showed me a book of silhouettes, ships and crafts in shadow. He asked me to identify them. Some were Soviet; the others, I did not know. When we finished, we walked to the car. Before they blindfolded me, I remember seeing an American frigate at the dock. They'd obscured her number. She was off-loading. They had marked the canisters in odd ways, warning emblems, I believe. These were the bombs, no? The big bombs?"

Then Kopali continued in Tosk, "You are Italian. I recognize your speech. You questioned me in Rome, at the headquarters, no?"

Christakis did not respond.

Christakis again spoke in rapid Greek to Stavros, "We are finished. Do you have any cigarettes for him?"

Stavros padded his breast pocket and held up his hands. He'd forgotten to bring any. He didn't smoke, but American cigarettes were prized currency that he should not have left behind.

Christakis didn't smoke either, but he reached into his breast pocket and produced a fresh pack of Papastratos. He handed them to Kopali who asked, "Do you have matches? They search us for matches, but how else am I to enjoy this reward?"

Christakis reached into his pants and handed Kopali two books of matches. He placed them in Kopali's hand, below the tabletop, out of Stavros's sight.

Kopali looked at Christakis, puzzled. Christakis revealed nothing. Then Kopali faked a fumble of the handover. He dropped both matchbooks to the floor and while he leaned over, he slid one into his slipper. He rose with the other matchbook and said, "Thank you. If it is not too much, perhaps you might send me more cigarettes, perhaps a carton? These they allow."

Christakis said, "Of course."

Then Christakis nodded to Stavros. Stavros rose from the table and went into the hallway where Smith was waiting on a metal chair reading a Greek sailing publication. He said, "We're done. We gave him cigarettes and matches."

Smith nodded.

The two men reentered the recreation room. Stavros and Christakis limply shook hands with Kopali, who had transformed into the barely ambulatory imbecile who'd greeted them an hour before. Smith said, "Wait here and I will escort you to your car."

Neither Christakis nor Stavros spoke in Smith's absence. Both were by now certain the room had been bugged. When Smith returned, Stavros asked, "Is there any chance we can talk to Kopali's attending doctor?"

Smith said, "I'll take you there. Like I said before, he's under orders."

On their way from the building, on the stoop at the entrance, they waited for twenty patients dressed in gray smocks and tattered army surplus coats to pass. Some were carrying hampers, others saws and trimmers, and one man held a net. Three staff dressed in white walked alongside. Smith said, "Olive detail."

Chapter 24

"What did you make of the doctor?" asked Stavros as he wheeled the Morris out of the hospital gate.

"He was on edge. He didn't want to talk to us. Nervous as a cat," said Christakis.

"Was he Greek?"

"No. I don't think so. Perhaps Bulgarian or Macedonian. His was a Greek name, and he spoke Greek like a northerner. It was difficult to tell," said Christakis.

"He wouldn't say who ordered the procedure. Only that the procedure was successful, and the patient showed remarkable improvement. A transorbital lobotomy, sounds like something from outer space. What did he call Kopali?" asked Stavros.

"A paranoid schizophrenic," replied Christakis.

"Right, a paranoid schizophrenic with delusions of grandeur," added Stavros.

The two men rode in silence for a few kilometers. Then Stavros asked, "What do you think is going on at the hospital? Is Kopali faking his treatment? Is he playing the system? What the heck is going on?"

"I'd say that Kopali is playing anyone and everyone he can. We should follow up on his profile and see what we can develop on Chernov. The other thing, the submarines, who knows? I'm sure he told the Italians and Americans. We'd be wise to stick with Chernov. I will ask for a surveillance team to begin around-the-clock observation. I'm sure we watch him now, but not nonstop, and not for targeting.

"Can you ask CIA for a team, too?" inquired Christakis.

Stavros wheeled the Morris, said nothing, and smiled at Christakis.

Two days later, there arrived at the Dromokaition Psychiatric Hospital of Athens a package. In it was a single, olive-green carton of Papastratos cigarettes. The carton was unopened and factory-sealed. The security officer passed it to Kopali without hesitation.

Kopali tore the cellophane from the carton, ripped the thin cardboard, and fingered the first pack. He glanced at a beautiful young woman making ready to enjoy a smoke. She wore pearl earrings and three strands around her long, arching neck. A man's arm reached into the picture, dressed in a white shirt and suit, flicking a lighter for her. Life was all smiles.

When Kopali removed the wrapper to open the first pack, he saw the edge of a miniature yellow note, a Sigurimi tradecraft. He tore the top from the pack and retrieved the paper. In Tosk, it read:

Walk away from the olive grove. Hide in the park until dark. Proceed due west. Guide by the lights of the Skaramagas shipyard gantry. At the old pier north of the shipyard is a trawler under Bulgarian flag. The vessel's name is Ofelia. *Ask the watch, "Is Vasil aboard." You must do this in two nights, 9 November. Welcome home, comrade.*

Kopali wadded the thin, water-soluble paper, chewed it, and swallowed. At the same moment as Kopali was opening his cigarettes, Stavros received a telex from Frank Wisner. It read:

I have ordered no medical procedure for Kopali.

Chapter 25

The Dromokaition Psychiatric Hospital encouraged painting as therapy. A few notable works hung on the gray walls of the recreation room, forgotten and askew. The oil paints, brushes, a small jar of acetone for cleaning the brushes, and a few used rags were stored in an unlocked wooden cabinet near the easel. Kopali took the acetone and a rag.

It was a chilly afternoon when the olive detail formed up on the ninth. The patients all wore loose, heavy coats, tattered and abused.

Kopali was smart. He was psychotic, but smart. He compiled profiles in his mind for every man in his detail. One, a slight man of undistinguished stature, was in Dromokaition because of his love of fire. He was a pyromaniac. He had set fire to his family's home. He'd tried to burn a police station. He'd watched every fire he started until the last ember was cold. This made him an easy arrest. He never spoke and preferred to grunt and giggle.

The sun set on November 9, 1951, at 5:15 p.m. The olive detail was forming up for the return to housing when Kopali stepped in line behind the pyromaniac. He inserted the acetone-soaked rag in the coat pocket of the pyromaniac and lit it. The confusion this created, the running and gleeful shouting, drew all three of the orderly staff. The pyromaniac fought off the orderlies. They would not deny him the ecstasy of immolation. He fanned the flames coming from his coat and treated them like they were a pet in his pocket. A fiery rat.

As a confused circle grew around the flaming patient, with some men cheering and others wailing and rocking, Kopali slipped unnoticed into the low shrubs of Mount Aigaleo Park. He was in the eastern shadow of the mountain and darkness fell fast. The orderlies, confused and rattled, didn't count their charges until they arrived back at housing. By the time they organized a search team, Kopali had found a hiding place soon to be on his way to Skaramagas.

Around midnight, Kopali began walking west, using the lights of the Skaramagas shipyard gantry as a guide. At two in the morning, he reached the small commercial port north of the shipyard and found the trawler *Ofelia*. It wasn't a large vessel, perhaps twenty-five meters. There was a single watch on deck. Kopali approached and gave the challenge in Tosk. The man standing watch only nodded and motioned Kopali aboard. Kopali climbed up a short gangway, then stepped down onto the deck. As he stood on the desk, smiling at his expected freedom, two more men arrived from the cabin. The first man put his hand over Kopali's mouth and the second yanked his arms behind his back, dislocating his shoulder. Kopali tried to scream in pain, but the muscular man's hoary hand muffled all sound. The man on watch tied a gag around Kopali, then slipped a canvas sack over his head. He retrieved heavy iron handcuffs and leg manacles from a deck locker, bound Kopali, then shoved him forward into the cabin doorway. Kopali stumbled and fell down the ladder.

As he lie squirming on the boat's passageway, the two men from above descended. They lifted him under his armpits and dragged him to a cabin. They threw him inside, and again he fell to the deck. He heard the door close and a lock bolt.

The captain of the trawler was a tall, bearded man dressed in the expected clothes of a fisherman. When the security men reported Kopali aboard and bound, the captain said, "Good. Let's make way. Ready the crew and shove off."

The trawler *Ofelia* chugged away from the dock into the Gulf of Elefsina. She came about full on a course south to the Strait of Salamis. Only yards from the dock, the watch lowered the Bulgarian flag and replaced it with the flag of Italy.

Chapter 26

"I'm glad you could come by. I want to fill you in on Ringchief. You hit it spot-on. Come in and sit," Fuller motioned to the solarium and the two chairs where he and Stavros had talked before. The safe house in Kifissia was buzzing. Men moved about the foyer with satchels and packs. They wore street clothes, and Stavros knew better than to ask what was up.

They took their chairs, and Fuller asked, "How you doing?"

Stavros nodded and said, "I can't complain."

"The boss says you may be onto something big, so I'm supposed to give you a pass on FIEND assignments," confided Fuller.

This was the first Stavros had heard of any change in his standing orders, but he'd expected it when he reported to Wisner the exchange with Kopali, and Wisner said to make the GRU rezidentura a priority.

"So, let me set the scene. You'll like this. Remember how slimy Ringchief felt? Like an eel oozing out of mud. We bring him here in the blind and put him into the cellar. The technician is there, in a mask, with the poly and a syringe of scopolamine. He laid them out on a desk with a pair of rubber gloves. They set Ringchief next to the desk and taped his arms to the chair rails. I don't think Ringchief knew what a polygraph looked like. He'd never seen one before. He thought it was an electric torture device. Before we can even start questioning, you know, establish a baseline. He sings. And it's just what you said.

"The Sigurimi have his father, his sister, his aunt, and an uncle detained in Albania. They told Ringchief all the terrible things they intend for these folks before they hang. He's scared shitless. But here's the kicker. The Sigurimi don't give a crap about the date and location of the jump—*they already know!* They want Ringchief to lead the group down a specific trail for an easy ambush. That's what they want. They promise to spare

Ringchief, release his family, and everybody lives Albanian happy ever after.

"Now what do we do? The Sigurimi have his family, he's come clean, the op is off. I sent him and his unit back to Heidelberg for *advanced training*. We'll let the Sigurimi think they are still running him. It might keep his family alive for a while.

"We asked him how the Sigurimi stayed in touch, how'd they communicate. You know what he said?" asked Fuller in a rhetorical tone.

"The Italians recruited him out of a DP camp. I feel sorry for all those displaced people, homeless, penniless, no future. But the camps are infested with agents, and there are no secrets. The Sigurimi spotted him, and when the Italians earmarked him for recruiting, the reds already had his number.

"Ringchief wrote home, like all the Pixies. They write enough to be novelists. He wrote home but addressed the letters to a Sigurimi drop. They used code, and that's how he informed them of his movements. That's how he informed on the group. Oh, and cigarettes. When they couldn't hand off a note with a brush pass, they used cigarettes. Notes in the pack. Never American, always foreign . . . Greek, Turkish.

"Damn, we should have thought of that."

Fuller sat in his chair and nodded his head. Then he slapped both legs, got out of the chair, and said, "I need to manage this little escapade." And he tilted his head toward the activity in the foyer. "Oh, before I forget, Wisner said to call on the secure line. He's back in DC, so he should be in the office by now. See the coms officer."

Stavros said, "Great. Thanks for the update. Let me know if there's anything I can do."

"Roger. Will do. I've got to shove off, you take care." When he shook Stavros's hand, Fuller's grip was a vice.

Stavros climbed the curved staircase to the second level. The coms officer pointed to a telephone receiver without a dial rotor in a small room. He said, "Close the door, it's soundproof. I'll get him. Just pick up when you hear the tone."

A minute later, a dull ringing tone alerted Stavros, and he lifted the receiver. Before he could speak, Wisner said, "Cheetah escaped last night."

Cheetah was code for Kopali.

Stavros said, "What do we know?"

"He walked away from some maintenance detail into the woods. Is there a park nearby?"

Stavros said, "Yes, a big one, it borders the hospital."

Wisner said, "I don't want him on the loose, and I don't know what's going on. If you find him, let's make sure he can't talk. Understood?"

"Yes, sir," answered Stavros.

"You'll never find him. If this was GRU or Sigurimi, they'll have him out of the country by now. By boat is my guess. But if you cross paths, put him down."

"Yes, sir."

Chapter 27

"It is a fool's errand. Kopali is gone. Probably with the help of whoever is running his doctor. We will never find him. It is better that we focus on the rezidentura and see if there is any truth in what Kopali told us, a hook. A young, blond hook? Or money? Kopali said he likes money. Money or property. He thinks he is worth more than the GRU pays. His wife is demanding. Her family is well-connected; his family is not. What are your thoughts?" asked Christakis.

Stavros sat at the small table in the Kafenio Mouria near the Ministry for Public Security. Before him was a glass of water, a Greek coffee, and a bowl of cuttlefish stewed in wine. Christakis had the same drinks with scrambled eggs. They sat away from other customers. The place buzzed with animated conversations in a fog of cigarette smoke.

Stavros said, "I'm sure you are right. Kopali had help. It was a setup. The procedure was fake, he was playacting. He fooled security."

Stavros was right. The escape had been set up, just not in the way he imagined.

"How's the knee," asked Stavros.

"Much better, thank you. I walked to the Ministry just this morning," reassured Christakis.

"Do you have more rallies or hunting planned?" asked Stavros.

"No. No. That was the last rally of the season, and it is too late in the year for boar hunting. We were lucky to take a boar when we did. Hunting is much better in September, mid-September," answered Christakis.

The two men were budding friends. Stavros liked Christakis, although he could not share his CIA affiliation. Christakis liked Stavros, but he could not disclose his SIFAR allegiance. Christakis knew Stavros was CIA, it was all but public information. Stavros assumed Christakis knew he was CIA from Greek intelligence. He was wrong. SIFAR worked with CIA's OSO who knew all about Stavros. Stavros, however, knew nothing of the Italian connection.

Christakis was younger than Stavros. He was in his late twenties. His reserved manner made him seem older. Stavros, at thirty-eight, saw himself as seasoned and experienced. And perhaps he was. But Stavros's experience, his time in the OSS, in Greece and China, his college professing, his time with the CIA differed from his current predicament. He knew how to survive in the mountains of Greece with a bloodthirsty German command trying to kill him. But setting an ambush on a hapless railroad, or even the improbable sinking of a ferry, didn't prepare him for the alleyways and shadows of Athens. If all the world's a stage, then the stage that was Athens was rickety, poxed with pitfalls, and poorly lit. Upon it performed professional liars, impeccable actors, and false innocents. Stavros was a blameless babe flung into the depths of deceit. He was smart, but he was learning on the job.

Americans were a confident lot. Their naivete, boundless resources, and privilege served them well. Indeed, their enthusiasm inspired many in the Old World. But their attendant overreach and impetuousness dogged them. These shortcomings went unrecognized. A quote, unreliably attributed to Winston Churchill, fit the moment: "Americans can always be relied upon to do the right thing—having first exhausted all possible alternatives."

The CIA ran hundreds of clandestine projects, a vast field of whirligigs spinning in the torrent. By 1951, their scope of operations was worldwide. Greece was a notable hub of Cold War activity, but far from the only theater. The ploy to target the GRU rezidentura in Athens rose all the way to the top, to the deputy director of plans. It was important, maybe critical. But Frank Wisner had many fish to fry.[31] Stavros was on a long leash, balanced over a deadly fault. Precariousness and oblivion and an incomplete picture. He didn't know what he didn't know.

The GRU was practiced and hard. They operated without moral restraint. The Soviet experience and the long, dark, cold Russian history that preceded it applauded authoritarian rule and Draconian measures. Killing a CIA operative in Athens was of little consequence. The GRU's one concern was, is the target more valuable to us alive, or dead?

The GRU made assassinations look like accidents. One method that was gaining approval and becoming popular in their playbook was fly-swatting. This involved an automobile, a target, and an immovable object—a wall, a building, another vehicle. They lured the target into the trap, the driver received a signal, and the automobile crushed the target against the wall. It was not pretty. GRU also enjoyed poisoning, but that required access. It required closeness. Closeness was vulnerability. Fly-swatting was gaining popularity. Gunshots and garroting were reliable methods but forswore the cloak of uncertain attribution.

Each service, the GRU and the CIA, employed methods of elimination, of neutralization. What separated them was institutional willingness and seasoning. Americans were new to espionage. Prior to World War II, there was no American national spy service. The Russians, the Greeks, the British, the Italians—these countries had cultivated spying for centuries.

The GRU, the Soviets, and the Greek KKE, ran clandestine operations for a long time. They built networks, or chains, and recruited agents, some with generational pedigrees. Athens was their home court. But the GRU's agenda was not the KKE's. They might be ideologically compatible, but tactical considerations varied. Greek ambitions were not Soviet ambitions. The Greek KKE's independent streak could cross wires.

The KKE had been in political freefall following their defeat in September 1949 under napalm on Mount Grammos. Their attempt to take Greece by force had failed for a second time. Their fighters, the residua of the Democratic Army of Greece (DSE), retreated to camps in northern Albania. The KKE had burned bridges with its biggest supporter, Yugoslavia, when it sided with Stalin over Tito in 1948. Stalin, long before, had handed Greece to Britain in 1944.

In 1951, a cluster of leftist political parties merged to form the EDA, the Greek United Democratic Left. The largest faction, by far, was a renamed and disguised KKE. Outlawed following the Civil War, the KKE's tenuous leadership controlled the EDA from exile. The remnants of the KKE in Athens, underground and secretive, vied for political prominence in the leadership vacuum. Small, angry sects fought over Titoism and arcane ideological nuance. One sect urged anarchy as the way forward. The working class, they said, was to lead the revolution. The proletariat needed only enlightenment by example to do that. The sect that called themselves The Torch preached direct action and assassination. They counted among their cell of faithful a few university students and fewer faculty members. And one hanger-on, a good-looking, money-strapped, blond, and ambitious fine arts undergraduate and part-time model.

The Communist Party of the Soviet Union and their agents in Athens did not equivocate. If killing needed done, it would be the GRU doing it, not impetuous Greeks. Extinguishing The Torch was to the GRU like crushing a cigarette butt under the heel without breaking stride.

Chapter 28

Calista, code name Alepoú, had a date. She rode the bus from her basement efficiency apartment near the School of Fine Arts to the Exarcheia neighborhood. She stared through the scratched window at businesses and apartments along Kaisariani and Venizelou. As the bus neared Exarcheia, graffiti, political posters and sloganeering plastered any and every available space.

Exarcheia had history. All of Athens had history, but Exarcheia attracted from Athens its political and artistic eccentrics. It had sheltered the crucible of Greek radical and unconventional thought since the late 1800s. One such sheltered radical was the self-anointed leader of The Torch, Achilles, a nom de guerre of his own selection. His given name was Theo, but Calista knew him only by his revolutionary aura.

Theo was a college dropout. His reason was that the National Technical University of Athens School of Architecture was but a bourgeois induction center. He trumpeted in strident and self-assured tones that universities stripped from him and all enrollees, fervor and revolutionary zeal. If Greece were ever to transform into a socialist then communist utopia, men of action would lead, not denuded sycophants in caps and gowns waving flimsy sheepskins. The other reason was that he didn't make grades. He was better suited to the performing arts.

The small collection of pariahs that made up The Torch made up his audience. But Achilles wasn't all made-up. He read *Das Kapital* and almost plowed through Commodities and Exchange before he began skipping. He hoped Chapter III, Money, or the Circulation of Commodities might hold the key, but there he discovered Marx had written in formulas and mathematics. Mathematics was the reason he missed grades. He read Lenin, his 1901 *What Is to Be Done?*, a communist gospel, and the 1919 *Dictatorship of the Proletariat*. Lenin was an author more to his liking—zealous, agitative and brief. Achilles used code phrases permissibly and, to some, convincingly. *Labor*

Theory of Value, Dictatorship of the Proletariat, Combined Uneven Development—these he sprinkled into his leadership lectures at cell meetings.

He wasn't bad looking. He was tall with intense eyes behind round metal spectacles. He wore the coat of a sailor, although he'd never set foot on a working vessel, save a ferry, and then only as a passenger.

Achilles told himself that he wasn't the only revolutionary to drop out of university. Stalin had dropped out of the Georgian Orthodox Seminary in Tbilisi after five years. Achilles saw his destiny as center-stage, intensely lit, and written in the blood of martyrs. Not his, other martyrs.

Calista saw in Achilles two things. As a fine arts major, she liked his performance, and he was not unattractive. And, as an under-funded undergraduate, she saw a meal ticket. Achilles saw in Calista a beautiful young follower, tantalizing but vacuous, with whom to explore liberated sex.

Achilles talked himself into combat. He had preached direct action for long enough, and now he believed his own sermons. He planned to assassinate a capitalist and provide to the downtrodden and anesthetized working class a stunning, awakening example of revolutionary heroism. He'd killed no one before, but how hard could it be? The details he was still working out.

Calista had an acquaintance, an economics professor for whom she modeled. The professor knew the schedule of the American Economic Cooperation Administration Mission. She had seen these papers at the professor's apartment where some of her favored modeling hung. She knew of Achilles's quandary. Which capitalist should he use as his revolutionary example? He had spilled his not-so-secret plan one night while trying to impress Calista enough to get her into bed. His line went, "My mind is heavy with revolutionary planning. My stress is almost unmanageable. The responsibility of leading a revolution is demanding. It would be healthy for me to have a physical release. Are you thus inclined, comrade?"

She wasn't.

But she knew an opportunity. She told Achilles she would visit the economist under pretext and snatched from her desk a schedule of the ECAM chief and deputy. Her date was to deliver the schedule to Achilles, dodge his advances, then report back to her OSO handler about the development. This, she hoped, would generate another stipend from the always flush CIA treasury.

One pariah in Achilles's audience was there by design. He was a quiet man who worked as a maintenance supervisor at the University of Athens. He was a bona fide worker and thus credible in the otherwise unsoiled sect. He was also a GRU informant, straight Stalinist KKE from start to finish. He sat three rows behind Calista on the bus to Exarcheia.

Chapter 29

"Do you take the ferry from Piraeus?"

"No. Perama. It is shorter, and Piraeus is always busy."

"I've never been to Salamis. It is a restricted base, right?"

"It is secure. I'm sure I could arrange your entry if you like. But today, my business is official, and I must go alone. Greece is receiving submarines from Italy. Perhaps we will talk this evening?"

Stavros said, "Sure. We need to discuss Meltemi." Meltemi was code for the campaign to infiltrate the GRU by doubling the rezidentura. "Did Greece buy these ships?"

"No. No. The submarines *Poseidon* and *Amfitriti* are war reparations. [32] Greece has already taken possession of the destroyers *Doxa* and *Niki*, as well as two minesweepers and a tanker. These too are reparations. I will be there to look important. I have no other function. I know nothing about submarines," lied Christakis. While he looked important in his formal dress uniform, he was going to Salamis for another reason.

"All right. We'll talk later. Call me at the hotel."

Christakis hung up the telephone without saying goodbye.

The ceremony at Salamis was formal and dry. Italian naval dignitaries and their Greek counterparts made windy speeches and stood for photographs. Greek reporters and cameramen hovered about the dais while the second level of officers, men like Christakis, stood in the lower crowd and mingled with their Italian equivalents.

In labored but understandable Greek, an Italian officer said to Christakis, "These events are tedious but better than shooting at each other."

Christakis answered in Italian, "The pains of peace." That was code. The men continued in Italian, hushed and guarded.

The Italian officer said, "The Service reports an unfortunate accident aboard one of our commercial fishing boats two days ago. A man overboard wearing iron jewelry."

Christakis said, "Unfortunate. Do we know how he and his doctor arranged the fakery?"

The Italian officer shook his head, "No. The GRU got to his doctor; they set up the phony surgery. He was waiting for details on his escape when we hijacked the plan. A hospital orderly was his contact, a Greek. We didn't get a name."

Christakis nodded to his acquaintance, broke contact, then continued milling about the crowd.

That evening, alone in his hotel, Stavros heard a knock at his door. It was Dimitra. She carried a small, cloth travel bag and wore her dig attire—dungarees, a heavy shirt with military epaulets, and a faded mid-length cloth coat. She wore her hair tied back and no makeup. Her eyes penetrated his soul, and she smiled at his surprise. She said, "Am I invited in?"

Stavros said, "Absolutely. Come in, relax. Sit here. He motioned to a gray, French country, high-back chair next to his writing desk. She entered and lowered her bag onto the chair.

"You are a surprise. I didn't expect you until this weekend. Is everything okay?" he asked.

"It is fine. I am two days early because the Ephorate wants to discuss my progress. We have just now set the grid, so I have little to report, but they want to know how I am spending Mister Marshall's money. Nosy, that's what they are. A clutch of nosy old men."

Stavros said, "I bet they just got bored without you. Most likely they want you to enliven their humdrum days. You are to be a splash of beauty and effervescence in their otherwise drab existence."

"Do I look like a beauty?" she said with a downward motion of her hands over the length of her body.

"I'm not an impartial judge," said Stavros.

"Kiss me if you don't mind engaging with the toiling rabble," she said.

Stavros smiled and kissed her. She put her arms over his shoulders and kissed him in return. The telephone rang and rang.

Chapter 30

"We've got questions about Chernov, right? Who, where, when, and with what? His identity is no secret; everybody knows who he is. There's no leverage there. If we can motivate him with money, we can fashion an approach. We just need to isolate him.

"If his motivation is young and blond, that's more difficult. We have no honey for the trap. And we're uncertain that he will respond to blackmail. He might not give a damn. Photos of him with a young woman may not present a problem, except with his wife. The GRU might see it as a breach of security and discipline, and he might fear demotion, or worse. That could be leverage. Hard to tell.

"Has your surveillance helped with any of this?

"Oh, and I'm sorry I couldn't take your call last night. Something came up," Stavros offered.

Christakis stared at Stavros with a look that said he didn't need to know anymore.

"The surveillance tells us everything we already know. He has a daily pattern of movement. He has an apartment near the embassy. But so far, we have yet to spot him with a female. He goes to the embassy early, and he leaves late. He travels in an official car with two security men. Sometimes for lunch he walks to a taverna and orders souvlaki, always pork. Always the same taverna, and always with his detail. He does this only on nice days, never in the rain. Two, maybe three times a week. These days are random. He takes his dinner at his apartment. He has a cook and a cleaner, both Russian. No doubt they are GRU vetted. We have no eavesdropping on him, not his apartment phone or his office. His mail arrives through the embassy in diplomatic pouches.

"So far, he is a blank slate. Nothing stands out," reported Christakis.

"But you know him, right?" Stavros turned the tables on Christakis. He was thinking about the photo in the CIA file. Now it was his turn to shake up their relationship with sensitive information.

Christakis didn't flinch. He hesitated, but he remained unwavering. He said, "I have met the man. This was before you arrived in Greece, before the Circle."

Stavros waited. Christakis offered nothing more. Stavros said, "Do you know him well enough to make an approach?"

"No. This would not be wise," answered Christakis. Then he fell silent.

Stavros pushed, "Would you like to tell me why it would not be wise?"

"I would like to tell you, but this is not allowed," answered Christakis.

Stavros respected what he assumed was a reference to Christakis's operational orders. Operational orders or an attempt to hide a compromising personal involvement.

"Do you know him well enough to add to our profile?" asked Stavros.

Christakis shook his head, and a chilly air of reservation descended on the park bench and their conversation.

Both men sat in silence. When the silence grew too heavy, threatening to break the bond, Christakis said, "Your CIA has photographs, no?"

Stavros nodded. "They have photographs and a report filed after the war that said you are an impostor. It was from a debrief of Gouzenko. Do you know the name?"

Christakis nodded.

"The report said the real Christakis died during the German invasion and that you assumed his identity. They assume you are GRU.

"In your defense, I told them that Greek names are hard to transliterate. And that a name like yours, spelled with the letter Chi, can be hard to render in English. The report was from six years ago and came to the CIA via the Canadians, then the FBI, so I'm not convinced of its reliability," said Stavros.

Christakis again fell silent. Then he said, subdued, "You saved my life from the boar. You could have let it kill me, and all your concern about GRU would have died with me. Why did you save me?"

"I didn't think about it. Saving you was not an operational decision. You seemed like a good guy, and you needed help. That's all," Stavros assured him.

"I cannot claim to be good, but I am not GRU. The CIA has incorrect information. Or, perhaps, incomplete information."

"Would you like to complete the picture?" asked Stavros.

"Not now. But I owe you my honor, and with that I swear I am not GRU and that you and your invisible employer are not my enemy. We are on the same side." Christakis turned to Stavros and his eyes belied truth and depth of commitment.

The men again sat in silence. The morning air was warming in the November sun. It was Friday and schoolchildren walked and skipped their way to class carrying their books in strapped bundles. A group of four young girls passed singing the Greek national anthem. Christakis said, "They must learn "Hýmnos is tin Eleftherían" by their third year demotiko. It is a national requirement."

"'Hymn to Liberty,' it's a magnificent, dignified work. Not all national anthems can claim that," said Stavros.

"It is from an 1823 poem by Solomos. He wrote it to honor our War of Independence, our liberation from centuries of Turkish domination. It resonates like the ringing of bells in the hearts of all Greeks. The anthem transforms everyday Greeks into warriors and iconoclasts. It is a powerful meditation, *ancient valor rising*."

This was the first time Stavros had heard Christakis say anything philosophical. He interpreted it as revelatory, an emotional opening, affirmation of friendship. He believed Christakis was not GRU. He believed the Greek was an ally. But Christakis was not painting a complete picture. The picture Stavros saw was more than an imprimatura but far from finished.

Christakis was an early pencil sketch on raw canvas in black and white with subtle shades of gray.

"How do you think we should move ahead on Chernov?" asked Stavros.

"We will keep watching him. I will see about introducing someone at the taverna. Perhaps we can recruit someone, a waiter or waitress maybe. Everyone as vulnerabilities. Chernov is no different. We must be patient and careful. What Kopali said is true. Chernov is an old wolf who has seen many tricks and traps," said Christakis.

"What's the name of the taverna? I may drop in for lunch some rainy day."

"Kitsoulas, on Filikis Etaerias off Antistaseos. Don't go there alone. Take a friend, a female. And don't look American."

Chapter 31

"Would you like to go to lunch some rainy day?"

"What are you talking about? Rain? Are you making for me a puzzle? Why would I go out in the rain? Don't be clever. Tell me what you want."

"I want company on a rainy day. It's work," said Stavros.

"Work . . . ah, a spy game. If it rains on Monday, we can go. After that, I will leave for Aphaia."

"How was your presentation at the Ephorate?"

"The men on the Ephorate are far removed from their ancient and storied excavations. To hear them tell their tales, one discovered the Acropoli, one Delphi, one the Lions of Delos. They amaze themselves. They stare at me like I am a curiosity and ask questions as they might an undergraduate.

"Still, if this is the price to pay for Mister Marshall's money, so be it. This I can weather. We have weathered worse, no?"

Stavros flashed back to the cavalry raid on the Nafpaktos jail, the joint OSS and EAM-ELAS operation that had freed Yiorgos, Dimitra's second in command. The searing image of Dimitra astride the black stallion, Diablo, rearing the horse to improbable height fired in his mind. All he said was, "Far worse. Then you'll go with me?"

"Yes, we have a date."

"One other thing, I can't look American."

Dimitra raised one eyebrow. She stared at Stavros like an entomologist might view a specimen under magnification. Now the puzzle that was Stavros captured her undivided attention.

Chapter 32

It was early afternoon on a rainy Monday when the tall, bearded, and bespeckled Orthodox priest entered the taverna Kitsoulas with a mysterious veiled companion in black. His cassock and the lace that brushed her shoulders were courtesy of the CIA wardrobe maintained at the safe house in Kifissia. When he showed them to Dimitra at the Grande Bretagne, she'd said, "This is a joke, no? This is your American holiday Halloween?"

He shook his head.

A man Stavros assumed to be the owner greeted them at the door. He was reverential. Stavros was certain this was treatment extended few other customers. He showed the couple to a table, told them of the daily specials, and asked if he could bring them a drink.

Dimitra did all the talking. Stavros was fluent in Greek, but no Greek would miss his American accent, and after all these years, his conversational constructions were often formal.

Dimitra said, "If you have a white wine, perhaps Gavalas, I will have one. My priest is fasting. He will have water. Only I will order a meal."

The owner nodded and left the table.

Stavros looked at Dimitra and muttered, "Nobody said anything about fasting. I'm hungry."

Dimitra said, "Your pain adds depth to your performance. Now remain silent."

Stavros was there to observe. So far, the taverna was typical. It was doing a brisk business for a rainy Monday in November. His eyes scanned the room as he sat with his back to the door.

The owner returned with a menu, one glass of Gavalas, and another of water. Dimitra thanked him, and he said that a waitress would be back to take their orders. Then he corrected himself. Nodding to the priest, he said, "Order."

Dimitra pushed her veil back over her head and sipped her wine with a satisfied smile. Stavros grimaced at the water. Five minutes later, a young waitress arrived at their table with a pad. She looked at Dimitra and asked what she would like. Dimitra ordered a pork souvlaki, and the waitress looked at the priest. Dimitra told her that her priest is fasting. But it was not serenity in the priest's eyes behind the fake spectacles, it was surprise. With her blond hair pulled back and wearing the working clothes of a waitress, Stavros hadn't recognized her. Now, looking into her green eyes, he saw the model in Penelope's photographs.

She said to Stavros, "You must return when you are not fasting. We serve excellent food." Then she nodded to the priest and set off with her order.

Dimitra caught his look of revelation and asked, "Do you know her?"

Stavros shook his head. Dimitra wasn't convinced.

The young waitress returned with the order, and Dimitra asked her, "Is your taverna always busy on Mondays?"

The waitress said, "I couldn't tell you. I don't work Mondays, mostly Fridays and Saturdays. I'm part-time. I go to school."

"What do you study?" asked Dimitra.

"Fine art, sculpting, and painting," she responded.

"Excellent choices. I wish you well," said Dimitra.

The young waitress nodded and moved away to another table.

She whispered to her priest, "There, you have all the information a spy should need."

Stavros said nothing and thought, *If you only knew.*

Dimitra drove the Morris, and Stavros removed his fake beard and eyeglasses. He shed the cassock and replaced it with his jacket. Dimitra removed the veil and tossed it into the rear seat.

They were on the way back to the Grande Bretagne so she could change, grab her things, and catch the last ferry to Aphaia.

She asked, "Do you want to tell me from where you know the young woman?"

Stavros stayed silent. He didn't want to lie to Dimitra. He knew that any mention of Penelope would start a row, an unwinnable fight. An outcome he deserved. But Penelope was now part of an operation. So, in his mind, dishonesty, and the sin of omission, transmuted into a matter of operational security. He said, "I've seen her in photographs. She's a model."

"Photographs? Of what kind? Where?"

"I can't say."

"You can't or you won't?"

"I can't say because it might prejudice a matter of security."

"When do you plan to tell me you are a spy?" Dimitra demanded. "You say you love me. You say you want me in your life. This can never be if we cannot share the truth. I am not a babe in the woods, Stavros. You and I have lived lives that require secrecy and security. You either trust me or you don't."

She was getting heated, and Stavros knew this couldn't end well. There was one way out.

He said, "All right. I work for the CIA. I have a mission. You guessed it. Bravo."

She was silent for many blocks, shifting the Morris and weaving through traffic. Then she asked, "Are you in danger?"

He shrugged.

"That is not an answer. Are you in danger?"

He said, "I don't think so, not now. It is early in the mission."

"Then you will tell me when this mission becomes dangerous. I might help in that case."

He said, "No. I don't want you involved."

"We are in love. We are involved. I may have valuable contacts. Do you not remember from where I came?"

As the Morris pulled under the hotel's portico, he replied, "How could I forget."

The image of Dimitra on Diablo replayed in his thoughts.

In his hotel suite, he superseded Dimitra on Diablo with Dimitra dressing. She was flawless. He watched her take off the black sheath, wiggling her shoulders out then letting it drop to the marble floor of the bathroom. In her underwear, she gathered the dress, folded it and put it in her travel bag. The ritual of women dressing, and undressing was to Stavros like catnip to a feline. He couldn't resist, not with a woman proportioned and composed as Dimitra.

With her eyes never leaving the mirror, she said to him, "I want you to be careful. I don't want to know the details and fine edges of what you are doing. But you must, if we are to have a future, you must tell me the big news. Do you understand?" Not waiting for an answer, she went on, "If you are in danger, you must tell me. If I can help, you must tell me.

"When we excavate, perhaps you can come to Aphaia, and I will show you our site. We won't start for another week, maybe two. It depends on the weather. The rain you called for today will slow us. Otherwise, I will return in a month for another session with the Ephorate. Perhaps we will see each other before then, no?"

She bowed her head and shook her hair, then flipped it back, gathered it and tied it. She slipped into her dungarees and work shirt, washed, and pressed from the hotel laundry. She turned to look at Stavros lying on the king bed, arms behind his head, watching her like a movie. All he said was, "Got it."

It was three in the afternoon, and the ferry to Aphaia left Piraeus at five. As they drove to the port, Stavros said, "Let me ask you something?"

She looked over at him, head cocked, and said, "What is that?"

"Now that you know the real reason I'm in Greece, does it change anything between us?"

"Change? How?"

"I don't know. I'm asking you?"

"The only change is that being a spy for the American CIA is more dangerous than researching a doctorate. I will worry about you more. That is all. Before you told me the truth, I worried about you, because your secret was obvious and all but said. Now I will worry about you with the full confidence that you are a spy and a laggard."

Stavros shook his head and smiled. This was the pontificating Dimitra who had swept him from admiration to agape all those years ago in the mountains of Chómori. Her chiding showed she cared, proof that he mattered enough for her to berate. Otherwise, she would never have wasted her breath.

At the ferry, he parked the Morris, got out, and came to her side to open her door. She stepped out, and he retrieved her bag from the second seat. She took it from him, and he said, "Good luck on the dig. I hope you get set up and find a treasure."

"Don't be ridiculous; that is not how archaeology works. You know as much."

"I know I will miss you," he said.

"And I you. But this will pass. We will see each other in time. You have my order to be careful. Athens is complex, much more than your childish American mind can ever grasp. For centuries, its people, its ways birthed complexity and confusion in every generation. Always new, always unforeseen, always adding mystery. You must look not at the first strata, the obvious, but at the second or third layer, much like a dig. When you visit Aphaia, I will teach you. Bring your notebook.

"Kiss me. I must go."

He did, and he watched her stride into the mass of passengers waiting to board. She parted the milling crowd of tourists, locals, merchants, and priests like the bow of a valorous trireme piercing Aegean chop. He thought, *What a woman!*

Chapter 33

The Greek KKE had faced exile and chaos following defeat in 1949. While the communists declined, the Greek right wing ascended. Radical anti-communist elements were not only tolerated under British tutelage during German occupation but promoted and supported. The British handed the Greek project to the Americans when they ran out of money in 1947, and the new paymasters took a different bent. Then another bent.

The American political mission counseled law and order and liberal, conciliatory politics as the way forward for the war-torn country. The Americans insisted on weeding out violent anti-communists and off-the-book death squads. Moderates replaced far-right ministers tempering the new Greek government. So long as the Americans were writing the checks, the Greeks had little choice.

Even before the Americans were in charge, in 1947, they and the British had engineered replacing Napoleon Zervas, then the elected Minister for Public Order. During the war, Zervas had enjoyed Churchill's favor. He led EDES, a small resistance movement with a rightist bent based in the western mountains. EDES sometimes fought, then sometimes collaborated with the Nazis. EDES also targeted EAM-ELAS, the bigger resistance force operating throughout Greece. As minister, Zervas conducted inefficient reforms of the gendarmerie and mass arrests of communists. This brought Dwight Griswold, head of the American Economic Mission in Greece, to the conclusion, "I feel he is making more communists than he is eliminating."[33] Zervas returned to the Greek cabinet as Minister of Public Works in September 1950. He was again weeded out a year later, this time by the Americans.

America's politicians in Greece were on one bent and the CIA on another. While the American Mission made headway toward a more civilized and inclusive political ecology, under the surface, things were different.

During German occupation, the far-right Greek fascists gravitated to the collaborationist Security Battalions. They did the bidding of the German occupiers and tortured resistance fighters while they pillaged, raped, and burned their way through the Greek countryside and towns. Other rightists, perhaps less terroristic, affiliated with the EDES resistance. EDES and Zervas were anti-communist and fickle royalists. EDES won the bulk of Britain's arms and ammunition. EDES commanders, though much less involved in fighting Germans, received high praise on BBC broadcasts and field decorations for their bravery. The BBC seldom mentioned EAM-ELAS, who fought the Germans more and whose commanders turned down decorations, requesting instead boots and guns. The eight American OSS commando groups that fought in Greece during the occupation, like the one Stavros led, paired with EAM-ELAS guerrillas. The EAM-ELAS coalition included communists. The Americans praised these partisans. EAM-ELAS never let them down, always had their backs, and never breached security.

When the occupation ended, and the Germans left Greece, the political war began. The Germans left in October 1944, and by December, Greeks were fighting Greeks in the streets of Athens. Many rightists, those not already enlisted, migrated into the Hellenic Army and the police forces.

By 1951, the leadership core of Greek rightists had clustered in a clandestine cell called Holy Bond.[34] Holy Bond originated in 1945 among the officer corps of the Security Battalions. From 1947 on, Holy Bond was a CIA front drawing a million dollars a year.[35]

Another rightist layer, this one above the board, was a Greek special operations unit working with NATO and the CIA. This was the Mountain Raiding Companies, LOK.[36] Formed early in 1947, LOK challenged KKE control in their mountain redoubts. Field Marshal Alexander Papagos purged LOK of "almost all men with views ranging from moderately conservative to left-wing."[37] The First Paratroopers Brigade of

LOK trained for CIA Stay Behind duties known in Greece as Operation Sheepskin. Holy Bond infiltrated LOK.

The Italians were engaged in their own Stay Behind commitments and recruitment. And, as Director Broccoli had told Christakis of his concerns about *certain disruptive elements* recruited into Gladio, he carried the same concerns for Greece. Christakis's mission for SIFAR was to uncover the undercover rightists and fascists making their way into Sheepskin and report to SIFAR. This was his primary mission, and doubling Chernov was secondary. Greek rightists and their fascist allies were a tough crowd and a tougher nut. Christakis knew to be cautious. His targets were killers, and death by their hands would not be quick.

Stavros was not in the CIA Stay Behind loop. Scuttlebutt was all he warranted. To him, Chernov was the big prize, and Stay Behind was a whole other universe.

Christakis worked for the Greek Ministry for Public Security, separate and apart from his ultimate loyalty to SIFAR. At the Ministry, Christakis analyzed reports and spent limited time in the field on undercover assignments. He specialized in mountain banditry, a criminal element laid low during the German occupation when resistance groups recruited bandits or shot them.

Mountain brigands were storied and revered, some of it true. Over the centuries, their reputation grew from unalloyed thievery to heroic lore. From humble beginnings as tax-dodging Greeks fleeing Ottoman rule in the fifteenth century, the Klephts burnished their repute four centuries later in the War of Independence. Bloody harassment of the Turks and selfless bravery won them the signature "noble bandits." Their colorful songs and dance enlivened Greek culture. They perfected a popular cooking technique, kleftiko, a pitted fire to hide smoke while cooking pilfered lambs. Klephts, or their popular legend, were a blurry notion of Robin Hood, Spartacus, and Al Capone. Christakis was not a romantic. Now, with the return of law and order, and foreign occupiers vanquished, the Klephts' glossy revolutionary patina was matted, and they had reverted to a dull if persistent criminality.

Christakis, like all diligent security operatives, maintained Klepht contacts and informants. Over five centuries of notoriety, the Klephts had dabbled not only in mountain thievery but in black markets, subversive organizations, and gunrunning. A well-connected Klepht could open doors otherwise bolted and tell of things never spoken of. Christakis drew a car from the motor pool and set off to visit an old acquaintance, Makris, on Mount Giona, near where the boar almost gored him. As far as the Ministry for Public Security knew, he was working his bandit beat. But Christakis was after much more than Klephts, and asking the wrong question might get him killed.

Chapter 34

"What you ask, this is a dangerous request. These men, they do not suffer two types, communists, and pretenders. I know you are not a communist, Alexis, but a pretender is an equal enemy to them. Should I arrange an introduction, you will need a wolf pelt of impenetrable strength and durability, one that protects you from disclosure and bullets. Do you have such? Can you act a role so well as to save your life?

"My advice to you, Alexis, is from the heart. All the years I have known your family, wept at their funerals, drunk at their weddings, my advice is you forget this idea. These men, the Holy Bond, they are insane with hatred. They believe they are gods on earth who alone can cleanse Greece of its communist infection. They are secret like the Filiki Eteria and, in their minds, just as ennobled. Are you certain you want an introduction?"

Makris was an old man now, blind in one eye and white everywhere that hair still grew. His long beard and scraggly mane framed his one good eye, the color of milk. His face was as rough as the mountainside where he lived. Makris was a Klepht and retired, at least from active banditry. His small, well-tended cottage of stone and terracotta stood on the eastern slope of Mount Giona at an elevation just below the highest tree line. The village of Viniani was five kilometers east. He rode there on this trusty mule, Astrofengiá, Starlight, every few weeks in the temperate months. When the winter snows fell, he stayed at home.

Makris claimed centuries of Klepht lineage and boasted of his great-grandfather's membership in the 1814 secret society dedicated to freeing Greece from the Ottomans, Filiki Eteria. In that society his great-grandfather had fought alongside Dimitrios Makris, a fabled leader of the 1821 War of Independence, and it was for this hero that his father named him.

Christakis listened to the old man and paused before he answered. In a calm voice, he said, "It is a day in Greece, Italy, and all throughout Europe where these men are not the friends of freedom. Their plans and actions will not help Greece, not now. They seek only power for themselves, not the people. Neither Klephts nor honorable citizens will withstand their rule. They are in league with the fascists who rained fire and blood on Greece so many years. Their loyalty is to something alien, not of this mountain, nor this region, nor Greece. I have a duty to uncover these men and with your help, this I intend.

"You speak of a wolf pelt. I will need even more. No? Dolon wore a wolf pelt, yet Odysseus and Diomedes found him crawling among the Greek dead on the shores of Troy at midnight. The wolf pelt did not send him back to Hector with news of the Greek ships. It delivered him into the hands of his enemy, there to lose his head.

"I live a wolf pelt. The Ministry is my pelt, pelt enough for these ghosts. Holy Bond may have others from the Ministry in their ranks. I have no way to know.

"Makris, I want you to consider only one thing. You are a man I respect and one who has helped my family. You are a friend. Should my pelt fail, will you be in danger from the introduction?" asked Christakis.

"Me? Ha! Me in danger! How do you endanger an old man whose family is long gone and has nothing worth stealing? You make me laugh, Alexis. Just as I would laugh at Holy Bond, should they come for revenge.

"My days are few. I would take three times the men with me, should they come. It would not be an economical mission for them. No, Alexis, the decision is yours. If you want an introduction, this *I* can arrange. If you want to live, this *you* must arrange."

"Please arrange it," said Christakis.

Makris nodded.

Christakis went on, "I have a car. Do you need anything else from the village while I am here?"

"No. The ham you brought me will last months, and the cheese I will nibble. I eat like a bird these days. I have Skylla. He is as old as me! But he still carries me. Ever year he fades, and every year I become a lighter burden.

"This year's winter is late. There are many years when snow would already block the path. But this year is late, and from the clouds, I see no threat.

"I expect this week a visitor. This will allow me to ask about an introduction. I will send with this visitor a letter instructing you. I know not how, only that you must expect it. If a meeting is possible, this letter will say how that will happen. If it is not. . . ." Makris shrugged.

"I learned you took a large boar this season. The other side of the mountain, no?"

Christakis nodded, "Yes. He wasn't free, he made me pay with my knee, but it is much better now."

"I need to thank you for the hind quarter. It is salted and hangs now in the shed," said Makris.

"I am pleased you can make of it some use."

"I will make of it all use! Nothing goes to waste in this house."

Christakis smiled and rose from the chair in front of the stone fireplace. Above the chestnut mantel, a battered Mannlicher M1895 rested on prongs made of deer antler. Christakis looked at the weapon. Battered it might have been, but Makris kept it oiled and buffed. Christakis asked, "Where do you find ammunition for the Mannlicher?"

"Ah! This weapon has been re-chambered for the eight-by-fifty-six-millimeter cartridge. These are no problem. Many rounds left from the war."

Christakis nodded. He took a step toward the seated Makris. He shook his hand, and said, "Thank you for your help. I hope to see you again before your winter incarceration."

Makris smiled a gap-toothed grin and padded Christakis's grip with his free hand.

Chapter 35

Stavros waffled. Meeting Calista, even without knowing her name, presented a quandary. One with many sides and just as many downfalls. The fastest way to know more about Calista, and how he might use her to double Chernov, was to talk to Penelope. But that approach was fraught. Penelope was like flypaper. Once touched, she might never pull away. But this, Stavros acknowledged, was a ship already set sail. Maybe Penelope was mature and cosmopolitan and had seen their night together as . . . what? The titillating start of a prolonged romance? A convenient pairing? A friendly but somehow professional fling? Stavros didn't like any of these formulations. Lust and hubris leading to guilt and regret. That's what had happened. But, he told himself, had he not gone with Penelope that night, he would never have known about the model. Thus, his lust was now his mission.

He thought of Penelope as a bright, ambitious, young woman with a crush on him. To go any further, to encourage her crush, would lead her to believe more was possible. Penelope and Stavros would go nowhere so long as Dimitra hovered in and out of his life.

Stavros needed to know more about the model. An approach to Chernov by his fantasy might prove productive. If Stavros could dangle the model, he would have an advantage. Perhaps dangle the model and offer money at the same time? It wasn't a plan, but it was more than nothing. He needed to know more about the model. That meant time with Penelope.

And what could he ask Penelope? He couldn't ask about the model—how to get in touch, what's she like, would she be honey for a trap? This was delicate. He didn't want Penelope to think she was being used, although that was what he intended.

Why did the model have a cab driver bring her and the mislaid file folder to Penelope's building? What the heck was the file folder about? It contained information about the American

Economic Commission, a weekly schedule, of what value was that? And why was Penelope playing coy about it?

The more Stavros tried to make his way through the rough, the thicker the tall grass. He'd have to see Penelope. Or maybe he could return to the taverna on Friday or Saturday as himself, not a fasting priest, and see if he might recruit the model. That would be risky. The taverna was a place Chernov frequented, and it was under surveillance. The GRU might spot Stavros, connect him to the model, and blow the entire approach. It would be best to make contact away from the taverna.

It would take longer, but he could request a team on the model, track her movements, find out where she lived, then make an approach. But to request a CIA team would increase the circle of players, something that Frank Wisner had warned against. This operation, turning Chernov, went straight to the top. No local leaks. That was boss's orders. Stavros could ask Christakis for a team, but again, that would widen the circle. No, this was a job Stavros needed to do. He'd follow her from work and go from there.

Stavros was a conspicuous tail. He was tall and memorable. He'd practice surveillance and countersurveillance in Washington, DC, against other OPC trainees and seasoned spies. But in Athens, he was inexperienced. And, in his training, he always paired with a partner. Christakis might help, but he shouldered responsibilities of his own.

If he could get an introduction through Penelope, he could meet the model without pretense. His thoughts circled back to Penelope, time with Penelope. It wasn't hard to be with her, just the opposite. She was an inviting dalliance of undetermined but poisonous blowback for Stavros. Poisonous but pivotal to the mission.

Stavros thought about the things that mattered in his life. Things that might suffer blowback. There was Dimitra, his job, his dissertation, his life, his stepmother and father, Marta and Alex, and that was it. Of these, besides his life, the downside to

Penelope was Dimitra. But Dimitra was a moving target. Where were they going? Marriage? Maybe, but doubtful. Cohabitation? Plausible, but where? Children? Unlikely without cohabitation.

He considered bringing Dimitra into the scenario, telling her everything. She knew now that he worked for the CIA. The rest, the details, were puzzle pieces scattered in a dark room. Stavros could turn on the light, bring Dimitra up to speed on everything, and get her thoughts. She would excoriate and shun him for his night with Penelope. After that storm, she might be a partner in the mission. But that wasn't fair. Dimitra was tough. Dimitra was no one's fool. Stavros had stood with her in battle. She had led fighters with confidence and boldness. She had woven a delicate escape route through KKE political landmines, an exit that others died trying to make. But it wasn't fair. She wasn't CIA, and she wasn't expendable. He admitted, if only to himself, this mission could turn deadly. The GRU played by strict rules, their rules. If he were blown, discovered and vulnerable, the GRU would care about only one thing. If Stavros would not turn on the CIA, *he* would be expendable. And Stavros could not be turned.

That evening, after two Napoleons in Alexander's Bar, Stavros called Penelope from his room.

"How are you tonight," he asked.

"I am fine. It is good to hear from you. How did your travels go?"

Stavros remembered his lie about traveling. He said, "All went well. Say, I'd like to ask you a favor?"

"Of course, what is it?"

"You offered to put me in touch with someone at the university who might help with my research. Can we have lunch and discuss that?"

"Certainly. Will Thursday work? I'm open," she said.

"That's good. Where do you want to meet?"

"Do you know the taverna Kitsoulas?"

Chapter 36

"Comrade Colonel, this report I thought you should see."

"Yes. Tell me what it says. I don't have time to read a report. Tell me the important part," prodded Chernov.

"Sir. Our informant in the KKE splinter sect, The Torch, says that he believes their leader is planning direct action against the capitalists. An assassination. He has no more information but believes their leader, a man who goes by Achilles, is planning this. This leader has dropped hints in his lectures that something big will propel the sect forward to the vanguard. He said that the cell should make ready for revolutionary discipline soon. Sir."

"How many followers does this Achilles have?"

"Twenty-five to thirty, no more, sir."

"Are they armed?"

"No. This is not reported."

"Then by the devil's hand, how do they plan to make a revolution?" asked a perturbed Chernov.

Before his aide could answer, the rezidentura held up his palm.

"Send for Kozlov. He is between active assignments. I'll talk to him tomorrow morning. Tell him to come sober."

"Yes, sir."

"You are dismissed, lieutenant."

Chapter 37

Christakis was back on Mount Giona as the letter from Holy Bond had instructed. He waited at a small roadside park north of Sikia, near where they had taken the boar. The park was a car pullout with spring water flowing from a modest stone monument and a battered picnic table. A wood rail fence and stonewalls defined the tidy space but were no impediment to coming and going. Sikia rose in the valley of the Mornos River at a lower elevation. It fell within the zone of deciduous trees, giving Christakis an excellent field of vision through the leafless oaks.

He sat exposed on the top of the picnic table and lifted his eyes to the sky when a golden eagle screeched. The air was crystalline. A faint scent of wood smoke drifted up from Sikia. He was unarmed, as the letter instructed. It was nine o'clock, and Mount Giona had just allowed the morning sun over its peak. The first rays warmed Christakis, and he faced east to gather its energy.

He heard them before he saw them. Two men, both carrying shotguns, approached from a hikers' trail that led down the hillside to the Mornos. They talked with no concern for stealth. They weren't hunters, at least not hunters of boar.

Christakis pretended to be a tourist who had stopped along the scenic roadway to relieve himself and drink of the cool mountain spring. He smiled and greeted the two men with, "Kaliméra."

Both men stopped ten paces from Christakis at the crest of the trail. The taller man spoke. He asked, "Are you Christakis?"

Christakis nodded.

"We have questions for you. Are you prepared?"

Christakis nodded again.

"Why do you seek Holy Bond?"

Christakis replied, "Brothers, may I ask your names?"

"You may ask, but we are the ones carrying guns. You will answer us. Do not evade."

Christakis nodded, "As you wish. I seek Holy Bond because I see the communists rotting Greece from within. I served in the Sacred Band during the war, in Athens and the Dodecanese, under General Tsigantes. I work now at the Ministry for Public Security, and I see and hear many things that would interest Holy Bond. I feel it is a matter of honor to seek Holy Bond and rid Greece of traitors."

"We know of your military service. We are not without intelligence. What is your position at the Ministry?"

"I am an analyst with responsibility for mountain brigands. Also, I represent the Ministry at formal events and conferences," replied Christakis.

"And what is your connection to the Italians?" asked the tall man, raising the muzzle of his shotgun level with Christakis's chest. The second man followed his lead.

Christakis flinched imperceptibly, but he flinched, his confidence shaken. At ten paces, he didn't think his inquisitors saw it.

"I am related to Italians from generations ago. My grandfather came to Greece to fight in the War of 1897, the Greco-Turkish War. He fought at Domokos under Ricciotti Garibaldi. The Turks routed his battalion, and he retreated with his surviving countrymen into the Tsamadoráchi hills.

"My great-grandfather was Greek, born and raised. He fought in the War of Independence with the Souliotes. He was wounded at Karpenisi and sent to a hospital of the Great Powers in Missolonghi. There, he nearly lost his leg, but he found an Italian nurse, my great-grandmother. They moved to Salento after the war, in the boot heel. My family lived in Italy until my grandfather's return."

"And when did you become SIFAR?"

"I do not know what you mean. I am Greek, I work for the Ministry. That is my attachment."

Christakis didn't like the turn of events. He could see the eyes of his inquisitor harden and the muscles of his forearm tense. His trigger finger twitched.

"We know. Do you think we do not have men in SIFAR, patriotic Italians who will rid their country of communists? You come to us under pretense, Christakis. If you worship as a Roman Catholic or as a Greek, now is the time to speak with your lord."

Christakis stood on the bench of the picnic table, then stepped to the earth. The tall man motioned for him to raise his arms. Christakis did. As he raised his arms, he made a looping circle with his right hand while pretending to hobble on his bad knee.

Twenty meters away, behind a boulder outcrop, he heard a masterly *Fermo! Fermo!* Dante launched like shot from a cannon. His ruddy coat was the color of earth and his attack so unexpected that neither man drew a bead. He was on the tall man in a second. His one hundred pounds of fury flew the last two meters through the still morning air, knocking the man from his feet. Then Dante's maw closed on his right arm with the force of a bear trap. The companion tried to take aim, but Dante was a blur as the two bodies writhed in the dust.

A shot rang from behind the outcrop, this one from a rifle. The companion fell dead before he hit the ground. Christakis ran to the struggle, picked up the shotgun, and leveled it at the tall man, still fighting with the brute. Christakis's whistle pierced the mayhem. Dante was just about to release his grip on the man's arm and go for his throat. But at the shrill command he withdrew and came to Christakis's side. Christakis could tell the dog was disappointed, he wanted to finish the job. Christakis said, "Good, Dante."

Basil and Atticus joined Christakis lording over the grimacing tall man.

"We should finish this swine," said Basil.

"Yes, but not now. For this one, I have questions," said Christakis.

The tall man tried to right himself, and Dante loosed a growl that rose from the bowels of Hades. The tall man lay again on the ground.

"We will blindfold him and take him from here. You know where," said Christakis.

Basil nodded.

Christakis asked, "Where did you leave your truck?"

"Up the roadway, on a fire trail."

"We should move him before anyone drives by."

Basil nodded to Atticus, who left at a trot to get the truck.

"For now, gag and blindfold him and tie him. We'll put him in the car's boot. We'll use the truck for the last leg; the car will not make it."

Basil nodded and shoved a wad of cloth into the tall man's mouth. He tied the man's arms behind him and his feet together with two ready-cut binds tucked into his belt. Then he pulled a dark cloth from his pocket, wrapped it around his head, and knotted it tightly at the back of the man's skull. Christakis and Basil lifted the man like a burlap sack of potatoes up and into the car's boot. They gathered the dead body of his companion and threw it on top of the prisoner. Christakis slammed the trunk lid, disappointed that it didn't strike an appendage.

Basil said, "He was carrying this." And he handed Christakis a freshly issued American .45 semiautomatic pistol.

Christakis said, "Finders keepers, just like the Americans."

Basil said, "You keep it. I still have mine from the OSS."

Christakis and Basil waited for Atticus as if enjoying the scenery from the picnic table. When they heard the truck coming, Basil asked, "What do you plan to tell Rome?"

"I haven't decided. Holy Bond has infiltrated SIFAR. We will tell Rome nothing for now. Let us see what this *malakas* has to say for himself," said Christakis.

Atticus arrived, and Basil carried the two shotguns to the truck and told him the plan. Atticus called Dante to the truck.

The animal jumped into the bed and circled it twice. Atticus reversed the truck and started back up the mountain. Basil and Christakis followed in the car.

Chapter 38

Stavros was in luck. The model was not working; she was nowhere in sight. The taverna was busy and he assumed his natural role, the American professor. He was eye-catching but not menacing. He sensed no alarm tolling.

He waited for Penelope outside the taverna under a denuded plane tree. Its leaves had departed for the year, but several orbs of spiky fruit still dangled. She was on time and rose on her toes to kiss him when they met. They walked in together. Stavros received a long glance from the owner. His height, the hardest thing to disguise, worked against him.

Today was a mouse day. Penelope wore flat shoes, a modest blue skirt, and a white blouse buttoned to the top. Her hair was back, held in a plain brown barrette, and she wore no jewelry save a gold cross on a thin chain.

"Are you teaching today?" asked Stavros.

"Indeed. How can you tell?"

"Just a lucky guess. You look like a teacher, a professor," he smiled.

"Yes. I dress for instruction. I am not much older than my students, and some boys are excitable."

"I understand their excitement," quipped Stavros.

She smiled and winked.

They sat at a table along the wall adorned with newspaper clippings mounted on wooden plaques, articles about the taverna, and awards from dining associations and travel publications. She saw him look over the mementos. She said, "This is a good taverna, popular with university faculty. We are near many embassies and often international staff eat here. Perhaps an ambassador? We may have a cosmopolitan lunch, no? You will know someone else who will be here."

Stavros cocked his head.

Penelope went on, "The model, Calista."

He tried to act unaware.

"From my photographs. The young woman. You know her, at least you know what she looks like, no?"

"Oh, her," he dissembled.

"Yes. She works here. If she is not busy, I will introduce you."

Stavros couldn't tell if this meeting was going well or headed completely off the rails.

"She works at noon, so we are a bit early," said Penelope.

Stavros regained his footing. He asked, "So, what does she do? She's a student, right? Isn't that what you told me?"

She's a student and she models, too. You can imagine why she is much requested. Those looks . . . I am so, so jealous," said Penelope in a fake, threatening tone.

"Okay, we've been over this before," said Stavros. "Penelope, you are a lovely and intriguing woman." Then Stavros clipped his flow of compliments, remembering where this monologue had led the last time.

She smiled and said, "Thank you. I was fishing for that."

Stavros chuckled.

"Should we talk about your dissertation?" she asked.

"Right. Well, if you can arrange it, I'd like to meet with someone versed in ancient navies. Fourth and fifth centuries BCE. I'm interested in shipbuilding and its military and political implications," said Stavros. "I'm trying to tie together social, economic, military, and, I suppose, cultural contributions. Do you think that's too broad?"

"I do not know. If you were standing for a degree at the University of Athens in wage development, my opinion might have value. But how am I to know what . . . what is it called, Park University?"

Stavros corrected, "Park College."

"Park College in . . . where is it?"

"Parkville, Missouri."

"Yes, Park College in Parkville, Missouri. How am I to know their oddities? Each university, each department, each discipline, they are different, no?"

Stavros nodded, "Yes, but what do you think. What is your opinion?"

"I think you have bitten a large piece of the apple," she said.

"In America, we might say, I have bitten off more than I can chew," said Stavros.

"Yes, yes. That is another way to describe your ambition." She smiled.

Stavros smiled back. She not only critiqued his dissertation, but his mission.

She said, "I will ask *the ancient ones* to see who might be best."

Stavros cocked his head.

"That is what we call those who study things old and obscure. The ancient ones," she said.

"Right. That's clever," said Stavros. Then he thought, *I guess Dimitra would qualify as an ancient one,* but he would pay if he tried to hang that label on her.

"Well, just keep me in mind. If you think of someone I might work with, let me know," said Stavros.

"Oh, I'll keep you in mind, have no worries," she cooed through a Cheshire Cat smile.

He smiled back, and he wished, in that instant, that he were unattached, that Dimitra was not in the picture. Penelope was coy and tempting and her transparent flirtation thrilling. He told himself to get a grip.

A waitress came to the table and asked about drinks. Stavros ordered a beer and Penelope a white wine. He said, "I guess you're done teaching for the day?"

"Yes, I have only one lecture in the morning on Thursdays. The rest of the day, I *should* work on my dissertation." Her emphasis on *should* suggested tenuousness and opened the door for speculation of what else she might do this afternoon. He felts his grip falter.

Their drinks arrived, but not with the expected waitress. Calista smiled at the couple and lingered on Stavros, eyebrow raised, signaling recognition.

Penelope said, "Surprise. Calista, so good to see you. Please allow me to introduce you to my friend and fellow professor, Stavros Theofanis."

Stavros said, "It is a pleasure to meet you, Calista." Then he cut himself off before mentioning her modeling. If he admitted that, she would know he visited Penelope's apartment.

He said instead, "Penelope tells me you are a student, in fine arts?"

Calista said, "Yes, fine arts, sculpting and painting. Do you have a relative in the church? A priest, maybe?"

Stavros blushed. Evidently his disguise had not been as good as he'd hoped.

"No?"

Now she looked at him with the eye of a sculptor. He could feel her sizing his cheek bones and measuring the distance between his orbs. He should have anticipated her honed observational skills.

She let it pass. She said, "It is good to meet you. Are you lecturing at the University of Athens?"

"No. I'm here researching my PhD."

"What topic?"

"Ancient navies."

"My father could talk your ears off. He builds ships in Salonika. He has worked at it his entire life. He is a master."

"That's fascinating. Perhaps I should interview him. Can I reach you through Penelope?" he asked.

"Penelope, yes. Or at the School of Fine Arts. Just ask for Calista, they will find me."

"Thank you. That's kind," said Stavros.

She looked at Penelope and said, "I can't wait on your table, it's not in my area. This taverna is strict about waitress assignments."

Then she looked to Stavros and said, "It was a pleasure meeting you and let me know if I can put you in touch with my father. He's about your age."

Stavros's jaw slackened and Calista was off.

Penelope saw his expression. She knew Stavros was thirty-eight, young to be twenty-year-old Calista's father. She comforted him. "Young people do not know their elders' ages."

Stavros said, "Right."

Penelope had called him an elder. It took his ego a full five seconds to rebound.

The regular waitress arrived and took their orders. They were finishing lunch when Calista came to their table and asked how they liked their meals. Stavros and Penelope smiled and nodded.

Calista asked Penelope, "Do you still want to shoot on Saturday?"

Penelope said, "If you are open. We can work for maybe two hours? In the morning? With the favorable light? The weather should be clear."

Calista said, "Then I will meet you at the park. Eight in the morning?"

Penelope nodded and smiled, and Calista nodded to Stavros and was off.

"Would you like to come to our shoot this Saturday?" she asked Stavros.

"Sure, if you don't think I'll be in the way."

"I want to photograph Calista in natural light, outdoors. It is not the best time of year for this. Better in springtime, no? But Calista radiates springtime, her energy is youth and rebirth. Fecundity, fertility. She is Kore," Penelope used the ancient name for Persephone. "Calista stirs the Eleusinian Mysteries."

Penelope had slipped innocently into her spiritual persona. Stavros marveled at her modulation, intrigued by her depth.

Just as quickly, practical Penelope reemerged. She said, "Wear rough clothes for Saturday, I like to shoot far from the civilized world."

Chapter 39

The cabin was dank, the air chilly and overburdened with the smell of kerosene from the lantern. Basil said, "This one is not so tough as he pretends. And he is no lover of dogs. I offered him Dante as a companion, and he pissed himself. He was brave for less than an hour, then he broke."

Christakis asked, "Anything about the SIFAR infiltration?"

"He knows nothing. He would tell us lies if he could, but he is too scared to even lie. He was told about you and SIFAR by a superior, someone he knows as Sentinel. They met in Athens, in a park. That's where they gave him this assignment. They have you pegged as a SIFAR capitano. He was to kill you."

Christakis looked at the shivering mass of man on the wooden floor, bound and gagged and squirming like a carp on the deck of a boat. He wanted to kill him and be done with the trouble. But an instinct told him that the prisoner might be valuable.

Christakis asked Basil, "How long can we keep him here?"

Basil nodded to the doorway, and the two men stepped outside into the bracing mountain air.

Basil lit a cigarette, inhaled, then let the smoke drift away. He said, "We can keep him here a week, maybe two. I don't think Holy Bond can find him, but tending to him, feeding him, giving him water; he will need attention."

"Can Atticus help?" asked Christakis.

"Oh, yes. He will help. He is not far away."

"We need time to communicate with Rome. The director told me to speak only with him. He gave me the Sheepskin mission. I am not sure who else knew. If only the director knew, SIFAR has a big problem," said Christakis.

"Uh-huh. . . ." Basil nodded.

Chapter 40

"Speak first with the informant. He is KKE and a patriot. He can tell you about the sect. Then uncover the chain they used to plan their actions. If they plan to kill an American official, we need to know who their target is, when they plan to attack, and how they organize for the attack. If they have a source of information, I want to know who or what that is.

"As for their leader, Achilles. . . ." Chernov drew a finger across his neck. "Make it an accident."

The man sitting on the other side of Chernov's desk was forgettable. He didn't look Russian. He looked nothing. He was medium height, medium build, not muscular, no facial hair, and he wore a gray fedora without adornment. His trench coat was neither new nor tattered, its luster faded months ago. Save for the bags under his eyes, the product of vodka and insomnia, his face was unmemorable.

Kozlov was a killer, GRU trained and practiced. His methods were not always by the manual, but he got results, and in short order. Chernov didn't like him, but he liked his results.

"Questions, comrade?" asked Chernov.

Kozlov shook his head.

"You are dismissed, comrade."

Kozlov met the KKE informant at a *kafeneion* near the Soviet Embassy. The loyal Stalinist told the GRU man Achilles played the role of aloof, pensive revolutionary, with no dirt under his fingernails. He was distant in the cell with one exception. He was under the spell of a stunning, blond art student. The informant did not know where she lived, but he knew the bus stop she used when going to cell meetings. Her name was Calista, and her father was a party member in Salonika.

The informant said that Achilles would be easy to find. He enjoyed posing at tavernas and kafenios in Exarcheia. The informant did not know where Achilles worked or how he paid his rent. He suspected Achilles was the son of money. He knew this type of man from the University of Athens where he managed the workers who maintained the buildings and fixed the plumbing. His was a position risen into from years of working in his trade as an electrician.

Kozlov asked about the assassination. The informant said, "I know nothing of his plan other than that he can be read like a book. He has a smirk. A look that tells of his adventurism. He has listened to his own words for so long that he now believes them. Also, he is trying to impress the woman. He is incapable of hiding his lust. In meetings, he lectures about discipline, but he is never far from the blonde.

"I have seen them talk when no other cell members are present. He is a kitten playing with a lion."

The informant advanced his hand under the table toward Kozlov. Kozlov saw the motion and crept his hand closer. The informant placed a miniature 21mm film cassette into Kozlov's palm. Then the informant whispered, "I filmed them with the Ajax, the girl and Achilles."

The Ajax-10 was a concealable, self-advancing camera. It was 2.75 x 2 x 1 inches and the standard for 1951 Soviet espionage. The film cassette was even smaller.

"Look for Achilles on Kallidromiou Street, any taverna or kafeneion. He will pose there like a parrot with his book and notepad."

Chapter 41

"I will see them Saturday. I should know more by the end of the day. What do you think, Christakis, is this all coincidence, or is it a setup? Calista working at the taverna where Chernov eats lunch? Penelope in the Circle and connected to Calista? The file folder? I haven't told you about that. That's another mystery," prodded Stavros.

The two men sat away from curious ears in comfortable leather armchairs at the far end of the Grande Bretagne lobby. Their eyes scanned the points of entry, the main doors, the elevator, and the entrance to Alexander's Bar.

They were meeting to update on Meltemi, the operation to double Chernov. Stavros didn't know about SIFAR or Holy Bond.

"Coincidence is possible. But in espionage, unlikely," stated Christakis.

"Right. I get that. So, what do you think? Develop Calista as possible bait? Or walk away because it smells fishy?" asked Stavros.

Christakis was only half focused on Chernov and Meltemi. His mind was on Holy Bond, what to tell SIFAR, and what to do with the prisoner. "Your next meeting. You are to go into the woods with two women and take photographs?"

Stavros nodded.

"All meetings should be so enjoyable!" chided Christakis. "Meet them and develop Calista so far as you can. The risk is negligible. I suggest you get to know Calista. See if she has potential. Is she inclined to help? If she is, does she understand the risk? What will you pay for her part? Tell her what that might be. She is a student, so her pay will be low. Do you wish for backup? Should I follow undetected?"

"Thanks, but I shouldn't need backup for a photo session."

"What park?" asked Christakis.

"Kesariani, west of the university. We are to meet at the Lion Cave. Penelope said from there we can climb up into the cedars. She wants to photograph in the cedars."

Christakis said, "You will be climbing to the southwest, into Cima Imitos, the preserve. Wear good boots."

"I guess you know the location?" asked Stavros.

Christakis nodded, then he asked, "Have you considered that Penelope is under discipline?"

"For whom?" asked Stavros.

Christakis shrugged.

The scales began falling from Stavros's eyes. He said, "She just doesn't seem the type. Who would she be working for?"

Christakis said, "There is no type. Your mind is relying on a presentation. Fake perhaps. Have you slept with her?"

Stavros stumbled and didn't answer. He looked away into the distance of the lobby."

Christakis said, "That is your illusion. Men are simple to fool. It happens, but do not let the illusion determine your actions. If she believes she has you in her power, you may have to allow her to continue to believe this. If she is playing you for a fool, play the fool."

This was hard for Stavros to hear. Christakis was right. Dimitra's words returned to him: "Athens is complex, much more than your childish American mind can ever grasp."

In that instant, Stavros realized how valuable Dimitra was to him. She had entered his life in a time when trust meant everything. They had fashioned combat together and shared secrets that could have gotten them or others under their command killed. He realized from the moment he became CIA that no other woman would be as trustworthy. Dimitra's value soared, and he cursed his stupidity for dismissing it to sleep with Penelope.

Christakis said, "Of course, all of this might be what it seems. A tempting college student. An innocent professor. A gullible American. Who knows? Athens is full of intrigue, and it doesn't take a spy to invent it."

There was silence between the men.

Then Stavros asked, "Have you heard anything from your team watching Chernov?"

"No. It is the same. His routine is just that, very routine. I wonder if Chernov has met the model Calista. Since both are Russians, maybe they have a single waiter they request. It would not surprise me if the waiter is a man, possibly the owner. Yes, I will bet it is the owner. He is always there, and he has the most to lose if the GRU were to seek revenge. Using the owner would reduce the chance of Chernov's poisoning. I'll have the team report on this specifically. It is ironic, no? The Russians are the ones who poison and thus are paranoid. I know of no other service who poisons. Do you?"

Stavros regained a bit of poise and joked, "I don't know what you mean. I am not attached to any government service or agency. I am only here to encourage cooperation and progress among our people."

Christakis grinned.

Stavros asked, "You've been out of town. Can you share what you've been up to?"

"No."

A moment passed with neither speaking. Then Christakis asked, "Do you know Sheepskin, some call it Red Sheepskin?"

Stavros shook his head.

"Better that we don't discuss it," said Christakis.

"Do you want me to dig around, talk to somebody, find out anything?" asked Stavros.

"No. No. Do not do that. There is no need. As the Americans say, keep your nose clean of it."

"Right, but it's just 'keep your nose clean,'" said Stavros.

Now Stavros was curious. He sensed that Christakis was preoccupied. He said, "You know, if you need any help, just let me know."

All Christakis said was, "Thank you."

Then a familiar silence.

Stavros drummed his fingers on the chair's chestnut arm.

"Well, I guess we can catch up on Sunday, if you plan to be around," said Stavros.

"Yes, I plan to be in Athens. If I am not, I will leave a message at the hotel, the same code as before."

"All right. Don't forget my offer. If you need anything, just let me know," said Stavros.

Christakis nodded.

Chapter 42

The GRU secure location was not as nice as CIA safe houses. In fact, it wasn't a house. In a dilapidated depot in Elaionas, a run-down industrial tract in western Athens, Kozlov began his interrogation of Achilles. The smell of cured tobacco thickened the air, and the brown mat covering the concrete floor held dust from thousands of leafy bales now long gone. The warehouse was cavernous. Filthy skylights allowed scattered rays to outline the pillars and trusses supporting the galvanized roof. Oddly, it reminded Kozlov of Saint Basil's Cathedral in Red Square. There the light entered through elegantly arched windows and traced the divine through smoky incense. But in this space, for Achilles, there was no divinity and no salvation.

It wasn't hard to make him talk. The informant was right; there was no dirt under his fingernails. He lived his self-selected, meager life on family money. Kozlov didn't say who sent him, and Achilles assumed it was the Americans. He assumed Kozlov was CIA. When he started talking, hoping to negotiate his way out of captivity, he offered to spy for the agency. He said he knew contacts in the KKE that the CIA would find valuable. It was the wrong thing to say to a GRU operative.

Kozlov's Greek was good, but he couldn't hide the Russian post-alveolar trill, the soft rolled *R* pronunciation. Achilles caught on, but far too late. By then, his offer to double as a CIA informant for the GRU rang hollow.

Achilles told Kozlov of the plot to assassinate the deputy of the American Economic Cooperation Administration Mission. It wasn't much of a plot, but Achilles wasn't much of a killer. He told Kozlov he had received the deputy's travel schedule from Calista, who got it from a professor. He told Kozlov he didn't know where Calista lived, but he knew where the professor lived. He had followed her and an American to her apartment one night.

Kozlov had the target and the critical connection, the chain; those were his orders. To Kozlov, Achilles was of no more value. Kozlov lifted a square bottle from the duffle bag on the matted floor beside him. Achilles assumed the bag contained instruments of torture to aid in his interrogation. One reason, along with being a coward, that Achilles had talked. The duffle contained such instruments, but Kozlov was both efficient and professional. No need to dirty his tools when words would do the job. Kozlov popped the cork and swigged, showing that the liquor wasn't poison. Then he motioned to Achilles. Kozlov held the bottle to Achilles's lips, and he drank. Then Kozlov offered Achilles another drink, and another. Kozlov matched him drink for drink. Achilles thought he was bonding with Kozlov, man-to-man, leader to leader. He saw his new life, after this peculiar initiation ritual, as an agent, of sorts. He wasn't sure for whom he would work, but he convinced himself he had passed the test.

Then from the duffle, Kozlov removed a syringe, and Achilles in the approaching fog of intoxication shuddered. The injection worked quickly; Achilles passed out and slumped in the chair. Kozlov untied the soft cloth strips binding him and checked for ligature bruising. Achilles was unmarked. The drug, RP 4560, was an experimental compound developed in France and passed to the Soviets by industrial spies. It would undergo development for three more years on its way to becoming chlorpromazine, or Thorazine. In 1951, the French thought they were developing an anesthetic.[38] The drug was undetectable in the victim's blood.

In his sailor's coat, Achilles made a fateful trip to the waters he pretended to ply. It was a short drive to Skaramagas through the moonless night. On a rickety unused pier north of the shipyard, Kozlov placed in Achilles's coat a half-consumed bottle of absinthe before slipping his unconscious body into the Gulf of Elefsina, where his lungs would fill with salt water. Death by drowning. An unfortunate accident.

Kozlov dismissed the two GRU men helping him with transportation and detainment. He drove to Anatolikis Thrakis #

38, Penelope's apartment. There he slept in his car to be on post and watch her movements Saturday morning.

Chapter 43

Calista took the bus to Penelope's apartment after her shift at Kitsoulas, where she helped close the taverna. It was an early night, and she arrived just before midnight. Two hours before Kozlov. She spent the night with Penelope, and they slept together, as they had since the OSO assigned Penelope Calista, code-named Alepoú. They were passionate in bed, aggressive and hungry, but detached. To Calista, it was an adventurous exploration of her sexual potential. To Penelope, the same, with a more willful and professional appeal. Penelope had begun work for the OSO as a contract agent three years before. She was an early University of Athens recruit. And, yes, Stavros was a target for development. Her mission was to spy on another CIA spy.

To say the CIA's OSO and OPC didn't communicate was an understatement. In November 1951, Frank Wisner strove to come to grips with the reach and scope of both organizations. He understood OPC's commitments. He had been OPC director and originator before his promotion to deputy director of plans. But the OSO, the espionage wing—the spies who were to find things out and not blow them up—was dense, provincial, and often worked far out of bounds. Spying often escalated into direct action, a job for which OSO spies were neither qualified nor recruited, and no one, before Wisner, held the reins.

The road to the Lion Cave was serpentine. Once in the mountain park, Stavros worked the Morris's steering wheel and gears to handle the tight turns and switchbacks. He was to meet Penelope and Calista at the cave, and from there they would hike to the photo shoot. Penelope and Calista took a taxi and Stavros said he would drive them back when they were done.

It was a beautiful morning, crisp and clear. A slight mist hung in the mountains, and Stavros savored the park's beauty. He arrived at the Lion Cave before the women and pulled the Morris to the side of the road. With the engine off, he could hear the caws and vocalizations of crows or ravens. He couldn't tell them apart. The Greeks called them Coronis. In mythology, they were harbingers of misfortune. But this he let pass on a beautiful morning with the sun just above the horizon.

The taxi arrived ten minutes later. Penelope got out with a shoulder bag, and Calista followed with her cloth duffel. Both women wore jeans, boots, and sturdy jackets. Stavros wondered whether this shoot would be in less suggestive attire than the prints in Penelope's bedroom. He said, "Kaliméra. Beautiful women on a beautiful morning, what could be better?"

Both women smiled as the taxi departed and another car passed a moment later. Stavros paid it no mind. Penelope, however, noted the diplomatic license plates.

They began their climb just as Christakis had predicted; they hiked southwest into Cima Imitos, a nature preserve containing the highest peak in the park. They walked a half kilometer on marked trails over rough paths. It wasn't mountaineering, but it was more than a casual stroll. From the summit, they paused for the commanding view of Kamini, the nearest Athens neighborhood. Farther east, fifteen kilometers in the distance, rays of the rising sun bounced off the placid Petalioi Gulf. The trio stood together in silent appreciation. Then Penelope pointed to a thicket of cedars. She said, "Let's start there. Calista, would you like to change?"

Stavros perked up. Penelope said, "You may turn your head, Professor."

Calista sat her duffle on a boulder, pulled off her cloth cap and shook her long golden locks. She wore nothing under her jeans and jacket except for a long-sleeved T-shirt and socks. She sat on a towel spread on the boulder and untied her boots. She was out of her hiking clothes and naked in less than thirty seconds.

True to Penelope's fascination with nature, Calista slipped into a long-sleeved silk sheath the color of ocean. The dress was slit up the left thigh and had a V-neck. It clung to every point of her body in transparent glory. She was barefoot. When

Penelope told Stavros it was okay to look, he did, and it mesmerized him. Calista stood on that chilly morning as a statue in the woods, like something from a myth brought to life. Calista said, "We should work fast before my teeth chatter."

While Calista was changing, Penelope pulled from her grip a telescoping tripod and set her camera atop. From behind her viewfinder, Penelope motioned Calista into the frame she sought. The light fell on the model from the early sun at a forty-five-degree angle. The two shades of gold, her hair and the sun, melded into a miasma of woman and nature. Just the shot she wanted. Penelope snapped a remote shutter release, advanced the film, then made frame, lens, and aperture adjustments. Shot after shot. She worked fast but meticulously.

Calista struck poses, both with her body and her face. She was risqué, and Stavros traced every movement with wonder. She wore no makeup. Yet her face and her wide green eyes were subtle and suggestive. Every posture, stance, and expression projected studied detachment. She came to life in the beholder's eye, unobserved, no camera intrusion. She was lightness and warmth against the hardness of nature. Somehow, she was discrete yet part of her surroundings. Stavros thought, *This kid's got skills. She's not only beautiful, but possessed. No wonder Penelope pays for her talent.*

He was right. But he didn't know fully her talents.

They had been shooting for ten minutes when Calista said, "I am cold. I can't hold poses while I'm freezing."

Penelope looked at Stavros and pointed to Calista's duffle. Stavros went to the bag and pulled out a wool blanket. He held it behind Calista, who took the corners from him and wrapped it around her. She was shaking. Penelope said, "Hug her."

Stavros didn't believe his ears. He looked at Penelope like a misguided teenager.

Penelope said, "Hug her to warm her. Do you not understand? This is your job."

Calista turned to face Stavros and opened the blanket. He did as ordered. He hugged her with his arms outside of the blanket. Her body was electric. He felt a charge, a bolt of energy that embarrassed him. Was this happening?

They hugged for three minutes while Penelope reloaded film. Calista stopped shaking and when Penelope said she was ready, Calista looked Stavros in the eyes and said, "Thank you."

He only nodded, but he wanted to say, *No. Thank you.*

This routine—pose, shoot, hug, and reload—played out four more times. Every time Stavros did his duty and with each turn, his anticipation grew. He liked this job. He believed Calista liked the way he did it. His male ego was thriving. After more than an hour, clouds blotted out the early sunlight that Penelope so valued. With the light gone, so was the magic. Calista dressed again in her hiking clothes, and the trio started back down the mountain trail.

Kozlov was not dressed for hiking. He wore city clothes from his night before with Achilles. City shoes, suit pants, and a baggy trench coat were not his friends on the mountain trail. He wasn't physically fit, either. His smoking, vodka intake, and paunch hadn't diminished his ability to kill. But climbing in Cima Imitos was outside his comfort zone. He muffled his smoker's cough and tried to stay undetected. This trio, this chain of information, could it lead to another link? Were they climbing the mountain to transmit? Did they have a radio in their bags? These suspicions were his motivation, yet now, nearly to the pinnacle, he could see. From behind an outcrop, he watched at forty meters. They were shooting photographs. No radio, no meeting, just the three shooting photographs. Should he kill them? They appeared to be unarmed, save for a camera. It couldn't be an accident; gunshots are seldom by accident. He carried his Makarov with its eight-round clip and one round in the firing chamber and had pocketed one extra clip. Killing three people with seventeen rounds wouldn't be a problem, so long as they were unarmed, surprised, and gave little resistance. But

Kozlov would need to be close. The Makarov was not a reliable weapon beyond twenty meters and much more effective face-to-face. It's .380 rounds were deadly if you could look your victim in the eye, but lacked knock-down power for longer range. What about the bodies? This trail was public, and although not well traveled in November, the bodies would be discovered. That was a matter of time. In the end, he decided he would neutralize the chain here and now and let the local authorities scratch their heads trying to find the killer. While the Greeks were chasing ghosts, he would be back in Mother Russia sitting out any investigation, cooling his heels, and awaiting another posting. He would leave Greece under diplomatic cover immediately, days, maybe weeks before they found the bodies.

Behind the outcrop, he pulled the Makarov from his trench coat and press-checked the slide. Assured the weapon was charged, he returned it to his pocket. He would approach the trio, now on their way back down the trail, as a fellow hiker. He would greet them, distract them with a meaningless question, shoot the man first and then the two women.

He rose behind the outcrop, straightened his coat, and heard a sound from behind, all too familiar and unsettling. The American Colt .45 semiautomatic pistol makes a muffled but discernible click when thumbing the hammer to cock.

Christakis didn't have to speak. Without looking, Kozlov raised his arms above his head. He was a professional, and someone else, probably a professional, had the drop on him. He'd committed no crime, done nothing wrong, and his embassy would get him out of this. If he died, he was a professional; this was his job. The state would care for his family, and they would honor him for his sacrifice.

Christakis spoke, "Turn toward me."

Kozlov complied.

"Take the gun from your pocket, two fingers by the grip, and place it on the ground to your side," Christakis ordered in a professional voice.

Kozlov complied.

Christakis asked, "Do you have any other weapons?"

Kozlov nodded, "A knife in my right pants pocket."

"Open your coat, remove the knife, then kick it toward me. Slowly."

Kozlov complied, and as he kicked the weapon, the trio approached on the trail.

Penelope saw the two men first. She knew the one holding the gun. He was in the Circle. He worked for the Greek Ministry for Public Security. She assumed he was friendly. The other man, she didn't know and never seen before.

Then Stavros saw them. He said, "Alexis, what's going on?"

Christakis said, "Bind him and gag him, then search him. First, secure the gun and the knife."

Stavros picked up the Makarov and handed it to Penelope. But she already held a gun, a CIA-issued High Standard. He recognized it immediately. She was in a combat stance, two hands on the pistol, and her weapon trained on Kozlov. Stavros assumed it had come from her camera bag.

Christakis handed Stavros two ties and a gag tucked into his belt.

Stavros tied Kozlov's wrists behind his back and knotted the gag.

Stavros padded Kozlov and found loose currency and a Soviet Embassy ID proclaiming the prisoner a cultural attaché.

Stavros looked at Christakis and said, "You really must tell me what the hell is going on." Then he looked back at Penelope with the same question in his eyes.

Christakis said, "He followed you up the mountain. I saw him press-check his weapon. He was going to kill you."

"Who the hell is he?" Stavros asked.

"GRU. I've encountered him before. He is an assignment killer."

"What the hell?" mouthed Stavros.

"Let us get off the mountain and we can talk it over in a more protected place," said Christakis.

Penelope remained silent, and Calista was dumbstruck.

Stavros looked at Penelope and again his eyes did the questioning, "Where did you get the pistol and why were you packing it on a photo shoot."

Stavros pocketed the Makarov, and the five hikers descended. Stavros steadied Kozlov, who made no sounds on the descent save muffled cigarette hacking. He made no sounds when ordered into the Morris's boot. Once in the boot, Stavros tied Kozlov's ankles. Then Christakis handed Stavros a blindfold and Stavros said, "Are you a Greek Boy Scout? You came prepared."

Again, Stavros's attempt at transplanting American humor fell flat.

With the four seated in the Morris, they made weapons safe and secured them. Stavros introduced Christakis with the nonchalance of a Sunday driver. Then he asked Christakis, "Where to?"

Christakis said, "One of your nice safe house villas might be best?"

Stavros looked behind him at Penelope, and Calista and raised an eyebrow.

Christakis saw the look and said, "We can go to one of ours, but yours are much nicer."

Stavros asked, "How would you know?"

Christakis smiled and shrugged. Christakis knew Stavros worried about CIA security protocols.

Christakis said, "You can blindfold us."

From the backseat, Calista spoke for the first time. "Oh, brother. Here we go again!"

Penelope said, "I believe we are on the same team. All of us. Except the one in the boot." "I know who sent *us*," she went on, nodding to Calista, "but who do you two work for?"

No one answered.

Finally, Stavros asked Christakis, "How did you get here?"

Christakis smiled. "A friend. It is always good to have a friend."

Stavros drove north. The Kifissia safe house was the only place he could think of that met their needs. They could unload the prisoner out of sight and keep him in a guarded holding cell. He told his passengers, "When we get out of the park, I'll make a call. Meanwhile, find something to use as blindfolds."

Christakis pulled two ready-cut black sheaths from his jacket and handed one to Penelope. Calista pulled her cloth cap over her eyes, shaking her head all the while.

Stavros said, "You don't have to put them on now; wait until I make the call. Hell, they may tell us to get lost."

This is what worried Stavros about working solo and reporting only to Wisner. Frank Wisner was the top dog, but he wasn't always easy to contact. And if no one else was in the loop, Stavros's mission would raise suspicions.

Christakis asked of no one in particular, "Do you think he was alone? Are we leaving behind a partner?"

Penelope said, "There was only one man in the car that followed the taxi. It was registered diplomatic. I glimpsed the driver, and it was him."

Stavros had underestimated Penelope. But who was she working for? She must be CIA. That pistol and that shooting stance were straight from the manual.

A kilometer farther north, they passed the embassy car pulled off the road. Stavros asked Christakis, "Should we search it?"

Christakis shook his head, "No. Better we secure the prisoner and get to somewhere safe. We can send a team back for the car."

They weaved their way out of the park and onto the main road along the eastern border of the university. As they headed north, Penelope said, "Pull in there," indicating a parking lot for the Department of Physics.

When they had parked, she said, "Stavros, come with me. I will get you a phone. It is Saturday and the department will not be busy."

They entered the low concrete building into a reception area. Penelope went to the first door with a light shining and asked to use the telephone. The absentminded academic, buried in notes and formulas, at first objected. Then Penelope showed him her Economics Department ID and flashed the young man a winning smile. He relented and pointed to a desk across the room.

Stavros made the call. He got the duty officer and asked for Hod Fuller. It was his lucky day, Fuller was there.

Stavros gave Fuller a cryptic description of their situation. He used code for how many people, their combatant status, and reached back to OSS days for a few choice phrases Fuller would remember.

Fuller said, "Bring 'em on. We'll sort things when you get here. How far out are you?"

Stavros told him fifteen to twenty minutes.

Fuller said, "Great. Blind them when you're ten minutes away."

Stavros said, "Roger," and hung up. He nodded to Penelope. She thanked the graduate student and they walked to the car. Along the way, without looking in her direction, Stavros said, "You and I really need to talk."

Chapter 44

The Morris pulled up to the gate of the Kifissia safe house. A young security officer motioned for Stavros to stop, then bent over as Stavros rolled down the driver's window. The officer looked inside the car and said, "General Fuller said this would be weird."

The security officer eyeballed the three passengers wearing assorted blindfolds but otherwise looking like they were out for a Sunday drive.

Stavros said, "Do you want to look in the trunk?"

"Yes, sir. That's protocol."

Stavros got out, went to the trunk, opened the boot, and Kozlov squirmed inside like a pudgy panda, a prize won at a carnival shooting gallery. The officer said, "Do you need any help, sir?"

Stavros shook his head.

The officer said, "See the chief of security when you get to the villa. He'll take it from there. When your visitors are in the house, they can remove their blindfolds."

Stavros thanked the young officer and followed the driveway to the villa. Under the entrance portico, another officer greeted them. He said, "Park here and leave any weapons and bags in the car."

They complied and left behind three pistols, two knives, and Calista and Penelope's carry bags. A security man frisked them as they exited the Morris. With everyone cleared, Stavros gathered his blindfolded *visitors* into a line with Christakis following Stavros. Christakis, Penelope, and Calista walked with their arms extended to the person in front. The sightless chain clambered up a set of semicircular stairs to the front door and entered the foyer.

Stavros was just about to tell them to remove their blindfolds when he heard clapping from the staircase to the left. It was Fuller. He said, "I applaud your presentation. It's a sight

I've never seen before. Quite a parade, Stavros. Quite a parade. Well done, Lieutenant."

Fuller was smiling like a hyena.

Stavros said, "Take off your blindfolds and meet Hod Fuller."

Christakis and Penelope unknotted their strips of cloth and Calista removed the cloth cap that covered her eyes. They all blinked at the light.

Fuller approached, shook Christakis's hand, and nodded to the women. His eyes lingered on Calista as she shook her tousled hair.

Stavros said, "Thanks for hosting us. I didn't know where else to go."

"You came to the right place, brother. We take in all kinds here. But tell me, what do we have in the trunk?"

Stavros nodded to Christakis, who answered, "I am Alexis Christakis, sir. I am an officer with the Greek Ministry for Public Security. I have some knowledge of the prisoner. He is a GRU assignment killer. He goes by many names."

"Okay. All right. I see we've got something to talk through. He's in the trunk, right?"

Stavros nodded.

Fuller motioned to an armed man at the front door. Then he said to Stavros, "Give this man the keys. He'll need to move the car to the back. Our cells are in the basement."

Stavros handed over the keys and told the security chief, "We need to search a vehicle, the one he drove. It's in Kesariani, about a kilometer north of the Lion Cave, parked off the road. It's tagged diplomatic. Best leave it where it is and make the search undetectable. It's a GRU vehicle, so check everything."

The security chief looked at Fuller, who nodded. Then he motioned for two other men and went to move the Morris.

Fuller said, "All right. Let's get comfortable and talk this thing through."

He pointed to the solarium and the area away from traffic where they could talk in private.

"Can I get you anything to drink? Is anybody hungry?"

Stavros said, "Can we get everybody some coffee, maybe some pastry."

"That's not a problem. I'll see to it. Stavros, walk with me. The rest of you can get comfortable," Fuller motioned to the seating in the solarium.

Out of earshot, Fuller said, "Thanks for bringing the blonde; she made my day. What the hell are you into?"

Stavros didn't know where to begin. He said, "I was working on Frank's assignment, the big fish operation you said he told you about."

Fuller said, "Right. Who are these other guys?"

"Christakis is a contact from the Circle, the influence operation I've been running since I got to Greece. Penelope is in it, too. That's where we met. Calista, the blonde, is an art student at the university. I'm still trying to place her in this. . . ." he almost said *clusterfuck*, then regained objectivity, "In this chain."

"So, the GRU man is who?" asked Fuller.

"I do not know. Christakis says he knows him."

"What about Christakis?"

"He's a good man. The CIA has an old file from after the war. Remember the Gouzenko defection?"

Fuller said, "Vaguely."

"Gouzenko defected in Canada. The Canucks questioned him, the Brits questioned him, the FBI jumped in, then years later, Hoover turned over a copy of a copy of the file to Frank. The information in the file is unverified. They say Christakis is an impersonator, a GRU plant in the Hellenic Army. I don't believe it. I've spent time with him, and he's organic. I'm sure the file was bullshit, or they misspelled a name or somehow got it wrong."

"Yeah, okay, so I'm going to assume your mission involves the GRU, and you've got a honcho in your sights," said Fuller.

"That's a fair assumption," said Stavros.

"Okay, so how does everybody else fit in?"

"I . . . I wish I could tell you."

"How about this, what were you doing this morning when you captured the GRU man?" asked a puzzled Fuller.

"A photographic shoot. Penelope is an amateur photographer. She teaches economics at the university and she photographs as a hobby. Calista is her model. I went at Penelope's invitation. We were on Cima Imitos this morning shooting, favorable morning light, and all that."

"All right, I do not know where Cima Imitos is, but I'm assuming it is a park of some sort."

"A preserve. Near the university in Kesariani," answered Stavros.

"So where did Christakis come in?"

"He was my backup." Stavros didn't mention that he hadn't asked for backup, and Christakis had followed on his own. Stavros went on, "Christakis and I have been working together on the big fish mission. He knew about a . . . prisoner? What do you call someone institutionalized? A patient? Anyway, Christakis and I have been working together."

Fuller said, "Well, this one may take a written outline and a program guide. Let's get some coffee into them and see where this goes. What do you want to do with the GRU guy?"

"I do not know. He was sent to kill us," answered Stavros.

"Okay. Let's get our story straight before we sit down with Mister GRU."

Stavros nodded.

They walked to the kitchen on the opposite side of the villa. Fuller said something to the steward, then returned to Stavros. As the two men headed back to the solarium, a security officer motioned to Fuller. Fuller told Stavros, "Wait here. I need to talk to him."

The security officer told Fuller that he knew the woman, the one with brown hair. He had seen her at the safe house in Kolonaki, the OSO operation. He said she was contract.

Fuller thanked him and rejoined Stavros. He said in a whisper, "We netted one of our own. The brunette, she's OSO, contract."

Stavros said, "Damn. I knew it. As soon as I saw her with the HDM, her shooting stance . . . I knew we'd trained her." He shook his head.

"The OSO needs to get their act together and stay out of the business of armed contractors. Aren't these the guys paid to snoop, not to shoot?"

"I think that's one of Frank's big headaches," said Stavros.

"Speaking of Frank, wait here. I'm going to alert coms. We may need to reach him. If OSO is in this, he's the guy who can make them talk. What time is it in Washington?" asked Fuller.

"Should be about o-four-hundred," said Stavros.

"Okay, I'll be right back." Fuller bounded up the stairway to the second floor. He was back a minute later. He said, "We'll get him on the line, just in case."

"Smart move," said Stavros.

"Now, let's get to know our guests, shall we?" Fuller smiled.

The two men arrived at the solarium at the same moment as two stewards with trays of coffee and pastries. The stewards set each person with a cup and poured coffee. When they were out of earshot, Fuller began, "Okay. Welcome to our humble establishment. Your comfort is our only concern. Except for the guy in the trunk.

"Let me say, I am nobody's boss. I'm ranking here, in this house, but I'm nobody's boss. I can, however, get on the telephone everybody's boss."

Looking at Christakis, he added, "I'm not sure about you."

"Anyway, everything that is said must remain within this group. Are we agreed?" Fuller asked.

Stavros, Penelope, Christakis nodded. Calista said, "I have no clue what is going on here."

Fuller said in his most reassuring tone, "Calista, is it?" She nodded. "Calista, we have a man in our custody who, I am told, tried to kill you. Let's make some sense of what is going on before we decide what to do with him. Is that fair?"

She nodded.

Fuller asked, "Can we count on your discretion?"

She nodded again.

"Outstanding. Now, let me start by saying, if you haven't already figured this out, this is a United States Government secure location. Three of us in this group, maybe four, maybe five, are connected to the United States Government.

"Stavros and I are connected, as are you, Penelope? Right?" asked Fuller.

"I'm not at liberty to discuss that," she replied.

"I am. And you are," said Fuller.

"Now, what about Calista?" he asked.

Penelope said, "She is an acquaintance from the university. I employ her as a model for my photography."

Stavros didn't like Penelope's attitude. He said, "You are running Calista. What's her cryptonym and to what purpose?"

Christakis sat in silence, taking it all in.

"Running? I don't understand what you are saying?" Penelope said.

Fuller reentered the conversation, "Perhaps you would understand if the deputy director of plans asked the questions? I can make that happen. Stavros is Mr. Wisner's eyes and ears in Athens, so. . . ."

Fuller turned his attention to Christakis. "Alexis, is it?" Christakis nodded. "Alexis, Stavros says you are solid. You saved his bacon this morning, so I'm betting you are on our side, the good guys. I'm not sure of your affiliation. I'm betting the Greek Ministry for Public Security is not as deep as you go. But . . . what say we assume we can trust you with sensitive United States Government information. Is that a correct assumption? Do I have your word of honor, sir?"

Christakis said, "That is a correct assumption. And you have my word of honor. Yes."

Fuller redirected to Penelope. He said, "Penelope, we know you are OSO contract. You are burned. I have that from a security man who knows you from another United States Government secure location, right here in Athens. So, what's your mission? And is this young lady an asset?"

"I am nobody's asset," piped up Calista. "I volunteered."

Penelope shook her head disbelieving the tell.

"Okay, now we're getting somewhere. The sooner we get it all in the open, the quicker we can begin our conversation with our guest in the basement," said Fuller.

Penelope fidgeted. Fuller rose from his seat, walked around the coffee table between them, leaned over, and whispered in Penelope's ear. He returned to his chair, then motioned Penelope with a twirling of his wrist.

Penelope said, "My mission is Stavros. Calista is an informant. She reports to me on a KKE breakaway faction we suspect is planning direct action."

"Wait, what?" blurted an indignant Stavros.

"Sorry, Stavros. They ordered me to develop you to see if you were KKE. You know? Because of Dimitra?" Penelope cringed.

"What the hell! Who gave that order?"

"It came down through channels," she said.

"Through OSO channels?" he shouted back. "Does Frank know?"

She shrugged. Then she said, "No. I doubt it. This came before the reorganization. Right after you got to Greece."

"So, why does Calista work at a taverna where the GRU rezidentura eats lunch?" asked Stavros.

Penelope shrugged, "Happenstance?"

"Right," said Stavros, not believing it for a second. "Then what the hell was the file folder all about?"

"I was checking you out. You found the first tell, but not the second. They teach us these things in OSO. You OPC guys are monkey-wrench types, OSO, more tweezers." Penelope smiled.

Fuller said, "All right, this internal squabble stuff can wait."

Stavros was slack-jawed.

Fuller turned to Christakis. "Alexis, you've been working with Stavros on a high-value target in the GRU. Do you have anything to add?"

"No, sir. Only that the GRU came after Stavros, Penelope, and Calista, because of another chain. Not the mission that you mention. That mission is not far along; it is still invisible."

"What chain is that?" asked Fuller.

"This is only a guess, but likely because of Penelope and Calista. Maybe connected to Calista's informant activities," said Christakis.

"Calista, would you like to fill us in?" asked Fuller.

"I reported a plan to assassinate an American official," she revealed.

"By whom," asked Fuller.

"By some renegade communist group at the university. They call themselves The Torch. I was close to their leader, a guy named Achilles. That's what he called himself. He wanted to shoot a capitalist, an American official. Penelope and I gave him a fake travel schedule."

"Did the GRU know?" asked Fuller.

She scrunched up her flawless face and shrugged her shoulders.

"All right, now we're getting somewhere," said Fuller.

Fuller turned to Christakis, and asked, "How do you know our guest is GRU?"

"That information I gained during a previous assignment."

"Would you like to tell us more," prodded Fuller.

"While I might like to tell you, I am sorry that it is not permitted," said Christakis.

"So . . . not permitted by the Greek Ministry for Public Security? If that's the case, I can get Tommy Karamessines on the line. He's a high-ranking United States Government official who I bet you know. I'm certain he knows someone at the Ministry. He works with your people. Do you know Tommy?" asked Fuller.

"We have met," answered Christakis.

"Would he permit you to discuss your knowledge of the GRU?" asked Fuller.

"No, sir. He cannot provide that permission," answered Christakis.

Fuller looked at Stavros. Both men were thinking the same thing. Christakis was working for another service, not Greek, not American.

Then, with a pert interruption, Penelope said, "Alexis, just tell them you work for SIFAR."

Christakis turned white.

"I'm OSO. We work with SIFAR. Operation CHARITY? I posted for six months in Rome right after OSO recruited me. I saw you at Naval Intelligence HQ. I looked you up when I saw you in the Circle. It's okay, we're all friends here." She smiled.

"You are SIFAR?" asked an incredulous Stavros. "How in the hell did that happen?"

His color slowly returning, Christakis said, "That is a long story. A story for another time, perhaps. I can only say that my knowledge of the GRU comes from an earlier Italian Naval Intelligence encounter."

Fuller and Stavros again looked at each other, and puzzlement passed between them. Christakis was deep, very deep, and Penelope was . . . deeper than they had given her credit for.

"Well, aren't we an onion with many skins?" said Fuller. Let's take a breather, take a break, walk around for a couple minutes. Then get back together to talk over Mister GRU. How's that sound? The patio is nice, if you want some air."

Calista asked, "Do we have to wear blindfolds?"

"No," Fuller said with a smile.

Fuller and Stavros got out of their chairs and Fuller said, "I'm going to check on Mister GRU. Give me ten minutes."

"Right," answered Stavros.

"Try not to strangle Penelope before I get back," said Fuller.

Stavros shook his head.

Stavros walked to the patio, ignoring the others. He was standing at the far end of the stonework staring into the distance, trying to modulate his anger when Penelope joined him. He paid her no mind.

She said, "I'm sorry. I was working. I was ordered."

He said nothing.

"I enjoyed our time together. I like you—"

He cut her off. "Don't even start. Save your breath for someone you can fool," he muttered.

"Stavros, I wasn't trying to fool you, I was just. . . ." Then he walked away.

Neither Calista nor Christakis was good at small talk. They stood together in the solarium, watching Stavros and

Penelope outdoors. Calista said, "I imagine they have some things to work out."

Christakis said, "It is hard for spies to make friends."

"Well, Alexis, I think this may have gone further than friendship."

Christakis nodded.

"So, you are Italian?" asked Calista.

"No. I am Greek. Generations past, my family lived in Italy. It is a long story," answered Christakis.

"Well, perhaps when this is over, you can tell me. I like long stories, over nice dinners." Calista beamed.

"Perhaps I will. And you? You are northern, no? How did you come to Athens?" asked Christakis.

"My family is from Salonika. I came to study art at the university. This is my third year. It is an excellent school, but Athens is expensive. So, I model and work as a waitress."

"You said you volunteered your information?" asked Christakis.

"Yes. I approached an Italian, an employee at their embassy. I asked him how to get in touch with the American CIA. I knew about The Torch and Achilles. I'm left-wing, I guess communist, but something about Achilles and The Torch wasn't right. So, I went to the CIA. They assigned me to work with Penelope. And they gave me some money, which I needed. So . . . here I am," she said. "You can't tell anybody, right? We took an oath, right?"

Christakis said, "Your secret is safe. You are a bold woman to take such steps."

"Bold and poor," she said, smiling.

It was hard not to be pulled into this woman's world. She was captivating in every way. Christakis felt himself slipping and struggled to regain his footing.

He said, "You know you may be in danger. The GRU are unforgiving. You should take every precaution.

"Is it possible that the GRU was behind the direct action?" he asked.

"Direct action? What's that?" asked Penelope.

"The assassination," said Christakis.

"Wow, I don't see how. Achilles was a loner and madly anti-KKE. The KKE and the GRU are friends, right? Both communist allies, right?"

"Correct. They are allies. But, they do not always see eye to eye," said Christakis. He let the conversation lapse. He thought the GRU may have been doing the KKE a favor, getting rid of a splinter. If The Torch had been planning an assassination, one that the GRU or KKE did not sanction, that might undermine their strategy in Greece and undermine the international revolution. Penelope and Calista were links in the chain, providing the fake travel schedule for the target. But the GRU didn't know it was fake. The likelihood that the GRU ran an informer against The Torch was high. The GRU plumbed the depths of every Communist Party and splinter. Without fail, they had placed a loyalist in this sect. It was just a theory, but Christakis saw the merit.

Fuller returned to the solarium with a file folder. He motioned for Stavros to come inside, and Penelope, Christakis, and Calista returned to their seats. When everyone was settled, he asked, "Any more coffee, anyone?"

He got no takers.

"Well, this may help enlighten us," he said, pulling a photograph from the file and placing it on the coffee table.

It was a clear shot of Calista and Achilles, taken in a hallway of a nondescript building.

Stavros said, "From the car?"

Fuller nodded, "I guess Mister GRU is slipping. It was under the sun visor. His tradecraft is trade-crap. Also, we found a bag with persuasive implements and a vial and syringe. We'll send it all out for analysis.

"Now, Calista, is this Achilles?"

She said, "Yes, but how did they get this picture?"

"They have their ways. This is how he identified you. By finding you, he found Penelope, then the three of you." Fuller looked around to Stavros, Penelope, and Calista.

"I will bet he went after Achilles first, head of the snake and all that. Achilles may have told him how to find you," he said, nodding at Calista.

"But what about Achilles?" asked Calista.

Fuller shrugged, "From the tools in his bag, I would say it didn't end well for Achilles."

"You mean he's dead?" asked an incredulous Calista.

"Our friends at GRU do not play softball," said Fuller.

Stavros got the sports reference, but it flew wide of the Greeks.

"All right. So, before we engage Mister GRU, what do we want to know?" Fuller asked of no one in particular.

There was a moment of silence. Then Christakis said, "Why?" He paused, then continued, "The GRU may have sought to neutralize a direct action that didn't fit the Soviet agenda. And they rid the KKE of a splinter. I believe the pieces fit."

"So, they were working our side of the street," said Stavros. "They were protecting an American official?"

"I doubt they cared about an American casualty. They cared about the timing and the public reaction, not the American," offered Christakis.

"Holds water," said Fuller.

"So, the GRU will want their killer returned," said Stavros.

"Right," said Fuller. "And if he has diplomatic status, we'll need to reach pretty high if we want to do anything other than give him back."

"Can we get anything for him?" asked Stavros.

Stavros looked at Christakis, both men thinking the same thought. Was this a lever to turn Chernov?

Penelope asked, "Should we threaten the GRU man? Life in prison, execution, these things?"

Christakis said, "He is hard. The GRU has been his home for many years, and he has worked many assignments. He has spilled much blood. We can threaten him, but. . . ."

Fuller said, "Let's see what he has to say. I expect little more than NRS."

Penelope cocked her head. Fuller said, "Name, rank, and serial number. If we get something, great. If we don't, we still must decide what to do with him. And Stavros, you and Alexis will need to weigh in. We'll need to know if he can be of value to whatever you're working on, right? Big fish, and all that?"

Both men nodded.

Fuller looked at Penelope and asked, "Does Mister GRU mean anything to any of your assignments? The ones you haven't told us about?"

She looked hard at Fuller and shook her head.

"Okay, so he knows you two." Fuller nodded to Christakis and Stavros.

"You don't have a direct interest, right?" Fuller nodded to Penelope. She shook her head.

"He doesn't know me, so let's keep it that way. Stavros, why don't you and Alexis question him? I'll have security bring him to a room, and you can go from there. Does that sound like a plan?" asked Fuller.

There were nods all around except for Calista, who was in way over her head. Then Christakis said, "I agree with the plan, but perhaps we should let him ripen, maybe just one day."

Penelope looked quizzically at Christakis.

Christakis went on, "These Russians, often they enjoy alcohol too much. This is common. If we allow him to sit for a day, he will feel the effects of its absence. It could give us an edge, a lever. Maybe not, but one day will not delay us, no?"

Fuller considered. Then he said, "All right. You two come back tomorrow afternoon, and we'll see if Mister GRU is cooperative. By then, a bottle sitting in front of him might be the honey we need to prod the bear.

"Well, I've enjoyed our time together. Can I get anyone anything before you go?" asked Fuller.

Everyone shook their heads.

"Great, I'll have your car brought around." Fuller rose, shook both men's hands, and nodded to the women.

As he walked away, Calista asked, "Time for blindfolds?"

Ten minutes from the Kifissia safe house, Stavros told his passengers they could remove their blindfolds. He told Penelope, "I'll drop you two at a cab stand or a hotel and you can find your way wherever you need to go. Will that work?"

Penelope nodded.

Stavros looked at Christakis and said, "You and I need to talk so I'll drive you home or wherever we need to go."

Christakis nodded.

Two minutes later, he pulled the Morris to the curb behind a cab stand. He turned in the driver's seat and said to Calista, "Calista, it was a pleasure meeting. You need to be careful. You can reach me at the Grande Bretagne and Christakis at the Ministry. I'm sure you know how to reach Penelope. Keep your doors locked and be aware of your surroundings. If you need a place to stay, Alexis or I can help."

Penelope said, "You're generous. But I can provide for Calista." She didn't say, *because she's my assignment.* She knew that would provoke Calista.

Stavros just smiled at Calista, never making eye contact with Penelope.

Calista slid out of the car, then squirmed back in and tapped Christakis on the shoulder. She said, "I want to hear the rest of your story. You promised."

Christakis nodded.

When the women were out and Stavros was back in the stream of traffic, he said, "Okay, I need to hear that story, too."

Chapter 45

"Okay, start from the beginning. Are you Italian or Greek?" asked Stavros. The two men were back in the comfort of the Grande Bretagne lobby in the same chairs as before.

"I am Greek," said Christakis. "My family is Greek, but they lived for two generations in Italy, in Salento. In the boot heel.

"Are you certain you want to hear this story? It is long," asked Christakis.

"Oh, yes. Whatever it takes. If we want drinks, we can get them from the bar. I need to hear the whole thing, and leave nothing out," said Stavros.

"Very well," said Christakis. "My great-grandfather fought in the War of Independence. He was wounded at Karpenisi in 1823. He was just sixteen. Three hundred and fifty Greeks against four thousand Ottomans, Catholics, and Albanians. The Greeks attacked the Albanians at midnight, thinking that surprise would secure a victory. It was a bold disaster. Do you remember what I said at our dinner in Amfissa after the rally?"

"What's that," asked Stavros.

"That we Greeks fight like tigers but think like mice."

"Oh, right," Stavros agreed.

"So, my great-grandfather was fortunate in two ways. First, he lived; most of the Greeks died. They took him to the hospital of the Great Powers in Missolonghi. A doctor wanted to take his leg. A musket shell had shattered the bone. But a nurse told the doctor she could save it. She asked for two days to improve his condition. She was Italian and a godsend. My great-grandfather's infection faded, and his love grew.

"He proposed during his recuperation. He was a bold Greek. He was hobbled, walking on crutches, of no value as a soldier and little as a husband. But he learned enough Italian to propose marriage and bargain his way into the young nurse's life.

This was my great-grandmother, Cecilia. She said yes. Part of the bargain was that they must live in Italy, near her family.

"Do you know Magna Graecia?" asked Christakis.

Stavros had heard the term but was not up on what it meant.

"Magna Graecia was a Roman term for the parts of Italy that were Greek. The ancient Greeks settled along the coasts of southern Italy from Sicily, up to the heel of the boot. This goes back to the eighth century BCE, before the Trojan War. Some say these wandering Greeks seeded the culture of ancient Rome. That region, to this day, speaks a dialect called Griko.

"My great-grandfather, Alexis, built a business in a small village near Brindisi, Torre Rossa, on the coast. His leg healed, but he still hobbled, so he became a merchant. He traded in shipping equipment and boat building products, and the family did well. He raised two sons and a daughter, and although he was in Italy, all his business was with Greeks.

"My grandfather, his first son, rose in the ranks of the local Greek politicians. He married, but his wife died giving birth, as did the child. Without a family, he joined with Ricciotti Garibaldi, the son of Giuseppe Garibaldi, the great man who molded Italy, a father of the fatherland. Together they recruited two thousand volunteers and went to fight the Turks at Domokos in 1897."

"I know Domokos, we staged an OSS action near there," said Stavros.

"Yes, yes. It is north of Mount Giona, on the southern edge of the Thessalian plain. Here the Greeks were not outnumbered—each army totaled forty-five thousand—but the Ottomans outmaneuvered them. The Greeks were in defensive formations and the Turks flanked them, placed their artillery close, cut their line of retreat, and won the battle. My grandfather and most of the surviving Italian volunteers made their way through the Turk lines into the Tsamadoráchi hills.

"I know those hills, too. We made our retreat through them almost to Karpenissi, then to Chómori," said Stavros.

"You went west. My grandfather went south. He and a group of the volunteers built a settlement outside of the village of Gravia, north of Amfissa and east of Mount Giona. He remarried, this time to a Greek, and his firstborn, a son, was my father.

"My father fought in the Balkan War as a young man. We Christakises go to war young. This is a pattern. I spoke of my father before, no? He was a farmer and an auto mechanic before the Germans came.

"I had one brother and one sister, both younger, again, before the Germans. I was born in 1924 and went to fight the Italians in 1940 at sixteen. I have told you this, about my promotions, but there is something I left out.

"They captured me. In the spring of 1941, before the Germans came to save the Italians, I led a platoon into a trap. It was a well-laid trap, not typical for the Italian commanders. We Greeks were better at guile and trickery, but this time, the Italians were best. I was not yet an officer, but as the ranking enlisted man, an intelligence unit interrogated me. I spoke to them in Italian, and I told them of my family's Italian roots. I was well-treated.

"They said it was only a matter of weeks until the Germans came. Then, the Greeks would collapse, and the worst would begin. It was odd. To this day I do not believe they sought to deceive me. I believe the Italians in charge of my custody did not like the Germans and were not happy about their assignment in Greece.

"They asked if I would work for them, against the Germans and the communists. For this, they would release me and the rest of my platoon. They said if I did not work for them, they would have to turn me over to the Germans when they invaded and took charge of Greece. The Germans were of no concern to me. I hated them. The communists? This was a time before EAM-ELAS. The Greek communists were still in exile and outlawed by Metaxas. I said yes. The Italians released me, and my men and I rejoined the Hellenic Army. We fought the Germans in Attica, then Crete. And when all was lost, I took a caïque to Turkey, then transported to Egypt with other Greek soldiers. When they expanded the Sacred Band to a regiment, I was assigned to the unit.

"In 1944, the Germans killed everyone and burned the settlement where my family lived. They are all gone," Christakis grew distant, and Stavros saw his eyes moisten.

Stavros asked, "So you contacted Italian intelligence."

"Yes, Italian Naval Intelligence," answered Christakis. "I sent reports about German movements after the Italians withdrew from the fighting in September 1943. But I was in Egypt with little information. KKE was active in our ranks, but Naval Intelligence was not interested. I believe Italy was in turmoil and their services were not functional.

"One day, a KKE man tried to recruit me. They promoted me to ypolochagós, a lieutenant. He too was an officer. I played along. I did not oppose the communists since they seemed to be the only ones fighting the Germans in Greece. Then the KKE began organizing mutinies. I reported these activities to my superiors and the Italians, but the Greeks sat on their hands, and the Italians seemed removed and uninterested. Greek commanders didn't control their forces in the Middle East. The British were in charge, and the Hellenic Army churned with politics. The king or no king? KKE or elections? What about Macedonia? What about Epirus? We fought political battles more often than military battles, and the words flew like bullets.

"When we deployed to Athens upon the German retreat, they ordered us to contain the communists. That is when the KKE officers in Sacred Band pressured to recruit me. They intended sabotage from within. I played along, and it was the first I met Chernov. He was destined for Albania, but at the time he was a GRU officer in Athens. He would return to Athens as the rezidentura in 1950, about the time you arrived in Greece.

"It was odd. The GRU did not favor the KKE uprising in December 1944, the Dekemvriana. I found out much later that in October 1944, the Soviets and Stalin cut a deal with Churchill for Greece to remain British. In exchange for Greece, Stalin got Bulgaria, Hungary, Romania, and half of Yugoslavia. A cagy Russian, no?"

"Now Italian Naval Intelligence grew interested. The GRU mattered more than lowly KKE army officers. So I fed the GRU information about the KKE Greek Army officers and kept the Italians informed as well. I saw nothing wrong, since it did not harm Greece. And if you might wonder, I am Greek; that is my loyalty.

"When I posted to the Ministry, the GRU took an interest. They wanted information on Greeks, British, and later, Americans. This I could not provide. I fed them incorrect and outdated information for as long as possible, just to stay in touch. But the GRU is well-placed and cross verifies everything.

"The GRU assigned Chernov to Albania, and he did not reach out to me for months. When he returned to Athens, he got in touch and when we met, I believe that is where the CIA photographed us together.

"I interrogated Kopali in Italy. This was the first I learned of Chernov's vulnerabilities, but we discussed it only in passing. I needed to talk to Kopali to confirm information about Chernov and see what he knew about sensitive shipments. Thank you for arranging that," said Christakis.

"So, where is Kopali now?" asked Stavros.

"Lost at sea," said Christakis.

Stavros just raised an eyebrow and shook his head. Then he said, "So you used me to neutralize Kopali?"

Christakis shrugged. He said, "I did. It was an assignment. Kopali was a security risk for Italy and NATO. I used you much as you will use me to get to Chernov. That is the business we are in, no?"

It was hard for Stavros to muster indignity over Kopali.

"And what is your present assignment?" asked Stavros.

"I cannot tell you. My primary assignment has nothing to do with you or the Circle or the GRU killer. My secondary assignment is doubling Chernov. That we can share," said Christakis.

"Does it have something to do with Red Sheepskin?" asked Stavros.

Christakis said nothing.

"Right," said Stavros.

"If you are not assigned, do not involve yourself. These are delicate matters with deadly consequences. If your CIA does not want you involved, stay away," said Christakis.

Christakis's admonishment was like throwing catnip on the ground and ordering a kitten not to roll in it. Stavros burned to know more. He might have remembered; curiosity killed the cat.

Chapter 46

"He has not reported in, comrade Colonel," replied the GRU aid.

"When was the last we heard from him?" asked Chernov.

"He dismissed the two men who helped him with Achilles. He told them he would wait at the address Achilles provided for the woman in his chain."

"Do we know the address?" asked Chernov.

"No, comrade Colonel."

"That is inexcusable!" bellowed Chernov.

"Yes, comrade Colonel."

"Do we know his vehicle?" asked Chernov.

"Yes, comrade. It was an embassy car. We know the plate number."

"Have someone at the embassy contact the Greek police and see if it is on report. Then tell only me if it is found. Is that understood?" ordered Chernov.

He didn't wait for a response and waved the aide from his office.

Chapter 47

"We should stay at a secure location tonight. The GRU knows my apartment. I'm sure it is from there that they followed us to the park. Let's stay there until we know what the GRU man has to say," Penelope said.

"Tomorrow is Sunday. I have classes and work on Monday. Can I go home then?" asked Calista.

"We will have to see. If the GRU is targeting you and me, we will both need to make some other arrangements," said Penelope.

"What does that mean?" asked Calista.

"We will have to take measures to ensure the GRU cannot find us."

"Like what?"

"We will discuss that when we know more," said Penelope.

The conversation in the backseat of the taxi was stressed. This was all new to Calista and nothing she had anticipated or bargained for.

"We'll go to the university, and I'll call my team. They can bring us in," said Penelope.

"Bring us in? Do you mean where you took me blindfolded before?"

"Probably."

Calista shook her head.

As the cab wove its way through the light Saturday afternoon traffic, the two women sat in silence. Penelope thinking one, two, and three steps ahead, and Calista stewing.

Calista asked, "Did you and Stavros have sex?"

"We don't need to discuss that," answered Penelope.

"Well, we do . . . sort of. You and I have sex. Is that part of your job? Is that something you are required to do? You know . . . under orders?" asked Calista.

Penelope brought her finger to her lips and shushed Calista. Then she leaned into the front seat and asked the taxi driver to take them to the university.

He nodded and smiled.

Chapter 48

"I thought I recognized you. You no longer have the Greek mustache, and you have more meat on your bones, Akula. It has been two years, or maybe three. I am pleased to know I am in safe care," said Kozlov with a forced smile.

Stavros looked at Christakis, wanting to ask out loud, *What the hell is he talking about.*

Christakis didn't answer and stared across the wooden tabletop at Kozlov.

Stavros said, "Can we start with something simple. What is your name?"

"I believe you have in your possession an identification card from the Union of Soviet Socialist Republics. It has my name and position at our embassy. My rank provides diplomatic immunity and consideration. By keeping me captive, you are violating international protocols and making for me a terrible inconvenience. I have important assignments to attend," smirked Kozlov.

"The ID card says you are Anatoli Ivanov. Let's pretend that is your actual name, for convenience, Anatoli. Here's another question: why were you going to kill us?" asked Stavros.

"This question, I do not understand. I was on the mountain, enjoying a morning hike, when Akula attacked me from behind. The next I know I am a prisoner of . . . who is it that is holding me? The CIA? This would be typical American menacing, no?" said Kozlov.

Christakis noticed it first. When Kozlov placed his handcuffed hands on the table, they shook. A small jitter at first, then more substantial. Kozlov return them to his lap. Christakis and Stavros both knew that the full onset of delirium tremens could take three to five days, but there were early signs and Kozlov made his second mistake. The DTs were a natural form of torture, the price an alcoholic paid for indulgence in its absence.

Christakis asked, "Are you treated well?"

"Yes, except for the ride in the boot, this is not a bad security location, a safe house. I believe that is what you American spies call such a place," answered Kozlov.

"Is your food and drink satisfactory?" asked Christakis.

"The food is average, for American cooking. The drink. . . ." and Kozlov shrugged.

"We will need to keep you here for a week, maybe two. Since you are not providing the details, we require. It will be good for you, no? Good to remove yourself from the vodka? I'm sure your attendants will make you as comfortable as you deserve," said Christakis.

Kozlov knew the DTs. He had tried to stop drinking two years before, while posted to Poland. His rezidentura in Warsaw was a teetotaler and yammered nonstop about the superior physical and moral standards of the *new Soviet man*. It didn't work; he broke down. The shaking, sweating, and shivering progressed to an irregular heartbeat. He lost his balance and couldn't stand. He crawled about his apartment. He vomited until there was nothing more, then retched in anguish. Within twenty-four hours he began hallucinating. He had cleared his apartment of booze before he began, so he drank from a bottle of rubbing alcohol. He was lucky, he only drank two swigs of it; more would have killed him. A GRU team found him unconscious when he failed to report for two days. They nearly booted him from the service, but Chernov came to his rescue, knowing his value as a killer. They reassigned him to Athens. In Athens, where practical results were more important than moral rectitude, Kozlov flourished at both of his passions, killing and drinking.

"I really must demand that you release me immediately. At minimum, I demand that you allow me to contact our embassy to report my detention," said Kozlov.

"Don't get your hopes up," said Stavros.

The Russian, translating from Greek, did not understand the American idiom. Kozlov looked puzzled.

Christakis said, "You do not have a prayer of being released. Not without cooperation. Let me describe a situation and maybe you can add some detail? If we discover enough detail, I think we should celebrate each detail with a drink. *Za vstrechu!* For the meeting, no? Do you prefer vodka or, since you are a cultural representative, perhaps a more localized beverage, tsipouro? That would be more accommodating to us Greeks, no?"

Kozlov saw now the outline of his torture.

Christakis rose from the table and went to the door of the small windowless room. He knocked twice and a security man opened it. Christakis whispered to him, then returned to the table. The three men heard the bolt close on the door.

Christakis said, "This is why you wanted to kill my friend and his associates. You can acknowledge by nodding or do nothing, you do not have to speak. This way, you remain true to your GRU oath. Since you have killed no one of our concern, no one that we know about, we have no reason to keep you further. You will leave here, get transportation to your embassy, and you will leave in a good mood, no?"

The bolt on the door slipped open and a masked security man entered with a tall bottle of clear liquid labeled Tsililli Tsipouro. He sat it on the table in front of Christakis and pulled three shot glasses from his pocket, sitting them before each man. Christakis nodded. The security man removed the handcuffs and Kozlov rubbed each wrist in turn and said, "*Spasibo.*" The security man left, and they all heard the door bolt.

Christakis worked the cork from the bottle, and a heady, florid fragrance filled the room. "It is a shame, this tsipouro is without anise. I prefer it with. And you?" asked Christakis.

Kozlov did not answer. Stavros saw him fixate on the bottle. There was something mechanical about his resolution, a dead eye fixation.

Christakis started over, "This is why you wanted to kill my friend and his associates. It is because you were under a mistaken belief that they provided information about an assassination target. You believed, incorrectly, that they were a chain supporting a splinter group who planned adventurist direct action. Direct action not sanctioned by the GRU."

Christakis picked up the bottle and allowed it to hover over Kozlov's shot glass. He stared at Kozlov. Kozlov blinked, then nodded imperceptibly. Christakis said, "I will need to be more certain of your affirmation."

This time Kozlov nodded for all to see.

Christakis poured the liqueur first for Kozlov then Stavros then himself. Then he said, *"Za vstrechu!"* The three men downed the shots, of which Christakis had poured miserly portions for himself and Stavros.

Stavros watched a flush come over Kozlov, and he thought the Russian's hand steadied as well.

Christakis smacked his lips and continued his interrogation. He asked, "I believe you knew not that the information about the target was incorrect? And that the information was planted to render the direct action impossible and spare the target, no?"

This time, Kozlov nodded distinctly and without hesitation.

Christakis poured another round. Again with smaller portions for him and Stavros. Kozlov didn't notice the difference, his focus landed fiercely on his own drink. The three drank again, and again Christakis said, *"Za vstrechu!"*

Stavros watched a glow come to Kozlov's bloodshot eyes. It was a soft beam of relief and emboldened spirit.

Christakis said, "This is good. Cooperation between men and nations. This will make the world a better home, no?"

Stavros followed Christakis's lead. Christakis knew this man much more than Stavros, and much more than Stavros would have guessed.

Christakis tacked. He asked, "Rezidentura Chernov, is he still hounded by his wife? She was the daughter of a prominent man. No? Chernov is a soldier making the wages of a colonel. This cannot be a proper fit, the two of them, no?"

Kozlov froze.

Christakis hovered the bottle over his glass.

Kozlov shrugged.

Christakis sat the bottle back on the table. He said, "Let me make this easier for you. Is Chernov a man we can buy? And are you a man we can buy?"

Now Kozlov looked frightened. His eyes darted, and all confidence drained from his face. With these types of questions, he saw little likelihood of release. In the muzzy initiation of his inebriation, he became alert to the hard end of this dialogue.

"Comrade, we will not kill you. You are killing yourself." Christakis poured another round of tsipouro. "You will take longer, this is true, but you will do the job.

"You may, however, go to one of our accommodation facilities in a country not to your liking, there to rot and die. I speak plainly. I am Greek, of this I have no choice. Perhaps my friend can speak in a more tactful way. Since you are a diplomat, this you will appreciate, no?" Christakis smiled and poured Kozlov another drink.

Kozlov bolted the shot and swallowed hard. His eyes became round, his fear deepening.

Stavros was uncertain where Christakis was headed. He recognized that the first phase of the interrogation was to whipsaw Kozlov, give him hope, then pull the rug from under him. Was Stavros supposed to reinstate hope?

Stavros said, "Anatoli, let us think positively. If you can help us, we can help you. And forget about release or your embassy coming to your rescue. To them, you are a ghost, gone forever. C'est la vie.

"All we need from you is a pledge, a two-part pledge. One, that you will kill none of our friends. And two, that from time to time you will check in with us about things of concern. Perhaps update us on GRU assignments? You know, things we will find out, but you might help us know quicker. That is all. For this, you will be freed and compensated. That part we can talk about once you've made a pledge."

The hardened GRU man was a realist. The threat of incarceration in God-knows-where was credible. He knew the Americans capable of this. Their repute for being soft and inexperienced in espionage rang true. But lifetime incarceration, this they could manage. He deserved his dilemma. He was sloppy and played loose with his tradecraft. The Torch were amateurs. Capturing and killing Achilles was child's play. Kozlov allowed himself to believe there was no counterintelligence. He failed to report his movement, and the GRU could not find him. Scales lifted from his eyes, and a troubled view of his world sharpened. He asked Stavros, "If I were to agree to such an arrangement, how would I explain my absence. My time with you will be noted."

Stavros looked at Christakis.

Christakis poured another round and said, "I have a prize for you to flaunt, a distraction. You are practiced at misdirection, no?"

Chapter 49

Stavros handed Fuller the two sheets of handwritten pledge with Kozlov's signature. At the bottom of each were a set of fingerprints. Fuller said, "Well done. Should each double be so easy, eh? I thought this guy would be harder."

Christakis said, "He has a weakness."

"Yeah, no joke. What name did he sign?" Fuller asked.

"Kozlov," said Stavros.

"Do you think that's real?" asked Fuller.

"Who knows? We've got his fingerprints," said Stavros.

"Okay, so I watched on TV and I've got some questions. What distraction will you provide? And what's with the shark reference, Akula?"

"Akula was my GRU cryptonym from a few years earlier."

Fuller stared at Christakis, then Stavros. Stavros shrugged and raised an eyebrow.

"The distraction is a man, a prisoner. He is a Greek fascist, a member of Holy Bond."

Fuller looked puzzled. He was not in the Stay Behind loop but had heard of Holy Bond. Stavros knew little as well.

Christakis could see their confusion. He said, "Holy Bond is fascist. They came from the wartime Security Battalions, the Greeks who collaborated with the Germans. Thieves and brutes and anti-KKE."

"And you know this prisoner, how?" asked Fuller.

"I was working another assignment."

"For SIFAR?" asked Stavros.

"Yes."

"So . . . I guess you can't tell us more?" said Stavros.

"No. I cannot tell you more. But the assignment was not counter to American or Greek interests," said Christakis.

"Is the OSO involved?" asked Fuller.

"No. Not that I've been told," said Christakis.

"Okay. You've got a prisoner. Where is he?" asked Fuller.

"A secure location. Perhaps not as refined as this one," answered Christakis.

"What's his condition and how long will it take to get him here. The longer Kozlov is missing, the more questions he'll have to answer," said Fuller.

"He can walk, and his injuries are not severe. A dog bit him. And he may have some bruising. I don't believe any bones are broken. He is over two hundred kilometers from here. The drive will take a day," said Christakis.

Stavros noted the dog bite.

"We can do better than that," said Fuller. "Can we land a Chickasaw anywhere near him?" asked Fuller.

Christakis looked puzzled. Fuller said, "A Sikorsky UH-19D helicopter. They fly one hundred miles an hour in straight lines. We could have the prisoner here in two hours and release Kozlov this evening. And that reminds me, we should send a team to retrieve his car, right? He'll need to look like everything is kosher. I hope the Greek police haven't found it."

"If they have, I can help," said Christakis.

"The helicopter can land half a kilometer from the location. The terrain is mountainous, and tree covered. But a clearing is nearby. I will need to go to direct the pilot," said Christakis.

Fuller said, "Stavros, go to help."

Stavros and Christakis nodded.

"We can work from Elefsina. I'll bring Kozlov, and we can put him together with his car and prisoner there. Then we'll set him free to do God's will and America's dirty work," said Fuller.

"I'll call Elefsina and get the bird fueled. You two brief Kozlov and get your butts to the airfield, pronto. If this sham works, it will be one for the books," Fuller assured them.

"Will you call Penelope, too?" asked Stavros. "She and Calista need to know what we're up to."

"Right. I meant to tell you that she and Calista spent the night at the OSO place in Kolonaki last night. I called to confirm that she was contract. It took a call to Frank before the OSO honcho would talk to me." Fuller shook his head.

"You briefed Frank on Kozlov?" asked Stavros.

"Right. He said he hopes you know what you are doing and best of luck. Sounds like you're riding lonesome, partner." Fuller smiled and added, "He said for me to help however I can but to stay focused on . . . that other thing."

Fuller didn't want to mention FIEND in front of Christakis.

Christakis knew of FIEND but not Fuller's pivotal role. The OSO and SIFAR kept their own irons in the Albanian fire. The Greek let it drop.

Stavros drove the Morris as fast as traffic allowed. He wasn't reckless, but he was determined. Keeping his eye on the street, he asked, "So your time in the GRU, were you always a double?"

"Yes. But remember, the GRU was interested in KKE, almost as much as other services. They keep track of their own. It is an obsession. It was easy to provide them harmless information."

"So . . . when you broke contact, did they not realize you were a double? Why didn't they kill you?"

"I believe they thought I was still under control, a sleeper. Someone they could activate later at their will. Now, I think they have forgotten about me. They have their hands full of CIA instead.

"I may still be on their elimination list, but for reasons known only to them, they take their precious time. I imagine they hope I will be promoted and advance in my position at the Ministry. This will make for them a greater return on their investment in me.

"Say what you will about the Russians. They are harsh and deadly, but they are also smart and play this game with eyes to the future."

"So . . . this prisoner? He has something to do with Sheepskin?" asked Stavros.

"It is better not to discuss. He will interest the GRU because of Holy Bond. The Soviets will want to know more about that organization. They do not tolerate fascists. He will be a prize for the GRU. They will bleed him of information, try to double him, and when that fails, they will make his death look like an accident. Regardless, these are outcomes to our advantage."

Stavros nodded. Then he asked, "So . . . the prisoner is on Mount Giona?"

Christakis nodded.

"Who is watching him? Do you have a SIFAR team there?" asked Stavros.

"No. Just friends. Men you have already met," said Christakis.

"I thought as much," said Stavros. "Will I see Dante again?"

Christakis grinned and said, "This is possible. He is possessive of the prisoner. I believe Dante thinks him a trophy."

Stavros chuckled.

Chapter 50

The Chickasaw was warmed up and ready when Stavros and Christakis met the flight crew on the tarmac. Christakis told them the destination, and the copilot plotted a course west-northwest on a heading of 296 degrees to the village of Lefkaditi. There they would pick up the Mornos River and fly north to the landmarks Christakis knew. When the Chickasaw lifted into the afternoon breeze, Stavros and Christakis realized it would be too noisy to talk, so they stared out the cabin windows and watched Greece roll by below the skids.

Their direct route was 134 kilometers, 83 miles. Soon the Chickasaw was at top speed with only a light headwind from the west. They rose out of the Thriasion Plain north of the Gulf of Elefsina, correcting to their plotted bearing. They struck a course between the mountains of Pyramida to the south and Paliokastro to the north. Both crags rose over seven hundred meters, and the chopper seemed to struggle for elevation. It wasn't the aircraft. The pilots, both veterans of Korea, did what all helicopter jockeys do. They stayed close to earth. If they experienced a catastrophic mechanical failure or drew enemy fire—unlikely on this mission—it was best to be low.

The ride was exciting. The treetops bent and waved only inches below the skids. Both young airmen had earned their stripes as MEDEVAC crew based in Pusan with the Third Field Hospital. The CIA needed skilled pilots and had recruited these—some say poached— from their station in Pusan. A year later, the young officers were in Greece. They liked Greece. The pay was better, and it was warmer than Korea.

They passed Mount Pastra to the south, its peak rising to over one thousand meters. Then they overflew a plain, reducing altitude to skim fields of orange trees and olive groves. The plain stretched to Elikonas where the mountains rose to 1,700 meters. Again, they climbed to clear the terrain. Greece demanded adaptive escalation to reach Mount Giona, at 2,500 meters.

Theirs was a reverse rollercoaster ride starting at the bottom and flying to the top.

After thirty minutes in the air, Christakis, seated on the port side, elbowed Stavros and motioned to the window. Stavros stared below and made out the ancient ruins at Delphi. That meant Amfissa was close and their destination nearing.

At Lefkaditi, they banked north to follow the Mornos River. The pilot motioned for Christakis to come forward. The men yelled to be heard over the engine's howl and rotor wash. They reduced speed and stayed above the river for five kilometers. Then Christakis pointed to a fire tower, and the pilot banked the Chickasaw to the east. Christakis searched the topology and spotted a small, remote church.

The Church of Holy Trinity was a simple affair, no bigger than a farm shed. Its only religious adornment was a cross leaded into the stained glass of its door. But the area around the church was clear and level, big enough, Christakis hoped, to land the Chickasaw.

Christakis pointed, and the pilot indicated he could see the landing zone. The pilot looked over at the copilot, who shrugged and gave him a thumbs up.

The aircraft set down in a whirling cloud of dust and fir needles. It was early for vesper services, so landing did not inconvenience the handful of locals planning to attend that Sunday evening. Stavros and Christakis belted on Colt .45 pistols and grabbed M1 carbines from the weapons rack in the cabin. With Christakis in the lead, they set off for the cabin and the prisoner.

Basil greeted them at the door with his shotgun in the crook of his arm. He said, "I heard you arrive. I am glad to see it is you and not Holy Bond. It is only me and Dante so. . . ."

"So you would have shot the prisoner and fled, no?" asked Christakis.

Basil shrugged.

"Good to see you, Basil," said Stavros.

"And you. I trust you are well, Lieutenant. What did they call you? Lieutenant Professor?" Basil chuckled.

Stavros said, "I really would like to know where you Greeks get your information."

"The only secret in Greece. . . ." started Basil.

"Is why Greeks cannot keep a secret," Stavros finished.

"So, you know. This is good," said Basil.

Christakis asked, "How is the prisoner?"

"He is alive, but he smells like death. I would have thrown him into the creek if I'd known you were coming. Would you like to do that now?" asked Basil.

"No time, my friend. Can he walk?" asked Christakis.

"Oh yes. He can walk. You should blindfold him until you reach the trailhead. Then let him see until you are near the church. Blindfold him again, then give him a thrilling ride in a helicopter. If I were coming, I would throw him out over the sea. I have no use for such a man," said Basil.

"I understand, my friend. But the swine has value for another mission, and I must thank you and Atticus for minding him," said Christakis.

"This we do for friendship and Greece," said Basil. "Oh, and thank someone else, no?"

He whistled twice, and Dante bounded from the cabin door and came to an excited heel next to Basil.

Stavros said, "Dante, how nice to see you. You are looking brutish as ever."

Dante took the acknowledgment as a compliment and sniffed the air in Stavros's direction. Christakis called the dog with a pat on his thigh. Dante looked to Basil for permission and with his master's nod, bounded to Christakis, his stubby tail wagging like an over-wound metronome.

Basil said, "He misses you, and your treats."

Christakis pulled from his jacket pocket a half-eaten pastry wrapped in a paper napkin. Stavros recognized it from the safe house in Kifissia. Christakis said, "Sedersi." Dante sat, his tail still wagging in the dust. Christakis gave him the treat and patted him on his blocky head.

Stavros started to ask if they had trained Dante in Italy, but decided it was a question better left for later.

"All right, let us move the prisoner, and another day we will play with the dogs," said Christakis.

The return to Elefsina was quicker than the trip out. The Chickasaw benefited from a tailwind. They landed at 1700 hours, and Fuller greeted them on the tarmac. Christakis and Stavros thanked the flight crew and grabbed the blindfolded prisoner under the armpits, pulling him out of the cabin. At flight control, they met a freshened Kozlov waiting with this car. They placed the prisoner in the boot, and the four men stood ready to part. Fuller first handed Kozlov his Makarov, then its ammunition clip. Fuller said, "You can charge your weapon when you're in the car, *capisce?*"

Kozlov nodded.

Christakis, Fuller, and Stavros still wore their Colts.

Stavros said, "We'll be in touch. You know the tricks. We'll need to talk next week to see how things went."

Kozlov nodded.

"That's when you'll receive compensation, as we agreed."

"Yes. I understand. What can you tell me about our guest?" Kozlov asked, nodding to the boot of the car.

"He is swine, fascist swine. If you do not already have a file, start one and title it Holy Bond. These are men who hate communists, all communists. Especially you.

"This one reports to a control in Athens known as Sentinel. If you learn more, you must tell me. This is our arrangement," said Christakis.

Kozlov nodded. He said, "I believe we are aware of this group." Then he got into his car, charged his Makarov, and drove away.

Fuller said, "I wonder what he'll tell the GRU?"

"It doesn't matter. If the GRU kills them both, it is no loss to us," said Stavros.

"Run him and see where it leads. Chernov is still the big fish, right?" asked Fuller.

Both men nodded.

"All right. I'll see you two the next time you need accommodations. If anything comes up, Stavros, you know how to get in touch," said Fuller.

The men shook hands.

Fuller walked away, then turned and said, "Oh, I talked with Penelope, Stavros. She said she wants you to call."

Then he turned again to leave and bellowed a laugh as he walked away.

Chapter 51

Stavros did not call Penelope, she called him. She got no answer. Then she took a taxi to the Grande Bretagne and waited in the lobby. She didn't know his room, or she would have gone there. She asked the front desk to call him, but the polite young woman behind the counter told her that Mr. Theofanis had asked not to be disturbed. It was late. At ten thirty she asked the concierge for a favor.

She handed him five dollars and said, "Will you please go to Mr. Theofanis and tell him Penelope needs to see him, and it is urgent. Then, use this word for recognition, *Meltemi*."

The young man knew Mr. Theofanis. He accepted the tip, went to his room, and seeing a light under his door, he knocked gently and announced he had a message.

Stavros came to the door. The young man gave him the message ending with Meltemi, the codeword for doubling Chernov. Stavros thanked him, closed the door, and said to no one, "Shit!"

He needed to talk to Penelope. She knew the codeword for Chernov. He hadn't told her, Christakis hadn't told her, Fuller didn't know, so someone in the chain had told her. And that meant only one other person, Frank.

They couldn't talk in the lobby; that would not be secure. And he didn't want her to know his room number. On the roof of the hotel was a swimming pool. It was closed this time of year, but his guest key would open the door, and it would be unoccupied. He called the front desk, asked if there was a young woman in the lobby and could the receptionist patch him through to her. A minute later, Penelope picked up a house phone and said, "Stavros, we need to talk. Now."

"Okay, listen. Come to the rooftop swimming pool. I'll unlock the door, and we can go outside for this discussion. I'm going there now."

She did as she was told and three minutes later stood before him on the deck of an empty covered swimming pool under a trellis of dormant wisteria. He stared and didn't speak. She said, "Frank told me the codeword."

"I don't believe you," replied Stavros.

"Stavros, really, he did. I got reprimanded for, you know . . . my mission, but he said to talk to you about Meltemi. He thinks I can help."

"Bullshit," said Stavros. "Who are you really working for?"

"Stavros, I'm OSO, that's it. Everything I said at the safe house is true. Calista is my asset. They ordered me to develop you.

"Listen, I think I have a way to double Chernov."

He didn't respond.

"We can use Calista, but maybe not in the way you might think."

He didn't respond. But she had his attention.

"Stavros, I didn't ask for the mission to develop you. They ordered me. They didn't order me to take it so far . . . I was to report on the possibility that you, and Dimitra were working for KKE. And given Dimitra's past. . . ."

He cut her off, "You know nothing of Dimitra's past. She is. . . ." He wanted to say, *ten times the woman and twenty times the patriot you will ever be*. But he pulled back. Penelope didn't need to see his anger.

"I get that, now. But before, I knew only what your jacket told me. Your file is impressive but might be open to speculation. Right?"

He didn't respond.

"Can we sit down?" she asked and nodded to a wooden bench on the far side of the pool.

Stavros knew this tactic. Get the target to relax, sit close to them and imply trustworthiness and intimacy.

He said, "No."

"I am not manipulating you. I am tired. I spent the entire night last night talking to Calista, reasoning with Calista. I got no sleep. And by the way, her codename is Alepoú."

"Vixen?" asked Stavros.

"Or fox, have it either way," said Penelope.

Stavros thought, dead giveaway and sloppy. OSO amateurs.

She said, "I'm going to the bench, you can come or not. I need to sit down."

He followed. She sat, and he stood.

"Stavros, can we try to clear the air about my assignment before we get into Meltemi? I need to say something." It wasn't really a question; Stavros knew something was coming, whatever he said.

He said, "Shoot."

She looked up from the bench with the tired but magnetic hazel eyes that had duped him before. She said, "I wanted for us to be together. I mean, after I figured out that you were not KKE. I think you are one hell of a man. I can go on, but you'd just think I'm piling on compliments to cover my lies. Most of what I told you about myself is true. I haven't shared that with any man, ever.

"I know you have every right to hate me, but somewhere in my childish notions I look forward to a day when all this is behind us when we might. . . ."

Stavros cut her off, "Penelope, that's never going to happen. I could never trust you."

She nodded, and tears swelled in her eyes.

She took Stavros in for less than a second. It was the oldest tactic in the woman verses man playbook. He said, "What do you think Calista might do for Meltemi. That's why we're here, right?"

In a choked voice, she said, "Right." She sniffled. "Well, Calista is talented. Her looks and personality will take her far.

But these are obvious devices. Chernov would smell a trap. But I'm wondering about Mrs. Chernov?"

"What do you know I don't know," asked Stavros.

"That's a tautology, Professor," said Penelope.

"Tell me about Mrs. Chernov," said Stavros.

"We know she is coming to Athens for a visit. She will be here sometime early next week, we think Wednesday. That's when embassy staff typically fly in from Moscow. We believe she'll be on that plane."

"We? The OSO?" asked Stavros.

"Yes. We have been listening. You can tell Christakis he can reassign his Ministry team watching Chernov. They might get in the way."

"So how would Calista, Alepoú, come into play?" asked Stavros.

"I'm thinking we dress her up. Then we put her in touch with Mrs. Chernov. Then we let her spin her wiles and make Mrs. Chernov think she's discovered that her husband has been funding a well-cared-for plaything," said Penelope.

"And why would that turn Chernov?" asked Stavros.

"Pressure. Money pressure. Mrs. Chernov will want the same, perhaps more. Her family is well-off. . . ."

"Yeah, I know. Well-off, connected, prominent, while Chernov is only making a colonel's salary," said Stavros.

"We can backstop our approach with some pictures. Photos of Chernov and Alepoú together. All dressed up. Nothing risqué; that might be too obvious," she said.

"And where would these photos come from," asked Stavros.

"From our imagination and my cutting room floor," said Penelope.

Stavros could not dismiss Penelope's idea. In it he saw merit and imagination. The key would be to put Alepoú and Mrs. Chernov together with the element of happenstance.

"You say Wednesday?"

Penelope nodded.

"How long is she staying?"

"We think a week. She'll take the same flight back a week from Wednesday," said Penelope.

"I need to talk with Christakis," said Stavros.

Penelope nodded. Then she said, "When you feel like it, I'd love to hear about Mister GRU."

"Right," Stavros nodded. "Are we finished?"

"Stavros. . . ." Penelope began.

He held up his hand and cut her off. He said, "It was a presupposition without a terminal answer. Not a tautology."

He had taken the bait. A glint came to her eye, and she smiled when he looked away.

Chapter 52

Vera Chernov was a heavy woman. She was in her early fifties with dyed blond hair and a prominent brow. When the couple married in their early twenties, she was not so heavy. Two children, potatoes, vodka, borsht, and age had changed things. Still, she carried about her an air of haughty superiority and disdain for lesser people. These she judged by their dress and manners.

Like all Russian women of means, she appreciated furs. Now, in Athens and among the world's leading furriers, she went shopping. Avanti Furs had served Athens for over one hundred fifty years. Their business reputation was stellar, and their brand was the ticket to bragging rights among Russian connoisseurs. Their storefront on Ipatias was only five blocks from the Grande Bretagne and faced a park called Metropolis Square. On a bench in that park sat a couple eating their takeaway lunch of souvlaki and chips.

Mrs. Chernov arrived in an embassy car with two security men and the woman eating her lunch bent over to get something from her purse. This was the signal. A stunning blonde in a lustrous full-length sable came out of the shoe store next door before Mrs. Chernov could scoot her heft from the car and walk to Avanti. The blonde entered Avanti a minute before Mrs. Chernov. A security man checked inside Avanti and came back outside. He nodded all clear, and Mrs. Chernov told the two to wait on the curb. Then the nearest security man held the door, and she entered the store.

Calista was a performer. And she was an observer of other's performances. It was one reason she had latched onto Achilles. Penelope had coached Calista on the manners of a superior woman, a woman of class and high society, and Calista was a quick study. Her performance wasn't perfect, but it didn't have to be. Mrs. Chernov saw what she expected to see. An intelligent, beautiful young woman with her life ahead of her and well-positioned to afford the best in furs.

Calista took off the sable and handed it to a pert attendant. She wore under it a fitted Bordeaux sheath. She was flawless. Mrs. Chernov watched her out of the corner of her eye and told herself that this woman would age, as surely as herself.

Calista waited for the attendant. She caught Mrs. Chernov's eye and smiled at her. Her electric green eyes nailed into Mrs. Chernov a bolt of envy.

The attendant returned with a white waist-length mink with a high, showy collar. Calista slipped into it with the ease of water flowing in a brook. She walked to the full-length mirror and did a half-twirl. Then she pursed her lips. She glanced over at Mrs. Chernov and said, "Excuse me."

Mrs. Chernov said, "Yes?"

"May I ask your opinion of this piece? I can see by your wrap that you know style, no?" asked Calista.

"Thank you for your confidence," said Mrs. Chernov.

"May I ask, where do you intend to wear this piece?" inquired Mrs. Chernov.

"My friend, he is taking me to the Maria Callas concert next month. Do you think it too garish for such an event?" confided Calista.

"In Moscow, yes. In Athens . . . I imagine it will be welcome and make you quite an attraction," answered Mrs. Chernov.

"Oh, yes. In Athens it would fit nicely. But the concert is at Teatro alla Scala in Milan, Italy. The military will fly us there.

"I just can't decide. I think it is too bulky around. . . ." Then Calista put both hands under her breasts and jostled them upward. She smacked her lips, "I just can't decide."

Calista turned to the attendant and thanked her. The attendant took the mink and returned with Calista's sable. Calista slipped into the fur and reached her right hand into her pocket for a pair of smart leather gloves. As she removed the gloves, a photograph fell to the floor and the courteous Mrs. Chernov reached to pick it up for her. It was a picture taken at an official function with her husband in uniform and Calista on his arm. Stunned and slack-jawed, she handed it to Calista who said with an innocent smile, "Oh, thank you. This is my friend."

Calista sashayed from the store with the intent of a languid fox.

Chapter 53

Christakis decided not to lie. He told Director Broccoli the entire story about Holy Bond and using the prisoner as leverage against the GRU. He told the director that compatriots of Greek Holy Bond had compromised SIFAR. Italians of the same fascist bent. And someone in SIFAR had tipped off Holy Bond about his mission.

Broccoli listened, then began a careful response. "These matters of infiltration I know about. We are working to find such men.

"Your mission is over. You cannot infiltrate Holy Bond. They know you are SIFAR.

"Now, I need to talk to you about another matter."

Christakis sensed gravity in the director's voice.

"They have asked me to allow you to liaison with the American CIA, in an official capacity. You will maintain your cover at the Ministry for Public Security, but from today forward, you are to report to whoever the CIA tells you to. Is that clear?" asked the director, his tone implying it was not a question.

"Your pay and benefits will pass to the Americans. Do you see a problem, Capitano?" This time, it was a question.

It struck Christakis dumb. He fell back on his military indoctrination. He said, "No, sir. No problem if this is the will of the service."

"Good," said Broccoli. "Capitano, your record is exemplary. The Americans and Italians are allies. We are both members of NATO. I will not ask you to double your service for us on the Americans. There is no need. When you leave Rome, you will return to Athens detached from SIFAR. I must remind you of your pledge to maintain the secrecy of our operations unless ordered to disclose them by a superior officer. A SIFAR officer. Do you understand?"

"Yes, sir," said Christakis.

"Alexis, this request came from the highest level of CIA administration. That is all I know. Italy is an independent country and SIFAR is its own service, but the Americans have what they would call a lot of pull. They pay the bills and write the rules. If it were up to me, I would never ask you to leave.

"Now you have a choice, no? You can accept your orders and work with the CIA or resign from all services. That would leave you with your position at the Ministry but outside of intelligence work. I believe at this work you are good, maybe exceptional. But if you do not want to further your career, now is the time to quit. You can take that up with the Americans in Athens."

Christakis nodded. Then he asked, "Who is my CIA contact in Athens?"

"Stavros Theofanis."

It was a three-hour flight from Pratica di Mare to Elefsina in a ponderous but reliable C-47. Christakis was the only passenger. He sat on the port side, looking out at the low hills of southern Italy. Then he recognized the half-moon Port of Taranto at the top of the boot heel and thought about his great-grandfather and his grandfather. They had made their lives and raised their families on this narrow appendage jutting into the sea. If his great-grandfather had stayed in Greece, Christakis would never have connected to Italy. Never received courtesy from his Italian captors, and never worked for Naval Intelligence.

Then there was open water, the Ionian Sea. He spotted two oil tankers en route to Taranto but couldn't make out their flagging. Then came the cliffs of Ákra Agíou Georgíou on Corfu. From there they paralleled the southwest coast of an island that Christakis thought of as half Italian and half Greek, though the Greeks would argue with that.

The Douglas droned on. As the snowy dome of Mount Giona rose on the horizon, his mind, still lost in thought, slipped back to his childhood. He had grown up near the village of

Gravia, just east of the peak. They had nicknamed the unnamed village Piccolo Brindisi, Little Brindisi. Most were hard-working farmers, Italian veterans of Domokos, and their sons and daughters, eking out a living on the plains east of the regal mountain.

His family was not poor. They did not want for anything. No family in their settlement had much more or much less than any other. His childhood had been a happy time until the war. He'd played in the countryside and hiked on the mountain with his brother like all the Greek boys and treasured all the memories: hunting, sports, girls. Then came the war.

For his mother, he felt the most remorse, infinite emptiness. She had been a saint. Her soft Italian cooing comforted him in a blanket of protection and safety. But her words stung like wasps when he transgressed. His stern father worked all the time, every day, a tireless provider. He deserved better than death at the hands of the Nazis. His sister, Eva, was only four years old. As a teenager, he had paid her little attention, but now he missed her like a part of his own body. These reflections, these haunting memories he buried. But the order from SIFAR triggered a personal inventory, tumbling his defenses. He took stock of his twenty-seven years and struggled to place himself in the grand scheme.

He was unmarried with no serious involvement. His women friends were for convenience, not attachment. Without a family to consider, it was not a factor in his decision, in his life.

If he accepted the CIA, things would change. SIFAR gave him a long leash. He knew little of CIA's doggedness, but he knew of their organizational confusion. Stavros and Penelope were a prime example. One OPC and one OSO, at odds and working at cross-purposes. One hand not knowing the other's purpose. It did not give him confidence.

He held nothing against the Americans. They had saved Greece from ruin and communist domination. To them empire was an economic arrangement, not GIs billeted on the Acropoli.

They promoted democracy and meant it. They weren't perfect, but in sum, they advanced civilization.

The Americans had money, endless stacks of money. They could buy anything. Anything but experience and savvy. Still, Americans were leaders. They commanded a dominant military and an indomitable notion of destiny. They thought in novel ways, bold ways. Not always the best ways, but they didn't recoil at originality. In the end, if he wanted to stay in intelligence, working for the CIA would be attaching himself to a rising star.

He thought again about family. If he wanted to start a family, now would be the time for detachment from intelligence. But the idea of family was painful. The Stoic in him said, if you do not have a family, they cannot take it from you. Then he told himself that he was still young. Perhaps after ten years with the CIA, he would still be of an age to marry and have children.

Then there was Stavros. He didn't know how to feel about him. He liked Stavros as a man, respected his skills, and admired his intellect. But had Stavros engineered this change? Without talking to him? That didn't seem in character. Stavros was a puzzle, a worrying puzzle. He would call Stavros from Elefsina and set a meeting for later in the day.

His ears popped as the aircraft descended on its final approach.

Chapter 54

"I didn't ask him to do it. Frank contacted SIFAR without my knowing. I just found out before you called," Stavros assured him.

The two men were again in the lobby of the Grande Bretagne. It was late, and they were alone.

Christakis believed the flummoxed Stavros.

"So, what is the plan?" asked Christakis.

"Frank said to keep working on Meltemi and manage The Circle. But first, we need to get you with Tommy Karamessines and get you enrolled, get the pay and benefits straight. You *are* coming to work with us, right?"

"Yes," answered Christakis. But his lack of depth and commitment worried Stavros.

Stavros said, "Listen. You are my friend. That comes first. I'm going to let you in on something that I think Frank is trying to accomplish. This is off the record, okay?"

Christakis nodded.

"Frank wants me in Washington. Back in October, he told me he wanted me there within a year. I think he thinks of you as my replacement. Someone, a Greek, who knows the down and dirty. His eyes and ears. I imagine, and this is only a guess, that Hod Fuller has told him about you. I'm sure you impressed Hod. Hell, you impressed me. That Holy Bond deception for Kozlov was a brilliant move. Inspired.

"So, this is just a guess, but I think Frank is moving me to Washington and you are my replacement. What worries me is that it's happening faster than I thought. I need to get some personal things sorted before I leave," confided Stavros.

"That would be Dimitra?" asked Christakis.

"That would be Dimitra," answered Stavros.

Christakis nodded.

"Dimitra and material for my dissertation," added Stavros.

Stavros was ten years into the future Christakis. Stavros was at the far end of a decision, CIA, or family. Marriage or career. But with Dimitra, things would not be simple. Christakis held his tongue.

"We'll go to the embassy and put you with Tommy tomorrow. It shouldn't take that long, a couple of hours, a day at most," said Stavros. "You've got Frank's seal of approval, and you know Tommy, so the skid is greased."

It was a new idiom for Christakis. He nodded.

"I'm told the Alepoú and Mrs. Chernov encounter went well. I've got to hand it to Penelope. It was a clever idea. She's devious, and I'm glad she's on our side . . . I hope she's on our side," Stavros flashed back to Dimitra's injunction about the *treacherous mouse*.

"According to Penelope, Mrs. Chernov is supercharged with resentment. Raging hot. She is demanding to be taken to a concert in Milan, and dressed for the event, and our target's life just became hell. Penelope wouldn't tell me the details, she said I did not need to know. But I think the OSO has a maintenance man in Chernov's apartment building who listens through the steam registers and pipes with a stethoscope. She said something about her contact not needing a stethoscope to hear their quarreling," Stavros shrugged.

"Alepoú? I assume she did well, and she is safe?" asked Christakis.

Stavros noted a weight of concern in Christakis's question. He said, "She's great. Back in school. Penelope said the only glitch was that Alepoú wanted to keep the sable fur. She tried to argue that she may need it to preserve her cover. Penelope wasn't buying," said Stavros.

"Did she quit her job at the taverna where Chernov eats lunch?" asked Christakis.

"Yes. That's my understanding. OSO compensated her for her contact with Mrs. Chernov. Penelope wouldn't tell me how much. We can find out, but I don't think it's important," said Stavros.

"So, you've been talking to Penelope?" asked Christakis.

"Only about Meltemi. Everything else is off limits," said Stavros.

"She will try to keep you engaged. She is a smart and complex woman, and you broke her heart," said Christakis.

"I doubt that. She'd have to have a heart for someone to break. But you're right, she is complex . . . and best kept at arm's length," said Stavros.

"What do you think about approaching Chernov? Is it time? And if it is time, who should do it and where? Chernov might like to hear about supplemental employment opportunities, no?" asked Stavros.

"I can do that," said Christakis.

"Really? Are you sure that's not just putting your name at the top of the GRU elimination list?" asked Stavros.

Christakis shrugged. "Who else would do it? Alepoú is blown; Mrs. Chernov can identify her. Penelope is not a choice."

"Alexis, I value your commitment, but I have to question your exposure. I think you're putting yourself at risk. Let's think it over for a couple of days. Let's get you papered and in the system. We'll figure out something. The concert is not until December, a month away, so Chernov will be on the hot seat for a while. Let's think about it, okay?" urged Stavros.

Christakis nodded to his new boss. Then he asked, "What is my cryptonym?"

"I don't know. We'll let Tommy fill in that blank. We've got fifty people at headquarters whose job it is to generate codenames."

"And what is yours?" asked Christakis.

Stavros looked up at the ceiling and pretended not to hear.

Christakis repeated, "Stavros, if we are to work together, I need to know your cryptonym."

Stavros replied in an inaudible mumble, "Professor."

"What! The CIA assigned that?" laughed Christakis.
Stavros nodded, "It followed me from OSS."
Christakis chuckled and shook his head.

Chapter 55

The ZIM swayed like a wayward whale frisking with a mate. The black Soviet limousine weighed over two tons, and the four GRU operatives inside added heft and a cloud of eye-watering cigarette smoke. The driver horsed the steering wheel like the helm of a schooner, straining to bring its bow into a Meltemi gale.

Kozlov's vehicle was better for the twisting, narrow roads that were his choice for escape. But his Pobeda was underpowered. It made Stavros's Morris look like a sports car. Kozlov picked up his tail north of Nea Penteli, about ten minutes from his designated rendezvous with Stavros and Christakis at Daveli Cave. The mountains, thirty minutes north of Athens, rose to eight hundred meters. The roads were dirt and gravel with endless switchbacks, hairpin turns, and few guard rails.

Kozlov had a problem. Even more of a problem than the four goons chasing him. The GRU had made him as a double. He was blown. They had debriefed his Holy Bond prisoner, used on him the latest truth drug and torture, and believed his account of being captured by a SIFAR agent and transferred to Kozlov. Chernov couldn't save Kozlov and didn't want to save Kozlov. Chernov detested the man, useful though he had been. And Chernov was distracted by his raging wife. There was no angel to save Kozlov; he was on the run.

Ten kilometers from the cave, Kozlov led by two hundred meters. He watched in his rearview mirror the ZIM following like a persistent bear, clawing its way closer on the straights, and falling behind on the curves. Then, at the end of a long stretch, the road rose into a berm beyond which Kozlov could not see. He topped the rise, and the Pobeda went airborne for an instant before he saw the sharp left bend. It took all his luck and driving skill, but he stayed on the road, made the turn, and sped downhill toward another switchback. When he completed the switchback, he viewed where he just traveled. He watched the ZIM fly over the hump toward the hidden curve. The ZIM was not so lucky.

The limousine launched and wallowed as the driver steered hard left. For a moment it rose on its right side wheels, and gravel flew. Then momentum, gravity, and destiny flung it into the abyss, tumbling down the rocks, erupting in flames halfway to the valley below, then coming to a blazing rest on its roof. Even Kozlov, a man who had witnessed bizarre death and destruction, gasped. It looked like a movie.

Kozlov was a professional. He had known this day would come, the day when he would have to disappear or face the consequences of a life of murder and deceit. He'd made plans and stashed his tools of escape. But the only tools in his possession were his Makarov and a few Greek drachmas. In Athens, in a dingy bus station, he had a locker. In it was a satchel with money, false identification, a fake passport, and a beard for disguise. Looking back at his planning, he realized a bus station, even one for local travel, would be watched. The GRU would watch every point of transit in Athens. He had run these exercises himself. He had a car, but its diplomatic plates were a dead giveaway. His chance, his only chance, was to meet his handlers, feed them a fake report, and take his compensation. He expected two thousand American dollars. After he had the money, he would kill them to end the trail, take their car, and run. He would charter a small boat to Izmir, Turkey. From there he could travel by train or bus to the city of Elazığ. He knew the GRU was thin in Eastern Anatolia. Elazığ was majority Kurdish who spoke Zazas, and the GRU struggled to fit in or recruit agents. If they found him, he could move on to somewhere in the Middle East. He'd cross that bridge when the time came. But now, he needed money. Once in Turkey, he could buy other tools.

Stavros and Christakis waited at Daveli Cave. They had parked the Morris farther up the rough road, out of sight. Christakis took an overwatch position on a crag above the cave entrance. He shouldered a standard issue M1 Garand with open sights that, from thirty meters, would be deadly accurate.

The Pobeda arrived, skidding to a stop, scattering dust and rocks. Stavros watched from the modest church built into the cave entrance. Agios Nikolaos, the church, and Agios Spyridon, the hermitage in the cave's depths, had occupied Daveli since the thirteenth century. This dank morning in November, they were empty and remote. A perfect rendezvous.

Stavros watched Kozlov get out of his car. He looked around and Stavros waved from the cave's entrance. Kozlov waved in return and walked the fifty meters up the gravel path to meet him. As he got closer, Kozlov saw Stavros's Colt in a holster on his right hip. Kozlov's Makarov was in his coat pocket. Kozlov couldn't see their car, and Stavros was armed. This wouldn't be easy. He asked, "Where is your SIFAR friend?"

Stavros motioned to the rock wall behind him. Kozlov let his eyes search the shear face until he spotted the ledge with a scraggly shrub and Christakis with his rifle trained on his chest. He said, "Am I not trusted?"

Stavros ignored him. He asked, "Are you armed?"

"Only with my Makarov. You are much better armed than me."

"Hand it over, grip first," ordered Stavros.

Kozlov complied, he had no choice.

Stavros took the weapon and stood back to his original distance. He asked, "How did it go?"

"I told them I discovered the Holy Bond connection following the chain from The Torch. I told them Holy Bond provoked the assassination plan and supplied Achilles with his weapons. They wanted to discredit the communist movement. They took the prisoner into custody, and I believe they are questioning him, as we expected."

"How is your cover?" asked Stavros.

"Good, so far as I can tell," Kozlov lied.

"Do you have anything for us on Rezidentura Chernov?" asked Stavros.

"No. Only that he is short tempered, and rumors are that he and his wife are fighting. GRU has ordered to make NATO a priority, but you would expect that, no? And there is one other thing. They asked about Holy Bond. They asked if I ran other assets in the organization. I told them no. They said they believed the CIA funded Holy Bond. They asked if I could confirm this? I said no."

Stavros noted the funding but didn't let on.

"Do you? Fund Holy Bond?" asked Kozlov.

Stavros just stared at the killer.

"I wouldn't expect you to answer," said Kozlov. "May I have my money now? It is best we make of this a short meeting, no?"

Stavros pulled from his back pocket an envelope and laid it on a boulder to his left. He ejected the clip of the Makarov and cycled the slide to eject the round in the chamber. Then he handed the unloaded weapon back to Kozlov. He placed the clip with the envelope and said, "You make take these after I leave. When I am out of sight, pick them up, leave here, and plan to be in touch next week. Are we clear?" asked Stavros.

Kozlov nodded. This required improvisation. He needed the money, most of all. But he needed their car, too. To get their car, he would have to kill Stavros and Christakis. But how?

Stavros turned to walk away and Kozlov waited until he was out of sight. He looked up at Christakis, who motioned with the barrel of the M1 for Kozlov to pick up his things and leave.

Kozlov picked up the Makarov and reinserted the clip, then he cycled the action to put a round into the firing chamber. He stooped to pick up the loose round Stavros ejected and put it in his pocket along with the Makarov. Then he picked up the envelope and looked inside. He didn't need to count the money. The American currency in twenty-dollar bills, no matter the exact amount, would be plenty to get him to Turkey.

He walked back down the path to the Pobeda. He sat behind the wheel and before he turned the key; he pumped the accelerator pedal six times, flooding the engine. He cranked the motor, and it wouldn't start. He tried again, still it wouldn't start. He stepped outside and looked up at Christakis, holding his arms outstretched in a pleading posture.

It didn't surprise Christakis that the Pobeda was a problem. He knew the vehicle's reputation for unreliability.

Kozlov yelled to Christakis, "I think it's the battery. I have cables. Can you help?"

Christakis climbed from his perch and joined Stavros at the car just up the road. He said, "Kozlov has car problems. Should we help?"

"What's the problem?" asked Stavros.

Christakis shrugged and shook his head.

"We can't leave him here. The risk of him blowing his cover is too great. Let's go see what he wants," said Stavros.

The two men got into the Morris and drove the short distance back to the cave. When the Morris pulled alongside the Pobeda, Christakis rolled down the passenger window. Kozlov approached and said, "I think it's the battery, but I have cables. And I have this. . . ." He pulled the Makarov from his pocket and aimed it through the passenger side door at Christakis. He said to Stavros, "Turn off the car. Put your hands on the wheel where I can see them."

Kozlov stood about a meter beyond the swing of the passenger door. Christakis searched for a way to render him off balance to take his weapon.

He said to Christakis, "Throw your sidearm out of the window, then get out of the car and kneel by the door."

"You," and he looked at Stavros. "Throw your weapon out of the window but stay in the car with your hands on the wheel. Where's the rifle?"

"In the boot," said Stavros.

Kozlov peered into the rear seat and didn't see the weapon.

"Let's get this over with," said Kozlov. "I want the car."

Neither Stavros nor Christakis believed he would stop there.

Christakis flung his Colt out of his window to the rear of the Morris and opened the door. Stavros pitched his Colt out the driver's window into a low bush.

Kozlov kept his weapon trained on Christakis, now kneeling and vulnerable. He circled Christakis to retrieve his weapon and as he did, his eyes strayed from Stavros. In a practiced silent motion, Stavros found the fake bolt under the Morris's dash and lowered the compartment with the Colt. He took the gun in his left hand so he could leave his right on the wheel, hoping Kozlov wouldn't notice his other hand missing.

Kozlov returned to where he could keep Stavros and Christakis both in his sights. Stavros saw Kozlov take aim at the back of Christakis's neck and brought the Colt around, firing twice through the passenger window. He hadn't fired lefthanded since his OSS training in 1943. He jerked the trigger using his fingertip, and his first shot went wide. But in the instant it took to reacquire his target, muscle memory from hours of practice returned. He curled his finger at the second knuckle, put the meaty part on the trigger, and squeezed. His second caught Kozlov in the right shoulder. A Colt .45 at close range is a mighty hammer. The bullet's 230 grains found its mark at nearly 900 feet per second. The force of the round spun Kozlov, and he flung the Makarov. Christakis grabbed it from the dirt. With Kozlov writhing like a winged chicken on the road, Christakis kicked him in the side. When Kozlov stopped moving, Christakis reclaimed his Colt, stepped away, then remembered the money. He kicked Kozlov again and lifted the envelope from his coat pocket. Stavros sprinted around the car's hood and the two men stood over their would-be killer.

Christakis said, "I'd like to finish him, but I think we can use him."

Stavros nodded. He couldn't hear a thing. The .45's discharge inside the Morris had left his ears ringing.

"When I heard your shot, I thought he'd missed me, but I saw no impact. Where did you get that gun?"

Stavros pointed to his ear and Christakis knew the problem. Christakis pointed to the Colt.

In a voice overly amplified and articulated, Stavros said, "Always have a backup. This Morris may be slow, but it's well equipped."

Chapter 56

"Back so soon? And this time with a medivac and a Soviet Embassy car. You two are busy beavers." Fuller greeted Stavros and Christakis in the foyer of the Kifissia safe house. "Discharging your weapon in the line of duty; now you've got some paperwork." Then he looked at Christakis and said, "Oh, and welcome to the CIA.

"Give me five minutes then tell me all about it. Security will take what's-his-name. They'll move him downstairs and patch him up. Is it serious?"

"Shouldn't be. Shoulder wound, through and through. He's lost some blood, but he should recover," said Stavros.

"Right. Let's talk it over. Give me a minute and I'll be right back." Then Fuller bounded up the staircase.

Stavros and Christakis moved to the solarium and sat in the far corner. Stavros, trying to keep things light, asked, "How did the Pobeda drive?"

Christakis shook his head. Then he said, "Thank you for shooting Kozlov. And coming prepared. We made a mistake by letting him get close without disarming him and by not bringing our weapons to bear when we approached."

Stavros nodded and said, "Yep. Next time, we'll know better."

Fuller joined them across a coffee table. He slapped his thighs as he sat. He said, "Sorry for the interruption. I needed to finish the call." Then he looked at Christakis and said, "Looks like you are about to be read in on FIEND. I guess you told someone you speak Albanian?"

Christakis nodded, "I speak Tosk, Gheg not so much."

"Right. We'll take care of that later. Now, tell me what happened with . . . what's he calling himself?" asked Fuller.

"Kozlov," answered Stavros. "We set a meet north of Athens. He showed up, we disarmed him, he briefed, money changed hands. Then we got sloppy, he tricked us, got the drop on us, but we recovered."

"What was the trick?" asked Fuller.

"Engine problem. His car wouldn't start. He got us close, then got the drop," said Stavros.

"How'd you get out of that," asked Fuller.

"The equipment guys hid a Colt under the dash of the Morris. He looked the other way, I grabbed it, and I shot him," said Stavros.

"So, why didn't you kill him," asked a puzzled Fuller.

"He is a gift, the swag you might bring to the host of a dinner party," said Christakis.

"Who is hosting this party?" asked Fuller.

"Chernov," said Christakis.

Chapter 57

The code was from two years earlier, but Chernov recognized it. Akula wanted to meet. As he left his apartment in Psychiko near the embassy, he saw a freshly scrawled, underlined number three in blue chalk on the white wall at the street entrance. Christakis would be at the meeting site that evening, and he wanted Chernov to come alone. Chernov didn't go anywhere alone since his promotion to rezidentura, but that he could finesse. It made him smile. He liked Akula. He thought the young man was smart and counted it a failing not recruiting him into the GRU. Perhaps Akula had changed his mind? It would be a welcome shift from how his luck was running. The meeting gave him an excuse, as well. He could stay out late and avoid his wife on her last night in Athens. She would fly back to Moscow tomorrow with the scheduled Soviet Embassy staff shuttle. Good riddance. He would divorce her, but the party honchos frowned on divorce. It didn't conform to the *new Soviet man*. He thought about having her killed, but. . . .

He was certain the photo and the blonde were a setup. *Clever*, he thought. Well executed and credible. His history with young blondes was a failing, and his tormentors played on that. Mrs. Chernov knew about his proclivities and allowed him a long leash. What other choice did she have? He was 2,200 kilometers away. But the insult of parading a woman half her age at a military reception and now, at a concert in Milan—it was too much. It was the straw that broke the camel's back. She demanded that he take *her* to the concert even though he pleaded there were no tickets, no reservations, no transportation. It didn't matter. She had seen the proof with her own eyes. He would buy her a coat and a dress, maybe some jewelry, take her to the concert, spend the night at the best hotel, or she would. . . .

She was a woman of means. Her family was prominent, even before the 1917 revolution. Since then, they had played their cards smartly and remained on Stalin's good side. They were in favor. His wife claimed to be on socializing terms with Nina Beria. But Chernov had never met her or her husband, the ruthless Lavrenty Beria, Minister of Internal Affairs. Beria could do him irreparable damage through GRU politics and could, with his signature, have Chernov arrested, tortured, and murdered. He didn't want to think of it. He was a GRU rezidentura. A position that should confer upon him authority and stature second to none. But he remained vulnerable to the timeless vice, avarice. He had married for his wife's prominence. Now his soul lay on Dante's Fifth Terrace, there to purify for eternity along with sinners of their companion failing, prodigality.

That evening, in the cool night of late November, Chernov dismissed his security detail over the objections of the officer in charge. He walked from the embassy to the Yagos Argyropoulos park only a few blocks east. It was a small park in a pleasant neighborhood, and late as it was, there were no children playing on the swings and climbing equipment. He passed the park often and had once read the plaque, dedicating it to the man who had translated Greek philosophy and theology into Latin for the 1439 Council of Florence. The council had tried to bring together the Eastern Church and the Roman Church for five years. It hadn't worked. Chernov, an avowed atheist, nevertheless respected the organizational skills of both sects and thought his Soviet brethren would be so lucky to last as long.

He stepped into the grassy area and lit a cigarette, a signal that all was clear. Akula, Christakis, stepped from behind a tree on the boundary. He walked to a bench and stood there for Chernov to join him. Chernov spotted no watchers but assumed Akula had positioned them out of sight. He walked to the wooden bench and nodded to Akula. He said, "It is good to see you, my friend. It puzzled me when I saw your code. I thought you were uninterested in furthering our relationship."

Chernov was a pro's pro. Christakis knew not to believe a word this man said. Yet, there was something in his voice that told Christakis he was looking for a friend as much as a recruit.

He put that thought aside. Christakis said, "I have something you lost."

"Oh, what is that?"

"Kozlov."

In the dim city light, Christakis saw a second of recognition in Chernov's eyes. Chernov asked, "This person, why do you think we have lost him? The name means nothing to me."

"You lost him because we ran him. He was our double, but not for long," said Christakis.

"We? Who? I don't understand?" said Chernov in fake puzzlement.

Christakis ignored him. He said, "You may have him back. For him, we want only one thing."

"And what is that?" asked Chernov.

"He is a down payment. A human token. Your next payment will be in cash, a great amount. For the cash, we expect your cooperation. You know the rest."

Chernov baulked. Akula wasn't here to make amends. He was asking Chernov to turn, to double on the GRU.

Christakis went on, "We will pay you one thousand dollars every month for your cooperation. The money we will deposit in a numbered bank account outside of the Soviet Union. You will access it as you see fit. I have with me five thousand dollars. This is yours for your pledge of cooperation. That is all I need from you, a pledge. No paperwork. If you'd prefer the compensation in some other currency, that we can arrange."

Chernov froze. He needed the money. He could take the money now and betray the promise later. He asked, "So you are CIA now?"

Christakis didn't answer.

"You have to be CIA; SIFAR is not so well funded. And yes, I knew of you and SIFAR, even before your gift of the Holy Bond scum. What type of cooperation would you expect of me?" Chernov asked.

It was a dodge, a play for time. He would take the money, but in his mind, he was processing what it meant. He would take the money, then decide what to do next.

"You know the cooperation we want. You are not new to this. Years ago, you expected from me cooperation, and I gave you what you thought you needed. Now, it is my turn to receive and your turn to give." Christakis removed the envelope from his pocket. He saw Chernov's right hand edge toward it.

"I will not provide information that puts my people in mortal danger. Is that clear?" said Chernov.

Christakis stared at him.

"Besides, we have been told not to kill CIA agents unless ordered from headquarters. It is a new day in Moscow," confided Chernov.

Christakis maintained his stare and pushed the envelope closer.

Chernov hesitated, then reached for the money. Christakis resisted his grasp and said, "You must sign the receipt."

"Yes, yes . . . I know the script." Christakis released his grip and pulled from his pocket a paper and a pad, an ink pad.

Chernov put the envelope in his jacket pocket. Then he initialed the receipt. When Christakis flipped open the ink pad, Chernov said, "Must we? Can you not extend some level of professional courtesy?"

Christakis stared and held the pad.

Chernov shook his head and placed his four fingers on the ink. Christakis said, "Your thumb, too, please." Chernov complied. He touched the receipt with all five fingers. Christakis covered the pad, blew on the receipt, then folded it and put it in his pocket.

Christakis rose from the bench and said, "We will be in touch. Look for code in the second sequence for our next meeting. We know you have frequent official duties requiring your attendance and we will accommodate. You will need these."

He handed Chernov the keys to the Pobeda. "It is on Karkavista, two blocks from your embassy. Your lost killer is in the trunk. Don't leave him too long, he has a wound. We wouldn't want him to die before you question him, no?"

Chernov nodded in resignation. He rose from the bench, turned toward the street, and before he walked away, Christakis said, "Enjoy your concert."

Chapter 58

"Mr. Theofanis, you have a call from a lady named Dimitra. Should I bring you a phone," asked the polite concierge.

"No. Please ask her to hold and I'll take it in my room." The concierge nodded and walked to the front desk.

Stavros gulped the last swig of his Napoleon, left a tip on the bar, nodded to the bartender, and left Alexander's for the elevator. In his room he dialed the operator and asked to be connected. The next voice was Dimitra. She asked, "How are you and what are you doing. I guess from the delay, you were in the bar, no?"

"Aren't you a breath of fresh air," said Stavros. "And yes, I was in the bar. Christakis left a few minutes before you called. I was finishing my drink. How are you and how goes Aphaia?"

"How many," asked Dimitra.

"How many drinks?" asked Stavros.

"Yes, how many?" she repeated.

"Only two, but it should have been twenty," he joked.

"Oh?" she queried.

"Right. Liquid therapy, and a victory celebration, of sorts. And I miss you," he said.

He didn't slur, but she could tell he was loose.

"Well, tell me more when you come to visit me this weekend," she stated matter-of-factly.

This was typical Dimitra. She never wasted an opportunity to order when a simple ask might do the job.

She went on, "We have been two weeks apart. That is long enough, no? We have completed the grid layout for the dig, and the weather this weekend does not look promising for excavation. So, if your duties permit, I believe you should come to Aphaia."

Stavros didn't hesitate, "I'll be there. First ferry Saturday morning."

She said, "Good. We have a date. Arrivederci." Then the line went silent.

Chapter 59

He was a fish out of water. Both men were fish out of water. Neither Stavros nor Christakis knew anything about jewelry. Especially engagement rings. Both men brought to jewelry style the same sensitivities that they brought to automobiles. They were looking for something shiny and two-toned. Maybe with some chrome. Then the young lady behind the display case saved them from themselves.

Along with furriers, Athens is home to world-renowned jewelers. Fanourakis in the Kolonaki neighborhood had designed and sold jewelry since its founding in 1860 in Heraklion, Crete. The sweet front-desk attendant at the Grande Bretagne had assured Stavros that Fanourakis would not disappoint any Greek woman. The young concierge standing beside her confirmed her recommendation with a nod. Stavros had recruited Christakis to come along to make certain he didn't chicken out. *Plus*, he thought, *Christakis might know something about women's jewelry*. Why he thought that was anybody's guess. He was dead wrong.

In the end, after a detailed discussion of traditions and the differences between royal engagements and common betrothment, Stavros chose simple gold bands, one for him and one for Dimitra. Had they been royals, he would have bought matching sapphire rings, blue cabochons surrounded by diamonds mounted on a wide platinum band. That was not Dimitra, and it was not him.

He paid for the rings, thanked the young attendant, and walked out of the store with a sense of relief. Buying a ring, the right ring, made him more nervous than meeting Kozlov. He was on the sidewalk and realized that Christakis had hung behind. He was still talking to the attendant and looking at another display, this one containing bracelets. Christakis pointed to one, a simple Greek key maze pattern, the symbol for eternal life. The attendant placed it in a padded box and stepped to the register.

Christakis paid and joined Stavros on the sidewalk. Stavros chided his partner, "Something for yourself?"

"No," answered Christakis, reserved as always.

"Well, don't keep me guessing. Who is the lucky woman?" asked Stavros.

Christakis sheepishly answered, "I may give it to Calista. I have not decided."

"You bought it, so I think you've already decided. Calista's a prize, partner. She's smart, beautiful, and she might have a future in this business. You would be great together," said Stavros.

Christakis nodded. He was finished talking about personal matters.

Stavros laughed out loud, slapped Christakis on the back, and the two men made for a line of taxis.

Chapter 60

Buying engagement rings was the easy part. Putting them in his pocket, meeting Christakis, and riding to Piraeus to catch the ferry was much harder. It was an odd ride. Christakis drove his Simca. He planned to drop Stavros, then drive to Calista's. They were going hiking on Mount Giona. The oddity was that Christakis had done all the talking, or most of it. Stavros had listened with one ear, but his mind was on meeting Dimitra, what to say to Dimitra.

He almost missed the question. Christakis said, "Tell me why." When Stavros didn't answer, Christakis looked over at his passenger with a smile. He repeated, "Stavros, tell me why. Dimitra is a beautiful woman and accomplished as few others. But why marry, why now? These are matters I too think about, though not as thoroughly as you. Tell me why?"

Stavros understood his friend's prodding. It was a good question, perhaps not one that men often discuss, but a good question. After an attentive lapse, he said, "Trust. Yes, she is beautiful and yes, accomplished. These alone would satisfy any man. But for me, for you and me, it's a matter of trust, right?

"It's the work we have chosen. Trust is the rarest commodity in our world. It can't be traded or horded or touched or felt, but it is our exchange, our currency. I will always trust Dimitra. From our time before until today, trust has always followed. Perhaps I didn't come to know its value until Athens, until today. That is the reason, my friend. Trust."

When they reached Piraeus, Christakis pulled the Simca to the curb. He said, "Good luck, my friend." Then he held out his hand and Stavros shook it.

Stavros said, "Thanks, and good luck to you. Tell Calista I said hello. And watch out for boars."

Both men laughed.

He got out of the car and started toward the ramp of the Aphaia ferry. As always, Greeks, tourists, clergy, and assorted islanders teamed waiting to board. He stood among the crowd, lost in thought, wondering how he had come to this moment. Then he lurched aboard when the crowd moved. It was a short sail to Aphaia. But in his heart, he yearned to begin a much longer journey.

Acronyms

Acronym	Meaning
Alepoú	Calista's codename
CIA	US Central Intelligence Agency
DDP	CIA Deputy Director of Plans, Oversees OPC & OSO
DP Camp	Post WWII Displaced Persons Camp
DSE	Democratic Army of Greece, left led
EAM-ELAS	Greek National Liberation Front-People's Liberation Army, left led, abbr. ELAS
EDES	National Republican Greek League, right led, pro-king
Ephorate	Board of directors for Archaeological Society of Athens
FIEND	CIA Operation to overthrow Albanian communist regime, a.k.a. BG/FIEND
Gladio	Italian secret "Stay Behind" armed force to resist Soviet invasion
GRU	Soviet Military Intelligence
Holy Bond	Clandestine Greek military rightist organization
KKE	Greek Communist Party
Klephts	Greek 'noble bandits' of the mountains, but bandits nonetheless
KYPE	Greek Intelligence Service, abbr. KYP
LOK	Greek Mountain Raiding Companies working in Sheepskin
Meltemi	CIA Operation to double Soviet GRU rezidentura
MI6	British Secret Intelligence Service
NATO	North Atlantic Treaty Organization
ONI	Italian Naval Intelligence
OPC	CIA Office of Policy Coordination (Propaganda, Commandos)
OSO	CIA Office of Special Operations (Spies, Intel Analysis)
OSS	US Office of Strategic Services
Sheepskin	Greek secret "Stay Behind" armed force to resist Soviet invasion
SI	OSS Special Intelligence Branch

SIFAR	Italian Armed Forces Information Service
SOE	British Special Operations Executive
The Circle	Stavros run CIA propaganda operation
The Torch	Small breakaway KKE cell
Valuable	British Operation to overthrow Albanian communist regime

Bibliography

Books

Anderson, Scott. *The Quiet Americans: Four CIA Spies at the Dawn of the Cold War - A Tragedy in Three Acts*. New York: Doubleday, 2020.

Aristotle. *History of Animals, IX. I. 2.*: Translated by Richard Cresswell. London: George Bell & Sons, 1887.

Binnendijk, H., and A. Friendly. *Turkey, Greece, and NATO: The Strained Alliance: A Staff Report to the Committee on Foreign Relations, United States Senate*. United States Congress, Senate Committee on Foreign Relations: US Government Printing Office, 1980. https://books.google.com/books?id=quMbbs-2EjQC.

Books, LLC, and S. Wikipedia. *Epic Cycle: Odyssey, Iliad, Epic Cycle, Cypria, Telegony, Little Iliad, Aethiopis, Nostoi*: General Books LLC, 2011. https://books.google.com/books?id=trSnSQAACAAJ.

Celik, Selahattin. *Turkish Counter-Guerrilla: The Death Machine*. Köln: Mesopotamia Publishing, 1999.

Congress, US. *Final Report of the Select Committee to Study Governmental Operations with Respect to Intelligence Activities, United States Senate: Together with Additional, Supplemental, and Separate Views. Report - 94th Congress, 2d Session, Senate; No. 94-755*, vol. v. Washington: US Govt. Print. Off, 1976. //catalog.hathitrust.org/Record/000770088
http://hdl.handle.net/2027/mdp.39015070725273 (v.1)
http://hdl.handle.net/2027/mdp.39015076851891 (v.2)
http://hdl.handle.net/2027/mdp.39015076851883 (v.3)
http://hdl.handle.net/2027/mdp.39015076851875 (v.4)
http://hdl.handle.net/2027/mdp.39015076851867 (v.5).

Davies, M. *The Greek Epic Cycle*: Bloomsbury Academic, 2001. https://books.google.com/books?id=I9JfAAAAMAAJ.

Davis, R.C. *Shipbuilders of the Venetian Arsenal: Workers and Workplace in the Preindustrial City*: Johns Hopkins University Press, 2009. https://books.google.com/books?id=wp6o6fKC7dcC.

Durrenberger, E.P. *Uncertain Times: Anthropological Approaches to Labor in a Neoliberal World*: University Press of Colorado, 2017. https://books.google.com/books?id=zqMvDwAAQBAJ.

Duthel, H. *Global Secret and Intelligence Services I: Hidden Systems That Deliver Unforgettable Customer Service*: Books on Demand, 2014. https://books.google.com/books?id=I84rBQAAQBAJ.

Faini, M. *Spies and Their Masters: Intelligence—Policy Relations in Democratic Countries*: Taylor & Francis, 2020. https://books.google.com/books?id=1eruDwAAQBAJ.

Farago, Ladislas. *War of Wits: The Anatomy of Espionage and Intelligence. Paperback Library: Silver Edition ;52-125*, vol. 284 p. New York: Paperback Library, 1962.

https://books.google.com/books/about/War_of_Wits_the_Anatomy_of_Es
pionage_and.html?id=GNZAxQEACAAJ.

Ganser, D. *NATO's Secret Armies: Operation Gladio and Terrorism in Western Europe*: Taylor & Francis, 2005. https://books.google.com/books?id=n0uRAgAAQBAJ.

Harlaftis, Gelina, and Christos Tsakas. "The Role of Greek Shipowners in the Revival of Northern European Shipyards in the 1950s." In *Shipping and Globalization in the Post-War Era: Contexts, Companies, Connections.* Edited by Niels P. Petersson, Stig Tenold, and Nicholas J. White. Cham: Springer International Publishing, 2019.

Iatrides, J.O. *Greece at the Crossroads: The Civil War and Its Legacy*: Pennsylvania State University Press, 2010. https://books.google.com/books?id=Vv1t3D_3vjkC.

Lane, F.C. *Venetian Ships and Shipbuilders of the Renaissance*: Borodino Books, 2018. https://books.google.com/books?id=_ombDwAAQBAJ.

Lulushi, A. *Operation Valuable Fiend: The CIA's First Paramilitary Strike against the Iron Curtain*: Arcade, 2014. https://books.google.com/books?id=gXvoBAAAQBAJ.

Maior, George Cristian. *America's First Spy: The Tragic Heroism of Frank Wisner.* Washington, DC: Academica Press, 2018. https://books.google.com/books?id=KrFtuwEACAAJ.

Rees, Q. *The Cockleshell Canoes: British Military Canoes of World War Two*: Amberley Publishing, 2008. https://books.google.com/books?id=uIOoAwAAQBAJ.

Simpson, Christopher. *Blowback: America's Recruitment of Nazis and Its Effects on the Cold War*, 1988. http://www.tandfonline.com/toc/rwhi20/.

State, Dept. *Foreign Crops and Markets*, vol. v. 65. US Foreign Agricultural Service, US Bureau of Agricultural Economics, US Office of Foreign Agricultural Relations: US GPO, 1952. https://books.google.com/books?id=I8doPsCx41sC.

USA, IBP. *Italy Intelligence, Security Activities and Operations, Handbook Volume 1, Strategic Information and Regulations.* Washington, DC: International Business Publications. https://books.google.com/books?id=ettFCgAAQBAJ.

USN. *Understanding Soviet Naval Developments.* United States Office of the Chief of Naval Operations, United States Office of Naval Intelligence, United States Department of the Navy Office of Information: Office of the Chief of Naval Operations, Department of the Navy, 1985. https://books.google.com/books?id=AUwSAAAAYAAJ.

Watson, B.W. *Red Navy at Sea: Soviet Naval Operations on the High Seas, 1956-1980*: Taylor & Francis, 2019. https://books.google.com/books?id=i6yhDwAAQBAJ.

Weiner, Tim. *Legacy of Ashes: The History of the CIA.* 1st ed. ed. New York: Doubleday, 2007.

Wilford, Hugh. *The Mighty Wurlitzer*: Harvard University Press, 2008. http://www.jstor.org/stable/j.ctt13x0h2v.

Conference Paper

Zajicek, Benjamin. "The Psychopharmacological Revolution in the USSR: Schizophrenia Treatment and the Thaw in Soviet Psychiatry, 1954—64." 2019. Accessed April 28, 2021, https://www.ncbi.nlm.nih.gov/pmc/articles/PMC7329222/.

Discussion Forum

Broccoli, Umberto. "True Intelligence Is Made at the Table." 2019-06-05, 2019. https://mediterraneinews.it/2019/06/05/intelligence-umberto-broccoli-al-master-delluniversita-della-calabria-la-vera-intelligence-si-fa-a-tavola-ed-ha-ricordato-markus-wolf-e-federico-umberto-damato-pa/.

Hearing

6-199 House Testimony on Aid to Greece and Turkey, March 3, 1948 - Library. 1948. The Ambassador in Greece (Peurifoy) to the Department of State. 1951.

Journal Article

"Shipbuilding in Ancient Greece and Rome." (2015-02-02 2015). https://woodensailingshiphistory.wordpress.com/2015/02/02/shipbuilding-in-ancient-greece-and-rome/.

Bithymitris, Giorgos, and Manos Spyridakis. "Union Radicalism Versus the Nationalist Upsurge: The Case of Greek Shipbuilding Workers." *Dialectical Anthropology* 44, no. 2 (2020/06/01 2020): 121-35. https://dx.doi.org/10.1007/s10624-020-09582-6.

Britannica, Editors. "Marshall Plan: Summary & Significance." *Encyclopaedia Britannica* (2021). https://www.britannica.com/event/Marshall-Plan.

Cook, J. M. "Archaeology in Greece, 1951." *The Journal of Hellenic Studies* 72 (1952): 92-112. https://dx.doi.org/10.2307/627997.

Fiste, Markella, Dimitrios Ploumpidis, Costas Tsiamis, Effie Poulakou-Rebelakou, and Ioannis Liappas. "Dromokaition Psychiatric Hospital of Athens: From Its Establishment in 1887 to the Era of Deinstitutionalization." *Annals of General Psychiatry* 14, no. 1 (2015/02/15 2015): 7. Accessed April 28, 2021. https://dx.doi.org/10.1186/s12991-015-0047-1.

Frydrych, Eunika Katarzyna. "The Debate on NATO Expansion." *Connections* 7, no. 4 (2008): 1-42. Accessed 2020/11/15/. http://www.jstor.org/stable/26323362.

Jacoby, Rolf. "The United States Information Service." *Aslib Proceedings* 7, no. 3 (1955): 133-35. Accessed 2020/11/15. https://dx.doi.org/10.1108/eb049557.

Lengel, Edward G. "The Greek Civil War, 1944-1949 | the National WWII Museum | New Orleans." (May 22, 2020 2021). https://www.nationalww2museum.org/war/articles/greek-civil-war-1944-1949.

Long, Stephen. "CIA-MI6 Psychological Warfare and the Subversion of Communist Albania in the Early Cold War." *Intelligence and National Security* 35, no. 6 (2020/09/18 2020): 787-807. https://dx.doi.org/10.1080/02684527.2020.1754711.

Mak, Dayton. "Raymond Hare: Our Man in Cairo During WWII." *Association for Diplomatic Studies & Training* (July 1987, 2020). https://adst.org/2017/07/raymond-hare-man-cairo-wwii/.

Masson, Philipe, J. Labayle Couhat, Gary G. Sick, and Karlan K. Sick. "The Soviet Presence in the Mediterranean: A Short History." *Naval War College Review* 23, no. 5 (1971/1/1 1971): 60-66. Accessed 2020/11/05/. http://www.jstor.org/stable/44641188.

McCormick, Gordon. "Soviet Strategic Aims and Capabilities in the Mediterranean: Part II." *The Adelphi Papers* 28, no. 229 (1988/03/01 1988): 32-48. https://dx.doi.org/10.1080/05679328808457569.

Nuti, Leopoldo. "The Italian 'Stay-Behind' Network — the Origins of Operation 'Gladio'." *The Journal of Strategic Studies* 30 (12/01 2007): 955-80. Accessed 2021/4/29. https://dx.doi.org/10.1080/01402390701676501.

Ploumpidis, D., C. Tsiamis, and E. Poulakou-Rebelakou. "History of Leucotomies in Greece." *History of Psychiatry* 26, no. 1 (2015/03/01 2015): 80-87. Accessed 2021/02/14. https://dx.doi.org/10.1177/0957154X14529224.

Spyridakis, Manos. "The Political Economy of Labor Relations in the Context of Greek Shipbuilding: An Ethnographic Account." *History and Anthropology* 17, no. 2 (2006/06/01 2006): 153-70. https://dx.doi.org/10.1080/02757200600666041.

Swartz, Peter. "US-Greek Naval Relations Begin." (2020). http://public2.nhhcaws.local/research/library/online-reading-room/title-list-alphabetically/u/us-greek-naval-relations-begin.html.

Team, To BHMA. "Greek Shipping Post-War Reconstruction (1946-1952) - Ειδήσεις - Νέα - Το Βήμα Online." *ToBHMA* (2018-06-04 2018). Accessed April 28, 2019. https://www.tovima.gr/2018/06/04/international/post-war-reconstruction-1946-1952/.

Reports

CIA. *CIA, Report, Director's Log, November 26, 1951, Top Secret, CIA.* 1951.

Thesis

R. N. Palarino, Maj, USA. "Greece and NATO: Problems and Prospects." US Army Command and General Staff College, 1980. Accessed 2021/4/29. https://apps.dtic.mil/dtic/tr/fulltext/u2/a093986.pdf.

Web Pages

"The Hidden Plots of a Supranational Military Power and the Intricacies of Their Servants." Searchers Without Masters. Last modified 2021. Accessed April 28, 2015. https://ricercatorisenzapadroni.noblogs.org/post/2015/07/14/letrame-occulte-di-un-potere-militare-sovranazionale-p2-e-gli-intrallazzi-dei-loro-servi-i-servizi-segreti/.

"Soviet and Eastern Bloc Defectors." 2021. Accessed May 1, 2021. http://research.omicsgroup.org/index.php/List_of_Soviet_and_Eastern_Bloc_defectors.

ABS. "Guidance Notes on Propulsion Shafting Alignment." 2019. Accessed April 28, 2021. https://ww2.eagle.org/content/dam/eagle/rules-and-guides/current/design_and_analysis/128_propulsionshaftalignment/shaft-alignment-gn-sept-19.pdf.

Barrett, Matt. "Matt Barrett's Greece Travel Blog: The American Club, Kifissia, ACS Cruise to Nowhere and Flisvos Marina." 2021. Accessed May 1, 2021. https://www.greecetravel.com/matt-blog/2008-10-07.htm.

Berger, D.H., Major USMC. "The Use of Covert Paramilitary Activity as a Policy Tool: An Analysis of Operations Conducted by the United States Central Intelligence Agency, Major D. H. Berger, USMC." 2020. https://fas.org/irp/eprint/berger.htm.

Bernstein, Carl. "The CIA and the Media." 2021. http://www.carlbernstein.com/magazine_cia_and_media.php.

Botsiou, Konstantina. "Who Is Afraid of the American?" 2020. Accessed April 28, 2021. https://ecpr.eu/Filestore/PaperProposal/56c182eb-9ec2-4516-92bc-10d98f6187e6.pdf.

Buro, Ozel. "The Knife Through the Heart of Europe: Gladio." @TC_OZEL_BURO. 2021. Accessed April 28, 2021. https://teskilatimahsusa.wordpress.com/tag/gladio/.

Chapin. "Foreign Relations of the United States: Diplomatic Papers, 1944, Europe, Volume Iv - Office of the Historian." Office of the Historian, US Department of State. 2020. Accessed April 28, 2021. https://history.state.gov/historicaldocuments/frus1944v04/d1275.

CIA. "Soviet Strategy and Intentions in the Mediterranean Basin." 2020. Accessed April 28, 2021. https://www.cia.gov/library/readingroom/docs/DOC_0000278476.pdf.

CİNOĞLU, Dr. Hüseyin, Dr. Oğuzhan BAŞIBÜYÜK, Dr. Oğuzhan Ömer DEMİR, And Dr. M. Alper SÖZER. "Gladyo İtalyan Gizli Örgütlenmesi (Gladyo Italian Hidden Organization)." Police Academy Directorate International Terrorism and Transnational Crime Research Center. 2021. Accessed April 28, 2021. https://docplayer.biz.tr/4915097-Gladyo-italyan-gizli-orgutlenmesi.html.

Fakalou, Ekaterini. "History of the Hellenic Navy." Academy of Athens. 2021. Accessed April 29, 2021. https://www.hellenicnavy.gr/el/istoria/istoria-tou-pn.html.

Handler, William M., and Joshua Arkin. "Naval Accidents 1945 - 1988." 2020. Accessed April 28, 2021. https://fas.org/wp-content/uploads/2014/05/NavalAccidents1945-1988.pdf.

Historian, Office of the. "Foreign Relations of the United States, 1945-1950, Emergence of the Intelligence Establishment - Office of the Historian." 292. National Security Council Directive on Office of Special Projects. National Archives and Records Administration, RG 273, Records of the National

Security Council, NSC 10/2. Top Secret. Although undated, this directive was approved by the National Security Council at its June 17 meeting and the final text, incorporating changes made at the meeting, was circulated to members by the Executive Secretary under a June 18 note. (Ibid.) See the Supplement. NSC 10/2 and the June 18 note are also reproduced in CIA Cold War Records: The CIA under Harry Truman, pp. 213-216. According to an August 13 memorandum from Davies to Kennan, Kennan was subsequently appointed as the representative of the Secretary of State. (National Archives and Records Administration, RG 59, Records of the Department of State, Policy Planning Staff Files 1947-53: Lot 64 D 563). See the Supplement. 2020. https://history.state.gov/historicaldocuments/frus1945-50Intel/d292.

Iliopoulos, Dimos. "Comparative Analysis of New-Buildings ("Handy-Size" Bulkers) between "Hellenic Shipyards" (HSY) and a Modern "Far Eastern Shipyard" (Fes) with Time Difference of 40 Years (1973-2013)." 2019. Accessed April 28, 2021. https://higherlogicdownload.s3.amazonaws.com/SNAME/a09ed13c-b8c0-4897-9e87-eb86f500359b/UploadedImages/2017-2018/iliopoulos_comparative_anal_2018_SECP_pdf.pdf.

ISSR, Italy. "Our History - Republic Security Information System." Information System for the Security of the Republic. 2021. Accessed April 28, 2021. https://www.sicurezzanazionale.gov.it/sisr.nsf/chi-siamo/la-nostra-storia.html#Il-sistema-nazionale-di-sicurezza-e-intelligence-nel-secondo-dopoguerra-1948-2007.

McCormick, Gordon H. "The Soviet Presence in the Mediterranean." Rand. 2020. Accessed April 28, 2021. https://www.rand.org/content/dam/rand/pubs/papers/2008/P7388.pdf.

Morgan, Charles. "Morgan Papers on Greece, 1935-1941." Amherst College. 2021. Accessed May 1, 2021. http://asteria.fivecolleges.edu/findaids/amherst/ma51.html.

Norris, Robert S, and Hans M Kristensen. "Declassified: US Nuclear Weapons at Sea During the Cold War." 2020. Accessed April 28, 2021. https://www.tandfonline.com/doi/pdf/10.1080/00963402.2016.1124664.

NPS. "Postwar Period: End of the OSS and Return to the Park Service (US National Park Service)." 2020. Accessed April 28, 2021. https://www.nps.gov/articles/postwar-period-end-of-the-oss-and-return-to-the-park-service.htm.

Studies, American School of Classical. "The Athenian Navy." American School of Classical Studies. 2020. http://www.agathe.gr/democracy/the_athenian_navy.html.

Wikipedia. "Osa-Class Missile Boat." Wikipedia. 2021. Accessed April 29, 2021. https://en.wikipedia.org/wiki/Osa-class_missile_boat.

Wikipedia. "Truman Doctrine." Wikipedia. 2021. https://en.wikipedia.org/wiki/Truman_Doctrine.

Wikipedia. "National Intelligence Service (Greece)." 2021. Accessed April 29, 2021. https://en.wikipedia.org/wiki/National_Intelligence_Service_(Greece).

Wikipedia. "Igor Gouzenko." 2021. Accessed April 29, 2021. https://en.wikipedia.org/wiki/Igor_Gouzenko.

Wikipedia. "Venetian Arsenal." 2021. Accessed April 29, 2021. https://en.wikipedia.org/wiki/Venetian_Arsenal.

Wikipedia. "Galleass." 2021. Accessed April 29, 2021. https://en.wikipedia.org/wiki/Galleass.

Wikipedia. "Efharis Petridou." 2021. Accessed May 1, 2021. https://en.wikipedia.org/wiki/Efharis_Petridou.

Wikipedia. "Expulsion of Cham Albanians." 2021. Accessed May 1, 2021. https://en.wikipedia.org/wiki/Expulsion_of_Cham_Albanians.

Endnotes

[1] Team, To BHMA. "Greek Shipping Post-War Reconstruction (1946-1952) - Ειδήσεις - Νέα - Το Βήμα Online." ToBHMA (2018-06-04 2018). Accessed April 28, 2019. https://www.tovima.gr/2018/06/04/international/post-war-reconstruction-1946-1952/.

[2] ABS. "Guidance Notes on Propulsion Shafting Alignment." 2019. Accessed April 28, 2021. https://ww2.eagle.org/content/dam/eagle/rules-and-guides/current/design_and_analysis/128_propulsionshaftalignment/shaft-alignment-gn-sept-19.pdf.

[3] Mak, Dayton. "Raymond Hare: Our Man in Cairo During WWII." Association for Diplomatic Studies & Training (July 1987, 2020). https://adst.org/2017/07/raymond-hare-man-cairo-wwii/.

[4] Chapin. "Foreign Relations of the United States: Diplomatic Papers, 1944, Europe, Volume Iv - Office of the Historian." Office of the Historian, US Department of State. 2020. Accessed April 28, 2021. https://history.state.gov/historicaldocuments/frus1944v04/d1275.

[5] Bernstein, Carl. "The CIA and the Media." 2021. http://www.carlbernstein.com/magazine_cia_and_media.php.

[6] Wikipedia. "Osa-Class Missile Boat." Wikipedia. 2021. Accessed April 29, 2021. https://en.wikipedia.org/wiki/Osa-class_missile_boat.

[7] Wikipedia. "Truman Doctrine." Wikipedia. 2021. https://en.wikipedia.org/wiki/Truman_Doctrine.

[8] 6-199 House Testimony on Aid to Greece and Turkey, March 3, 1948 - Library. 1948.

[9] Lengel, Edward G. "The Greek Civil War, 1944-1949 | the National WWII Museum | New Orleans." (May 22, 2020 2021). https://www.nationalww2museum.org/war/articles/greek-civil-war-1944-1949.

[10] Wikipedia. "National Intelligence Service (Greece)." 2021. Accessed April 29, 2021. https://en.wikipedia.org/wiki/National_Intelligence_Service_(Greece).

[11] Wikipedia. "Igor Gouzenko." 2021. Accessed April 29, 2021. https://en.wikipedia.org/wiki/Igor_Gouzenko.

[12] "Shipbuilding in Ancient Greece and Rome." (2015-02-02 2015). https://woodensailingshiphistory.wordpress.com/2015/02/02/shipbuilding-in-ancient-greece-and-rome/.

[13] Wikipedia. "Venetian Arsenal." 2021. Accessed April 29, 2021. https://en.wikipedia.org/wiki/Venetian_Arsenal.

[14] Wikipedia. "Galleass." 2021. Accessed April 29, 2021. https://en.wikipedia.org/wiki/Galleass.

---

[15] Weiner, Tim. Legacy of Ashes: The History of the CIA. 1st ed. ed. New York: Doubleday, 2007. Page 66.

[16] The Ambassador in Greece (Peurifoy) to the Department of State, 21 December 1951, FRUS (1951, V), 526; see also Stefanidis, Asymmetrical Partners, 241. https://ecpr.eu/Filestore/PaperProposal/56c182eb-9ec2-4516-92bc-10d98f6187e6.pdf

[17] CIA. Cia, Report, Director's Log, November 26, 1951, Top Secret, Cia. 1951.

[18] Wikipedia. "Efharis Petridou." 2021. Accessed May 1, 2021. https://en.wikipedia.org/wiki/Efharis_Petridou.

[19] Morgan, Charles. "Morgan Papers on Greece, 1935-1941." Amherst College. 2021. Accessed May 1, 2021. http://asteria.fivecolleges.edu/findaids/amherst/ma51.html.

[20] Aristotle. *History of Animals, IX. I. 2.*: Translated by Richard Cresswell. London: George Bell & Sons, 1887.

[21] "Soviet and Eastern Bloc Defectors." 2021. Accessed May 1, 2021. http://research.omicsgroup.org/index.php/List_of_Soviet_and_Eastern_Bloc_defectors.

[22] Anderson, Scott. *The Quiet Americans: Four CIA Spies at the Dawn of the Cold War - A Tragedy in Three Acts.* New York: Doubleday, 2020. Page 213

[23] Britannica, Editors. "Marshall Plan: Summary & Significance." Encyclopaedia Britannica (2021). https://www.britannica.com/event/Marshall-Plan.

[24] Weiner, Tim. *Legacy of Ashes: The History of the CIA.* 1st ed. ed. New York: Doubleday, 2007.

[25] Wikipedia. "Expulsion of Cham Albanians." 2021. Accessed May 1, 2021. https://en.wikipedia.org/wiki/Expulsion_of_Cham_Albanians.

[26] State, Dept. *Foreign Crops and Markets, vol. v. 65.* US Foreign Agricultural Service, US Bureau of Agricultural Economics, US Office of Foreign Agricultural Relations: US GPO, 1952. https://books.google.com/books?id=I8doPsCx41sC.

[27] ISSR, Italy. "Our History - Republic Security Information System." Information System for the Security of the Republic. 2021. Accessed April 28, 2021. https://www.sicurezzanazionale.gov.it/sisr.nsf/chi-siamo/la-nostra-storia.html#Il-sistema-nazionale-di-sicurezza-e-intelligence-nel-secondo-dopoguerra-1948-2007.

[28] Ganser, D. *NATO's Secret Armies: Operation Gladio and Terrorism in Western Europe*: Taylor & Francis, 2005. https://books.google.com/books?id=n0uRAgAAQBAJ.

[29] Celik, Selahattin. *Turkish Counter-Guerrilla: The Death Machine. Köln: Mesopotamia Publishing, 1999.* Ganser cites page 151. Ganser page 66.

[30] Ploumpidis, D., C. Tsiamis, and E. Poulakou-Rebelakou. "History of Leucotomies in Greece." History of Psychiatry 26, no. 1 (2015/03/01 2015): 80-87. Accessed 2021/02/14. https://dx.doi.org/10.1177/0957154X14529224.

[31] CIA. *CIA, Report, Director's Log, November 26, 1951, Top Secret, CIA.* 1951. This report is 239 pages long with each page reporting 2-4 action incidents for the week of November 26, 1951.

[32] Fakalou, Ekaterini. "History of the Hellenic Navy." Academy of Athens. 2021. Accessed April 29, 2021. https://www.hellenicnavy.gr/el/istoria/istoria-tou-pn.html.

[33] Iatrides, J.O. *Greece at the Crossroads: The Civil War and Its Legacy*: Pennsylvania State University Press, 2010. https://books.google.com/books?id=Vv1t3D_3vjkC.

[34] Holy Bond (Ieros Desmos Ellinon Axiomatikon, IDEA).

[35] Simpson, Christopher. *Blowback: America's Recruitment of Nazis and Its Effects on the Cold War*, 1988. http://www.tandfonline.com/toc/rwhi20/.

[36] Mountain Raiding Companies (Lochoi Oreinon Katadromon, LOK).

[37] Duthel, H. *Global Secret and Intelligence Services I: Hidden Systems That Deliver Unforgettable Customer Service*: Books on Demand, 2014. https://books.google.com/books?id=I84rBQAAQBAJ. Page 321.

[38] Zajicek, Benjamin. "The Psychopharmacological Revolution in the USSR: Schizophrenia Treatment and the Thaw in Soviet Psychiatry, 1954–64." 2019. Accessed April 28, 2021, https://www.ncbi.nlm.nih.gov/pmc/articles/PMC7329222/.

www.ingramcontent.com/pod-product-compliance
Lightning Source LLC
Chambersburg PA
CBHW051503150726
47997CB00001B/97